"So now that I'm gr

"Debatable." Hannah

"Would you like me

back, and the thrumming of her body became a great deal harder to resist. This would-be dandy was the last person she should be toying with, but she could see his pupils dilating, smell that tantalizing mix of lime and wood…

She stepped closer, saying, "Oh, Mr. Weiss, that doesn't constitute grown." An unbidden sly smile rose to her lips as her eyes traced his form, and somehow, without even thinking, she'd moved so close, they were mere inches apart. So close that she could reach out and stroke his cheek, feel the slight dark stubble against his jaw. "And if you're aiming to impress me, well, let's just say, at this point in my life, very little does in that department, and I don't have the time or energy today to watch you flounder about."

His lip tipped. "I wouldn't flounder," he said, catching her eye. There was such heat in his gaze.

"And you truly believe anything between us would be lackluster?" he asked.

"Yes," Hannah lied.

Weiss snapped his fingers. "How about a wager then?"

FALL IN LOVE WITH
FELICIA GROSSMAN!

"Felicia Grossman gives me everything I'm looking for in a historical romance—her books are powerful and passionate and swoon-inducing!"
—Eva Leigh, *USA Today* bestselling author

"Felicia Grossman writes with passion and sensitivity, imbuing her characters with humor, heart, and strength."
—Mimi Matthews, *USA Today* bestselling author

"Felicia Grossman is a shining star in historical romance! No one writes love stories with more heart, more swoons and more sizzle."
—Joanna Shupe, *USA Today* bestselling author

"Felicia Grossman's passionate prose shines on every page."
—Rosie Danan, author of
The Intimacy Experiment

MARRY ME BY MIDNIGHT

"This book is fun to describe in list form—a gender-swapped Jewish Regency "Cinderella"!—but it's even more enthralling to see those magpie elements fused into a dazzling union."
—*New York Times*

"Grossman bibbidi-bobbidi-blasts us into a new corner of Victorian England, proving that the best fairy tales don't need to fit into a box (or even a shoe) but rather defy them." —*Entertainment Weekly*, Grade: A

"A masterful, original take on a beloved fairytale."
—*Kirkus*, Starred Review

"Historical romance fans should snap [this book] up."
—*Publishers Weekly*

"Inviting and immersive...This novel will appeal to readers seeking a steamy historical romance about reputation and representation, with a fresh fairy-tale twist." —*Library Journal*

"Grossman's choice to set [the book] at a particularly delicate time for the Jewish community in the U.K.—when legislation was being debated that would eventually guarantee Jewish men the same rights as all English men—adds a special poignancy. In this troubled atmosphere, Aaron and Isabelle's decision to choose love, courage, and kindness over everything else resonates that much louder and feels that much sweeter."
—*BookPage*

"A captivating setting, a masterful weaving of history and romance, and an utterly besotted hero make this novel a must-read not just of the summer, but of the year."
—*Vulture Magazine*

"A swoony twist on a classic, with a lady lead who wants to seize control of her own happily-ever-after and an unsuspecting but kind-hearted man who adores every part of her." —*Paste Magazine*

cinnamon roll of a hero as they navigate family, community, loyalty, and love."
—Amalie Howard, *USA Today* bestselling author of *Never Met a Duke Like You*

"[A] scorching and swoonworthy reimagining of Cinderella set in the 1830s London Jewish community... An excellent start to the series, and a much-needed addition to the historical romance genre!"
—Mimi Matthews, *USA Today* bestselling author of *The Lily of Ludgate Hill*

"With a fresh perspective on the well-worn long Regency era, Felicia Grossman blends history, fairy tales, and sexy tropes into a delicious concoction sure to captivate newcomers and veteran romance readers alike."
—Manda Collins, bestselling author of *A Governess's Guide to Passion and Peril*

"Spectacularly Jewish, fiercely feminist, and sizzling with erotic tension... one of my favorite books of all time."
—Jean Meltzer, bestselling author of *Kissing Kosher*

"[At] once timeless and completely fresh—a wholly, beautifully, Jewish story that feels reminiscent of my favorite fairytales. An unlikely partnership blooms into love between a fierce, driven heiress and a sweet, cinnamon roll hero that breaks the mold. This is a must for any historical romance reader looking to step into a side of Regency that's often overlooked."
—Rosie Danan, author of *The Intimacy Experiment*

Wake Me Most Wickedly

Also by Felicia Grossman

Once upon the East End
Marry Me by Midnight

WAKE ME MOST WICKEDLY

FELICIA GROSSMAN

A Once Upon the East End Novel

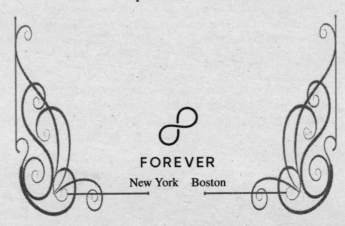

FOREVER

New York Boston

Forever
Hachette Book Group
1290 Avenue of the Americas, New York, NY 10104
read-forever.com
@readforeverpub

First edition: April 2024

Forever is an imprint of Grand Central Publishing. The Forever name
and logo are registered trademarks of Hachette Book Group, Inc.

The publisher is not responsible for websites (or their content) that
are not owned by the publisher.

Forever books may be purchased in bulk for business, educational,
or promotional use. For information, please contact your
local bookseller or the Hachette Book Group Special Markets
Department at special.markets@hbgusa.com.

ISBNs: 9781538722565 (mass market), 9781538722572 (ebook)

Printed in the United States of America

OPM

10 9 8 7 6 5 4 3 2 1

For Isaac "Ikey" Solomon and Hannah Solomon,
alev hashalom

Content Guidance

This book contains attempted (nongraphic) sexual assault, nonconsensual sexual contact, depictions of emotional abuse, and discussion and depiction of antisemitic language and behavior. Nothing in this book can be construed as medical advice. If you are experiencing an allergic reaction, please take all prescribed medications and seek a physician's care.

Chapter One

May 1832
Whitechapel, London, England

Night was the best time to hunt—especially if you relied on stealth, not strength, to snare your prey. The few lamps flickered in the heavy fog, camouflaging Hannah Moses against sooty boards hastily nailed over a broken door. A sliver of light from an upstairs window made the cracked stones of the alley glitter.

A gust of unseasonably cold wind rippled through Hannah's skirts as she moved toward the almost empty street, splashing damp debris through the moth holes in the bottom of her petticoats and the hem of her worn gray cloak. Her big toe, having burst through her hastily repaired stockings, burned as the chill seeped into her boots. With a grunt, she wedged herself between the slats of a rotting fence, the soggy wood high enough to conceal her presence.

Come on, come on. She tapped her half-numb foot against the ground and rubbed her hands together, her fingers still icy through her woolen gloves. Craning her neck, she peered onto the road just in time to see a weathered drunk toss up his supper. The man proceeded to keel over, face-first, giving the scavengers a good peek at his pockets.

They were upon him in a flash, mostly boys, with a few girls in the mix, jabbing and pulling at each other to get to the body fast enough. While some of the older ones shoved, a few smaller, cleverer ones slithered between the limbs, picking off buttons and laces—whatever could be sold the next day.

Probably to her shop or another of its ilk. Hannah's lip twitched at the predictable cycle of London's lesser neighborhoods, even as her boots pinched and another gust of wind rattled her bones. Gritting her teeth, she wrapped her cloak tighter around her arms.

Where was he? She'd been waiting almost a quarter of an hour and she had better things to do than—

"Hello, Hannah." The dark rumbling whisper came right in her ear, along with his hot, whiskey-scented breath.

"Oy, finally." With a scowl, she turned back into the alley that had only just appeared to be a dead end to find Ned Phyppers, leaning against the fence next to her.

"What have you got for me?" he asked, reaching out and tracing a rough finger down her cheek.

Hannah rolled her eyes at the gesture. "It's a bit cold for that, isn't it?" But she didn't resist as he moved his body over hers, blocking their faces from onlookers.

When he bent to kiss her ear, she told him, "He's in the tavern, two streets down. The Speckled Toad." She gasped as he nipped at the lobe. Closing her eyes, she gave her best impression of a besotted moan—a little show for the benefit of any onlookers.

"He's there now?" he murmured, taking full advantage of his position to kiss her again, this time on her neck.

"Will be until at least two." She nodded, gritting

her teeth as he slid the sleeves of her gown down her shoulders, exposing her to the damned cold. "The barkeep is making sure he's in good spirits." Biting back a sigh, she pressed herself against him as both a continuance of their charade and because it was truly freezing. "He'll be alone, in the left corner, facing the fire. Go in through the side door and don't make too much of a fuss," she added as he placed a hand on the small of her back, before sliding up her stays.

"Since when do you tell me how to do my job?" he asked as his fingers teased her nipple. She cursed under her breath, forcing herself not to slap his hand away, and instead focused on excising the twinges of guilt she still somehow felt, even after all these years, over what would happen to the hapless people she located for Ned and his customers. A foolish inclination, but one that somehow lingered no matter how hard she sought to squash it.

"I'm not telling you how to do anything. I'm just conveying the owner's message." Hannah closed her eyes once more, this time striving to lose herself in the pretense of being wanted and being able to want someone back.

"Keeping him happy is your concern, not mine." Ned pushed off the fence and crept toward the mouth of the alley, leaving her cold as she readjusted her buttons and cloak.

"It'll be yours, too, if you ruin my contacts and have to use someone not as reasonable nor agreeable for your information." She straightened her hood, shielding her face.

"If my men get too rough, I'm sure there are ways you could smooth it over." He reached back and stroked her cheek.

She rolled her eyes again, this time plucking his hand off, as they were done. "I think I'm getting a bit long in the tooth for that." More than a little. Funny how quickly time marched on when one always fought to live day to day. Her thirtieth year had come and gone, bringing little lines at the corners of her eyes and thin whisps of gray between the dark brown hairs ensnared in her brush. Not that she'd ever been a great beauty in the first place. Ordinary at best, without much else to recommend her besides her now well-honed sense of self-preservation.

"You still have your charms." In three quick steps Ned was before her once more, leaning in, hand back on her breast—as if to translate the actual meaning of her "charms"—before continuing. "And if this goes well..." His lip curled as he fiddled with her collar.

However, he did not meet her gaze. Did not look at her face. Not that she expected more. After all, they were both using each other. An honest arrangement between fellow creatures of the night. Though *he* had all the power and needed to be handled with extreme care if she wanted to keep her other business open— and her heart still beating in her chest.

Another blast of icy wind swelled between the buildings, as if spring was just another promise the world would fail to keep.

"It's late." She drew back, before giving his arm a quick squeeze through his jacket. "And you need to be getting on with it. You have work to do." Holding her head high, she brushed past him onto the street.

Leaving instead of being left.

"That I do. Next time, perhaps," he called after her, and she forced herself not to turn around.

Next time. There would most certainly be a next time. And maybe, if she took a sip or two or three of whatever he'd been drinking, she could turn off her mind and just enjoy things. Something that had been a great deal easier when she was younger.

A drop of rain plunked on her head, and she pressed herself flush against the pavement beside closed shops and boardinghouses, avoiding the gutters as she traveled westward. Home. To the far edge of Whitechapel and the pawnshop her parents had built after fleeing Odessa, changing Moscovich to Moses. Before things had gotten worse—for all Jews, not just those of ill repute and poor girls whose parents had too many mouths to feed. To the shop they'd run together, as a family, until it was just her and her sister.

Only, unlike her, Tamar was made for something bigger. For the future that had nearly been hers once. With new gowns and fine food and pretty jewels. Not to mention respectability and reentrance into the Jewish community—a place that tolerated them when her parents donated enough money for a plaque on the synagogue wall, only to denounce them when they'd become the gentiles' monsters to slay. Now they pretended the Moses sisters didn't exist altogether.

And while she'd love Tamar to stay with her forever, the longer her sister lingered in Hannah's world, the harder it would be for her to transform her path into something better. Which meant she really needed to get on with gathering the dowry she'd promised. One that would catch the eye—and hand—of a certain type of man. One that would erase all the unsavory bits of her family's past and her own present.

Or at least blind her sister's potential in-laws to them.

Shivering, Hannah rubbed her arms, hugging her body closer as a drenched rat skittered across her path. She moved forward and a second darted by. Followed by third and a fourth. Frowning, she crept behind a stack of crates to see what had frightened the creatures. She peered into the street and started.

Before her stood three men. Two she knew rather well. Unfortunately. Her shoulder still throbbed from their last encounter. She rubbed the spot on her jaw that had boasted a bruise for three days as well. They'd taken half what she'd made last week too. Something that would not happen again. Sheltering in her hiding spot, Hannah squinted at the sole stranger.

Young, probably closer to her sister's twenty years than her thirty-two. She wrinkled her nose. A dandy. With a shiny top hat and golden buttons just begging to be ripped off his too bright wool coat.

"Now, let's not be hasty or irrational about this," he said, his gloved palms raised to the men in almost supplicant surrender, his voice surprisingly calm.

"Oh, no one's being hasty. No, sir." Mick, the one who had punched her full in the mouth when she refused to give him an extra cut of her earnings, gave a dark chuckle. "Cool and slow, we are."

"Yes, we're the most logical men you'll ever meet," George—Mick's partner—the man who had twisted her arm so sharply behind her back, her sleeve ripped—added.

"I can see that," the stranger responded, his full lips twitching. Shockingly, he stepped toward them, not away, his posture bold, almost relaxed. "And I have a great respect for that logic and for both of you. Which is why I answered you honestly. I do not have any funds on my person. However, perhaps, if you provide me your addresses, I could send a card and we could agree to a mutually convenient meeting time and place for me to pay the very reasonable fee I owe you both for..." He raised a finger, cocking his head. "What did you call it?"

"Walking out of our territory alive," George growled.

"Yes, that's the terminology." The stranger nodded, threading his fingers together, not even flinching at the menacing noises emanating from the other men.

Oy. The dandy was certainly brave. She had to hand it to him on that front. Foolish, but brave. And probably soon to be quite injured. Not that she'd feel sorry for him. There was no good reason for someone like him to be on these streets at this hour. This was his own doing.

"An excellent, succinct description of the service you're offering me," he continued, "a very valuable service indeed. A—" The man's words cut off as he broke into a hasty, slightly clumsy sprint in the opposite direction.

Hannah's lip twitched as he darted around a trough and into an alley, making enough noise to wake the dead, if not half the East End. Though the way he jumped over a fence, clearing it completely as the tails of his rather audacious blue frock coat flapped in the wind, was rather impressive. Especially as he managed not to get his ridiculous long gold watch chain caught.

However, his pursuers knew the area a great deal better and were already traveling around the corner to head him off. Hannah rubbed her sore arm.

She should go home, get in bed, and forget about all of this until they inevitably pulled the stranger's body out of the Thames in a few months. That would be the best course of action.

And yet... she bit her lip.

Yes, the stranger likely had earned whatever was coming to him, dressing like that this far east, not to mention wandering alone in the middle of the night. But the idea of those two momzers taking her blunt and getting his as well... she balled her fists before ducking and skirting down another alley, cutting through the troughs and racks behind the goyishe butcher's shop, near tripping headfirst on the latch to his cellar door.

Oy. She was a draikopt, always looking for trouble, wasn't she?

Though looking at that now broken latch gave her an idea. Speeding her steps, she made it around the corner just as he emerged and, better, before Mick and George cut him off. Grabbing his arm quicker than he could cry out, she pulled him down with her, into the darkness.

They landed on the floor of the cellar in a heap, the door still ajar.

"What the—" he started before she clamped a hand on his mouth as muttering drifted from above.

Heart in her ears, she held as still as she could, barely registering the warm sensation of the stranger's body against hers. Nor the woody, yet somehow rather pleasant scent of whatever undoubtedly expensive cologne he was wearing.

No, she didn't dare move until his pursuers' voices had long ceased and the chittering of rats once again filled the air.

Only then did she remove her hand.

"Thank you for that," he said, straightening his jacket.

Shielding her eyes, she squinted, pointing above. "Don't thank me just yet. We still have to get out of here."

"Oh, I think that can be arranged," he murmured. And before she could inquire as to what he meant, he'd wrapped his arms around her waist. With an almost achingly gentle touch, he hoisted her up through the open door, keeping her skirts smooth and intact.

Hannah scrambled to her feet and backed away just as he leapt upward, catching the edge of the opening, and swung his legs past the edge so he landed neatly on his feet. Graceful as a cat. A large one. With a wolfish grin.

"There we go." He brushed his hands together and removed his hat.

A ripple of emotion she couldn't quite identify tingled through her veins as they stood face-to-face, until the moon finally peeked out from behind the clouds to give her a full view of him.

Hannah bit back a gasp. Handsome wasn't the half of it. Cropped brown hair beneath his neatly clipped and properly inconspicuous yarmulke; full red lips; deep, near black eyes with impossibly long lashes; a strong, firm jaw—if not for his rather outsized, thick eyebrows, he'd have seemed almost unreal, a storybook prince instead of a man. However, even those were not a flaw. They suited him. Somehow.

More than any feature on her face had ever suited her. Even when she was young and fresh and naïve enough to believe fairy tales were real. Or that she could thrive as anything but a villain.

Oy, she needed to leave. She coughed into her arm as she worked to stare at the debris-filled cobblestones instead of him. "Yes. Well. I would, um, advise you to move along." She indicated westward, to where she presumed he was traveling, or at least where he belonged.

In Aldgate proper, or farther, where the princes among their people had started settling alongside the gentiles they tried to emulate. Something at which he almost succeeded. "Stick to the populated streets. Ones with taverns," she added.

He cocked his head, almost as if he was trying to read her thoughts. "Sound advice." But he stepped toward her, close enough for her to study the shape of his ears and the flecks of ash in his brown hair, and the smooth planes of his face.

"I—" Any and all words caught in her throat as his eyes bored into her, smoldering despite the chill, taking her breath.

"Thank you for that as well." He pulled off his gloves, stuffing them in his coat pocket. "And for rescuing me. It's not every day the damsel rescues the knight." His lips settled into a rather self-satisfied grin, which shouldn't have made her stomach flip, but for some odious reason it did.

She rolled her eyes. "I'm hardly a damsel. And you're no knight."

"How do you know that?" He reached out to stroke her cheek.

An action done by another man less than an hour ago. However, this time, it sparked not merely desire inside, but something akin to longing. Not for the past and the opportunities she'd missed, but for now. For him. This handsome stranger.

Which was ridiculous. She didn't know him. And what she did know of him, of his set, made it clear that if he knew who she was, what she had done, what she continued to do—

Pulling herself backward, Hannah indicated to

the white edge of his tzistzis, which had presumably popped out from beneath his trousers during his jump. "They don't make us knights. Even if we try to dress like Beau Brummell on the outside." Blood pounding in her ears, she turned away from him. "Go home."

And before he could respond, she broke into a run, racing around the corner, not stopping until she reached the door of her pawnshop.

Quick as she could, she scrambled upstairs, past her softly snoring sister. Fingers trembling, she managed her buttons and stays, before splashing water over herself at the basin. She didn't dare meet her own reflection in the glass.

When she slid into bed, pulling the prickly, faded wool blankets over her head, she forced herself to sleep and not give him another thought.

There would be no dreams about the past, the present, or the Jewish prince she'd left behind.

Chapter Two

November 1832
Aldgate, London, England

What was the point of having a day of rest when one never enjoyed that luxury? When one needed to plot and plan and judge every situation, every interaction to extract the greatest benefit? When one's family's future depended on a compelling performance that never ended?

Conversation rose within the packed center of the synagogue at Duke's Place even with the concluding prayers having not quite finished. The men swarmed, done with half listening, ready and eager to argue and debate over food and drink. An activity enjoyable in theory, but a field of snares for one without a scholarly pedigree and with only the frailest of fortunes. Not to mention a distinct lack of firsthand knowledge of a world that was supposed to be his birthright.

But when one needed to hobnob with the community's most venerated, well...he'd make do.

Rising along with the throng, Solomon Weiss neatly folded the tallis that had belonged to his grandfather and slipped it into its thick, embroidered brocade bag.

The prior "Solomon" had been his mother's father, a man who'd died in Frankfurt before he was born. A man who, no doubt, had been a great deal more accustomed to playing his role in the community.

Or one would suppose. Solomon had never met the man, but considering the only prayers he'd ever heard in their house as a child had come from his mother's lips, the assumption seemed reasonable. His grandfather's knowledge would probably come in handy now.

Tucking the object beneath his arm, Sol smoothed the front of his newly remade velvet-lined frock coat. It was a rich deep blue—bold enough to garner attention but not so flamboyant to appear desperate—or at least that was the concept.

Cracking his back, he turned to the closest person he had to a friend, his hopefully soon-to-be business partner's husband, Aaron Ellenberg. "I thought that would never end."

"It's the same length every week," the other man muttered, straightening his fine silk cravat, his gloved hands a touch awkward. Though that was to be expected. After all, until six months ago, Aaron had been a mere custodian in this same synagogue. Now, however, he'd married the wealthiest heiress in Europe, securing his future and the future of any relations to come. A position Sol had sought. Though, in the end, even he had to admit that Aaron was better suited for both the role and the woman.

Damned lucky momzer. Especially as—though his salary was nothing to sneeze at—he'd not yet received the business partnership offered by Aaron's wife when she'd turned down his suit. And wouldn't until he snared more clients of his own. A task that had proved difficult when he still had responsibilities to grow and maintain his family's bank. Hence his repeat appearances at the synagogue. Even if the visits hadn't been quite as fruitful as he'd have liked.

However, he was starting to enjoy the rhythms and the company. Same with the daily morning prayers Aaron had started dragging him to a few times a week. He still couldn't forget his purpose.

Sol wagged a finger at his once rival, now friend. "That's what they want you to think, but I have it on good authority that the rabbi's sermons are getting longer."

Aaron's lip twitched as he adjusted his top hat over his yarmulke. "'On good authority?' What authority is that, pray tell?"

"I have my sources." He moved toward the aisle, searching for an opening to enter the river of exiting congregants. Sol winced as the fabric of his breeches rubbed against the nasty scrapes and bruises that he'd received the prior morning. This was what he got for permitting his horsemanship to get so rusty.

"Flesh and blood, or figments of your imagination?" Aaron grumbled. The other man then reached out to right an elderly gentleman whose cane slipped, before giving him a silent nod.

"Details, details." Sol glanced toward the now vacant raised bimah. "The point is, they never should have been permitted to lecture us in English."

"Why?" his friend asked as they finally found a spot in the shuffling sea of bodies.

"What?" Sol stopped short with the crowd nearly trampling two gentlemen debating a point about Abraham and his father.

A tap on his shoulder returned his attention to his friend. "Why shouldn't sermons be done in English?" Aaron gave him a soft nudge with his elbow. "Enlighten us with your wisdom."

"There is no 'us,' there's only you." Sol rolled his eyes. Glancing around first, he lowered his voice. "And if you must know, it's because sermons are much easier to sleep through when I understand nothing, instead of having to block out drivel. And god knows, given my schedule, I need the sleep." He put an arm on his friend's shoulder and guided him around the group that was still holding up the flow outward. "Now come on, your wife is probably waiting for us."

Aaron released a small snort though his expression became a touch wistful. "My wife is probably preening for compliments in her new gown, but if you want to spoil her fun..."

"No, I want *you* to spoil her fun as she loves you and merely tolerates me. I'm hungry and tired and don't see anyone useful to charm—" He craned his neck just to make sure he wasn't missing any opportunity. "Nope, no business to be had or connections to make. At least not at the moment so..."

"Please, she sings your praises. But I'll go fetch her." The other man gave him a brief nod before scurrying off, so the couple could leave and eat, and he could... well... lie down, he supposed, as his brother didn't exactly observe Shabbos in their home.

Not that he could judge Frederick for it—it hadn't been as important to his brother's mother, their father's first wife, and observance certainly had limited use, especially given the new, primarily gentile clientele his brother had acquired. Besides, as the elder and head of the family, Frederick had a great deal on his mind and more responsibilities than Sol could imagine, and certainly didn't need him questioning his choices.

Sol rubbed the back of his neck as he searched for Aaron and instead spotted a group of bankers congregating near an alcove. Ones whose favor he and Frederick could certainly use.

Straightening his collar, he turned and—*thwack*.

A cloaked figure, head bent, flew right into his chest, stealing his breath. Planting his feet to hold his ground, he reached and grasped the falling form before him.

"Whoa, careful now." As gently as he could, despite the rather sharp pain in his ribs, he worked to steady what now appeared to be a woman. "Are you all... right?" he asked, the last word breaking off as her hood slipped from her head.

Wide eyes, set off by heavy lower lashes, blinked at him in surprise, and a jolt of recognition blasted through his body. The wispy dark hair; the firm pointed chin; the full, plump, very kissable lips, pursed in determination—in an instant he was back in that alley, nearly six months ago, when, snooping in the shabbier sections of town had almost turned deadly before a rather quick-thinking stranger had saved him.

"You," he whispered. "It was you—"

But his pronouncement was interrupted by her lurching away, until a horrifying rip snicked through the air. "Fuck. I'm stuck." She glared at him before yanking at her shoulder seam, the scruffy wool fibers tangled with a gold button on the cuff of his coat.

"You most certainly are," he murmured, pleased by the rather fortuitous turn of events. After all, while he hadn't searched for her these past few months—business and heiress-hunting and danger and the like—he'd thought of her, his mystery woman. More often than he should, given how much was riding on the success of his current endeavors. "Or more, I'd say you caught me."

Again. His pulse began to thrum with a pleasure not unlike the sensation of penning a new deal or obtaining a new ally. Or better, making his brother truly proud.

"I certainly wasn't bloody well trying to," she grumbled, still not meeting his gaze, her gloved fingers slipping on the fabric of his sleeve. "I have enough tsuris without your type mucking things up further."

"My type?" He cocked his head, appraising her as she gave nervous glances from side to side, even while her lips curled into a rather surly scowl. Odd, as she'd barely flinched that night on the streets with the two toughs.

Dark eyes narrowed as she finally met his gaze. In the light of day, she was even more arresting than he remembered. Bold, firm features and the plump, expressive lips with a wry, sardonic set that made his pulse beat just a touch faster.

Pausing in her work to get free of him, she stuck out her chin. "The type that tries too hard."

Sol had to laugh. Though not loudly enough to call attention to the woman's predicament. He wasn't cruel, but she certainly didn't pull her punches. Yes, sir, she was all excitement and challenge. Damned if he wasn't drawn to her, despite all his better, nobler inclinations.

"Fair. Though at least I'm clever enough to know it," he said as she returned to the tangle with her rather long, gloveless fingers. "Besides, it still yields success," he couldn't help adding.

"On schmucks," she retorted without stopping her work.

"Which, fortunately for me, is what most people are." He gazed at the top of her worn bonnet, devoid of the feathers and bows that would've set off her dark brown hair so nicely. Likely she couldn't afford them, but if he was lucky, perhaps she was an heiress in hiding? "And really, why would anyone with half a brain be content at the bottom of the heap anyway?"

"Perhaps because they've realized that the 'heap' is not the center of the universe. Perhaps because—oh, for fuck's sake." She muttered the words as her frenzied fingers tugged the fraying strands around his button.

A nicer man would assist her, but he wasn't that nice. Certainly not that selfless. And he didn't want to let her go. At least not yet. Not when her body was so deliciously close.

"A fair point. Though if you have no desire for the esteem of the community, why are you here?" He leaned forward, studying her in the afternoon sun, which spilled through the tall arched windows, bathing her in light. She was around his height, making it so easy to stare into her face, even as she focused on her rather frantic work, unwinding the threads. He swallowed a little as her hand pressed against his chest, heating him even through the fabric of his garments.

Focus, Sol, focus. He cleared his throat. "It isn't as if your presence is required. You could be at home with your feet up instead of rubbing elbows with all of us."

After all, even with his limited study, he knew that, unlike men, women had no obligation to attend Sabbath prayers and make the quorum. And she didn't seem like the sort who enjoyed gossip or preening. And to his inexplicable delight, pretty as she was, she didn't appear costumed for a husband hunt. He seemed to be the only one in attendance aware of her charms.

Not pausing her hands, she lifted her chin to him. "Trust me, rubbing against you was never my intent," she told him, her tone dry.

"Pity," he murmured, just as, to his great disappointment, she managed to free herself, leaving all their garments intact.

"Oh no. I'm not for you, sir. Not if you want to be welcomed by the fancy set." Shaking her head, she took a step back, the ghost of a sardonic smile twisting her full lips. "Good luck on your climb, though, I hope you make it to the top and the view is everything you're seeking."

And before he could respond, his dratted so-called friend came rushing up them. "Sol—" Aaron started, boots clattering over the floor, nearly bowling down a group of scholars surrounding one of the rabbis.

"You've returned," he muttered dryly as the other man caught his breath. Sol turned around, ready to introduce him to the woman and—nothing.

The space behind him was empty.

"What—" he started, whipping his head around, searching the halls for any sign of her and her cloak. But...nothing. He craned his neck, scanning over and over, but to no avail. "Where did she—"

"She's gone." The normally jovial man's mouth was set in a firm line. "Thank goodness."

Sol paused his search and squinted at his friend. "What do you—"

Aaron slid his arm around Sol's shoulder and guided him toward the exit. "You don't want to be seen with her," he whispered as he pushed Sol forward with an aggressiveness he'd not seen in the man. Well, at least not unless he was provoked and his wife was involved.

"Who is she?" he asked as he glanced over his shoulder one last time. "I mean, I didn't even get her name. How do you—"

"Trust me. You'll thank me later," Aaron said through gritted teeth and a sharp prod to Sol's back.

"But—" Sol tried again as Aaron shoved him out into the street, slamming the door shut behind them, his questions still unanswered as she'd vanished once more.

Chapter Three

A snow-laced wind splashed muddy water over Hannah's boots as she trudged eastward through the streets, clutching her cloak to her body. She would not think of the man—Solomon Weiss, she now knew—for one minute more. His name was one she needed to forget despite the swirl of recent community interest around him, so thick it had trickled down to the likes of her. No matter that she had been supremely unsuccessful at forgetting that night in the cellar all those months ago. Opening the alley door behind the pawnshop on Lime, she trudged up the narrow back stairs toward the living quarters above.

No good could come of ever thinking of him again. No man with such clear designs on respectability was of use to her, and if the gossip was to be believed, he was not suitable for Tamar. Or at least not worthy of her beloved sister. His branch of the once prominent Weiss family was rumored to be bankrupt and had all but left the community. From appearances, they'd had recent success, but rumors said they were due to his brother's forays into the gentile world, not from any connection to theirs.

Her Weiss—she bit her lip—the younger Weiss had

been allegedly hired by Lira & Berab Sureties, a consolation prize after he'd failed to marry the heiress who owned half of that venerable company. Thus, he was probably again on the hunt for a wealthy spouse. One whose dowry would no doubt be used to pay his family's legendary debts.

And Tamar deserved better than to be used like that. Besides, she was still short the sum needed for a suitably tempting dowry, as the cost of doing business— the bribes she paid to both the authorities and the various gang leaders who ran their territory for "protection"—had recently increased. She'd make it up, though. Soon.

Hannah brushed dirt off her skirts before reaching out to grasp the knob leading to the rooms she and her sister shared. Creaking the door open, she set about untying her cloak and tossing it on the hook.

Tamar, stretched out on the patchy velvet chaise, her stocking feet hanging off the back, a book hiding her face, didn't even look up in greeting.

"I hope you didn't steal that," Hannah called as she moved toward their small kitchen, glancing toward the box where she kept their savings for Tamar's dowry.

"No, it's merchandise," her sister returned, pages flipping sharply. "Or it will be if the owner doesn't come back for it."

"Be careful, then," Hannah chastised. "It won't sell if you bend the pages too much." She propped open the lid of the large, heavy pot suspended over yesterday's still smoldering fire. Something that ought to have been tended by the young gentile girl to whom she paid good money to do such things. With the lightest touch, she poked, just enough that the flames licked the iron bottom. "Has Betsy been in?" she asked as an acrid burning scent hit her nose.

Tamar gave a noncommittal noise. Stepping back from the hearth, Hannah wiped her hands on her skirt before striding over to her sister, who still hadn't moved since she arrived home. She tilted her head to read the title of whatever was so interesting.

Sense and Sensibility by a woman named Jane Austen.

"A bit goyishe, no?" she asked as she folded her sister's discarded shawl, depositing it beside her feet on the chaise.

"Yes, but that doesn't mean it isn't enjoyable. The story is lovely." Tamar closed the volume and clutched it to her chest as she rose. "It's about two sisters. Their family has fallen on hard times after the death of their father. One is very romantic and the other's practical, but in the end they *both* find love with the perfect person for them and live happily ever after."

"I thought you just started reading it while I was gone?" Hannah moved to the window to adjust the fading curtains, ignoring her sister's emphasis on the word "both." While Tamar, with her brains and looks and ambition, could win the heart of anyone she desired, especially with the proper dowry, that was not Hannah's story. And never would be.

Besides, even if such a thing were possible, it wasn't as if she wanted the obligations of a romance. Tamar was enough of a challenge to protect, especially as she grew older. She needed someone else to fret over like a hole in the head. Hannah scratched her ear. "How are you possibly that far along?"

"It's my fourth time reading it." Her sister gave a dreamy sigh. "It's still wonderful."

"If you truly like it that much, after the week, it's yours." Hannah bent down and gave Tamar a kiss on the cheek. "I suppose if the owner comes back, we can buy you a copy."

"Really?" Her sister's face lit up with such joy that it was impossible to resist. Especially as she looked more and more like their mother every day. Same thick lashes she'd dreamed of growing into someday, same deep, dark, nearly black eyes that could always see right through her, same smile that she'd last seen—Hannah's throat closed as she pushed down those memories and instead focused on the family she still had.

"If it's what you truly want," she said, her voice hitching a touch. She bit her lip as she calculated the price. Ned, who she'd not seen hide nor hair of in months, had sent his lackey to collect protection payments the prior day, and he'd mentioned his boss having a few extra assignments. There'd be a price to receive them, but she'd done worse. And this was for Tamar.

"Just be sure to keep it and the others tidy." She indicated the large stack her sister had amassed on the makeshift shelf, before returning to the pot simmering over the fire. She propped open the lid and sniffed the contents—sheep with its bones and potatoes and carrots and onions and barely a handful of spices she'd tossed in before sundown the day before. "I think the cholent's done."

"Oh good. I was getting hungry." Her sister scurried to take her seat at the table. "How was the service? Or more, what did you find out? About whom?"

Drat.

"I—" Hannah started, her mind racing to find a believable excuse for her failure.

"Don't tell me you didn't see anyone who sparks your interest." Tamar pursed her lip in a pout.

"It's not my interest that should be 'sparked,'" Hannah retorted. "It's yours. I just want—"

"To make sure the matchmakers don't 'cheat us' and pawn me off on a man 'with nothing to offer because we don't know any better.'" Her sister gave a rather adept simulation of the glare Hannah reserved for their unruliest customers as well a sharp wag of her finger.

Hannah rolled her eyes. "I don't sound like that."

"You most certainly do," Tamar said with a laugh. "And it's all you talk about, making sure I'm not put with someone who's a fool or has no trade or has done something awful, or what have you."

"Obviously. I don't want you to be saddled with the male version of me." Hannah snickered at her rather accurate joke, even though an odd dullness crept under her ribs.

"No." Tamar shook her head, a look of horror marring her beautiful face. "Not at all. I don't mean—"

"I know." She waved off the cloying pity she most certainly didn't earn or need. "And I have a trade. As for the rest, it's early yet. We aren't officially speaking to anyone about matches until the spring, so you don't need to worry—"

"And until then? What am I meant to do? You barely let me help in the shop anymore." Her sister's tone had transformed from consolatory to accusatory in a flash. Though not unfairly. Hannah had been restricting Tamar's work.

But for her own good.

While the business was mostly legitimate, they still dealt in some stolen goods. Though nothing as risky or

profitable as their parents, there was always danger in
what they did. And it was best for Tamar to keep herself
safe. After all, she was still young, a mere twenty, and
Hannah had vowed to her parents she'd always protect
Tamar.

"I'm not a child any longer," Tamar added between
gritted teeth, as if she could read Hannah's thoughts.

"I know. Which is why we're searching for a match
for you." Hannah ladled the thick mixture, the potatoes
only slightly burnt, into two bowls. Moving to the table,
she slid one before her sister before taking up her own
seat and mumbling the motzi over the leftover bread
from the night before, even as her sister broke off her
own large piece. "And I'm making progress. Remember, last week at Bevis Marks, I overheard some very
useful information about who of the respectable families still has money and who is desperate for it and
might be willing to marry the likes of—"

"I could be the Queen of Sheba and the Sephardis
wouldn't bother with me." Tamar heaved a slow sigh.
"You know that."

The guilt returned, vanquishing Hannah's appetite.

Their situation was because of her. They were not of
the Sephardi side in the Jewish community—those families who had been invited back to English shores several generations back and now had the wealth and trade
links to show for it. If enough money was involved, a
Sephardi man might be persuaded to look past the
"inelegant" and "less-civilized" traditions and names
and accents of their Ashkenazi brethren—those who, in
the gentiles' eyes, had immigrated too recently to claim
any shared pedigree. Even if Sephardi and Ashkenazi
had recently united as one Jewish community.

But Hannah's mistakes had rendered such a match impossible. The Sephardic members of the community worked so hard to please the gentiles—for their communal safety, they'd argue—and to those same goyim, she and her parents represented the monsters of their folktales.

No self-respecting, well-regarded Sephardi would link themselves with them.

No matter how large a fortune Tamar could offer.

"If you didn't get names, did you at least see anyone to watch for? Someone handsome? Anyone who caught your eye?" Tamar's questions burst through Hannah's cycling thoughts.

She near spit her water across the room as the image of Solomon Weiss rose in her brain. Oy. Ducking her head, she patted her mouth with her cloth napkin.

"Because if I'm going to marry, I would need someone handsome. Along with all the rest, of course." Tamar smiled slyly, taking a large spoonful of cholent.

"With your looks, you'll have handsome. I was more focused on 'all the rest,' as you call it." When she could breathe again, Hannah narrowed her eyes—Tamar's list of requirements seemed only to be growing with each week. Soon she'd need a man more paradigm than possible. "Things that you also claimed were critical to your potential spouse, including whether they're well read."

"So you do listen, it seems. However..." Tamar screwed her lips to the side. "You're acting oddly." Her eyes narrowed as she leaned over to peer at Hannah. "What happened today? Was it the women again? Did they see you and talk about our—"

"No." Hannah shook her head. She'd never been a

social favorite, even when her parents were around. "Charm" was a skill that had always eluded her. And now, after everything, the whispers and pointed looks didn't touch her in any way—she didn't even flinch each time she passed by the empty space on the bookcase that had once held a donation plaque with her family name.

Not that she didn't notice the grooves from the nails still marring the wood. Even twelve years later. Probably because the Great Synagogue had ripped it out so quickly after the news of their arrests was splashed across all the gentile papers—heralded as some triumph for humanity. Their community's most respectable members had jumped all over themselves to show the gentiles that, unlike her and her parents, they weren't ogres too. Or at least merely the tamed sort. That they, like their most favored Sephardi counterparts, could become "good Jews."

"I was careful and stayed towards the edge of all crowds," Hannah assured her sister. "No one of note noticed me, and even if they did, it isn't as if I care what they say. I only want to go there to help you—which I am happy to do—*very* happy." She rubbed the back of her neck. "Anyway, it was—it was very silly. I tripped."

Worry lines sprouted on her sister's brow. "Are you injured?"

Hannah rolled her eyes. "It would take a great deal more than a few bumped limbs to daunt me."

"Yes, yes, you're the toughest of the street toughs." Tamar gave a dismissive wave before leaning over the table, inspecting Hannah again. "How's your arm by the way?" Her sister gave a knowing point of her fork to the elbow she was still nursing from an encounter with

Mick and George. The pair had become more aggressive since Ned spent less time on the streets, having risen in the criminal world, though she'd managed to hide all her take this time, so the injury was born out of their frustration, not her loss.

"My arm is perfectly serviceable," she said, resisting the urge to give the still tender joint a rub.

Her sister bit her lip. "You know. When I marry, perhaps you could come and stay—"

"When you marry, you will live happily ever after, far away from here, and I will not do anything to make trouble for you." Hannah set her jaw, refusing to engage in the old argument. Yes, the life she led might not be respectable, but it was hers. And she'd earned every bit of it. The good and the bad. And it was where she'd have to remain. Even if it was likely that one day she would be without her sister.

The two fell into silence as they ate, or more, in Hannah's case, stirred their meal.

"Did anyone help you when you tripped?" Tamar finally asked.

"What?" Hannah blinked at her.

"It would be rather awful if they ignored you," her sister continued, twirling her utensil between her fingers. "Even if our father hadn't attended the synagogue at Duke's Place, we're still Jews, still like them. And he did attend and support their efforts to maintain and help those less fortunate in our community. Which...I suppose we now are."

And yet those efforts had never been enough. Not truly. Not that she would say it out loud to Tamar. After all, her sister was young enough to have witnessed only the community's kindness, not the less charitable feelings she and her parents had engendered before it had turned its back on the Moses family when they'd needed it most. When they'd rushed to denounce them and apologize for their "crimes" to any gentile who'd listen. She swallowed.

"I'm invisible, remember?" she told her sister, crumpling her napkin. "That's why I'm going instead of you. Once you show up, people will talk. How can they not with your face? But with me, I can get us what we need. No trouble."

"Except for the gossips last week." Tamar sniffed. "And your tumble today." She cocked her head at Hannah. "And you didn't answer my question."

"What question?" Hannah frowned. *Oh, right.* "I wouldn't call it 'help' though he prevented me from hitting the ground." She rolled her eyes once more, thinking back to the incident.

" 'He'?" Tamar's lips twisted into a knowing smile. Leaning forward, she rested her hand on her chin and stared at Hannah expectantly.

Hannah, in turn, resisted sticking her tongue out at her sister and gave a dismissive sniff. "Solomon Weiss. Part of a banking family which was once very successful but lost it all through bad investments. They've been trying to rebuild for some time and have supposedly had limited success through gentile clientele. Which is probably why he helped me as he most likely doesn't know who I…" She bit her lip, not able to say the words out loud. Or more, admit the truth. She rubbed her wrist. "Anyway, I have no idea what he was doing there."

"Looking to get back in?" Her sister gave a shrug. As if it were so simple and easy.

"A waste of time and energy," Hannah grumbled.

Tamar opened her mouth, presumably in protest.

"His, not yours." Hannah said hastily. Especially as Tamar hadn't quite left. Not by choice at least. She still heard the woman at the Jewish Orphan's Home chastising her when she felt at her lowest: *You're making a mistake, robbing the child of her chances, her community, her people. Leave her with us, before you ruin her like your parents ruined you—*

Hannah had cut off the atrociously overdressed woman, condemning them for how they'd done nothing for her parents—and likely would do nothing for Tamar—before hauling away her sister.

That night she'd vowed not just to care for Tamar, but to give her anything and everything she could ever want. And she would not fail now. Hannah reached across the table and squeezed her sister's hand. "What you want won't be a waste for you. I'll make sure of it."

"Right." Tamar leaned back and stared at her, making Hannah squirm a little for once. Not a pleasant feeling at all.

"So this Solomon Weiss—he was kind to you?" Her sister squinted.

"I suppose so." Hannah shrugged, before settling back and taking another bite of cholent.

"Was he handsome?"

Hannah near spit out her food. "I wasn't paying attention," she managed to say as she pounded a fist into her breastbone. "I got caught on his jacket and the dratted man just stood there chatting while I—"

"Chatting with you?" Tamar asked.

"At me? To me? With me? One of the three? It was

damned distracting," she grumbled, before gazing up at her sister's rather odd expression. "What?"

"Nothing." Tamar smoothed her skirts and took a long sip of water. Hannah grabbed another piece of bread and chewed on it for a moment, working to keep her mind in the present and not back at the synagogue, where her fingers had near grazed his chest. This time, she'd been close enough to learn that he smelled not just like wood, but of limes. And mint.

And had lashes so thick and black that—

Her sister cleared her throat. "So he spoke to you while you got yourself free and..."

"And nothing." Hannah coughed again. "I left."

"Without saying good-bye?" Tamar frowned at her.

"He was a stranger." Hannah grabbed her own water.

"You didn't introduce yourself to him?" her sister asked. As if such a thing were easy. Or advisable. Not that there was any use saying so out loud. Tamar would only argue, and Hannah wanted to spend one Shabbos without a headache.

"There was no reason to," she said instead, rubbing her temples proactively. "Though Aaron Ellenberg rushed up to him at the end so I'm sure he knows better now."

For the first time in years, a hard lump filled her chest, more pressure snaking its way behind her eyes. Which wouldn't do. The past was done with and couldn't be changed. She had learned to live with the consequences of her and her parents' choices. And she'd survived.

Despite them and their opinions. And she would not be ashamed nor care nor—

"Hannah." Her sister's voice was achingly soft.

Hannah pinched the bridge of her nose. "It's all right, Tamar. I won't let it affect your prospects." She inhaled. "I'll be careful. And with the money I'm gathering for your dowry, I'll no longer be a liability to your future. You will have what you want." She gritted her teeth. "This spring. At the latest."

And before Tamar could argue, she rose and gathered her empty bowl and glass, moving them to the wash area for after Shabbos.

Chapter Four

Much to Sol's chagrin, Aaron did not immediately tell him the identity of his mystery woman when they left the confines of the synagogue. No, the blasted man forced him to wait while he dutifully attended to his wife and her grandmother, making sure the latter was escorted to the home of a cousin for her luncheon and bidding the former farewell so she could spend time with her good friend, the rather surly daughter of the community's midwife.

By the time they marched westward, snow had mixed with the rain, splattering debris all over his new boots, which were supposed to fool the world into believing his family was securely back at the "top of the heap," as his mystery woman had put it. Because like attracted like, and if he was going to rise, the big machers needed to think he was one of them already.

He'd make sure the boots were polished when he got home. Sol frowned as they approached the large town-home his father had built, and his brother was still in the process of restoring. The building sat right between the western edge of Aldgate and the eastern side of Mayfair—a stone's throw from a respectable gentile area the man couldn't quite breach, but which could easily be seen from the enormous windows of the tall upper floors—beneath the imposing sloped roof, which would need maintenance if this weather kept up. Sooner rather than later, as only last month, a large brick had come off and near crushed his head. Yet another reason for them to bolster their coffers again. And quick.

Their accounts were still recovering from a few new ventures his brother had undertaken last year. Not that there was any cause for concern. You had to spend money to make money, and if anyone understood how to balance it all correctly, it was Frederick. If not, they'd have been bankrupt long ago.

Trotting up the stairs, with Aaron close behind, he rushed inside the large open door that Martin, the family's butler, already held open, rubbing his hands together.

"Thank you," he breathed as the man assisted him with his overcoat. "It's getting a touch nasty out there and—"

"Ah, Solomon, you're home." His brother's matter-of-fact tone cut him off. "Hopefully you'll apply yourself properly to something useful this afternoon." Sol glanced to the parlor entrance to find the elder Weiss standing in the center of the large, paneled doors, the mirrored buttons on his best jacket gleaming beneath the brightly lit chandeliers. His honey-colored waves glinted in the light, highlighting the seriousness of his strikingly handsome face.

"Frederick. I didn't know you'd still be here," Sol said as he approached his brother, his heart pounding. His brother typically spent his Saturdays making calls to gentile acquaintances as part of his efforts in restoring the banking business their father had destroyed before his death. That very same event had also saddled Frederick, a mere seventeen years at the time, with a seven-year-old half-brother to raise.

Nearly two decades later, not only was the business once again profitable, but its profile was also on the rise—to heights no one could have previously imagined. A feat that ought to give his brother his due after his many years of hard work, sacrifice, and schemes. As admittedly, his brother had superb and often underestimated instincts in spades.

A boon for them both, as Sol possessed far less natural ability and charm.

"I see you've brought Mr. Ellenberg." His brother's gaze narrowed, inspecting Aaron. "Are those new gloves? Good choice, covering those hands of yours."

Aaron only stepped forward, extending the aforementioned hand to Frederick. "Good Shabbos. How are you?" His brother accepted after only a moment's pause, though from Sol's vantage point, the shake was limp and noncommittal. He winced—loyal to a fault, his brother had not quite forgiven Aaron for besting Sol in the courtship of the man's wife.

"I'm splendid. Happy to spend the day with the best sort of company." His brother stepped back and to the side and indicated a well-dressed gentile man and woman standing near the green silk fainting couch in the parlor. "May I introduce Lord Crispin Gladwell, the Viscount Penrose? And his sister, Drucilla?" Frederick returned his attention to the couple, his smile now wide. "Mr. Ellenberg has married into the Lira family, of Lira & Berab Sureties. My brother is very well acquainted with them."

"How do you do?" The man—Gladwell—or Penrose—

oy, he needed to get better at gentile naming conventions—
stepped forward, his tone cool, as his gaze flitted first
over Aaron before landing on Sol with a sharp intensity.
"Interesting business, sureties. Lots of speculation and
divination involved, as I understand, for very little return.
At least not for the people whose hard-earned money you
so freely take in exchange for your papers."

Hard-earned money.

Sol's jaw clenched. Something a viscount knew all
about, no doubt. How again did the man purchase his
bespoke garments? With funds yielded from the labor
of farmers—people who worked land only his family held? Land that had been—what? Gifted to them
by some long-dead king or queen for an undoubtably
"noble" service? One that involved only "righteous"
violence, no doubt.

Yes, the viscount's fortune was completely virtuous
in ways that his business could never be.

Not that he—or Aaron or even Frederick, who was
still seen as more Jew than gentile despite his recent
Baptism—could argue that point. They did not make
the rules of the game, only played with what limited pieces they were allotted. Pieces that the likes of
Penrose could take away over any insult or threat, large
or small, perceived or real.

He exhaled and gave the man his most pleasant, deferential smile.

"I like to think of it more as a protective industry.
We help businesses and the people who build them protect themselves against hardship," Sol told him, threading his fingers.

"For a healthy cut of their profits." The man gave a
dismissive sniff.

He saw Aaron clench his fists. "My wife's family and partners provide a service, one which harms no one, and certainly does not take any more than their fair—"

"That's a lovely gown, Lady Drucilla," Sol interrupted. "The way the trim on your gloves coordinates with the edging on the sleeves is so clever." He moved quickly toward the woman, his voice loud enough to drown out anything else Aaron might have said.

"Thank you so much." The woman's face lit with a warm smile. "I'm just relieved to be out of mourning for my dear, late husband and wearing color again. Gentlemen usually don't notice those things." She glanced over to Frederick. "Though your brother always does. From the moment I returned to London, and we first met." Her cheeks flushed.

Suddenly the source of Frederick's poor behavior was clear. Penrose was more than important, not merely for their banking goals, but for, perhaps, a chance at the life his brother had missed out on by raising Sol. A life he most certainly deserved. Time to shuffle the conversation in the right direction.

"Frederick has the most refined taste in all of London. Especially for artistic objects—he has quite the collection," Sol told her, hastily gesturing toward his brother's prized antique mirrors hanging on the wall.

"Oh?" Penrose arched a golden eyebrow.

"My brother flatters me. I'm a mere appreciator of beauty," Frederick said, coming to his side, his dark frockcoat swinging open to reveal its fine, royal blue velvet lining.

"I can tell." The viscount paused, this time leveling that inspecting glare at his brother. "However, Drucilla and I must be going." He snapped his fingers, and Martin arrived with a heavy overcoat for him and a fur-lined cloak for the sister. "We have several more calls to make. Your neighbor, Stoudmire, he and Drucilla were quite fond of each other when they were young, and his father is a marquess, you know? A good man. While he's a second son, he's retired quite admirably from His Majesty's service." He gazed at his sister.

"Yes, he was a most loyal and diverting companion. And so kind. He's a benefactor to my charity for impoverished children," she said. "It's so lovely that you're neighbors."

Penrose shot Frederick what could only be described as a triumphant smirk. "Thank you so much for your hospitality, Mr. Weiss," he said.

"The pleasure was all mine." Frederick gave the man an impeccable, dignified bow, before turning back to his sister. "I do hope to see you both at the opera next week. *If* you're attending." The hopeful smile on his face made him look at least ten years younger than his six and thirty years.

"Oh yes." With renewed enthusiasm, she turned to her brother and clasped her hands together, crushing her fluffy white muff. "Please? I would adore hearing Mr. Weiss's opinion of the production, from our box."

"That would be lovely," Penrose said, his words a touch forced. "Until then. Mr. Weiss, Mr. Weiss, Mr. Ellenberg." He gave them a tip of his hat and quickly marched from the building, nearly shoving his sister out in front of him.

"New friends?" Sol spoke first, breaking the rather heavy silence in the parlor.

Frederick, however, ignored the remark and brushed

past him to glare directly at Aaron. "Don't you have a floor to sweep somewhere?" He wrinkled his nose. "Outside my house?"

Sol winced. Oy. His brother really didn't intend to be unkind, though given the expression on Aaron's face, he'd have some smoothing over to do.

His friend folded his arms across his chest. "I was just leaving," he growled, reaching out to grab his coat from Martin.

But Aaron couldn't leave. At least not just yet. Not without telling him about her—the woman, his rescuer.

"No, you were not." Sol grabbed his arm. "You have information to give me."

Frederick released a huff from the other side of the room. "Can it not wait until tomorrow? At *his* house. Or should I say, his wife's?"

Rolling his eyes, Aaron gave Frederick another sharp frown. "Why don't you walk me to the door, Sol?"

An excellent solution. "I'll be right back," he told Frederick, but his brother had already turned his back, retreating into the parlor with a dismissive wave over his shoulder. Sol strolled quickly after Aaron, working to outpace him in the event the other man decided to leave without giving Sol answers.

"Rebecca said you should put more salve on your side," Aaron told him when he had caught up. "You've been rubbing at it, and I asked," he added before Sol could inquire. "And Isabelle thinks you should get more sleep. You've been working stunningly long hours as of late, between the sureties' company and the bank. She's concerned about your health." He raised a brow, not needing to say *and I don't like my wife to be upset* out loud.

Sol frowned. "I'm perfectly fit."

"You nearly nodded off this morning, and I've found you sleeping at your desk too many nights now," Aaron said. "*And* you risk hurting yourself in exhaustion. Look at what happened at your morning ride."

"I fell asleep once. And the incident with the horse wasn't from exhaustion, I just haven't been riding in some time. I should've practiced more." He'd loosened his grip too much on the reins in a careless act that Frederick had berated him for—rightly so, as he had more important things to worry after than his foolish brother's inattention.

Aaron straightened a fringe on the rug with the toe of his boot. "We just worry and care about you."

Which was touching. More than touching. The other man was truly kind. Annoying at times, like now when he was discussing things Sol felt no need to dwell on, but very, very kind. Sol ran a hand through his hair. "Sorry about Frederick. Penrose is an arse, and it can't have been easy holding back in his presence." He sighed. "Please understand—he holds a grudge for a long time and his behavior is because he is unduly outraged on my behalf as you bested me in the quest for Isabelle's hand. I'll talk to him, I promise."

His friend's lip twitched. "I'll keep my comments regarding your brother to myself, and I don't hold you accountable for what he does so you need not apologize."

"Good!" Sol exclaimed, glad to have cleared the air so quickly. He moved to physically block the door. "Now, before you leave, you have to tell me: who is she?" Aaron might be a hair taller, but Sol was broader and would use that bulk to his advantage if needed.

"I appreciate the directness," Aaron said.

"I thought you might." Sol folded his arms. "Especially as my charm doesn't typically work on you. Must be the lack of refinement on your end." He couldn't help teasing with a wink.

Aaron coughed into his hand. "No comment."

"Then I'll repeat my question—who is she?" Sol asked again as Aaron buttoned his overcoat, pausing only to bite his lip.

"Her name is Hannah Moses," he finally answered.

Hannah. Her name was Hannah. She seemed like a Hannah. Bold but graceful and—

Sol wrinkled his nose as the back of his brain prickled. "Why does that name sound familiar?"

"Because it's infamous. At least her parents are." Aaron glanced over at the parlor before lowering his voice. "It happened about a dozen years ago, when we were practically still boys. She—Hannah—wasn't that much older, probably no more than nineteen or twenty. Her parents were notorious fences, ran a pawnshop at the edge of Whitechapel."

Sol swore under his breath. If there was ever a person he should stay away from, it would be one who engaged with the seedier parts of London, feeding into the gentiles' worst imaginings of their ilk.

"I take it they were not discreet?" he managed to ask as a wave of disappointment washed over him.

Aaron released a hash laugh. "No. Which was the problem." His mouth set in a grim line. "While most in the community understand that not all of us can always meet the gentiles' definition of being 'upright' if we want to feed ourselves, the Moses family was not merely surviving."

Aaron sighed, then continued. "And they were certainly not thinking of the community and its safety when they acted. They were known to revel in how many characteristics they embodied of the monsters we're believed to be." He shook his head. "Worse, they were arrogant and careless. Tried to extract too much from a gentile of influence, with a sister who'd decided certain people needed to be taught a 'lesson.'"

Sol gulped. "Oh no."

Though considering the bravery she'd shown when she'd saved his life, the story wasn't particularly surprising. Really, he should have known. Why else would she have been out at night like that if she wasn't one of the community's villains? And while he didn't quite share Aaron's single-minded desire to protect the community at all costs—a good reason his friend was the one on the Commission of Delegates—the communal body, who, in addition to advocating with the Crown for the community's safety, solving internal disputes, and organizing their various factions, maintained tight control of the community's image to the outside world—he most certainly understood why a woman like Hannah was not only someone of no use to his or his brother's goals, but also someone he should *not* want to be around.

"The gentiles loved the trial. Both the outcome and the exaggerated reporting, which made several of their papers quite wealthy. Not to mention that writer who penned a popular serial changing the facts to make the woman's father resemble the fiends of their fairy stories even more. Wrote him as relying on the corruption of gentile boys for his criminal ways. Which, given the writer's connection to the trial, had many of his readers believing the truth in those allegations. And made them even more disappointed there were no hangings." Aaron shook his head in disgust.

Oy. Just oy.

"But that's not here nor there. In the real story, the Moses family greed saved them in the end," Aaron continued, shoving his hands into his pockets. "The parents paid a pretty penny in bribes to be sent to Norfolk Island. The older daughter—your Hannah—was given a lesser sentence, and only spent a year or two in prison. Though from what I've heard on the Commission, she was as up to her ears in everything as the parents."

Sol released a few choice curses in his head. Yes, sir, there could be no speaking of Hannah ever again. Especially not with Frederick's clear interest in the viscount's sister. Any whiff of a connection could kill his brother's chances. He opened his mouth to thank Aaron but—

"Older daughter?" he asked instead.

"Yes. There's a sister. Much younger. A mere child at the time. The community begged Hannah to let us take care of her, raise her properly so she'd have a chance at a good life," Aaron explained.

"Let me guess, the elder Miss Moses didn't take kindly to that?" His lip twitched despite himself because the woman he'd seen was hardly the type to acquiesce to anyone.

"No." A ghost of a smile graced Aaron's lips as well. "Essentially told my grandmother-in-law that she and the community could hang, and given what we 'allowed' to happen to her parents, that she and her sister had no use for our—well, let's just say the words were not polite and reflected a certain animosity." He cocked his head at Sol. "What?"

"I'm just surprised she didn't end up floating in the Thames," he said, giving in to laughter. Because Aaron's wife might be frightening, but her grandmother, a leader in the community despite not holding a delegate position on the Commission, was downright terrifying. Hannah was truly brave, or foolish, or both.

And for some ridiculous reason that only made him like her more.

"I'm sure the possibility crossed her mind several times, but Hannah Moses still lives, as we've all witnessed." Aaron smirked.

"Though if the two had met at services today..." Sol shook his head at the possibilities.

"Oh yes, that might have made quite the entertainment." Aaron's smirk became a full grin, the man probably picturing the scene. Sol worked to do the same but failed to remember what Mrs. Lira even looked like despite walking with her a mere hour ago, as his mind could only conjure images of Hannah. And the way her plump, full lips settled into a rather delicious smirk every time she gave as good as she got in verbal sparring.

Shaking his head, he said, "But back to Hannah." He pushed off the door and took a step toward Aaron. "What happened to her and her sister after?"

"As far as I know, she took the girl back to the family's old rooms and started running that pawnshop again. As if nothing had happened. Albeit she's had less monetary success and taken seemingly more care, as there hasn't been any trouble since, but you know the danger in it. Especially given how many gentiles those places serve." Aaron sighed anew. "Barely involve themselves in the community. The older one attends on the holidays, but always hides in the shadows. I'd forgotten she existed until she bumped into you by that alcove...Funny that."

"What?" Sol blinked at his friend.

"Nothing of importance. It's just the same exact spot where I crashed into Isabelle for the first time. Must be something in the design." Aaron tapped a finger to his lips before seemingly dismissing his thoughts with a brisk wave. "Anyway, I have no idea what she could possibly have been doing at services today. Or more, I can't think of a good and honest reason for her to be there. Which means that you should be careful."

He leveled a warning gaze at Sol, who ducked his head, scratching the back of his ear.

"About what? I don't even know the woman," he said, wincing a little at his dismissive words. Villain or not, Hannah had saved his life, which had to mean *something*.

Not that she appeared to be holding out for his gratitude. Or even seemed to want it. She hadn't been able to get away from him fast enough at the synagogue, and if that wasn't a sign that he needed to forget her, then that, coupled with Aaron's information...

Still, he hadn't truly thanked her.

"No. You don't." His friend frowned. "I'm just—Isabelle is only now getting her bearings with the Berab brothers, and you're still making a name for yourself. I can't imagine the dramatics they'd engage in to avoid being associated with someone like Miss Moses, and after all your hard work, you see..."

Sol could only nod. Because yes, he saw. Isabelle's former animosity with her business partners was the only reason she'd offered him a role—and with the families of Lira & Berab Sureties no longer at odds, he had no reason to assume she'd back him should he become embroiled in any sort of scandal.

"And I'm sure Frederick would have a fit if he knew you'd even spoken with her. Especially with the way he was fawning over that gentile woman," Aaron added, rolling his eyes. "Though now I suppose I don't need to wonder anymore about his recent Baptism." He smiled sardonically. "I hope he gets everything he wants out of it."

Sol winced at the judgment in his friend's tone.

"Perhaps," Sol said with a shrug. "Lady Drucilla is clearly a lovely woman, and if my brother is successful in courting her, I'll happily welcome her into our family."

"First, her brother must allow it. Something I'm working quite hard to make happen." Frederick's voice boomed from over Aaron's shoulder.

Sol winced at the sight of his brother back in the hall, glaring at his friend once more. Hopefully he hadn't heard too much.

Or really anything. Especially about Hannah.

"I see you're still here, Mr. Ellenberg. I suppose Sol is responsible—he's always been easily distracted." The dryness in his brother's tone could curl paper. "A problem we've been working to address his entire life. I worry, you understand, given how frivolously he's been spending his time since he's made your acquaintance."

Sol's face heated—how long had he lingered with Aaron, when he ought to have been working, Shabbos or not?

Focus, he had to focus. He had promised to deliver Frederick a real win. And he would—soon.

"I was just leaving," Aaron said, brushing past him. "It was good sitting with you today, Sol. I look forward to next time." Martin popped into the entry to open the door before Aaron swished out into the now fleetly falling snow.

Sol stared after him, forcing his mind away from the one person he needed to forget.

Chapter Five

Hannah had barely unlatched the door to the shop on Monday morning before the small front space was filled with customers. Some were shabbily dressed, popping in on their way to work as laborers or dockhands. Others yawned from a night on the streets, where they found other ways to earn their keep.

All needed funds. And all hoped that she would accept whatever objects they were willing to part with to get them. Whether the object was theirs or not—that was the question.

Not that the provenance of her wares precisely mattered, Hannah thought, reaching out to inspect the bottom of a fine porcelain bowl. However, *expensive*, stolen goods—like what she was holding—were hazardous to one's health, no matter the potential profits or thrill from the risk.

"Not for me, unfortunately." She pushed the bowl back at the bedraggled man in front of her. Not quite a regular, but he'd been around a few times before, selling her some little trinkets—pieces of ribbon, a plain tin ring, a decent knife. None originating with him, but all small and ordinary. Nothing big like today.

"What's wrong with it?" His pale eyebrows knit

together in obvious frustration. "No chips or breaks, see?" He held it aloft, as if proving his words would solve the argument.

"No, but—" She reached out and turned it on its backside. "It's got markings here and here, but only one from the maker. The other is for some other purpose, probably identification, if you catch my meaning."

"It's small." He pouted as she laid the bowl back on the counter.

She rolled her eyes. "It's big enough. I, for one, am not in the market for a one-way ticket to New South Wales. And you should know, I'd name *you* in court faster than you can say 'prison hulk.'"

The customer leveled a surly glare at her. "As if they'd believe the likes of you," he snapped before turning to the side and spitting on her newly swept floor. "All you do is lie."

"Maybe they would, maybe they wouldn't, but is that truly a risk you want to take?" Her lip curled even as the insult pinged off the emotional parapets that enabled her to survive the day without throwing a punch, or worse, shedding a tear.

Not that she'd ever do the latter.

"Rent's due, Hannah." Now he was pleading. Which was not only rather odious but bad for business. She glanced at the line behind him to find it had dissipated, with only the jingling of the bell and a trail of wet footprints to signal those who'd been there before. Hannah swore in her head. Hopefully the afternoon rush would be more fruitful.

"Not my problem," she told him, before shoving the stolen goods back at him. "And another piece of advice, I'd not take this elsewhere. At least two shops have been informing the magistrates for extra coin. Moreover, another three are so foolhardy, the constables will've nabbed the lot of you by sunset. Next," she called even if it was at an empty space.

The man grumbled, but accepted both the bowl and the halfpenny she hid in her sleeve for such occasions, before shuffling out of the now vacant store. This time, with an audible sigh, Hannah retreated to the back room, hidden by a thick, heavy curtain, where she could shelve the pawned and sold goods, and do some accounting, leaving her sister to tidy up the front section.

"That was kind, but it won't pay his rent," a male voice rumbled in her ear after Hannah opened the ledger to record her purchase of a worn perfume bottle from an earlier customer.

Whirling around, she came face-to-face with Solomon Weiss. She swallowed a gasp, working not to appear off-balance, despite the odd shift in the ground beneath her feet.

"No, it won't, and it wasn't. But I'm not kind and neither is he. What it'll do is put something in his stomach, which will make it less likely for him to come back here later, with a knife." She sniffed to hide a shudder at the memory of a similar encounter. One that had cost her father not only all the funds on hand, but two of his teeth.

Her chest tightening uncomfortably, Hannah forced back the past as she returned her attention to the present.

"Who let you back here anyway?" she demanded, making her voice as sharp and imperious as possible. Unfortunately, the effect was slightly lost when she backed into a table covered in vases and ornamental boxes, nearly knocking over the lot.

"The girl out front with the broom—said she was your sister—told me I could come back here when I introduced myself." He indicated behind him. "Does that happen often, the knife bit?" he asked, knitting his brow.

"I wouldn't stick around and find out if I were you." Hannah glared at him, folding her arms over her faded, once pale blue gown—a garment she suddenly noticed was, well, quite drab and hideous. Especially compared to his smart, deep green overcoat, which set off his fine features, highlighting the contrast between them even more. "As for my sister, she's too kind for her own good and no doubt you manipulated her in some way as you most certainly shouldn't be here." She wagged a finger at him. "Unless you're perchance buying or selling something."

To her surprise, he lowered his gaze almost sheepishly before looking back up at her. "I came to properly thank you for helping me last spring, something I should have done far earlier. I also wanted to apologize for the other day. I was flippant, as well as bordering on inappropriate, given the location."

When she didn't respond, he gave a shrug, his voice suspiciously nonchalant. "But now that I am here… may I look around?" He was already weaving to her left toward her merchandise. Not that it was unexpected. After all, rich or poor, macher or pariah, none of their people ever got anywhere, let alone survived, by asking for permission.

"Does this look like a shop in which you can 'look around'?" She closed the lower cabinets, silently thanking her own vigilance in locking up the more valuable—and thus more dangerous—wares. The ones that could only be sold to very special customers, if at all.

"It is rather dark." He glanced at the single lamp in the corner, the only light in the entire room. "Here and in the front. Why do you cover all the windows?"

Because I'm a bloody criminal and I'm trying not to get caught. Again. What do you think? Hannah wrinkled her nose at the man, unable to decide if he was putting her on. Because if he was here, he had to know who she was, right?

"The sun fades the wares," she said instead, removing a tin pocket watch from his hand and setting it back in its place.

"A fair point." He took a step back, cocking his head. "And I'm sure it has nothing to do with that man and his stolen bowl and the coin you slipped him despite the fact he was trying to make you his fence."

Oy. If this was an example of their sekel, no wonder the Weiss family business had failed.

"I'm already his fence. Just when he has things that won't get us both transported." *Or worse.* She leaned back against the small desk she used for accounting, cocking her head right back at him. "Does that shock you?" she asked, hoping her voice held enough threat to send him running for the front door. Because he had no business being there. None at all. And he needed to leave.

"Should it?" he returned, with yet another shrug, his voice and his expression obnoxiously unreadable. Perhaps she should rethink the lighting.

"What would you like, Mr. Weiss? Or more, why are you here?" she asked, gritting her teeth.

His lips broke into a full, earnest smile that was both

so handsome and so genuine that something odd inside her ached.

"You know my name," he said.

"Don't flatter yourself." She worked to ignore the dratted note of happiness in his voice. "I know many things. It's part of my job. Information is power, after all." As if his name was hard to learn. She had ears. "If you truly wanted to thank me or apologize—which you really *don't* need to, as it's highly unlikely we'll cross paths again—you could've sent a note," she pointed out.

The man didn't even hesitate to say, "I most certainly owed you both the apology and thanks. And I didn't want to write; I wanted to see you."

False. That had to be false. No one, save Tamar and her parents, ever wanted to see her without getting anything in return. And what could she possibly give this man that he couldn't get better somewhere else?

"Well, now you've seen me, and you've said your piece, I suggest you leave. Real customers, ones who pay, will be coming soon." She wrinkled her nose. "Don't you have a job you should be doing?"

Even if he didn't, he ought to have some reason to leave and stop forcing her to think uncomfortable thoughts—like how this was the longest conversation she'd had in years with anyone outside her family that didn't involve the other person making demands of her. Or more, the most interest anyone had shown in her outside her use to them.

"I had a meeting earlier, in Aldgate, so this visit was actually convenient." He glanced around again, this time threading his fingers together behind his back, rocking on the toes of his somehow, despite the snowy weather, still shiny black boots.

"I'm surprised that you would come anywhere near here," she grumbled as she searched her mind for some verbal jab to make him flee. "Though seeing you at Duke's Place was a surprise as well. I thought your family had moved beyond such things."

"I value the community. It was very important to my late mother and I…" He paused, and his brow furrowed.

"What?" she asked, despite the fact that whatever he was thinking should not matter in the slightest nor intrigue her in any way.

"Nothing." He gazed back at her and shook his head. "It's just that you aren't the type who is impressed with platitudes."

Hannah gaped. What did he mean by that? Or more, why did it matter? "I'm not the type who is impressed period, especially not by the likes of you," she said with more bite than intended.

"Fair enough." His chest rose, the fabric of his shirt pulling taut against muscles she was determined not to notice, before he wagged a finger at her. "But you do value honesty and I'll give that to you."

She rubbed the back of her neck, ducking her head, inexplicably unable to meet his gaze any longer. "It's all right. You really don't need to."

"I know, which is what makes me so kind." His soft smile became a grin, a near wolfish one, which, at her age, shouldn't make her heart speed, but…

Hannah forced herself to give him a haughty sniff. "I'm not sure 'kind' would be the word I'd use."

"Then nice at least. Or maybe charming?" His dark eyes twinkled through the dim room, and she couldn't quite think of a smart response. He cleared his throat.

"But anyway, I was at services to make business and personal connections. Something very critical for me and my family right now."

"Oh." She nodded as her heartbeat returned to normal with that dose of reality. Not that his answer hadn't been expected. That was the entire point of why his presence here, with her, was so ludicrous.

"Do you want to know why it's so critical?" he asked, as if her answer mattered to him in the slightest.

"Have I given you any indication that I do?" She straightened a strand of hair that had come loose from its hasty pinning.

"You haven't given any indication that you don't. And answering a question with another question signals interest, I should think," he pointed out, wagging a finger at her once more. Somehow, the act, which should be odious, was charming on him. In an obnoxious way. "Yes?"

"I'm waiting for you to tell me." She folded her arms, stroking the soft, old seams of the remade linen—too light for the weather but her wool needed mending. "Obviously, you're going to; thus you might as well get on with it so you can leave me to my business, one which is clearly very different than yours." She ground her teeth, her stare daring him to contradict her.

Instead, he merely shrugged. Then he took a step forward.

"Fair," he said. "You see, my father was a good man but not good with finances. So when he died, my brother and I discovered the business was...not well. It has taken years, but we—well, mostly my brother as I was rather young—have built it back to a stable, in fact profitable, state. But my brother made many sacrifices along the way. So now that I'm grown—"

"Debatable." The retort popped out despite, well, everything.

"Would you like me to prove it?" His grin was back, along with the ill-advised thrumming that was getting a great deal harder to resist. This would-be dandy was the last person she should be toying with, but she could see his pupils dilating, smell that tantalizing mix of lime and wood...

Oy, perhaps she should acquiesce more the next time Ned came around, despite the risk, or seek out Will, or Charlie, or any of the goyishe criminals with whom she knew exactly where she stood, where the limits were clear and well defined.

But instead, she stepped closer, saying, "Oh, Mr. Weiss, that doesn't constitute grown." An unbidden sly smile rose to her lips as her eyes traced his form, and somehow, without even thinking, she'd moved so close, they were mere inches apart. So close that she could reach out and stroke his cheek, feel the slight dark stubble against his jaw. "And if you're aiming to impress me, well, let's just say, at this point in my life, very little does in that department, and I don't have the time or energy today to watch you flounder about."

His lip tipped. "I wouldn't flounder," he said, catching her eye.

There was such heat in his gaze.

"I'm sure you think so," she said, and he laughed heartily, sending warm shivers down her spine, before she regained enough control to ask, "What?"

"You're both exactly how I thought you'd be and, at the same time, wholly unexpected." And there was that damned sincerity again, bringing forth emotions that she had no idea what to do with, except make him leave.

She drew back. "Go away, Mr. Weiss. I don't know why you're here or what you want, but I promise you, you will not get it from me." Damn it all, was her voice shaking?

She ground her jaw to steady herself and sharpened her tone as she glared at him, the dratted man who had no business being there. "You say you're grown, well, then you ought to recognize some truths of the world. This is not a place for you, and I have nothing to offer save a few lackluster minutes of amusement. And I'm too old to waste time on lackluster."

He arched those thick brows. "How old are you?"

"Thirty-two. Quite a bit older than the likes of your employer," she couldn't help but add.

"I'm also older than her. And her husband," he said, then added. "I'm twenty-six." As if it mattered. As if their situation wasn't the same—he was far too young for her. Even if she was inclined.

Which she wasn't.

"Good for you," she said. "If you stay out of places like this, you might one day grow old enough to study the Zohar." She turned her back to him and made a show of fiddling with a tray of loose buttons, willing him to take the hint and leave her be.

"And you truly believe anything between us would be lackluster?" he asked instead.

"Yes," she lied.

Weiss snapped his fingers. "How about a wager then?"

"What?" Hannah spun around, gaping at him.

Rummaging in his pocket, he pulled out a coin and held it up to her. "A sixpence." He reached around and set it on the table, brushing against her arm. "If we—"

"I cost much more than a sixpence," she snapped. Both because it was objectively true and because she had been a blasted fool to think their exchange was anything more than yet another demand to be made of her.

"I'm not purchasing anything. Or *anyone*," he said, sounding affronted. "I am gambling."

She could find no hint of teasing or sarcasm in his tone.

He raised a single finger. "One kiss. If it is 'lackluster,' you get the sixpence, and if it isn't, you'll owe me one."

Oy. He was tempting. Too tempting. And tempting led to wanting. And wanting what she couldn't have led to nothing but trouble. And he couldn't afford trouble. Especially not now. She swallowed. "I don't gamble."

"Coward." But Weiss smiled as he spoke and folded his arms over his rather expansive chest.

"No—*smart*," she said. Except when she stared behind those thick lashes into eyes that were all mirth and, if she were a more romantic person, magic, she found herself reaching into her apron pocket, pulling out a coin, and laying it next to his. "Fine. A sixpence. And either way, you leave."

"Excellent. We have a deal." And, oy, why was that grin so affecting? Or more, attractive?

And before she could think, she'd moved to him again. They were close in height, so she didn't need to stretch up to meet his mouth, instead throwing her arm around his neck to yank him toward her.

With a groan, he grasped her hips, pulling her against him as he held her close, his lips crashing into hers with a raw fire that near took her breath away. Moaning, she opened, taking him in, reveling in the broad, firm strokes of his tongue, which promised not only lust but a pleasure that would be deeper and more tantalizing. More terrifying.

His movements weren't careful and practiced, but pure. Without artifice or force, a passion just simple and true and natural.

She clutched at his shorn hair, knocking his hat to the ground, practically dislodging his yarmulke, unable to get enough of this, of him. Everything in her body craved more, of his taste, his heat, of him and only him, fully and completely. Which was—*no.*

Half dazed, Hannah wrenched herself back from his body. Panting, she clutched the table for purchase as her mind spun.

"So are you going to take that sixpence?" he asked, grinning from ear to ear as he retrieved his hat and perched it back on his head, all calm and collected and—

Momzer. Complete momzer. Hannah searched her brain for a cutting remark to hurl back at him because that couldn't stand, nor could the kiss have been so—

"Why don't you call it a draw?" a female voice called from behind her. Hannah spun around to find her sister smiling slyly just inside the curtain, broom in her hand. "I didn't want to interrupt, but you have a visitor. At the back door."

"Tamar." Hannah coughed a little, her face heating. She placed herself between her sister and the man whose grin only seemed to grow. "Mr. Weiss was just leaving."

Taking care to stay between them, she pushed him past her sister and into the front of the store as Tamar followed. Fast as she could, Hannah swung open the door, letting the chilly air brush over them both, as if it could soothe all the lust burning inside her.

Mr. Weiss locked eyes with her yet again, that knowing look, both irritating and charming, still on his face.

He nodded his head. "Good day, Miss Moses." He leaned over and indicated to Tamar. "And Miss Moses. Thank you so much for your hospitality." Then giving a little salute, he disappeared into the crowded street, leaving her staring after him as the wind whipped snow up around her feet.

With a sigh, she retreated back into the store and crossed to the rear entrance into the alley. Hopefully, her "visitor" would offer her an extra job, not demand more payment.

Given her luck, it would probably be the latter.

Chapter Six

Two days later, Sol stood at the threshold of Penrose's drawing room, surveying the man's guests. With dinner concluded, he could at last discern the true nature of everyone's relationships without the buffer of assigned seating.

Lady Drucilla had thread her arm through Frederick's and was in the process of introducing him to a group of ladies, presumably friends, leaving Sol to fend for himself. Or rather, in the words of Frederick, not do anything foolish, as Penrose had yet to give his brother permission to formally pursue Lady Drucilla. The man was doing his best to thrust Stoudmire, the marquess's son, in his sister's face every chance he got.

Which meant Sol needed to be in top form with his flattery and guided deployment of mild, genteel questions.

So far, so good. He'd received many of their smiles at dinner. As well as a few compliments.

Not surprising. He'd dressed in his second favorite jacket—the color more muted than the brilliant blue he'd worn to the Great Synagogue. But this was a more useful garment, as it had enough layers to hide the still-healing gash his now former valet had given him during the prior day's shave.

A little deeper and poor Frederick would've been forced to miss the gathering for shiva.

Shame he had such nervous hands, as the man had been quite amusing. Sol had asked his brother to find the man another position, and hopefully whatever he was doing now suited him better.

Sol scanned the room, catching the eye of a woman he believed to be the daughter of one of Penrose's fellow noblemen. She immediately ducked her head behind her fan and giggled to her friend next to her. Well, if that wasn't an invitation... too bad there wasn't dancing. He was good at dancing, as it put people at ease and allowed him to charm them even more easily.

An unbidden image popped into his head. Not of him with one of these women at a gentile ball, but instead, of the last person he should be picturing.

Hannah.

His hand on her waist. And she wouldn't be tittering. No, her eyes would be merry with amusement, clear and focused on him when he pulled her close—oy. No.

Mercy. That would never happen. Never in a hundred and twenty years.

He had planned to expunge that blast of lust between them earlier, not add fuel to the fire. Yes, she was... well, beautiful. And clever. And perceptive. And loyal, if the way she'd leapt between him and her sister was any indication.

Nothing like the selfish, careless troublemaker she was rumored to have been twelve years ago. But she was still not for him. She'd betrayed the community, and her family and—what was the matter with him? He needed to focus on Penrose's guests.

No matter how, well, incredible their kiss had been.

After all, he'd had to goad her into the act in the first place. Brutal for his confidence and a clear sign that she did not feel the same fascination for him as he did for her—a clear sign he needed to let any remaining interest in her go.

Sol strolled toward the young woman, only to be halted halfway by an older lady in a dark silk gown. "You're Frederick's brother," she practically accused, her face in a distinct frown.

Oy. Time to charm.

"I am." He gave a slight bow. "Solomon Weiss, at your service. I was just admiring your fan and how well it coordinates with the lace on your gown. I'm so pleased to make your acquaintance..."

"Lady Rochester," she said, face still stern, before giving a small bob of her head. Not a graying blond strand fell loose from the meticulous styling. "Lady Drucilla is my cousin." She glanced in the woman's direction. "She has certainly been spending a great deal of time with your brother since she came out of mourning."

"Frederick has been most grateful. He holds Lady Drucilla in the highest esteem," he said with a nod as he focused on assessing what words would appeal most to the woman before him to gain her favor on his brother's behalf.

"I'm sure he does." She wrinkled her nose in judgment, as the woman in question leaned closer to his brother, laughing prettily.

"She's quite lively and cultured, you know? She had her pick of husbands her first season and made an excellent choice." She raised a brow in challenge. "Even now, she's still a diamond, with her youth and beauty.

And her brother is one of the leading peers of the realm, held by *all* in the highest esteem." She emphasized "all" in a distinct contest to his claim.

"Are you aware he's one of the leading figures in Parliament?" She narrowed her eyes. "Your brother is in *banking*, is he not? Such filth in that industry, preying on the innocent."

Double oy. Time to spin the conversation. He cleared his throat. "As the elder, my brother took on both our father's business and responsibilities upon his death." Clasping his hands together and lowering his voice, he leaned forward a touch. "Did you know my brother raised me when our parents died? He was merely seventeen at the time—an age when lesser men are losing family fortunes in card games. Can you imagine?"

"I did not." And there was reluctant interest in Lady Rochester's eyes now.

Peeking over her shoulder, he found Frederick watching him, his face unreadable, though his hand was quite close to Lady Drucilla's as she chatted happily with another woman.

"There is no one more loyal than my brother, no one more willing to sacrifice for those he loves," he said, his voice speeding up. "And he gets results. After all—"

A large hand clamped down on his back, halting his words. He glanced behind him to see Roger Berab, one of his boss's two brothers, standing beside him.

"He did so well with Sol, here." Berab picked up where Sol had left off, his tone smooth. "He works in our family's business as well. And my brother—who is not an easy man to impress—already trusts him with some of our most sensitive matters." To Sol's annoyance, the woman seemed to relax at the mere sound of Berab's posh accent.

Or perhaps it was the man's countenance. While his wit had never particularly impressed Sol in the past, he was still undeniably handsome, though certainly not more so than Sol and his brother. Especially as Berab was getting a touch long in the tooth.

Technically he was the same age as Frederick, but his brother wore his age exceedingly well and appeared at least five years younger. A family trait.

"And to that end, I need to borrow him for a moment," Berab continued, interrupting Sol's thoughts. "If you will excuse us, Lady Rochester, you do look lovely tonight. I was so glad to be seated near you and Lord Rochester this evening. Your husband's mind is brilliant, and listening to his thoughts is always a privilege."

And with a flash of a charming smile and a sharp grip on his shoulder, he led Sol away from the group before he could get another word in. "Her husband has the sense of a fruit fly," Berab murmured once they were farther away. "Come along."

"What are you doing?" Sol hissed at the older man between gritted teeth.

"I'm helping you," Berab told him plainly, before shoving a glass of some too sweet after-dinner drink in his hand. "God knows why, other than I'm bored, though you or your brother making fools of yourselves here admittedly might hinder my own personal plans."

He took a discreet sip from a sliver flask that Sol barely had time to register before it was tucked, out-of-sight, in some internal pocket.

Sol narrowed his eyes. "I didn't know you were

invited." Or more, he'd not seen him at dinner. Though the table *had* been crowded, his and Frederick's seats naturally far from the hosts and their more honored guests.

"What, disappointed you're not the only Jew in a room full of gentiles?" A small smirk played on Roger's lips.

"I thought that was *your* preferred circumstance," Sol couldn't help murmuring beneath his breath.

"It wouldn't be if there were more of us who didn't require so much minding to stay out of trouble." Berab gave Sol another pointed look before motioning for Sol to follow him into the hall. "Though my brother believes you're trainable."

Sol raised a brow. "How generous of him."

Taking another swig of his drink, he led him into a small library. "Don't bother with the shelves. Half of the volumes are false facades," Berab said with no small amount of disappointment before nodding to a chair, presumably for Sol, as he swept toward the back of the room as if he owned it.

"As I'm generously speaking with you, let's get a few things straight." He leaned against a shelf, his tone sharp, changing personas once again. If the Berabs ever went bankrupt, this one could easily find work on Drury Lane. "I get invited to a great deal of places. Money does that. Especially when it's money that you reliably know how to keep without resorting to ignominious means."

Sol bristled at the dig. "Yes, that's far worse than kidnapping and physically attacking any competition," he retorted, relations with his boss be damned. After all, *this* Berab—with his youngest brother—had resorted to such means in their efforts, however wasted, to win Isabelle Lira's hand.

Berab gave a mild shrug and continued. "Your brother's trying to win a large pot with a mediocre hand. Best not to give away any of his tells." He gave Sol an insultingly knowing look.

Sol rolled his eyes. "I'm not a shmuck."

"Not completely, as if you were, David would've found a way to get rid of you already, no matter what Isabelle wants and how unfortunately powerful Ellenberg has become in the community, despite his lack of...everything." Berab sniffed.

"However, I have yet to fully form an opinion," he continued, giving Sol a once-over that was probably meant to be intimidating, but failed. "Right now, I'm just giving you some friendly advice."

His lip curled a little. "But why listen to me? It's not as if I know anything about this world or mine, both of which you want to join and neither of which you have any experience in. I certainly couldn't help you with those goals you seem to be failing at as of late."

Oy, the man was a putz. A self-important, smug putz. Even if a great deal of what he said was true. The Berab family moved within the Jewish community with an ease and comfort of which Sol could only dream. And the gentiles liked Berab's wealth and his Sephardic "lineage" a great deal more than the new-moneyed Ashkenazi Weiss brothers.

But the other man was still a putz.

Sol resisted folding his arms, and instead kept his posture deliberately relaxed. "It couldn't be you have your own motivations."

"Mine are not at cross-purposes with yours." Berab

shrugged. "Besides, David may have taken a shine to you, but you're merely an employee so it's no skin off my nose if you drown. Provided you don't splash about too loudly beforehand."

"How kind of you," Sol said, raising a brow as he put on his best imitation of Berab's smug but charming tone and accent.

"I am, aren't I?" The man's smirk turned into a full smile. "Your delivery wasn't half bad." Berab finished off his drink. Setting his glass down, he motioned for Sol to follow. "Walk with me for the rest of the evening. If you're a good boy, I'll give you a few introductions to those who might suit your purposes and overlook…" He pursed his lips. "Well."

"You really are benevolence incarnate." Sol shook his head but couldn't help smiling.

Berab raised a finger to him. "Definitely wear that smile when I present you," he said. "And I do owe David. Since I'm the best at this sort of thing, I should be the one to help you along," he added. "Besides, as I said. I'm bored and the reading material is lackluster."

Ah, and now the man's actions made more sense.

"At least you're honest," Sol said with a shrug.

"When I want to be," Berab returned, his word, tone, and expression eerily reminiscent of himself. Perhaps they were more alike than either wanted to believe. "What?"

"Nothing." Sol shook his head. "Or if I say it, you'll be insulted."

He paused and gave another knowing smile. "No, I suspect I'd actually not be." His smile turned rueful for a moment before he snapped his fingers at Sol. "But come along. We'll need something to drink as we're going to have to discuss matches. You were right to pursue Isabelle, even if you failed. The right wife would do wonders for *all* our purposes."

Naturally. And it wasn't as if he could say no.

And if all the women he imagined when Berab said the word "wife" looked like Hannah? That could be changed. Easily.

Chapter Seven

The last customer had left, and moonlight drifted through the small cracks above the drawn curtains of the closed shop as Hannah finished one job and mentally prepared for the next. Thankfully Ned had come by not merely to collect his take of her profits—but with an offer of an actual assignment. Just when she needed it.

"Going out tonight?" Tamar asked from her perch on the end of the front counter, her broom abandoned against the wall.

"Hopefully. Ned's late with the details, though." Hannah brushed past her sister, bending down to rummage through the lower shelves, reshelving unsold legitimate and quasi-legitimate wares from the afternoon. As she'd told Sol—who she'd not thought of at all since the kiss two days past—no one browsed in their shop—or more, no one was permitted to. If not, they'd have been shut down and carted off long ago.

"It seems like you're getting a great deal more excitement in here. At least this week." Her sister swung her booted feet back and forth, creating an irregular pounding rhythm on the wood right next to Hannah's ear.

"I don't run information for excitement; I do it for

money. Money that we need in order to give you a good life." She yanked the most sellable and popular merchandise—watches, paste jewelry, small trinkets that could be given as gifts or bribes, depending on one's point of view—to the front so she could easily grab them when requested. "And as for the 'excitement' you've been noodging me about, that will most certainly not be happening again."

"Why?" A smirk settled on Tamar's face. "You both certainly seemed to enjoy it."

Too much. Though wasn't that always the way? Solomon Weiss was . . . well, he did not belong in her world and she certainly had no place in his.

Hannah rubbed her wrist, pushing back older memories of how she'd once longed for such a thing—what she was now attempting to give Tamar. And how hard she'd tried and failed to transform herself into the sort of woman who could grasp it. However, frustration and desperation not only had led to risks she should've known better than to take but had caused her to carelessly lash out and wound the pride of those whose power she misjudged.

"It was fine." She rose and brushed off her apron. "All right, more than fine, but that's beside the point."

"What is the point?" Her sister cocked her head but did not move from her position, even as Hannah reached for the rag and wiped down the chipped black wood around her.

"The point is that Solomon Weiss is of no use to either of us," Hannah said as she scrubbed. "He doesn't meet our criteria for your husband, he's certainly not sniffing around to be a customer or supplier, and he doesn't have the sense or the access to information that would help me in my other endeavors. Without any of that, earth-shattering kisses or not, he's nothing but clutter in our world and needs to stay away."

" 'Earth-shattering'?" Tamar's voice rose nearly an octave.

"It's a turn of phrase, not a literal fact." Hannah folded the rag before lugging it and the bucket into the back room, even as something odd in her gut twisted. Probably from eating too quickly that morning or not enough on her break—something that was indeed the man in question's fault.

"It's too bad he doesn't meet our criteria. He's handsome. Very handsome," her sister called. "And probably knows how to read."

"If you want to amend what we've discussed, be my guest and I can chase him down," Hannah returned, keeping her tone light.

After all, what would it matter if Tamar really was interested in the man? If he made her sister happy, good for her. She deserved happiness. And while he wasn't exactly what they'd wanted for Tamar—he was on the edge of the community instead of its center—that certainly could change with the right maneuvering. Besides, he seemed nice enough and would probably be good to her and was definitely the marrying kind so—

"I don't think I'm what he's seeking," Tamar said, hopping to the floor, the heels of her boots thumping against the creaking floorboards.

"Nonsense. You're what everyone seeks. The dowry is just going to help the right people notice it," Hannah said, giving her sister a kiss on the cheek, forcing her mind away from the dratted kiss.

Which rationally couldn't have truly been that wonderful. It was just that she hadn't felt that sort of desire, that sort of passion, that sort of want since... well, she didn't know since when, but it didn't matter because no good could come of it. With a huff, Hannah hid a pair of candlesticks of dubious origin behind a line of books.

Oy. Not good. Not good at all. She was not going back to Duke's Place anytime soon; that was for sure. She'd highlight the best choices from the information she'd gathered or even suggest Weiss again for good measure. Which would prove she truly didn't care. Not. At. All.

She stomped out the door to sweep the stoop. After she was done and good and sweaty despite the night chill, Hannah went around to the alley in the back and near jumped out of her skin at the man waiting, leaning against the cracked plaster outer wall of the tannery next door.

"You startled me," she said as Ned emerged from the shadows, skirting the stream of foul waste liquid that drizzled down the center of the small passageway.

"One would think you'd be more aware." He straightened his warm coat and pushed off the wall against which he was leaning. He sauntered over to her with his usual arrogant air, before fingering the front of her cloak. "Been a while, Hannah. Had some other business to attend, but I'm glad to be back in communication with one of my favorite helpers."

Normally, she'd have pretended to enjoy his overtures and pressed herself against him, but for some reason she could not quite manufacture interest that night. At least not for him. No matter how useful it was for her pocketbook and how almost certainly it was going to be a requirement for her assignment.

Tired, she must be tired. It had been a long day. Hannah stepped back from Ned's body and rubbed her aching back. "Who am I to find?"

"A man," he said, twisting from side to side. The stink of cheap gin wafted in her direction, strong and full. Bollocks. While Ned was amiable enough on most nights, made more pleasant with a touch of the drink, when he was fershnikit, he could be...well, not so pleasant. She should've brought a knife.

Not that she could inflict serious harm with it, he was far too skilled to best, even foxed. But she could keep him off balance. Ah, well, she'd just need to proceed with care.

She dug her ankles into the ground. "There are thousands of men in London, and if we want to be paid, I need a bit more information."

He rubbed his hands together, moving toward her anew. "You do like money, don't you, Hannah?" He leaned forward, his hot breath right against her cheek.

The blood in her veins began to pound as he ran a hand down her cheek.

"As I've told you many times before, I'll reduce the fees for your shop if you decide to make our other arrangements more plentiful and convenient," he said, his words slurring.

"We both know that's the last thing either of us wants or needs. Just cut to the chase." She rolled her eyes, though there was an odd hardness below her breast in the place that usually thrummed with excitement over the money and what it would do for Tamar's prospects. How much closer it would bring them to their goal.

Because she did want her sister to succeed, even if that meant leaving her and their home. And almost certainly needing to distance herself for the sake of her new life and her new family. That would be fine. She would not diminish her sister's happiness to bolster her own. While she cherished their time together, she'd always known that it, like the days they'd spent with their parents as a family of four, like everything in life, was temporary. And what came after would be fine.

After all, her life might not have been all her choosing, but she'd made it her own. And she'd survived the worst parts of it. Again and again. Besides, unlike her sister, she had no way ever to integrate herself elsewhere. Even if she had the opportunity. Not with all she'd seen and knew. Oy, she needed to learn to drink the way Ned did.

"Just give me the name and description," she muttered to him when Ned didn't respond to her quip.

"I have it written down." He pushed open his coat and pointed to the top of his trousers. "Right in my belt. You know how to get it."

Double oy. She did not want this today. Hannah closed her eyes, willing herself to remain calm. "I'm not fishing it out just to have you fall over on me. You're too far in your cups for this, Ned."

"Since when did you earn the right to tell me what I am or what I'm not?" he taunted. "You used to be a great deal more fun. Don't make me regret coming back here." He waited for a moment, as if he expected her to approach, before shaking his head. "What's the matter with you?"

"Nothing. I'm just ready to work, that's all. Get us paid, like we both want." She clenched and unclenched her fists as her brain churned in search of some way to make him just, for once, permit her to win.

But no solution came, and Ned was clearly in a mood himself.

"Oh, I intend to have you work, just in more than one way tonight. Thus, if you want it, come get it." His lip curled into a triumphant smirk, as if he could read her mind.

Hannah bit back a sigh. Not what *she* wanted, but what choice did she have? It wouldn't be the first time she'd had to swallow her pride to handle such a situation and it would certainly not be the last. She had just hoped, perhaps foolishly, that after all these years, Ned would somehow be different. At least with her.

Completely foolish. After all, he was a true predator, just one who permitted her to run with him. She was a scavenger at best, and could become prey upon anyone's whim. She would never make the rules—she could only choose to obey them or skirt them. Something she'd learned well, and she could never let herself forget.

"Now," he demanded. "You're going to prove to me your gratitude and loyalty, as both have been a touch lax as of late. Not that it isn't expected from your kind."

Her spine stiffened at the old insult. He certainly knew where to find chinks in the armor she'd forged for herself and had no problem poking at them. Before she could force herself to move, he wrenched her hair hard enough that her eyes watered.

"You better make this good," he muttered. "You owe me," he added, snapping his fingers at her as she coaxed the small scrap of pride that wouldn't die to settle and her feet to move. "And if you don't deliver, remember, there's always your sister. It'd only take a minute, and I'd have her down here, in your place, earning this job for you. Which might be a better idea, given your attitude this eve'n. And after all, while you're withering, she's grown up nice."

Everything inside Hannah stopped. "What did you say?" Her words were an unfamiliar whisper.

Ned didn't seem to notice, though; he was still talking. And gesturing. "I've seen her about and it's clear she could be just what I'm owed. Her tits are almost as—"

Hannah didn't think, didn't hear, barely saw anything but a flash, as the temper that had once cost her and her family so much flared to life. She'd be damned if he even breathed in the same direction as Tamar. Before she registered what was happening, she'd leapt on the man, pummeling him. However, the element of surprise only took her so far. In a flash, his fingers were wrapped around her neck. Squeezing.

Hannah gasped for air.

"Ungrateful cow." The words filled the cold air as she grew dizzy and limp, darkness edging and—the grip loosened for a moment just before Ned's fist collided with her cheek, sending her reeling back into the wall. "There'll be no more jobs from me," he told her before giving her a swift kick, so she fell, a mixture of cold rain and wastewater soaking her stockings. Ned stood over her and chuckled for a moment, before turning away.

"Good luck with the competition," he called as he sauntered out of the alley. "Word spreads fast and you've proven your lack of usefulness to anyone who'd hire you. And don't expect anyone I do business with to be using your shop again now, no matter how much you pay," he added for good measure.

"Fuck." She murmured the word out loud as she struggled to rise against the wall. The side of her head was throbbing as well as her cheek and neck.

And worse, what Ned said was true. There would be no more jobs now. People with her skills and desperation grew on every corner. Her ability to comply with no fuss had been one of her best assets and without that reputation...she shook her head. Not to mention the fact that Ned had quite a bit of influence in the criminal world. There were plenty of other pawnshops and fences for him and his associates. Gentile-owned ones with more agreeable proprietors. Hannah leaned her forehead against the outer wall of the shop.

The only solace she could take in the situation was that this time, her temper was only going to cost them money, not their lives.

But they needed the money. *Tamar* needed the money. Because without it...Hannah shook her head and the world spun. She closed her eyes for a moment before reaching out to clutch the side of the building and haul herself to her feet.

She'd not cry; she'd not. She hadn't cried in years, not since her trial, when, after seeing her parents for the first time in nearly seven months, her mother had put a hand to her lips, signaling that she was not to say a word, as both her parents outright lied, insisting that they, not Hannah nor Tamar, had bought and sold the obviously stolen silver bowl.

The witnesses all agreed in bought-and-paid-for testimony. Only one had refused and testified against her, but he could only attest to her handling of a smaller object, consequential for no more than a minor prison sentence.

In the end, the fortune that her parents—a penniless girl who'd fled an unwanted groom and the boy who loved her so much, not even Siberia could keep him away—had accumulated managed to save her from a noose. But they were still gone. And it was still her fault.

Like it would be if she couldn't give Tamar a better life. She suppressed a sob. She should've left her in the Jewish Orphan's Home, shouldn't she have? The woman had been right. She was no good for her sister and would ruin every—

"Pardon me," a deep voice bellowed through the darkness.

Blood pounding in her ears, Hannah forced herself away from the wall and into the middle of the alley, widening her stance even though the ground still spun. "Who's there? Don't come any closer, I have a knife."

"If you had a knife, it'd be lodged between your former associate's shoulders with a constable ginning up testimony from your neighbors," the voice said. "A scenario that would probably make many people happy. Getting rid of two birds with one stone."

"I'm not a murderess," she retorted, despite the fact that it would probably be best if she were one in the current situation.

"Anyone can kill under the right circumstances," the stranger said, stepping toward her. Through the dim light, Hannah could make out the form of a very tall man, with fine, polished boots and a thick wool midnight black cloak, a large hood completely engulfing his head in darkness. Almost like a phantom.

Except phantoms weren't real. And far less frightening than humans.

The stranger wagged a finger, encased by thick, black leather gloves, at her. Expensive gloves. "And with you and your temper, Hannah Moses, I think those circumstances are more plentiful than with most."

Her heart stopped at the mention of her name.

"What do you want from me?" She breathed the question, not that the answer could be anything good.

There was a pause, as if the man was contemplating her, though she could not be sure as his face was still completely hidden.

"My employer is interested in hiring you," he said finally.

"For what?" she asked as calmly as she could, even if all her warning senses, the ones that had kept her alive in places so many others didn't survive, were telling her to run into the house as fast as she could and bolt the door.

"For what you did for Mr. Phyppers—to find information," he told her. "However, not all of us are certain you're right for the job."

"I'm not even certain I'm interested in the job," she retorted, her shoulders sagging a touch with relief.

A gust of wind swept in, raising moisture from the mud as it rapped against the crumbling plaster of the buildings sheltering her and the man.

"What does it pay?" she couldn't help but ask. Because, while it was clear that this man was trouble, she still needed the money, sooner rather than later. And circumstances being what they were...

"More than double what your previous employer paid," he said. "If you're good enough."

"He wasn't my employer, just someone I did jobs for from time to time," she mumbled, before the rest of the statement washed over her senses. "That much just for finding information?" she asked, her heart skipping a little, despite herself.

She shouldn't even be considering this. She had no idea who she was dealing with, even if she was good and finished in all her usual channels. Even if she was being offered an opportunity, here and now.

"It will be important information," the man said, breaking her thoughts.

"Will be?" she asked, peering again, in vain, through the darkness.

"The job we'd need you for isn't ready quite yet," he explained. "But my employer's interested in having you, on his staff, so to speak."

"Who is he?" she asked. Because if she knew that, she might be at least able to protect herself a little bit. And hopefully hide Tamar completely.

"That's not something you need to know." The stranger's voice was a touch sharp. Hannah frowned as she worked to analyze his voice. He wasn't young, certainly older than her, but not by too much. And he was clearly more educated as his accent was almost posh. Not from these parts, and yet he'd come upon her nearly undetected. How?

"Here." The man reached out and shoved a small, dark velvet bag into her hand.

"What is—"

"We're going to do a little test job," the stranger told her. "This is half a very fair sum, and just a taste of what's to come, as well as your instructions. If you succeed in a discreet and thorough manner, you'll get the rest. And a spot for future jobs. How does that sound?"

"Too good to be true," she retorted. And yet...She

turned the small sack over in her hand before fiddling with the tie.

The stranger pointed a finger at her. "You're a clever one," he said. "That's why my employer is interested," he added, and she shivered a touch.

How exactly did his employer know her? Had he been watching her? She'd need to proceed with care. She pulled out the instructions and squinted through the darkness before starting. "This is a fancy location."

"My employer likes to think of himself as someone who is quite at home with a certain set," the stranger said. "But don't let that fool you; neither he, nor anyone on his staff, is someone with whom to trifle."

"Noted," she said, folding her arms and silently cursing in her head. Because whether or not what the man said was true didn't actually matter, only that he and those around him believed it, and would thus have no compunction making her life very, very difficult if she didn't do what they wanted.

Oy. Her night was just getting better and better.

"Don't look so grim; you're getting an opportunity, right when you need it most."

"And those situations always work out so well," Hannah grumbled.

The man gave a harsh, cold laugh. "Your safety is not my concern," he said with a shrug. "But it, and that of your sister, will be much more secure if you say yes," he added in the same tone, this time making her shiver more than the snowy breeze that rushed between the buildings. "So do we have a deal?"

She stared up though the darkness, trying and failing one last time to catch a glimpse of his face through the cloak. It would be all right—she'd make sure of it.

She'd work hard to place as many defenses as she could between Tamar and whatever danger this brought, as well as stay alert to any danger for her.

Besides, it wasn't as if she had a choice. She sighed. "Fine."

"See? That wasn't very hard," the man told her. "I'll be back in a week to check your progress." He turned from her, his cloak swirling in the wintry breeze.

"Happy hunting, Miss Moses," he called over his shoulder before leaving her alone in the darkness.

Chapter Eight

Sleep did not come easily that night. Sol tossed and turned for hours, his mind unwilling to quiet as his thoughts darted between worry over his brother's situation and the unbidden memories of that damned kiss. A kiss like none he'd experienced prior. Not that there had been too many—given how often they were outside the community, he and his brother had taken care to truly behave in the manner gentiles called "upright"—but there had been enough.

But none had haunted him. Until hers.

He stuffed his pillow over his head and groaned. He was the worst. The absolute worst, for all the reasonable, correct reasons Aaron and now Roger Berab—who he didn't quite trust but who was still no fool—had given him. Especially given Penrose's disapproval of Frederick and—argh.

His brother had a problem, and it was his duty to assist in solving it. By whatever means Frederick asked of him. Which meant he needed to fulfill the request his brother had made of him months ago: pay off their remaining debts and raise his standing in the world.

He could not see Hannah again, nor think of her.

Gritting his teeth, he forced his eyes shut and fell

into a restless half sleep for all of an hour. He glanced at the mirrored clock on the wall. Not even four. With a groan, he padded out of bed and splashed his face with water from the basin, stretching his now sore back. A walk would do him good. Just a little one, around their neighborhood. He'd clear his head, sleep, and wake in a few hours with his brain doing what it needed.

After running a comb through his hair, he donned a shirt and a pair of trousers, struggling a touch with the cuffs. Glancing at the tiny flakes of snow swirling in the wind outside his bedchamber, he pulled on a dark but warm overcoat before creeping as quietly as he could down the back staircase and into the early morning darkness.

However, his path didn't remain close to his home and instead meandered east, so before he knew it, without even truly thinking, he was standing in Hannah's back alley, staring at the windows above and wondering which was hers.

A door creaked open, startling him into a near jump.

"You have got to be joking." Carrying a bucket on one hip, wearing what appeared to be merely a shawl over a thin night rail and boots, her hair in a simple braid down her back, Hannah herself stepped onto the cracked stones. "What are you doing here?" she demanded.

"I was—" He gasped as a flicker of moonlight illuminated angry purplish bruises and skin so swollen that her left eye didn't quite fully open. "What happened to your face?" he blurted out, before cursing at himself in his head.

She sniffed, her lips curling into a dismissive, half

smirk. "I fell," she said. "My skin bruises easily. Don't worry, no one will see it, or this—" She pulled down her shawl to reveal a series of even deeper marks around her neck, resembling human fingers. Her eyes bored into him, almost as if she was daring him to react. To prove to her—rightly—that he should be hurrying away as fast as he could, not itching to draw nearer.

And yet that was not the reaction he was suppressing. Instead, it took everything in him not to snatch her in his arms and promise to fix it all. Even if he probably couldn't and certainly shouldn't, given his promises to Frederick.

"Bruises fade as easily as they come to me," she continued, breaking him from his thoughts. "And if you leave, you won't have to see either." She glared at him.

"I—" he started as his overly tired brain searched for the right answer, the right way to respond.

"You don't belong here," she pronounced. As if to emphasize her point, she dumped the bucket in the trough, before slamming it on the ground.

"And you do?" he asked, his voice thick, because who belonged in a world where *this* was the price of doing business? Yes, he'd been in a few scrapes over the years. While his brother had used his natural charm and education—traits that Sol sorely lacked—to put on a respectable front for their business, he'd ventured into the darker places to use less genteel means. Including the occasional fisticuffs when necessary.

Though it had been a long time since he'd been caught cheating at cards.

"This is my home," she said as she snatched up her broom and began to furiously sweep the single step. "And this is who I am," she added in a voice that made his heart crack a little. She sniffed. "After all, I struck the first blow."

Every meeting, every encounter, every thought in this woman's direction was a mistake. Neither of them had any place in the other's life.

And yet, in that moment, all he wished was for the right words to take her pain away. Because that was what he was usually so good at—words. Even if they were often empty. Even if it shouldn't matter. Even if it was foolish.

"I hope the hit was to a lower area," he said, joking instead.

When she gave him a full smile, it warmed his body a great deal more than his coat. Even if it shouldn't.

"My, my, Mr. Weiss—"

"You can call me Sol, you know," he corrected, grinning back at her, despite, well, everything.

"Mr. Weiss," she repeated, with a roll of her good eye. He flexed his gloved fingers, which itched to reach for her. She brushed her braid behind her shoulder. "I didn't know that you were so bloodthirsty. What will all those community leaders back at the Great Synagogue think?" And there was a bitterness to her voice that both cut him and piqued his curiosity.

He opened his mouth to quip back—carefully, in the direction he wanted to lead the conversation—but she wasn't finished.

"As for your question, sadly, no, that was not the area I went for first," she said, rubbing the back of her ear with her free hand. "I was a touch... overcome... to have remembered that. A mistake I don't usually make."

"Overcome?" he couldn't help but ask.

She stopped sweeping and lay the broom against the wall, before releasing a great sigh. "I was angry," she said, this time giving him a sad shake of her head. "Fatal flaw, it seems." Her smile dimmed. "Though, I suppose not so fatal as I'm still alive. Again."

"Again?" he asked, arching a brow.

"Trust me, you do not want to know—just like *I* have no desire to know anything about you," she said, brushing the question off with a flick of her hand. "Besides, I've learned to control things since." She twisted the end of her braid around her fingers. "Or at least thought I had."

"I'm sure your reasoning was sound," he offered, not knowing quite what else to say. An alarming development, especially since, unlike the people in his life with better judgment, he wasn't quite sure he cared if there even was a reason.

Meshuggeneh. That was what he was. Maybe the bump he received from avoiding a runaway carriage when leaving Penrose's was more serious than he'd believed.

"It was because of your sister, wasn't it," he stated more than asked, recalling her protective stance when the younger woman had entered the storeroom. She didn't meet his gaze, signaling that he was correct— that whatever had happened, it had to do with defending her sister. And he liked her all the more for it. He cleared his throat. "I understand. I have a brother, who has always protected me, at great personal cost. I know a good sibling when I see one."

"Mr. Weiss—" she started, her body language clearly indicating she was ready to flee. He searched his brain for some way to make her stay, even though he shouldn't. Even if nothing he was doing made any sense in all his plans and schemes. He patted around in his jacket and his hand fell on the salve, the one for his own bruises. He fished it out, the glass of the bottle shimmering beneath the night sky. He pulled off the cap.

"You need this," he said, taking a step toward her.

"What is that?" she asked.

"Salve," he said, shaking the bottle in the light. "To help you heal." He dipped a finger in and held it up to her. "May I?"

She bit her lip but didn't retreat. "You're going to noodge me until I say yes, aren't you?"

He grinned at her. "You said you didn't want to know anything about me, but you seem to have acquired quite a bit of knowledge."

"You make yourself rather easy to learn," she said with a roll of her eyes.

"I'll take that as a compliment," he said, before reaching out and brushing his fingers over her cheek.

The breath Hannah sucked in seemed to echo between them.

Sol froze. "Does it hurt?" It never hurt him.

"No," she whispered, shaking her head. She closed her eyes. "Just keep going."

His heart beat in his ears as this time, the tip of his fingers softly brushed against her neck. Her lashes fluttered and his throat grew tight, but he didn't stop until he'd covered every bruised inch, and she was still standing there, before him, beneath the night sky.

"There we go," he whispered. He lifted her shawl back on her shoulders, retying it. Swallowing, he placed the cap back on the bottle and stuck it once again into his pocket.

"Why are you here, Mr. Weiss?" she asked as she finally opened her eyes again, her lips pursing into a pout. "Don't you have a nice bed and a warm fire and adulation from your peers to dream of?"

"I do." He nodded. "Yet none of them seem to be holding my attention as of late." He moved even closer, so close he could take her in his arms. "Do you know what is?" he asked as he halted, mere inches from her.

Hannah shook her head. "Don't," she said as she placed a finger to his lips.

But the moment his lips met her flesh, all reason fled. His fingers captured her wrist. He brought it to his mouth, kissing the soft skin in earnest. She moaned but didn't pull away. "This isn't a good idea for either of us. This isn't what either of us need."

"I know," he whispered as he pulled her close, wrapping her arm around his neck. She pressed her body against his, and like before, it was as if everything in the world had righted itself, even if it was all so terribly wrong.

"Weiss," she breathed, just before he took her mouth in his. She opened for him like before, and it was everything. Her fingers threaded in his hair, and he groaned as his tongue mingled with hers, deepening the kiss, while he near melted into an endless pool of need. He couldn't seem to get enough of her body on his, the sensations so glorious, time nearly stopped.

"I can't seem to keep away," he murmured as he pressed his forehead against hers.

"Try harder," she snapped, pushing herself off him.

Before he could say anything else, she ran into the building, leaving him alone in the alley, the sun starting to light the way eastward, the opposite of where he belonged, even if he suspected that, try as he might to resist, he'd return.

The staff was already rushing around the kitchen, and had already tended his fires, when Sol snuck back into the house. Oy. Now he was late and his brother would be irritated with him and for what?

A woman he needed to forget, no matter how fascinating he found her.

With a sigh, he touched up his shave, with only a few nicks, before splashing a bit more water on his face to calm himself down. As the clock chimed, he threw on a jacket, buttoning it as he trotted down the stairs and into the dining room, where his brother was already eating his morning meal and looking over the gentile scandal sheets.

"Well, look who's awake and dressed," Frederick said, not glancing up. He brushed a light brown curl off his forehead. "You do have impeccable timing, brother. I was becoming concerned the schedule you've set for yourself was destroying your appetite."

Sol slid into his seat just as a plate of cold fish and toast was set in front of him. He mumbled motzi beneath his breath so that Frederick couldn't hear and be made uncomfortable.

"It'd take a great deal more than a few late nights for that," he joked. "And enjoying a meal is one of my better skills. I even manage to use the proper utensil sometimes." When his brother rewarded him with a half chuckle, Sol's stomach settled a touch—but not enough to erase the guilt over how his late night actions might have endangered Frederick's efforts with Lady Drucilla.

A better brother would have tried harder to stay away—would have, after failing to secure a union with Isabelle Lira, found a better plan than working months on wooing clients for Lira & Berab Sureties while balancing the books for the Weiss Bank.

A better brother would have married for the good of their family.

Losers crumble, Sol. Winners find a way. His brother's words from so long ago, spoken after he'd taken a particularly bad fall from a horse when he was eleven, echoed in his head. And Frederick had been right. If he'd given up, yielded to his injuries, he'd never have mastered the ability. Never have had the enjoyment of trotting around the park in the early afternoon, nor the access it brought both brothers. When he paid enough attention not to fall.

"I'm sorry, Frederick. I know I haven't been pulling my weight as I promised." He fiddled with his knife. "I understand now that time is of the essence, so whatever I can do—"

"I have already told you what to do, a hundred times." His brother finally looked up from his reading. "Yes, you failed with the Lira girl, but that doesn't mean there aren't at least fifty better women that could gain us far more than she. You'd already be betrothed to one if you would just put in the proper effort." Frederick heaved a sigh before frowning. "Though...perhaps I've expected too much of you? So much responsibility at such an early age *is* a great burden."

Sol swallowed as memories roared back. How, days after his father's death and a year after his mother's, the nurse—a woman, he would learn had not been paid in over three months—handed him over to his older brother.

He'd seemed so tall, so adult, even though, in retrospect, he'd merely been a floppy-haired teenager with dark circles beneath his eyes.

In that moment, Frederick had become his anchor in the world. He'd knelt in front of Sol and placed his hands on his shoulders, staring right into his eyes.

We may be down, but I promise, we are not out. Together, we will rebuild everything so we're the envy of everyone. Because losers crumble, Sol. Winners find a way.

Sol glanced down at his food, his appetite leaving. "I'll try harder. Attend more events. I spoke with Roger Berab last night, and he's promised to assist me with the smart gentile set, so perhaps he can also introduce me to a potential wife. I don't completely trust him, but my successes also benefit his business, so he has every reason to help."

Frederick's eyes narrowed, and the temperature in the room seemed to drop ten degrees. "One would think you've now become more loyal to the Liras and Berabs and that Ellenberg fellow than you are to the family, given how much time and attention you pay them. Given how much you defer to their opinions."

"It's not that, I promise." Sol raised his palms as his chest twisted. "You—the family—we always come first. Always. I would never choose them over us. I'd never want to hurt you or jeopardize your happiness. I wouldn't be able to live with myself."

"Don't be melodramatic, Solomon." His brother sniffed, then looked at him in sympathy. "It's no wonder you fall prey so easily to those who seek to use you. Your emotions make it easy for others to manipulate you—Roger Berab likely thought you easy prey." He smiled softly. "It's for your own protection that I insist you stay away from him. Luckily all is not lost. There's no engagement, but I did gain Penrose's permission to court Lady Drucilla."

Thank god. Sol's lungs finally filled for the first time since he sat down. "That's wonderful news, Frederick."

"And while a Lira-sized influx of funds would have smoothed things with the viscount, I can forgive those failures. After all, you're young. Perhaps my expectations of you of late *have* been too great," Frederick added, dotting his mouth with his napkin. "However, the viscount has made it clear that he would prefer a different husband for his sister. And I fear, if my house is not completely in order, the case for his candidate will only improve, despite his sister's feelings."

"What more do you need me to do?" Sol asked. "Whatever you need, Frederick, I'm here."

His brother gave him a bemused shake of the head. "That won't be necessary. While I appreciate your eagerness, this courtship is delicate, and given your foolishness with Roger Berab last night, I'd be best served if you merely stayed out of scrutiny, and trouble, for a little while. It'll be good for you. You've been tired as of late. All that time you've been spending with those people and their sureties' company." Frederick tutted a little. "You're yawning at all hours. Thankfully our customers haven't noticed. Yet. Especially as the attention I'm garnering has piqued the interest of some of our old enemies. You know how dearly there are those who want nothing more than to see us fail."

Sol winced. Despite his baptism, and distance from the community, he knew there were those who would always view Frederick as fundamentally a predatory usurper. If he was a better brother, Sol would stop his own practice, but...he could not help but hold on to that last remaining link to his mother or the comfort he found in their traditions.

"Regardless, you've been...careless as of late," his brother continued. "Not that you've ever been particularly conscientious but these past few months...you've not quite been yourself. Unaware. You were nearly run down by a carriage last night stepping into the street. And didn't you fall off a horse recently?"

"You sound like Aaron," Sol said before grimacing when he met his brother's glare. "I didn't—I was just—Aaron merely mentioned the riding accident, and suggested it was due to lack of sleep, and you think alike—not that you are like him in any way—"

"See, this is what I mean," Frederick said with a tut and a shake of his head. "You've forgotten all your training. All the work we put into you."

"You're right." Sol nodded. "I'll be more selective with social obligations. I'll throw myself into my work and go to sleep early as many nights as I can."

Frederick gave him a long, appraising glance. "Remember what we have been working toward. Be careful not to take any actions which would be controversial in the eyes of the viscount and his set. While they are more open-minded than most, most still don't trust us. Actually, it's rather amazing Lady Drucilla has been so open to me." His brother's eyes softened in clear fondness for the woman. "The fact that she's so willing—" He shook his head.

"We must be extremely careful and not abuse that generosity. I understand why you childishly cling to such displays of your birth. Like your mother used to." He narrowed his eyes. "But I'd ask you to confine your indulgences to our house. That includes hiding that thing in polite company." He pointed to the yarmulke on Sol's head.

He supposed it wasn't an unfair request. He could keep the obligation with a hat, after all. And while it felt right for him, even before his Baptism, his brother had seen the traditions as humiliatingly backwards at best, and as a burden at worst. It wasn't fair to upset him when he was already under so much strain.

"I promise." Sol ran his fingers over his utensils as unease stirred in his stomach. He didn't want to remind his brother of his failures—or suggest Frederick had not considered all the angles—but he wasn't sure Roger Berab had ill intent.

Pushing a confidence he did not quite feel into his voice—despite the fact that this was the man who'd taught him that very trick, he added, "And the Liras and Berab families can be social assets as well as business. That's why I sought to align with them in the first place. Many titled gentiles use their surety company, and they're very keen on politics. They have goals of their own that require the proper respectability of people like Penrose. Jewish emancipation is not dead despite the failure of the Duke of Sussex's most recent bill in Parliament. Another bill offering Jews the ability to vote and hold office could be brought. It's not in their interest to upset anyone right now."

"Good." His brother gave his first approving nod of the morning. "Though truly, you should take care not to make any additional alliances without first consulting me. Your heart is in the right place, but the head can be easily fooled," he added. "And remember, first and foremost, you are needed here. Courting Lady Drucilla will take a great deal of my time and energy, and *our* family still has a business to maintain. After all, before you can get what you want, you need to see that you keep what you have."

"I can most certainly do both," Sol said. He squeezed his hands together under the table. "I will do both," he vowed. "What else?" His blood thrummed a little.

"You will marry an *heiress*. The right sort. But not yet. Not until my marriage is secure and celebrated. We cannot have anyone detracting from Lady Drucilla. And the woman you marry will be one I select for you. Trust me—the Berabs are only looking to use you. And that Ellenberg fellow ... well ... there's a reason he failed at five apprenticeships." His brother took a sip of tea before narrowing his eyes. "They work you too hard. You need a rest."

He snapped his fingers. "I know," he said, "you've taken ill. That's what we'll say. After all, it isn't far from the truth." He nodded slowly, as if he was deciding on the best course of action. "You'll stay out of sight when guests are in the house until the middle of December, at the earliest. A decent time for both banns and a wedding and for you to refocus on your priorities."

Sol frowned. December? He was supposed to keep this charade up until the middle of December? Technically, that would keep him out of sight for the rest of the gentile "season," but it was still almost a full month away. And even if he was overdoing his work at the sureties company, he still had responsibilities if he wanted to keep the position. His brother hadn't thought it through quite clearly.

"But how can I retain my position at Lira & Berab if I'm ill for that long?" he asked.

"You won't stop all work. You can still do plenty. There are messengers, aren't there?" His brother stirred his tea before leaning forward, his eyes wide, imploring him. "And this is your health we're discussing. Your life. You can do that for me, can't you?" Frederick gave him an almost pleading smile. "It could be fun. Like that time I stayed in with you when you had that head cold and I read you a story every night. You cried if I wasn't there and were eight, if I recall it correctly."

"I remember," Sol said softly. His heart squeezed. He had been scared and miserable. He'd still had night terrors of his father lying dead in his bed. And while Frederick was new to him, he'd been there. The one constant in his life. At a time when his brother should have had the world at his feet. He could have been studying, or with friends, or at an opera. But he wasn't. Despite being far too young to play parent, he'd been there, night after night.

Giving up his youth. Giving him his youth.

Mercy, he was being selfish, wasn't he? If Frederick needed him to spend a few weeks sitting in his room playacting an invalid, so be it. He could have his work delivered to him and eat from trays. It was a nice room, after all. With a window. And his own tub. What more could he ask for?

He glanced back up from his plate. "I can most certainly do this for you. I promise. I won't let you down."

"Good." His brother gave him a bright, almost youthful grin and Sol's chest filled with pride.

"Now, eat your food." Frederick pointed at his plate. "You don't actually want to become sick, do you?" He gave Sol another bemused half smile, which he returned before taking his first bite. Yes, he would do this.

For Frederick.

Chapter Nine

Not even a week in his room and Sol was already bored.

It wasn't as if he didn't have enough work, organizing files and accounting for two different companies. That took most of his waking hours. Especially as he was having trouble balancing either. Isabelle and David Berab never seemed able to agree on when to bill or how to tally each company's maximum protection. As for the bank, his brother had hired a new man who clearly needed more training. They were flush with extra interest that he couldn't trace. New clients, most likely, but where that information was...he'd have to ask Frederick.

When his brother wasn't busy. Or away from home. A rarity as of late.

And when the sun went down and he'd finished his tray, well, that was the most difficult time. As he'd not exercised except for pacing back and forth, his limbs were bursting with raw energy, making it near impossible to settle. Even harder to gain more of the sleep he so desperately needed to help his brother.

Worse, his mind wandered. Unfortunately, in the direction in which it most certainly should not. To

Hannah. Whose face and kiss and smart, tough, and—intentionally or not—funny mouth that knew a hundred deliciously inappropriate words and wasn't afraid to use them. Who protected herself and hers, right or wrong. She would not leave him be.

Even more troubling, when he tried to imagine the wife Frederick would select, he could only see Hannah, inviting him to do extremely inappropriate things in all sorts of places.

Which would not do. This was exactly why he was stuck in his room—because his head would not go where it should. And he shouldn't leave until he could force himself to want the right woman.

A proper, useful woman, who would help him be a better member of the Jewish community and a better asset to his brother and Lady Drucilla in the gentile community. A woman they all needed.

And yet his mind would not forget Hannah, no matter how hard he tried, even though they barely knew each other. They'd had, what, a few interactions and kisses? And while the kisses were glorious, they were—unwanted. Or at least neither he nor Hannah should want them. Something they'd both actually agreed upon and yet...

Sol pressed his fingers to his temples, working to calm the beginnings of a legitimate headache. Sitting at the edge of his bed, he hung his head and sighed.

He *would* love Frederick's selection for him. After all, no one knew him better than his brother. And even if he didn't immediately love her, he'd learn to. Like most couples. He'd make their lives good and secure, and the future of their family would be bright.

Rising and stretching, he paced to the window to

stare out into the night for the thousandth time. The same stars, the same moon, the same empty street. Except—Sol started as he peered, not at the sky, but at the ground below.

A single figure darted from behind a lamp. Ducking low, the person hid behind a gate across the way. Then two figures approached and stopped in the middle of the lane.

Rather large, bulky people, who stood with confidence despite the hour and darkness. Their heads bent toward each other and they split in two directions, their feet pattering away. The original figure sprang up and ran toward the house—his house. To the wall just below his window.

Two bare hands slapped down, and with a few high-pitched grunts, a cloaked head popped over, followed by a torso, and... skirts? So was it a woman in the narrow piece of property just under him? Whoever it was, they were trespassing. But somehow, instead of rousing servants to discreetly rid them of the invader, he remained at the window.

Squinting, Sol peered downward as the figure sank lower. She looked up and the hood fell back. The moon shone upon her face, and it was almost as if his blasted, inappropriate, unhelpful thoughts had conjured her.

Hannah. In their side garden. The bruises on her skin seemed to have thankfully faded. Either the salve had worked, or what she had said about healing quickly was true. Either way, he was grateful. And curious.

What was she doing there? Why had she come to him? And why was she being chased?

Not that such wasn't most likely a typical occurrence for someone like her. And she likely could handle herself just fine. Which meant he should probably ignore her and go to bed. Even if he wasn't actually tired.

He glanced at the road. Her pursuers hadn't returned. Yet. He leaned out the window, and cupping his hand over his mouth, he called down as clearly and as quietly as he could. "What are you doing here?"

Her chin tilted up with a start, fear flashing in her wide eyes before they narrowed. She swallowed a few times, and a forced calm came over her features. Hard to spot, but Sol was an excellent poker player—Frederick had taught him well from the time he'd become his guardian.

"Hiding, obviously," she said, jutting out her chin in challenge.

Yes, her mask was quite clever, but a bit irksome considering that while they might not know each other well, they certainly weren't strangers. Though again, perhaps those meetings, the saving of his life, the kiss, had not meant as much to her as they had to him—blast it all, he was a fool. And probably delirious from lack of sleep. But instead of returning to bed, his mouth opened again.

"Why are you hiding?" he asked, leaning forward.

"I was following someone, and they caught sight of me." She glanced over her shoulder. "And they're going to find me again if you keep making noise. And just after my face healed. I think perhaps it's time you went to bed like a good little boy."

Sol resisted a snicker, his body humming with heightened desire at the deliberate verbal shove. Oy, he was a schlemiel.

"Why don't you come inside then?" he asked, unable to help himself.

She squinted up at him. "Have you lost your, as the goyim like to say, 'bloody mind'? You...are inviting me...in there"—she pointed to the house as if he needed a demonstration—"in the middle of the night?"

"What? You offered me protection in someone's building not so long ago; why shouldn't I return the favor? Especially as this time, the place is mine to offer." He shrugged as if her answer didn't matter despite the dancing in his stomach. "And one could argue that I barged into your home, twice, without permission."

"You didn't get in the door the second time," she countered before biting her lip. "How do you know I won't rob the place?" Her hips swished a little as she stood there, hands across her chest in challenge.

A joke about how that wasn't her family's part of the trade sat on the tip of his tongue, but Sol bit it back. Humor wasn't enjoyable if it was at someone else's expense.

"I trust you," he said instead. And wonder of wonders, he did. Despite, well, everything.

"You shouldn't," she muttered. "You have no idea who I am or what I'm capable of."

"Perhaps." He shrugged again. "But you'll recall, last time we disagreed over what I knew or didn't know, or what I was capable of, I seem to remember that I came out on top." He scratched the back of his head as if pondering. "There was some money involved, I believe, perhaps a wager—"

"It was a draw. And you were certainly not on top of...oh, all right." She near growled the words, waving her hands in clear frustration. "I'll come in, but only because it'll be useful to my endeavors."

Sol bit back a grin, and indicated below. "Meet me by the door just around the corner in two minutes," he told her. He barely waited for her nod before he was padding, as quickly and as quietly as he could, down the back staircase. Cracking the entrance open, he beckoned her inside. Without a single word of thanks, she reached up and kissed the only mezuzah his brother hadn't removed from the house, before following him inside, her hood now back over her head.

Pulling the door closed behind her, he ran a hand through his close-cut hair. He didn't have a plan, did he? Not what to do with her nor how to keep her hidden in a way that wouldn't cause trouble for him or Frederick.

Heart pounding against his ribs, he forced himself to think.

All right, first get her away from any possible encounters with the servants. He trusted them, but good gossip was good gossip, and this would no doubt be the best sort. Which left... his personal rooms.

Of all the inappropriate places... not that he could say that, of course, especially after her continual digs at his age and maturity, or lack thereof.

Instead, he inclined his head for her to follow him back up the stairs. She frowned again, before shrugging in agreement. He ushered her inside his chambers, taking a last check at the empty hall before closing the door behind them. She spun around to face him, lines popping on her brow.

"Are we—is this your bedchamber?" she asked, her eyes darting back and forth from the bed to him, before giving him a rather knowing half smile. Or more, given the way she seemed to operate, a testing one.

Well, he would pass. She would not frighten or goad

him into... whatever she wanted him to do. Probably into proving all the irksome assumptions she'd made about him. If she thought that was going to happen, she had another think coming to her.

Head held high, Sol retreated to the sitting area near the fire and indicated one of the chairs. She shook her head in the negative and instead rubbed her elbows.

"I couldn't just take you into the main parlor," he said, taking his own seat, crossing one leg over the other as she moved to the fire, rubbing her hands together, the light making the strands of hair that had come loose from their holdings glow.

"Why not?" she asked, spinning around to face him again, her tone genuinely curious, and her large eyes wide and inquisitive.

The question was so sincere that it took him by surprise.

"My brother wouldn't like it," he blurted out before he could stop himself. "He's courting a gentile woman and..." He rubbed his neck, cursing in his head. He was supposed to be charming, damn it. And good with conversation.

"And he has a reputation to protect. Wouldn't want him to be—What do the gentiles call it?—'ruined' in some way, would we?" Hannah's lips curved into a rueful smile before she pursed them in a small pout. "Can men be ruined?" She paced, tapping her chin. "I suppose if it was possible, it would certainly apply to our men—no matter how much you dress like or resemble them. And I would definitely say that I'm the type to ruin reputations, in our community and outside." She gave a derisive sniff. "A very sound decision on your part then, bringing me up here."

Sol stared at her.

"I—it isn't like that," he tried, raising a hand to her.

"What is it like, then?" She cocked her head and squinted at him in clear skepticism.

"Um, it's me, not you," he offered with a half shrug, the phrase sounding even more inadequate out loud.

"Oh?" Hannah's lip curled in amusement once more. "So you're disreputable?" And now there was a distinct twinkle in her eye.

His belly warmed and he matched her expression. "I wouldn't say that exactly." He rubbed the back of his neck. "I'm more…" He sought for the right words to name the problem he'd become despite his best intentions.

"More what?" she asked, her cloak swirling as she turned around, inspecting the room instead of holding his eye.

"A bit too Jewish for the gentiles, I suppose, despite being a touch lacking in Jewish knowledge and practice. Though I've been enjoying changing that." Something he'd have to pause, he reflected sadly. At least until Frederick's marriage was secure. He dug his thumb into his palm. "Especially now, with my new position at Lira and Berab and its close ties to the community. While useful for our purses…" he said as she ran her hand over the marble edge of the fireplace. "It's made that aspect of me, and by extension Frederick, harder for certain gentiles to ignore."

She glanced over her shoulder. "So where does that leave you?"

"Trying to be on my best behavior." He rubbed the short hairs on the back of his neck as she palmed the books he'd left next to his chair—Smith, Malthus, what he should be reading, as well as the slim volume by

Keats he preferred. Nothing particularly embarrassing, nor particularly interesting. "Going out less. Certainly not to the opera or gaming halls or making appearances at gentile dinner parties and balls."

"Do you like going to those places?" she asked.

All of a sudden, he felt very exposed. He glanced down at himself in only his trousers, his shirt half unbuttoned, his feet shoeless.

Mercy. Though if she wasn't going to comment... he inhaled. "I prefer balls to dinner parties—the dancing is rather nice even if my knowledge and skill are limited." He gave her a wink, which she rewarded with an eye roll. "Opera is fine," he continued, "although gaming is truly the least preferable. I'm smart enough to know that the house always wins."

"And you like to win." It wasn't a question. She moved on to the center of the room, brushing past him and the bed until she came to the screen in the far corner. She peeked behind and started. "Is that a bathtub?" she asked, a note of what could only be described as longing in her voice, such a switch from the previous bravado.

"Yes." He nodded as she pushed the boards aside, exposing the large decoratively stamped tub.

She ran a hand over the edge. "We had one. When my parents were around. I loved soaking in it. When I was little, my mother used to wash my hair for me, and when I was older, my father used to buy me expensive soaps as a treat... he knew how much I wanted to feel... it's been years since I've been able to..." She spun around to look at him. "I do wash. Every day, in a basin." There was a twinge of color in her cheeks. She turned back around. "Do you prefer it cold, or hot?"

"Hot. It's a nice way to wake." He moved to stand next to her. "And occasionally to go to bed. The servants are fairly efficient."

"Never had many of those," she murmured. "Even when we were flush, there were only so many people we could trust. But my parents still managed it." She shook her head a little before returning her gaze to him. "How hot exactly?" she asked, her voice curious.

"Not scalding, but pleasant." Something in Sol's chest twisted. He loved bathing, but he'd never really considered how few people had that privilege. He'd certainly appreciate that more from now on. "It feels very nice. Especially after I exert myself."

"You exert yourself?" She glanced around the room again. "In here? How?" She waggled her dark eyebrows at him. "That sounds rather naughty, doesn't it?"

He burst out laughing. "I wish. Though if given the opportunity . . ." he couldn't help but tease her.

She rolled her eyes. "Please, nothing that takes less than six minutes requires actual exertion."

Less than six minutes . . . what did she mean by . . . Sol frowned and turned the words over in his head and . . . *oh.* She really was sharp. And if not nice, at least very, very amusing. And the firelight, with her big, dark, almost innocent eyes and wicked mouth, very alluring.

"Ouch. You wound me." He laughed again. "I'm perfectly fit, and trust me, anything I do, I do well. Especially that. Everyone is right satisfied. Guaranteed." And while that might be a touch of a tall tale, given his limited experience, it was at least a decent bet. Because when he committed, he always succeeded. "I'm a very good listener. And observer," he added.

"I'm sure." She moved away from the tub and

strolled toward him, a very deliberate sway in her hips. His heart picked up speed even as his mind whirled, trying to stay in whatever delicious yet terrifying game she was playing.

"I *am*," he whispered, moving to meet her. "And I already have some theories about you." He stood in front of her, face-to-face, at the foot of his bed.

"You don't need theories. Everyone knows everything there is to know about me." She released a harsh scoff, even as she showed her teeth in a facsimile of a smile.

"No, everyone knows what the gossips and papers said about you and your family ten years ago," he told her. "There's a difference." And despite how terrible an idea it was, how much he needed to stay away from her, a vast part of him longed to dig, to find out who Hannah was, on every level—to know her, this intriguing woman—to truly know her.

Her tongue darted out and wetted her lip. "I haven't changed that much. At least not in the ways that would please the likes of you," she said, her voice a touch husky—with desire, emotion, or just for sport, it was hard to gauge.

"That I don't know," he told her before biting his lip. "But what I do know suggests I have a great deal to learn, things that I can't find out from anyone but the source."

She made a skeptical noise.

Sol cocked his head, considering. What would make her believe his interest genuine? Or at least pique her curiosity so she'd meet him halfway, give him a little bit—enough to satisfy whatever itch he longed to scratch with her, or at least find a way to get her out of his mind. He pondered her for a moment. What would she respond to best?

Right. Sol cleared his throat. "For example, the papers certainly did not say anything about your ears. However, I have it on good authority that they are sensitive—very sensitive."

"What?" She blinked at him. "What are you on about my ears?"

He bit back a laugh. "You rubbed your right one that day at the Great Synagogue."

She waved a hand at him. "I probably had an itch."

"Maybe, maybe not." He smiled a little at the memory. "It was when Aaron burst on the scene, before you disappeared."

"So?" she asked.

"So you did it again when I came by, and I was noodging you." He nodded slowly, letting her remember too. "It makes you feel better."

"Maybe, maybe not, like you said." She twisted the tie fastening her cloak. "But either way, I don't—"

"And when I was kissing you, I ran my thumb along its edge and you arched into me and moaned," he finished.

She stared at him. "I—"

"It was a lovely sound," he assured her. "Lovely enough that I wondered what it would be like if I did that with my tongue instead of my finger." And he leaned in and paused, his breathing hitching, waiting for her. Because he'd not engage without mutuality, but god, he longed for it.

"This is a bad idea," she whispered, but didn't pull back. Didn't press forward, didn't kiss him, but she did not pull back.

He snorted. "Oh, it's completely meshuggeneh, I agree. After all, I promised my brother I'd make sure everything I did benefitted his goals—*our* goals. And I love him. I owe him everything." He swallowed. "And I have been rather decent at keeping that promise so far. I've been very, very, very good at avoiding situations that could get us both in trouble. However, it appears a situation came to me."

And in that moment, he wanted this trouble, more than he'd wanted anything in his life. So much that his brain, which often never stopped churning, now had only one clear focus—her. Only her.

"A situation?" She raised both brows. "That's what you call this?" Her tongue darted across her lower lip again, just as her mouth twisted into that bemused little smile that made his desire ache even stronger and hotter.

She stared a touch longer at him before tucking her lips in, only half hiding what suspiciously sounded like a giggle. And Sol near jumped for joy. He'd got her. Maybe not a kiss yet, but it would come. She wanted it as much as he did. He just had to give her a good chase first. Because, like him, she most certainly enjoyed the chase.

"Yes. One that has made my night very interesting." He cocked his head. "So are you going to let me prove it?"

"Prove what?" she asked, narrowing her eyes, the suspicion back.

"That the papers and gossip don't know all of you. That if I kiss your ear, you'll moan and squirm against me?" And if she wanted, he'd lick several other of her bits and parts. As many as she wanted.

Hannah tilted her head. "And what if you're wrong?" she asked. "What if your mouth on my ear does nothing for me?"

He snorted. "I'm not wrong."

"Aren't you sure of yourself?" She rolled her eyes before folding her arms. "Fine. Even if you were right—"

"I'm right," he said. "Very right."

"Debatable." She sang the word a little. "But even if you are, what if I could make you moan and sigh and what have you, longer and louder."

He laughed again. Oh, she was so very, very, very good at this game, wasn't she? A deliciously formidable adversary.

"From my ear?" he asked, because yes, he'd like that but there were other places, several others, where he'd dreamed of having her tongue since they parted.

"No," she whispered, leaning forward. "From kissing your neck." Her fingers flitted out, from the holes in her glove, tracing the air just before his Adam's apple. "This part, right here."

"Is that a bet now?" he asked, his voice thick, because yes, that was definitely one of his spots. At least one of the more accessible ones at the moment.

"What does the winner get?" she asked. "Because I don't have a sixpence on me this time."

"How about another kiss?" he offered.

Her smile broadened. "You can have one if you win," she told him. "I want something else."

He swallowed. She didn't mean...

"What do you want?" he asked, a thousand possibilities sparking in his mind, dizzying his brain and body. Oy, perhaps she really was more than he could handle.

She stepped back from him with another smile and untied her cloak before folding it and laying it on the bed. She returned to him, standing as straight and as regal as a queen.

"A bath," she told him. "If I win, I get a bath. A deliciously warm one."

Chapter Ten

Oy, she was in over her head—and not just because she'd almost been caught.

Tracking down the valet of some marquess's younger son was not as easy as it sounded. Why a man like that, one with a good job, had gotten himself into the sights of the stranger who'd hired her was another question. He must owe a lot of money to someone. Nevertheless, those details were not of her concern.

No, her concern was finishing her task, so to secure more jobs in the future as Ned had been good to his word and no one else would hire her now. At least that had been her sole concern, until—against her better judgment—she'd allowed herself to be lured into blasted Solomon Weiss's house.

Now she desperately needed to stay above the undertow pulling her out to sea. Or more fittingly, into the grimy river. Drowning her in a heady mixture of lust and what could only be deemed chutzpah, coming from a place in her she'd believed lost long ago.

"A bath?" he repeated.

"Yes." She straightened herself, so they were practically eye to eye, forcing her well-honed and well-earned toughness into her voice. "I want a bath." That at least was the truth. She did want a bath. Very much. Even though, given the time it would take to draw one—not to mention the manpower—it was probably not possible.

But for a little while, she wanted to believe in the impossible, to believe she was on equal footing with this altogether too charming and too wealthy and too tempting man. Because he *was* a man, no matter how many times she called him a boy. And a dangerous one at that. At least to her.

"All right." He nodded. "If you react less than I do, you shall have a bath."

They stared at each other for a long moment, neither moving, neither backing down from the challenge that had been issued. The shared stubbornness inflamed that palpable, ill-advised desire that they should be trying to kill. Somehow.

"Who attempts first?" he finally asked, shifting on his bare feet. His rather well-formed, clean, long toes, which she shouldn't be staring at. Oy, she was a mess. Since when had she noticed a man's toes before? If there was ever a sign she should run...however, her own, rather ordinary, booted feet wouldn't move.

Traitors. Ah, well, it was up to her brain to keep her pride safe, she supposed.

"I'd say that since you started this discussion, the honors are all yours." She punctuated the statement with her most flippant hand gesture.

For a long, awful moment he did nothing. Had she pressed too far? Had he merely been teasing with no intention of following through?

Instead, he stalked around her, so he was at her back. He wrapped a thinly clad arm around her waist, holding her to his chest, taking full advantage of the similarities in their heights to—*oh—my god*—he bit down gently on the outer edge of her ear, his tongue quickly following to sooth the skin, his breath sending a hot flush down her spine and—it was good that he was holding her because her legs began to buckle under the weight of the sheer deliciousness of it all.

Careful and achingly slow, he traced the tender skin of her ear. Hannah closed her eyes as the moan she was trying to hold back—because, god, she wanted that bath—burst from her lips. And in an instant, her back arched and she was pressing her hips against him as he held her.

Want—hot and real and naked—rippled through every inch of her body as his fingers danced across her stomach below, tracing patterns lower and lower, as above his mouth curved around, taking her lobe and gently sucking. The room spun as Hannah near panted with desire. She fisted the edges of his expensive but all too flimsy shirt, creasing the fabric that probably cost what the shop made in a month. When he grazed her again with his teeth, well, her senses fled and she cried out his name, probably too loud to protect his "virtue" or whatever goyishe phrase his brother probably used.

Though he took care of that, taking her mouth in his, claiming her and the sound in a resounding victory.

At least for round one.

"First, let's agree there's no more 'Weiss.' I believe you've, or perhaps we should say 'I've,' earned 'Sol,' or at least 'Solomon.' And second, how was that?" the momzer asked as he pulled away, leaving her body tingling and, worse, craving. An odiously handsome grin curled his lips. "Fairly successful, don't you think?" He radiated a smug pride that for some reason made her want him more.

Or to at least show him how much better it could be.

"It was good," she admitted, folding her arms across her chest. She still had her pride, after all.

"Just good?" he asked, reaching out and playfully tugging a stray strand of hair that had fallen from its worn and bent pins before smoothing and replacing it with a gentle tap.

And the tenderness in that gesture, the care, amid all the lust twisted something in her gut. Her vision blurred and it took everything in her to pull herself back to the moment, back to the here and now and its possibilities, limited though they might be.

"More than good," she admitted despite herself. "But I can do better." Because she could. She was the dangerous one, after all. She'd made herself powerful, in or out of her own territory. And she would prove it, damn it. No matter how ill advised.

He—Weiss—Sol—placed his hands on his hips with a grin. "Let's see."

"Lie on the bed," she told him with the most imperious tone she could muster.

His chin tilted and he raised both brows. "I don't remember the bed being involved in any of our prior negotiations."

Hannah wet her lips. Yes, she was going to retake control. "It wasn't not involved." She shrugged. "There's no rules against me utilizing it for leverage."

"'Leverage'?" Sol laughed a little. "That's an interesting choice of words." But he obeyed, climbing on the high posted bed, covered with thick red fabric that near glowed in the firelight. He lay back on his stack of fluffy pillows, legs splayed forward. With a stretch that pulled his shirt tantalizingly tight against his chest, he placed his hands behind his head and stared at her. "All right, now that you have me here, what are you going to do with me? How does this 'leverage' work?"

Without a word, Hannah hitched her skirts and climbed, first next to him. And then, with all the boldness she could muster, she placed one leg on each side of his, straddling his body, her skirts high enough they pooled above her knees.

Heart in her throat, but with hunger still heating in her belly, she bent down over him. Instead of going right for his neck, however, she moved higher. Not fully taking his mouth in hers, she brushed her lips against his, teasing him, just a little, but also reveling in his taste.

"I think this might be cheating," he murmured, closing his eyes even as he leaned back, his arms falling to the side. She trailed downward until she found the spot, the one she just knew would drive him meshuggeneh. After all, turnaround was fair play.

"Hannah," Sol whispered as his hips turned beneath her, grinding into her, making her innards turn to molten jelly as she pressed against him. With a groan, he grabbed her hair with one hand, pressing her down as they kissed, while snaking the other around her waist, sending even more delicious tingles through her.

"God, Hannah," he moaned, throwing his head back, his back arching, raising her off the bed. "God, that's good."

With a smile, she pressed her lips together, moving upward, to kiss his jaw. "So good that you'll admit defeat."

"I—" he started before a low chuckle rumbled

from his belly right against hers. He tilted his head and pressed a soft kiss into her forehead. "I'm not sure I'd go that far. It's against my nature to call this anything but a draw. However, I certainly believe you deserve a bath."

Sol glanced at Hannah as he rebuttoned his shirt. He was going to have to wear shoes, lest he wind up with feet full of splinters. Not that it would matter in the grand scheme of things, but he wanted to enjoy being the one to make her happy. Enjoy giving her this. Enjoy being the cause of that real smile he was beginning to long for.

Especially as it was clear, given all the responsibilities in his life, that no matter how much wanting to was starting to overtake him, he would not be able to give her much more. The sun would soon rise, she'd leave, and probably never return. And even if seeing her again wouldn't jeopardize Frederick's own courtship, even if she'd been a woman of means, he couldn't go to her. Which, though for the best, made something within his chest ache.

Because he might not know her, at least not well, but he knew she deserved better than this. Better than what he could give her. No matter what she'd done in the past. But this would have to do. Especially after the dreamy look he'd caught on her usually cynical face when she ran her fingers over the edge of the tub. He just couldn't deny her.

"Now?" She squeaked as she adjusted her skirts back over her legs. "I'm going to have a bath now?" She peeked over her shoulder at the tub and back at him.

"Now is as good a time as any, is it not?" He reached over and smoothed her tightly pinned braids. Oh, what he would give to truly run his fingers through her hair. He stroked her cheek. God, if only.

"I suppose." She bit her lip and glanced toward the door. "But won't you..."

"Wake the household?" He shrugged as he slid off the bed, adjusting his delightfully mangled garments. "Not if I do it right."

"You?" She wrinkled her nose. "What do you mean, you?" She crawled to the edge of the bed and sat, her legs hanging down, casual and natural, as if she belonged there, watching him. Being with him.

"I'm going to draw you a bath." Obviously. How else was it going to be accomplished?

"You can't draw me a bath," she insisted. "You'll break your back." She waved a hand over him.

Sol snickered. She had to be joking. Well, now he was most certainly going to have to do it, two buckets at a time, at least.

"I will most certainly not break my back." He flexed his arms a little. "I'm young and strong." And not exactly a small man. Broad too.

Hannah gave him a long, withering glance. "And not at all used to physical labor."

"No, but I exert myself." Quite a bit, especially sparring with Aaron. He pushed up his sleeves so she could see his arms.

Her eyes twinkled and she glanced down at her lap before wrinkling her nose. "You don't know how," she argued. "And it takes time. You need to make a fire, heat the water in a kettle, and then carry it to the tub."

"Yes, I worked that out in my mind." He rolled his

eyes. Even he wasn't that dim. "And the kitchen fire is already going." He rubbed the back of his neck. "And given the time, no one will be about for at least an hour. I should be able to do it." Correction, he *would* be able to do it. Not only to reward her, but to show her that he was just as competent and capable as she.

Or could be, with the right motivation.

She chewed on her lip for a long moment, not moving from her position. "Why?" she asked, and the confusion in that one word nicked at his innards, sharp and pure, like the edge of glass.

"Because I want to." And it was the truth. More and more as the seconds ticked by.

"All right." She shook her head and gave a bemused sniff. "Draw me a bath."

After more huffing, puffing, and pulling than he was used to—not that he could or ever would admit the same to Hannah—shvitz dripping down his neck, Sol finally filled the tub with the last two buckets of hot water. In just under an hour too. Not bad. Not bad at all.

"It's ready," he told her, turning to where she had moved—from the bed to a chair by the fire, her legs tucked under her, one of his books in her lap. God, she fit so neatly there, so comfortably. He twisted his fingers, resisting the urge to take up residence across from her.

She closed the volume, and he craned his neck to read her selection. Keats. Interesting. He'd have thought she'd want one more business-minded, though the idea of her reading something just for herself, in his room...

"Hmm?" she asked, lifting her chin and interrupting his thoughts. Thoughts he most certainly should not be having.

"You can just change behind the screen." He indicated to the area. "I promise I won't look." Because he wouldn't. Imagine, sure, but not look. She deserved the bath without him acting like a lust-struck fool. This was about her. Not him.

"Won't disturb you either," he added, meeting her skeptical gaze. "You can just sit in there, in privacy, and enjoy. I promise." As if to show her, he retreated to the far side of the bed, giving her plenty of room to go, undisturbed.

Hannah stared at him, lips parting almost as if she was going to say something. What he didn't know, however, whatever his senses imagined, made his heart twist and long to reassure her somehow. To hold her. Foolish as that was.

But instead, she merely rose and moved out of his view. Which was almost certainly for the best. Sol, in turn, grabbed the book by Smith and flipped to the most boring section, working to focus on his responsibilities instead of all the images that the rustling on the other side of the room was inspiring. Or memories of what had occurred on the bed. Or shadows of a future that could never actually be.

"This is lovely," she called several minutes later. "I've never…it's very nice." There was a bit more splashing and sloshing and more unsuccessful attempts to tamp down the images in his head.

Light laughter flitted over the screen, the most beautiful and erotic sound he'd ever heard. Oy. He forced himself back to the pages. This was about her, not about him. It should be as if she had her own, personal time, not with him intruding. Because it wasn't as if she wanted—

"Sol?" she called a moment later.

"What?" he asked, his voice a bit thick even to his own ears.

"This is, well, an experience," she teased. "But I think I'm going to come out smelling like you."

He frowned, parsing the words. "Oh, the oils. Yes. Lime and sandalwood. Not a ladies' scent, unfortunately." He cursed himself. She deserved that too. Something that would be right for her.

"Don't worry, I like it," she returned. "You should be proud; you've guaranteed that I'll keep thinking of you. At least until I get all grimy again."

And the twisting was back. The regret at the fleetingness, and the fact that he couldn't give her more. They would each go back to their own lives, his that he'd most certainly not earned, and hers that had been foisted upon her by an accident of birth, a few bad choices, and a touch of bad luck.

Two rather bold, proud people, but one could afford these emotions more often than not, while the other had to pay for them. Sol swallowed again and again as the water sloshed, and the garments that had been placed atop the screen slithered back to the other side.

When she emerged, her hair was a little damp at the edges. She crossed the room and retrieved her cloak, fastening it over her garments, her face flushed, probably from the remaining heat of the water.

"Well, thank you," she said, finally facing him, hands clasped in front of her, posture stiff as if they were strangers again. "That was, that was wonderful."

"My pleasure," he returned, rising off the bed.

She reached out a hand to him, fingers twitching, but they didn't touch. "You're covered in shvitz."

He smiled. "Don't worry, I'll clean myself off." He brushed at his shirt.

"I like you both ways," she told him, before glancing toward the window, the moon already beginning to fade. "But I should go. Your house will be waking, and I can't be here."

"I don't suppose I'll find you under my window again?" he asked as he hopped toward the door to hold it for her.

She halted and gave him a sad turn of her lips. "My work doesn't usually take me this way."

"Right," he said, because there was nothing else to say, was there?

This was just one last stolen moment between two people whose worlds were splintering farther and farther away.

"Be safe, Hannah," he told her, a tightness in his chest.

"You too." She gave a nod before she slipped out and down the stairs.

Sol closed his eyes and forced himself not to run to the window and watch her disappear. Instead he pictured her, in the chair across from him, and wished for more.

Chapter Eleven

It had taken another few outings for Hannah to find the stranger's mark. But she'd succeeded and been paid. With both funds and a note promising additional work in the future. Something that couldn't come too soon. Especially as the only other job she'd been offered was to act as a lure in a burglary. Much more dangerous than her usual work, even if the crew was all Jews. But if no one else came to her—it was something she might have to consider. Later.

Meanwhile, in the intervening time, she'd not thought about Sol.

Fine, not thought about Sol *much*.

At least not during the day and when she was out and about. Just a touch at night, when she was in her bed, staring at the ceiling, when something like regret choked off her air. Which was ridiculous. What had she to regret? That she hadn't kissed him more? Or done more than kiss him in those moments before she left? When she wanted with everything in her being to stay?

Despite the fact that he couldn't possibly truly want her. And even if he did, she couldn't want him because it would be wrong. Both for him and Tamar—the person for whom she cared most. And while she owed him nothing, Tamar was an entirely other story. The only story.

Which was why she should've never gone inside his home in the first place, never tempted herself. No matter how painfully kind he was to her. And how much heat there was between them.

Because heat and want weren't care. And they weren't respect. And they weren't even like. They certainly weren't the basis for—no, heat and want only brought trouble. She should know. Hannah brushed her skirt, shaking out that memory, locking it away whence it came, and instead stretched her back as she dusted off the main counter with a rag.

It was nearing closing time, and she and Tamar had been on their feet all day despite the fact that the stream of customers was noticeably lighter than it had been in years. An aberration, hopefully, because if Ned made good on the rest of his threat...or more *when* Ned made good on the rest of his threat well...oy... the stranger better have more jobs. They still had rent to pay and food to buy, not to mention it cost money to make money.

Hannah pinched the bridge of her nose. Best not think of that now. Not while what little business they still had was about.

"Ho, look now." Her sister whispered, hand on Hannah's arm, as the door swung open and a tall, commanding form entered. "The trade is hot," she whispered, excitement in her voice.

"It is." Hannah nodded before giving the man her brightest smile as he dropped two mismatched silver buttons in front of her. "What have we here?" she murmured, holding each up in a faux inspection even though it'd been clear from the start that only the larger, but coarser, of the two was fit for resale. The smaller, though finer, piece was worth quite a sum; however, the hallmarks of its theft could be spotted a block away, including the telltale ripped, not worn, stray thread hanging from the back. Which, given that he had the dress and weaponry of a professional, made the lack of care odd to say the least.

And it rankled her suspicions.

"Sorry, sir," she said, pushing both back to him. "Unfortunately, we don't have a place for either of these today. But please, feel free to come back anytime."

The customer paused, staring at her, making Hannah shiver a touch. However, he did not argue. Instead, with a glare and a grunt, he took his leave.

Hannah tugged and twisted a loose lock of hair as her blood still pumped in her ears. Not just from the interaction, but because of the one it recalled, so many years ago. The one that destroyed the life her family had created for themselves—the one she'd worked so hard to rebuild for her sister.

If you like these, just wait. There's more. The voice echoed in her head, taunting her. If she had only said, "Not today," back then instead of inviting him to return, thinking not of the danger but of the gowns and perfumes and supposedly eye-catching enhancements that could be used to entice men to want her in the light as well as the dark, opening her family's door to the vengeance, if only, everything would be—

"Setup?" Tamar asked, breaking her free from the memories of the past.

"Almost certainly. Though not a particularly clever one." Hannah grabbed the broom from against the wall, her hands still shaking. "Nevertheless, that's the fourth attempt this month. Is something happening in the gentile world?" she asked. While there was a possibility Ned was behind it, such a scheme felt too subtle for him.

"Not that I know of." Tamar shrugged as she tested the lockboxes. "Though the Kellys had to close."

Hannah paused. That was news. And not the good kind. "Why?" she asked. After all, the Kellys had been in the trade at least as long as her family. And while smaller in size, they boasted a slightly more reputable clientele as well as a more desirable space. Enough so that they sneered and whispered every time the sisters passed.

And moreover, they were at the top of the pecking order in the neighborhood. So if a reordering was going to occur, they'd be warned.

"Moved." Tamar gave a shrug before picking up the rag that Hannah had abandoned for the broom.

"Moved?" She frowned. "Where would they move to?"

"Don't ask me." Tamar sniffed before lowering her voice. "There was a constable poking around. Asking a great deal of questions. No arrests though. It's doubtful they'd fall for someone like, well, the one who just came in here but . . . yes, there was definite interest from the law."

And that sent a chill down her spine. While the new metropolitan police force didn't have quite the same antagonistic relationship with her family as the Bow Street Runners had—the self-righteous men who'd salivated for years, waiting for their family to slip and be made an "example of" so they could prove how much they protected the "innocent"—they certainly weren't friends. Nevertheless, though violence was supposed to be their primary target, the "decline in morality" in certain parts of the city was definitely piquing their interest. And certain people were more curious than others.

"You're being careful too, right? Asking enough questions?" Hannah leaned against the broom, searching her sister's face.

"Yes, of course. I'm not a fool, Hannah," Tamar snapped. "And I'm not a child. I know what stolen goods look like. And which we can fence and which we can't." She huffed in exasperation. "You know I'd be better at the work if you actually permitted me to help."

"You should be doing better things with your time. Making friends, reading books, being loved and adored. The business is my responsibility, not yours," Hannah said, and reached down to brush a loose strand of her sister's hair out of her face. "You're too smart and beautiful and good to waste your days with this dreck." She slipped her hand into her pocket, pulling out a glass-tipped hairpin whose owner never returned for it, and sliding it into Tamar's hair. "And I promise, soon all your days will be spent in ways befitting who you are." As soon as she could afford a proper dowry. Which meant more dangerous work as soon as she heard from the stranger.

Which meant getting Tamar away from the world that would always be hers.

An unbidden image of Sol Weiss popped into her head. Oy. She was a mess. *His* world was certainly not for her. If he knew, truly knew and understood what she had done and did—Hannah shook her head. It didn't matter. She would never see him again.

And she had better things to do. Clearly.

The bell jangled. "Can I at least answer that, or are you just going to lock me in a tower until you find a prince to shove me at?" Before she could respond, Tamar strolled to the door and stood in front of it, blocking the customer from view. After a brief exchange, a small woman squeezed past her and barreled toward Hannah, another woman with a cross expression in tow, while Tamar took up the rear.

The first shoved a parcel across the counter and glanced up expectantly. Hannah blinked down at the very young, familiar, attractive face.

"Miss Lira? What are you doing here? And wearing..." She bit her lip, unable to find a polite way to describe what one of the wealthiest women in Europe had decided to adorn herself with to visit her shop.

"She's Mrs. Ellenberg now. And she thinks she's 'blending in' with the 'common folk,'" the second woman said, folding her arms over her muted and slightly stained gown. "I told her dressing in a fine but faded cloak, five times too large for her and made for someone three times her age, to hide her newest gown was the opposite of what she was trying to achieve, and yet here we are..."

"No one recognized us on the street," Mrs. Ellenberg insisted.

"That's because we barely walked a block," the other woman retorted. "And your carriage is not as hidden as it should be in this neighborhood so it would behoove us to be brief." She turned back to Hannah. "We apologize for the intrusion. I—I'm Rebecca Adler, by the way—we were tasked in hiring a discreet messenger, but someone got curious." She gave Mrs. Ellenberg a nudge and the other woman rolled her eyes.

"Tasked by wh—" Hannah started before being quickly interrupted by the small woman with the large presence.

"I've never been in this part of London on foot and certain people are worth meeting. I promise, we will be quick," Mrs. Ellenberg said, her words speeding as if in demonstration. "That's for you," she added, nudging the parcel in Hannah's direction.

"What is it?" she asked, staring at the small item wrapped in paper.

"You'll have to open it to find out," Mrs. Ellenberg said. "As I said, it's for you."

"For me?" She blinked.

"That scrap on top says 'Miss Hannah Moses.'" Tamar gave a little sniff at the title. "And since you're the only one of that name here..."

Hannah blinked again, feeling as if she were observing a very odd play. "Who's it from?" Or more, who could it possibly be from? Because these women had never bothered with the likes of her, and no one else in her life gave her anything of value. Probably thought she would sell it. Probably right.

"You should open it and find out," the second woman—Rebecca Adler—said. "And we should be going." She threaded her arm through Mrs. Ellenberg's. "It was very good to meet you."

And before Hannah could say anything else, the two women, giggling, exited the shop, leaving her to stare after them, the bell tinkling in their wake.

"Well, we won't know what's inside if you just let it sit like that." Her sister pushed the object toward her. "Go on, open it."

Finally Hannah unwound the string and pushed

the paper down to reveal a small bottle. She palmed it, turning it over. "Perfume."

"Clearly." Tamar picked it up and held it to her nose, closing her eyes. "Oh, it smells nice. More than nice. Expensive."

Hannah rolled her eyes before holding it to her nose as well.

Oy, it really was beautiful. Bold and robust, but not overpowering, floral but still substantial and not overly delicate. "Who's it from?" she asked, running her fingers over the smooth glass.

Tamar snorted and retook the bottle, stroking it between her own fingers. "Who do you think it's from?" She shook her head, her dark curls bouncing. "Come on, Hannah. You're supposed to be the one with all the sense. Look who delivered it? And I saw what the two of you were doing in the back room the other day."

Her chest tightened. Because yes, she wanted it to be from him and only him, but wants and needs were two different things. And she needed to think about Sol Weiss the same way she would a sore tooth. She glanced down at the bottle again. "It...could be from someone else."

"Well, it looks like there's a note." Her sister poked at a small piece of paper sticking out of the discarded wrappings.

Limes might be nice, but I still say you need something of your own.

—S

"S"? Seriously? If he thought that was clever or careful, he was a fool. Hannah clenched her jaw. He had no business sending her such a gift—she squeezed the paper so hard, it near ripped. Tamar leaned over, and as quick as she could, she shoved the note into her apron pocket.

"Was I right?" her sister asked, scooting herself up so she was practically in Hannah's face.

"Let me smell that again." She snatched back the bottle and opened it again. It smelled so pretty.

"Careful, don't get fershnikit on the fanciness." Tamar laughed before jabbing Hannah's side, but she couldn't muster her sister's merriment.

He needed to forget her. They were not for each other. Because gifts and kisses were lovely but there was always a price. One she would no doubt be the one to pay—something she'd learned long ago. And with the way things were, any price was much too high. He should really just go to a professional if he wanted a "practice mistress," or whatever goyishe accoutrement he was aiming for, given his brother's affinity for that world. They had actual skills and would establish proper boundaries assuring everyone's safety and had the time and the wherewithal and—she dropped the bottle into her pocket.

"I'll never get drunk on delusions of being anything I'm not," she said with a sigh before glancing out the window at the sky. "We should close."

"You should go and thank him," Tamar said, leaning her elbows on the counter.

"No." Hannah shook her head. "I should go to bed. Or . . ." She frowned. "Return it. I should return it." And tell him specifically that things were over between them, and he couldn't be bothering her anymore. Especially if he truly wanted to stay out of trouble as his brother wished. She gave her sister a nod as she pulled on her cloak.

"Right. Because that's what will happen." Tamar rolled her eyes before nudging Hannah toward the back door. "I won't wait up."

Sol stared out the window into the night sky. Had she received the package? Well, she most certainly had. Aaron had confirmed it. That wasn't really the question he was asking. No, it was more, did she like it?

Or if he was being truly honest with himself, what would she do next?

"What are you trying to accomplish?" That had been Aaron's question when Sol had initially tasked him with fetching a selection of perfumes. He'd visited "poor, sick Sol," while delivering paperwork from his wife's company. Sol, in turn, had done his best coughing performance for his friend, feeling only a modicum of guilt over the lie while he asked for this one favor.

"I just want to...make her smile?" Sol had rubbed the back of his neck, unable to articulate a clearer explanation of his motives because damned if he knew. "I know that sounds rather silly and I know Isabelle and the Berabs—and of course Frederick—won't be pleased if I involve myself with her, and I will end things. Soon. Very soon. After all, I am going to marry who Frederick chooses. Before that, I only wanted to, well, do something nice?"

"You're playing with fire. I should go to Isabelle and have her put a stop to this nonsense as, obviously, I can't convince you to do so for your own good," the other man had grumbled before returning the next day with half a dozen bottles for him to choose from.

Sol had tested them each, finding one that was close, but still none quite suited.

"It should smell like moonlight," he'd said, ignoring his friend's, albeit justified, complaining. Because that's what Hannah was to him. Moonlight and danger and bravery and magic. And if he couldn't give her more, she deserved at the very least a gift worthy of her. Not that he could explain that to Aaron without sounding even more foolish than he already did. He'd only repeated the "moonlight" notion with a shrug, and gave him poor, sick, Sol eyes.

"I have no idea what that means." Aaron had thrown up his hands but returned with a new bottle the following afternoon. It had helped that he'd done all his paperwork for the company ahead of schedule and probably put a smile on Isabelle's face. Something he may or may not have mentioned while asking his friend.

Luckily when Sol had sniffed the new bottle, it was perfect. At least to him.

But would it be for Hannah? That was the true question.

"You shouldn't be sending me gifts," a female voice said.

Sol whirled around, eyes searching the dark of his room. He pinched himself, but no, he wasn't dreaming—she was there, standing against the door. Wearing the same cloak and dress as she had the night that they'd last parted.

"How did you get in here?" he managed to ask.

"I entered through the same door I did before." She indicated the hall.

"It's supposed to be locked," he muttered, shaking his head. "Someone was supposed to lock it," he repeated. If not, he'd have to start doing it himself because a robbery would certainly not help Frederick's suit of Lady Drucilla, nor convince Penrose they were respectable.

"It was," she confirmed with a shrug but didn't elaborate. Apparently, locks weren't a bother for her. She folded her arms and tipped her chin. "Don't send me more gifts." She gave him a rather stormy gaze that made him flinch a touch inside. "I'm not the kind for gifts."

He rolled his eyes. "Everyone is the kind for gifts." He peered at her, searching the contours of her face for the true emotion behind what he was beginning to realize was quite an elaborate mask. "You didn't like it?"

"That's not what I said. The perfume is not the problem." She somehow hardened her glare.

"So it's me that's the problem?" he asked softly as his chest burned. Perhaps he'd read, well, everything wrong. Perhaps the time indoors was getting to his mind. Perhaps—he hung his head for a moment. "I apologize, Hannah. I made a mistake. I thought you—"

"No." Hannah gave him a swat on the shoulder.

"Ow." He rubbed his arm. "What did you do that for?"

"Because you're—you're not hearing me. At least not right. Oy. Will you just listen for a moment?" She shook her head before sighing. "You're not the problem. I am. I'm not the sort of woman you buy pretty things for. I'm not the type of woman one woos. Nor am I an opera singer or actress who a fashionable gentile would hire as a mistress. I'm not even a street professional with regular clientele who merits extra appreciation. I'm not the type that men…" She glanced down as she trailed off.

"Men what?" he asked, even if a part of him already suspected the response.

She lifted her head. "Men have only wanted me either, at best, as a momentary substitute for someone better or, at worst, as a chance to show their dominance over something weaker. Not as someone to covet. I have made my peace with it, and so should you."

Sol gawked at her. Did she truly believe that? Truly? Yes, her life had certainly not been easy and the world had punished her many times over, but still. This was Hannah. Bold, clever, passionate Hannah.

Ridiculousness.

She ran her own business for goodness' sake. And climbed walls. And picked locks. He shook his head, half in disbelief, half in anger. How could she not see? How could she not know? And how had no one made her understand? How had *he* not made that clear?

Not that she would listen if he said all that out loud. No, best to take a different tack. He wagged a finger at her. "You seem to question my judgment quite a bit. Especially for someone who keeps losing bets to me."

"I didn't lose," she snapped before taking a long, deep breath, as if fortifying herself. "I didn't tell you the other night, but I suppose I should now." Her fear was visible. "I killed my parents."

Stifling the questions and reassurances he wanted to offer her, Sol knit his fingers, forcing himself to listen and think, not act.

"No, I have not been informed of their demise, but we've received no letters in twelve years and so many people don't survive the voyage across the sea." She pressed her knuckles to her lips and held them there. "And I know you believe the papers didn't have the whole story, but the truth, the true story, the reason they are there—the reason they are no longer with us—is that I was selfish, and deluded, and above all, couldn't control my fucking temper." She stroked her ear. "A gentile came to the shop. One from a good family. He was desperate and equally angry at himself and he, well..."

Sol stared at her. "He didn't—"

"He railed about the indignity of needing to go to the 'Jews,' which is common," she explained, caught in the memory. "But then he, well—I never was a beauty—no matter how desperately I wanted to be one and worked so hard at it. I begged my parents for the money to buy what didn't come naturally—but I still knew the truth. There was a man—a boy, really—one who I thought cared for me, before I realized he was only willing to spend time with me in the dark, if you get my meaning. But in the light..." She pursed her lips. "The week before, well, everything, he'd announced his betrothal to one of the community's darlings. And so, when that gentile said...well, while my hair is certainly not greasy, my eyes are deeply set and my nose is anything but small, and he was correct that the most pleasing thing about my appearance is my bosom. The truth is his words, that day, cut past all my training, all my defenses. I knew how I was supposed to behave, how I was supposed to always be calm, always deferential— how my safety depended on it. I knew my family's safety depended on it. *All* our safety depended on it."

There was a pause, and she bit her lip. "But when he asked if men put a sack over my head when we—"

And he could not stay where he was. Could not leave her alone any longer. "Hannah," he whispered as he stepped forward.

She held up a hand to halt his progress. "I mocked him. Asked him how, if he was so much better than me, did he end up the one begging, not the other way around." A small, sad half smile flickered over her lips. "And then I raised the rates and told him he could try another shop if he thought he could do better."

"I suppose he didn't?" Sol asked, even though he knew the answer, knew how the story would end. And what one bought of temper had cost her.

"No, he did not." She shook her head. "And my parents died for it." Her mouth set in a hard line. "I know who I am." She stabbed a finger against her chest. "My place in the world. My character. My desirability. And its limits. Especially to someone like you." Hannah's nostrils flared, her voice shaking.

"The hell you do," he said. And before she could say anything else, he took her mouth in his.

Chapter Twelve

She was not supposed to touch Sol again.

She should be resisting his touch. However, she was doing neither. But no, not only did she not pull away as he cupped her chin, taking her mouth, instead she threw her arms around his neck and welcomed his embrace, drinking him in.

Because god, she wanted him, and for some inexplicable reason, he seemed to want her as well. Even though she was the last thing he should want or need. Especially given how reckless she was around him, with both her body and her words.

It was so easy to tell him those things she could barely admit to herself. And instead of being repulsed, he made her feel safe and seen and not at all wrong.

"What do you want, Hannah?" he murmured as he kissed down her neck, before moving over to her ear, going right for the lobe. She threw back her head and groaned at the sensation, her body tightening with lust.

"I don't have wants," she managed to say as he took full advantage of her position, pulling down her cloak and the top edge of her gown, his mouth trailing down every new area of skin exposed.

"Everyone has wants," he whispered as her nipples

grew hard beneath her stays, aching to be free, for more of the attention he was lavishing across her neck and collarbones, so close but yet so far from the aching points. "All you have to do is ask."

If it were only so simple. If only he would behave like any other man—if only she could make him such in her mind. But she couldn't tell him that because she didn't quite understand it herself. Because by all logic he should be.

"What do *you* want?" she asked instead, pulling back.

"You," he said simply. He stepped forward and cupped her chin. "Just you."

The man was bloody out of his mind.

She gave a harsh laugh. "That's quite the line," she retorted, tucking a loose strand of hair behind her ear.

"It's true," he insisted, his voice firm, his dark eyes serious.

A lump swelled in her throat.

"Why?" she whispered.

"Because when I'm with you, I'm the me I want to be," he said. "Bold and brave and clever."

"And you aren't usually all of that?" she asked. After all, he was one of the precious few who moved seamlessly between their elite and the gentiles, the most respected outside the scholars.

His brow creased. "Perhaps. Or at least I can project the illusion of being so," he said slowly. "But I'm not particularly skilled without my brother's help and guidance. And I'm always careful to craft my responses to push an agenda—whether my family's or my employer's or even the community's, depending on the situation." He tutted. "I suppose I also know my place and, well, act accordingly."

"I thought I'd perfected that sort of thing," she teased, giving him a half smile, even if the joke stung a touch. "Another reason we do not belong anywhere near each other. My place, and what I need to do to thrive there, stand in complete opposition to everything you are and want."

"That's debatable." He reached out and ran his knuckles over her jaw. She shivered. "I think you underestimate your options. *Our* options." She opened her mouth to argue, but he shook his head. "I don't want to fight with you, Hannah. Not tonight, at least." He held out his hand and she grasped it, threading her fingers through his.

"What do you want?" she asked, her heart speeding up once again, as he brought her knuckles to his lips.

"I want to give you pleasure," he told her before frowning. "No. That's not quite accurate. I want to give you more than that, but I'm afraid that's all you'll accept, at least right now, and..." He inhaled. "I'm sorry, I'm doing this all wrong."

"Is there a right way to do this?" She forced a laugh. "Besides, while there's a decent possibility you might be one, you're certainly not talking to an innocent here. Most propositions I accept involve a great deal less flattery."

If they involved asking at all.

She gave him her best saucy wink to show that she didn't care. That none of it mattered anyway.

Because she was used to this, damn it. The script was comfortable now that she'd accepted her role, and she didn't need him to try to change—

"But what if I—I wanted to be different." He pulled her toward him, still holding her hand. "I want us to be different. Even if I'm not sure what it means yet for the future." He wrapped his free arm around her waist. "I just know that, right now, I want you. Not despite anything you've done in the past or present but, in a roundabout way, because of it. I just want you, exactly as you are, for no other reason than because you are who you are."

Oh, they were being such fools. He should find himself a nice, sweet, young woman who could give him what he needed—and she, should leave him to it.

Freeing her hand, she gave him a pat on the cheek. "I think that might be the nicest thing that anyone has ever said to me."

"Not nice." He nipped at her fingers. " 'Nice' is counterfeit."

"Kind, then," she amended. Because that was all he could be to her. A kind man who had offered her the facsimile of connection, showing her respect and lust and dare she say, admiration.

Sol bent down and kissed her forehead with an aching tenderness before pulling back and gazing into her eyes. His lip curled in that handsome, knowing sideways grin that she was beginning not only to crave, but to adore. "Kind is not how I feel towards you."

"How do you feel?" she asked, a delicious tightening happening in her core.

"Hungry," he said, clutching her closer. "Very hungry."

"Hungry I can handle," she quipped before taking a deep breath, working to be as brave as he believed her to be. She wet her lip. "Because I'm hungry too." And it was her turn to show him.

Grabbing ahold of his unbuttoned shirt and pulling him toward her, she opened for him again, reveling in his taste as his tongue joined with hers, firm and bold, with so much promise.

"What do you want?" he whispered as he moved to her ear once more, his kisses much more frantic than languid this time. Her knees near knocked together as he clutched her to him. "Tell me what you want. I'll give you anything."

A thousand secret wishes and desires, ones she could never, ever speak, rushed just below the surface, but Hannah shook them back. This was only for tonight. Once again, she'd live in the moment for as long as she could. No expectations, no regrets. If she said that to herself enough times, she might finally believe it. She reached up and ran her hand over his brow.

"Make me come," she told him, gazing into his eyes. "Make me come so I no longer remember my own name, only yours."

It was his turn to blink. And this time, fully smile.

"With pleasure," he said. "I may have less practical experience, but I am very willing to learn."

Before she could ask how he wanted to accomplish that, her cloak was somehow on the floor and her gown undone. She glanced up at him and to the pile, and back again. "How did you do that?"

"I'm a man of many talents," he said with that charming smugness that turned her to liquid. "Silver tongue and fingers."

She gave him a long look.

"I promise I can make you shiver with either." The smile turned wolfish. "Your choice."

Oy, she was in trouble. She should flee because while the wolf was the last thing she needed, god help her, it was the creature she craved.

"Those are quite the bold words," she managed.

"They're a promise," he said with a defiant tip of his head.

"Then by all means, show me." And before her courage could leave her, she slid her chemise over her head so she was naked before him. Swallowing, she willed herself to not cover herself. After all, if he truly wanted her, this—marked skin, round stomach, sagging breasts—was who she was, and she couldn't change no matter how much she'd wished to over the years.

Sol only blinked, his eyes hot, near wild, stirring the same in her.

"On the bed," he growled.

"Like this, I presume?" She lay back on the pillows, working not to think about what she actually looked like, but instead the way he looked at her. At the foot of the bed, he unbuttoned the rest of his shirt then slid it off his wide shoulders, muscles that a man of his wealth should not need, before he dropped it on the floor.

All she could do was gaze at him. And marvel.

Sol most certainly had a handsome face—she'd noted that the first time she'd laid eyes on him. Not just his full, expressive lips and twinkling brown eyes, but his bold, determined jaw and graceful brow. However, it was nothing compared to seeing all of him, nude, in the firelight. He didn't flinch as he stood before her, a hunger in his eyes as intense as her own.

Carefully, he slipped onto the bed next to her, gazing downward. "You're sure of this?" he asked.

"Very." She nodded. "Are you sure?"

"Very," he repeated. He shifted and, his mouth was on hers. He tasted of wine and lust and something sweet, but tart, almost like apples. She rocked up on her elbows to meet him, already greedy for his mouth, his tongue, his hands, his everything.

"While again, I may not be the expert here, I think you're supposed to relax. Let me do the work" He nudged her back into the bed then began to trace his lips down her body. She writhed under him as he kissed her shoulder, her neck, and lower, pressing herself into his touch.

"You like that?" he asked, a definite smugness in his voice. He moved back up and toyed with her ear, eliciting another moan.

"Yes," she managed to breathe as her back arched of its own accord. His lips against her skin were everything.

"I think you might like this even better," he taunted before taking one of her breasts in his mouth, lapping at her nipple.

Hannah gasped as he took the other in his hand, applying a gentle pressure that had her squirming anew, her core aching as she wrapped a leg around his, holding him closer to her, reassuring herself with the thickness of his own reaction.

Reminding herself that this was real. At least for now.

Sol continued, raising her desire higher and hotter with slow, lazy circles, punctuated by the grazing of his teeth, setting every fiber of her body on edge with want, stronger and hotter than she'd felt in a long time, perhaps ever.

"Please," she whimpered as her legs turned to molten liquid.

"Please what?" he asked. "Are you ready for me to

kiss lower? To lick lower? Make you come? Or do you want me to play with you more?"

"If you play with me more, I might stop breathing," she panted, amazed that this supposed novice had so easily entranced her. "Please. More. With your tongue."

"With pleasure," he repeated, kissing her forehead before sliding down again, spreading her legs with his body. He pressed his lips down her belly, his tongue tracing a path lower and lower, to each of her hips, then to the joint of her thighs.

She squealed as he nipped at the soft skin just above the area where her nether curls began.

He tipped his chin up and smiled at her. "I'll have to note that you like that for next time."

Next time. Hannah bit her tongue so she wouldn't correct him.

There could be no next time.

Even if she were another type of woman—one without her responsibilities to Tamar, one who wasn't a criminal—there were other circumstances to consider.

Sol would never achieve the success he so desperately wanted were he to continue to link himself with her. His position was tenuous enough—he needed someone monied, someone the community and gentiles would approve of, someone like Isabelle Ellenberg, as his wife.

One of the good ones.

Which she was certainly not.

"What's wrong?" he asked, pushing up on his hands, his brow twisted in concern.

"Nothing." She shook her head before running the back of her hand over his cheek. "I'm just enjoying this. You're a surprise. In many, many ways."

His inhaled and paused as if he was going to press, ask her something else. But he didn't. Instead, he lunged and kissed her on the lips once more before retaking his position between her thighs.

Hannah closed her eyes, willing herself to relax and merely enjoy this—him. Because she of all people knew how fleeting these little moments of happiness were.

His tongue lapped at her skin, parting the curls, and she near screamed again, dipping her head back, allowing herself to be lost in the sensation as he teased her, feeding her moans and hip swivels, driving her to the peak, only to pull back again and again, chuckling into her flesh at her moans of frustration, until she grabbed his head, holding him into her.

"There you go, love," he murmured against her body. "Take what you want."

And she did, god help her. She held him to her, guiding him as she stroked his sheared black hair. Moving against him until she reached that peak again, this time tumbling over it fast and hard, his name spilling over and over from her lips.

"Yes, love," he breathed, kissing her thigh. "Say my name."

"Sol," she whispered, nearly entranced. "Sol."

He sat up and took her hand, squeezing it. "What do you want, darling? Tell me and I'll give it to you. Anything."

And the promise, so clear and so earnest, made something within her ache. Or more, made her long to give him anything in return. But she couldn't. Or more, she had nothing left to give.

She needed to take this for the gift it was and enjoy it. And right now, the gift was this—this moment.

Which she would make sure they each remembered forever. For good or ill.

"I want you inside me." She bit her lip. How did she say this? Because no doubt he'd be concerned over certain things. "I don't have a sponge and I'm assuming you haven't prepared a sheath, but perhaps you could pull out, if you, um, concentrate." She swallowed. "If you want to. And if you want to actually—" Oy, she sounded ridiculous.

"I want to," he said, bending down and giving her a sweet, small kiss on the nose. "And I can pull out," he told her. "I can be careful. No matter how hungry I am." And there was the grin again, which warmed her so.

Even if she should surely be impervious to it by now. Hannah bit down on her back teeth—she would be impervious to it and him. Soon. No matter what.

She scooted herself up again. "Sol?"

"Yes?" he asked.

"Kiss me again," she told him.

The smile lit his handsome face. "With pleasure."

And he did, this time with languid, slow, aching strokes, first against her lips, and the inside. He moved his hand between them, caressing her skin, teasing.

"You're going to be the death of me," she managed to whisper in his ear.

"We can't have that." He gave her another peck. "I want you very much alive and thinking of me and only me."

Before she could respond, he moved fully on top of her, spreading her once again. He teased her entrance a little. "Are you sure this is all right?"

"I want this. And you," she told him because that at least was true. "All of you."

"Excellent." He grinned at her, sliding inside, filling her. And the pressure was exquisite, so much and not enough and everything. She clutched him to her, nuzzling against his flesh to create the memory of just the two of them together, joined. She kissed the joint between his neck and his shoulder, and he began to move.

She rose to meet him, taking her pleasure as he took his, two bodies as one, the rough hairs on his chest gliding over her skin. And almost too soon, she was ready again. She buried her face in his body, near biting his flesh as the shudders took her.

And then it was his turn. "Hannah," he cried, his voice strangled as he pulled out of her, turning slightly to the side to spend. "Hannah," he whispered as he grasped her to him, moving them both back down on the bed. "Stay with me."

"I can't," she said, shifting a little. "You know I can't."

"Not all night." He coiled an arm around her, pulling her back down. "Just a little. Please. Just be with me."

Hannah blinked up at him and the wolf was gone, replaced by soft dark eyes and a good man. Who was not for the likes of her. But she couldn't deny him, not when he stared at her like this, like she was someone actually worthy of him and his desire.

"All right," she sighed, laying her head on his chest. "Just for a little while."

Chapter Thirteen

Clanking in the kitchens roused Sol.

He pushed himself up from his now empty bed, staring out the window at the still gray sky, as the night stars quietly blinked out. Stray footfalls and an occasional grind of an axle floated up, but the world was still mostly asleep. Even the workers and servants were just beginning their day.

Hannah had left over an hour ago—rising from the bed and refusing to even permit him to assist with her buttons. It was the sensible time to leave, before anyone in the house could spy her. Facts he knew and had accepted. Even if everything in him raged at the idea of her being hidden away, of her having anything but her due.

They'd talked late into the night. Every bit of him bursting with desire to share anything and everything with her and encouraging her to do the same. To his surprise—and joy—she'd given him her secrets too. Well, some of them.

He'd told her of his father, of Frederick, and of the few fleeting memories of his own mother.

"She liked to laugh. She used to crawl on the floor and play with me. At night, she'd sing me songs. Mostly in German. A few Hebrew prayers. Really just the Shema. Last thing before I went to sleep." Reaching a hand behind his head, he'd stared at the bed curtains. "She was quite young with soft curls and perpetually flushed cheeks and loved flowers. At least I think so. I was small and my memories of her are...I hope they were real."

"I'm sure the best ones are. My sister's memories of our parents are like that, so I try to make sure to strengthen what she has." Hannah's voice had been wistful. "My mother was a beauty, you know? People forget that because of the rest. But she was. Like my sister." She'd rolled on her side. "Unfortunately for you, I favor my father, whose looks suited him more than me—but he was...striking. Though the papers called him cold and 'reptilian.'"

"He must have been clever as well as handsome, then," he said, stroking her soft skin. "Is this all right?"

She nodded but didn't tell him any more of her family; instead she stretched a little and pointed to the chair near the fire. "That book, the poems..."

"The Keats?" Sol asked as he wound his fingers through a lock of her now loose hair. "Did you like it?"

"Yes." She bit her lip. "Perhaps you could read some?"

He bent and kissed her forehead. "My pleasure."

And he had. For over an hour as she fell asleep in his arms. She'd been so lovely, her long brown hair splayed over his chest and her smooth shoulders. He could've lain there for days, weeks, months, watching the rise and fall of her back as she breathed, her skin against his. Never before had he been so content and calm and, well, happy.

But as she'd pointed out, he couldn't keep her.

Which was...wrong. That was the only way he could describe it. Wrong. Even if almost everyone in his life, including Hannah herself, would disagree.

That should likely move him. More than move him. Convince him to leave her alone.

Yet he couldn't convince himself that they were right, and *he* was in the wrong. No matter how foolish that was. Because he saw her—saw her value. Even if no one else did. Thus, in those wee hours of the morning, when it was as if they were the only two people in the world, the thoughts that had dogged him since they'd met turned into dreams, visions.

Ones in which they had a life—one where they could be together, with their own home and their own family. Taking care of her sister and his brother, of course— but connected—together.

Both independent yet part of a greater whole. And people would respect her. He'd see to it. He'd thrust himself back into the Jewish world—while protecting Frederick's place in the gentile—and she'd be able to go to synagogue and sit in the center of the balcony and no one would say a bad word about her ever again. A future that, though almost certainly impossible, made his meshuggeneh heart yearn.

Dangerous to say the least. Especially as the woman in question seemed quite determined to crush that same organ. Or at least chew off her own hand before risking hers.

Yes, the wisest thing would be never to go near her again. Except no one had ever accused him of being wise.

Still, he'd have to proceed with the utmost caution

from here on out. For Frederick's sake, for Hannah's, and for his own.

Sol stretched and rose from his bed, pacing over to his wardrobe to at least half dress for the day. Maybe he'd even wear shoes. He buttoned his shirt before pulling out a navy cravat, when a knock came at his door.

"Come in," he called, donning his jacket. One of his brother's footmen entered, bearing a tray.

"Your breakfast, Mr. Solomon," he said as he placed it down on the small table by the fire. The maid who'd followed him in set about poking at the flames to bring them back to a comfortable roar.

"Thank you," he told her before turning back to the man. "Thank you so much, Gregory."

The man gave him a small nod as the maid rushed over to futz with the curtains.

"Lovely morning, isn't it?" he called to her.

"I suppose," she returned, continuing her work. He turned back to the footman.

"I enjoy a little nip in the air, especially this time of year. Not too cold, but enough so everything is fresh and crisp, like a tart, tender apple." Sol smiled. He could never resist apples. Baked or raw, all ways, an absolutely perfect food. His mother had liked them on the holidays. At least he thought she had. Did Hannah enjoy them as well? If she did, perhaps he'd charm the cook to get a few extra and take them to her.

Or maybe he'd find a way that they could share a full meal together. Something she'd enjoy.

"Sir." The footman cleared his throat, returning Sol back to the present. "If I may, your brother wishes to see you in an hour. In his study."

Sol blinked at the other man, working to gauge whether this would be a good meeting or a bad one. After all, he'd been inside for over a week so he couldn't have done any damage, right?

Unless someone had found out about Hannah. He bit his lip. No, there would've been a snide comment or two from the staff if that had happened. The tension in Sol's shoulders eased. He should be fine—though if ever there was a sign that he should proceed carefully while Frederick was still courting Lady Drucilla....

"I'm sorry," he apologized, giving an exaggerated faux yawn. "Still a bit foggy in the head. From this dratted illness."

"Hmm..." The footman frowned. "I would eat up, then, and finish readying yourself for the day. He'll expect you to be...presentable..." The man glanced down and Sol followed his gaze.

Right. Shoes.

"Of course." He nodded at the man. "Let him know I'll be there, fully dressed, with a smile."

"Very good, sir," the footman said before exiting, the maid in tow.

Yes, this was good, Sol decided. He would see Frederick, help him with whatever he needed, and then, if things were going according to plan with Lady Drucilla, perhaps start laying the groundwork for a plot of his own. One with no guarantees of a happy ending, but as long as he didn't hurt his brother, it had to be worth a try. Did it not?

With a nod to himself, Sol lifted his teacup and took a sip, the hot liquid fortifying him. Yes, it would all turn out right in the end. Together, he and Frederick would make it so.

An hour later, Sol hovered in front of the door to his brother's study. Lavishly decorated, and adorned with several of Frederick's prized mirrors, the once dusty and crumbling chamber was an homage to the wealth Frederick had accrued reviving their family business. But Sol knew no matter how much success his brother had achieved, Frederick was not yet satisfied. He needed more. Needed to carve a true place of his own in the world—one of honor and respect.

Feeling something much like guilt, Sol again considered the unaccounted income he'd noted in the books for the Weiss Bank—and whether he ought to raise the matter with Frederick, when now, more than ever, he needed to step carefully. The prior year, his brother had stretched them a bit too thin in his eagerness to win the favor of—and more so, prove his "goodness" to— certain influential gentiles by lavishly donating to their pet charities. Sol had made the mistake of questioning if they truly had the funds for such expenses, and, well, even though it was clear his brother still loved him, their relationship had never been quite the same.

His fault.

He'd not shown enough respect—not taken enough care before speaking on the topic. He'd been presumptuous. After all, who had taught him the business in the first place? Who had spent years of sacrifice keeping them from ruin? He'd been arrogant and disloyal. Even now, the shame at his doubt still ate at Sol's gut.

And yet… Sol again could not account for an influx of funds.

With only a twinge of trepidation, Sol rapped his knuckles on the door. "Frederick, it's me," he called through the thick, diamond-cut wood.

"Enter," his brother said. Sucking in a breath, Sol pushed into the room, moving stand directly in front of the large black desk, hands clasped behind his back in what was hopefully a sign of deference and respect.

"Good morning," Sol said, focusing on his brother instead of his own reflection. Frederick's collection was impressive, but Sol had always found the mirrors a touch eerie. Not that he didn't have his own oddities. And his brother kept this singular, harmless one hidden, displaying only key frames in rooms impeccably tailored to show their beauty.

Frederick didn't look up from his correspondence. Instead, he adjusted his spectacles and motioned with his free hand. "Please sit."

Sol obeyed then glanced behind his brother when his head stayed down—he met his reflection in a towering mirror, grapes and thick leaves and clawed birds carved through the frame.

"Is that new?" he asked.

"Relatively," his brother said, finally looking up and glancing behind him. "It came about two months ago. From Poland. Supposedly belonged to some sort of prince."

"It's unusual, isn't it?" Sol asked. And a bit dark, he held back from saying. And menacing. If an inanimate object *could* be menacing.

"I'd say so. But an excellent addition to the collection." Frederick swiveled around, reaching up to stroke a raven's head stretching from the bottom of the frame.

"Very much." Sol nodded, shifting in his chair. "Your collection is unparalleled."

"It is, isn't it?" Frederick smiled, giving the mirror one last happy gaze before turning to him, hands folded on the desk. "But enough about that. I'm in need of your assistance."

"Anything." Sol scooted forward in his seat. Hoping to demonstrate his trustworthiness—and perhaps alleviate those unwarranted doubts—he added, "Is it the books? I had noticed additional income that is unaccounted for. I presumed they were new clients just not properly entered by the new manager. I took the liberty of assigning them temporary account numbers and reversing the calculations. Once I did that, they balanced. Nothing is late either, not our payments to creditors and customers nor payments into us. We're having a rather solid quarter. Once you marry Lady Drucilla, I'm sure new business will pick up in other sectors. Especially after the winter."

"Yes, you've managed to do your duty to the company at a relatively decent clip, especially for you. This plan to play sick was a stroke of genius." His brother smiled, tenting his fingers. "Perhaps, instead of finding you an heiress, we'll invent a disease to keep you in your bedchamber from now on. Something de rigueur from the Continent." He barked a little laugh at his joke.

"Perhaps," Sol agreed, smiling as well, though not without his stomach feeling oddly unsettled.

"Something to consider at least. However, right now, I need something else from you." His brother waved his hand, the gold buttons flashing against his jet-black jacket, only accented by his deep purple cravat. "A very important task, you understand."

"Anything." Sol clasped his hands together. "You can trust me, Frederick."

"I hope that is the case." Frederick adjusted his spectacle. "While I want to forget, you understand that it is hard to ignore your prior poor choices." His brother's gaze turned chilly. "Can I trust there haven't been any new occurrences? That you aren't keeping dangerous secrets from me?"

Sol swallowed.

He should confess. Tell his brother about Hannah. It was only right—first and foremost, he owed his brother his complete allegiance and honesty. And surely, if he explained, his brother wouldn't force him to promise to never see her again? But before he could open his mouth, his brother interrupted him with a sharp laugh.

"I'm just joking, Solomon," Frederick said. "There's nothing in my house I don't know about." His lip curled. "Nothing."

Sol blinked.

"But we don't need to discuss your poor choices— I will let you prove yourself with what I need from you now." His brother rapped his hand on the desk once, twice, three times. "There's a very important package I need delivered, personally, to a client late this afternoon. However, I shall be attending another engagement with Lady Drucilla and her brother. A critical outing, with an old friend of the late viscount whose blessing we need if we are to continue our courtship."

That was all?

"Of course I'll take the package," Sol said. What was so hard about that? Did Frederick really not trust him with so simple a task?

Frederick pursed his lips. "It's a bit of a ways south, located in a rather nasty place on the docks." His brother gestured outside. "Normally, I'd send a footman to deliver it, but it contains sensitive material, and the path can be dangerous. Though I suppose there's danger everywhere in the city these days. After all, the Marquess of Brackley's son was attacked the other day—robbed, right down the lane."

"Is he all right?" Sol asked as his mind spun. *Brackley*. Wasn't that the marquess whose son, Stoudmire, was the one Penrose wanted Drucilla to—

"Oh yes." His brother waved a hand. "Just injured, nothing fatal. Left to his father's estate in the country to recover. Such a pity we won't be seeing more of him. Childhood friend of Drucilla. Perhaps we'll visit him after we wed." His brother folded and unfolded his fingers. "I expect that to be soon enough."

Sol nearly jumped for joy. Yes, everything was coming together for them. They just had to hold on a little longer, and all their dreams would come true.

"That's wonderful," he said. "And I will support you in every way possible." He'd be exactly what his brother wanted and needed. No matter what.

"I know," Frederick said with a smile. "And in the meanwhile, we both need to be careful. Both with our safety and our presentation. Especially now that I'm on the brink of proposing. Our enemies might see this as a last chance to strike out."

His brother wasn't wrong. Once he married himself into the gentry, he'd have access to privileges no Jew, no matter how monied, could touch, whether or not he was seen as a villainous usurper.

And it couldn't come a moment too soon. He pursed

his lips, unable to ignore how Stoudmire's situation might be viewed.

A prominent gentile attacked? Who was a rival of Frederick's? People might jump to conclusions.

Ask any gentile on the street—Jews were either stealing good gentiles' places in proper society, secretly manipulating their surroundings to oppress the innocent, sucking resources like nuisances, masterminding unscrupulous criminal activity, or a combination of all the above.

It didn't matter where they came from—the city, the countryside, or out of England altogether—find an unhappy gentile and he'd explain why Jews were the villains in his tale.

If they were useful, they might have a temporary reprieve. However, if the choice was between one of them and one of their own...Frederick was right to be concerned. Sol shivered at the thought of Hannah, out on those same streets and coming to see him. Alone.

Oy. He needed to speak with her. Warn her.

Sol glanced toward the window. "It's early yet. I can go on foot so I'm not too conspicuous nor would our carriage be spotted and draw attention." He frowned at his bright coat and shiny boots. "I'll wear something subtle, so I blend."

"Excellent. Though watch your back. Stick to well-traveled areas." He brother reached inside his desk drawer, retrieving a folded paper. "Here are the directions." He tossed the sheet to Sol, who grabbed it and stuffed it in his pocket.

"And here's the parcel." His brother also held out a small, flat pouch—documents, no doubt. "You should leave soon. It looks like rain, and you certainly don't want to be in a storm after dark."

No, he did not. "Don't worry, I won't fail you," Sol promised him. "Good luck tonight with Lady Drucilla."

His brother gave him a thin, tight-lipped smile before returning to the papers on his desk.

Sol braced his shoulders, then left the room. He'd not let his brother down; he'd not.

Chapter Fourteen

Hannah placed both hands on her lower back and pushed, stretching her now sore, aching muscles. She should've asked for another bath before she left, even if she'd already stayed too long nestled in Sol's arms, the sound of his voice and his silly little stories lulling her into a sort of contentment she hadn't felt in years, if ever.

Oy. This was why she should never have returned, never told him what she'd told no one else in the world—secrets that he rightly should've loathed her for but somehow didn't—and she certainly should not have kept the damned perfume when all was said and done. These things weren't for her, and getting used to them would only make her soft and weak.

She'd sell the bottle, she consoled herself, and be done with this all.

It was wisest course of action. Especially as she'd not heard from the stranger. And true to Ned's word, her regulars had been silent.

"Are you sure you're able to work today?" Her sister moved behind her to swipe a rag over the glass panes of their living area windows. She gave Hannah a sharp nudge with her elbow before sniffing the air. "And you smell fancy. Quite the improvement."

She was definitely selling the perfume.

"I smell like I always do," she lied. Fighting a yawn, she shook her arms out before moving over to the stove to give the fire a poke. It was nippy inside and out. She glanced out the window—it looked like more sleet was coming. "And I'm fine. I made breakfast and swept and already served the morning rush. And now I'm on to lunch."

"You fell asleep standing up," Tamar scoffed before holding up a finger as Hannah attempted to protest, because she had certainly not.

Well, not for more than a few seconds.

"And you can't stop yawning," Tamar added just as another one came on. "Go rest, Hannah."

"I told you, I'm fine." She rubbed the back of her neck. She couldn't leave Tamar to run the shop—it was her responsibility. Besides, her sister, while eager to help, hadn't developed an eye for what could or could not get them hauled into court, nor did Hannah want her to. And considering the number of risky goods she'd been forced to reject as of late, Hannah couldn't risk not being the one fronting the store.

"You're tired," Tamar said. She glanced around then lowered her voice. "And you need your strength."

"I'm fit as a fiddle," she lied again. "Don't worry, I'm well enough to work so that when business picks up, there'll be plenty of money to add to your dowry." She made her voice sound bright despite the worry gnawing in her gut as she pictured their dwindling finances.

Tamar rolled her eyes. "Yes, that's what matters to me so much, the dowry, not that you're going to fall over, hit your head, and never wake."

Better that than allow you to be lured into a setup.

Like you almost did first thing, when I was in the back room for two minutes. Not that she could say that out loud. Her sister had been so upset when she'd rushed out and canceled the transaction, pouting in the back room for over an hour. Though pouting was much better than being extorted, or worse, hanged.

"You need rest, Hannah." Tamar's voice interrupted her thoughts. Her sister wrinkled her nose as she gave Hannah a head-to-toe gaze. "You're off lately. Is it that man?"

"What man?" She moved to the window and futzed with the curtains.

"You know which one." Her sister glared at Hannah.

"I thought you liked him?" Hannah asked as she retrieved another of Tamar's shawls which had fallen on the floor and folded it before shoving it into her sister's arms.

"I do," Tamar admitted with a slight scowl as she clutched the object to her chest and marched back into the kitchen after Hannah. "But I liked him better when he came around here instead of making you sneak off in the night." She wagged a finger and Hannah had to bite back a laugh.

Oy. Perhaps she'd sheltered her sister a touch too much. Sweeping her skirts to the side, she leaned against the gnarled worktable, where she could chop but also see the stove, the quick, neat rhythm from the knife focusing the ball of nervous worry that would not leave her senses.

"Tamar. You know—I'm—I sneak off in the night with quite a few men, right?" She paused her work for a moment to study her sister's face. "I mean, we haven't discussed..." She swallowed.

Her sister scoffed and rolled her eyes. "I'm not a child, Hannah. I know quite a few things."

Hannah bit her lip so she wouldn't snicker at the bold proclamation.

"So you know this is no different," she said instead, gentling her voice. "It's a temporary arrangement for mutually beneficial pleasure, which will end very shortly as I'm too busy for such a thing."

Tamar squinted at her. "Truly?"

"Yes. Of course." Hannah brushed her skirts before moving to the stove. "It's most certainly over now." Stirring the pot, she waved away the steam.

"If you say so." Tamar's voice was soft as she rose off her seat and drifted toward Hannah. "This is going to end in hurt, you know?"

Hannah reached out and gave her sister's arm a squeeze. "Darling, no one can hurt me." She sniffed a little. "Except maybe you—and you would never. But he's just a man, not family. So there's no danger."

"Isn't there?" her sister asked, her tone sharp.

"No, there's not." She nodded firmly. "He and I understand each other perfectly. What we're able to offer each other is only temporary and can never, ever be anything more." She grimaced because it was true. No matter what they shared, no matter what he said, he could most certainly get better elsewhere. She bent down to clean some grease that had dripped into the grate.

"I didn't say you were the one who was going to get—" Her sister, having moved back into the parlor, cut herself off by releasing a shriek.

Grabbing the poker, Hannah raced from the kitchen, only to stop short at the man calmly sitting on the fainting couch in their makeshift parlor. Reading that damned *Sense and Sensibility* novel. His tan trousers and plaid wool coat were a bit more subdued than usual, but they didn't take away from his handsomeness.

Worse, he appeared completely relaxed and at home. Almost as if he belonged. Which he certainly did not. Almost as irksome as the fact that he'd gotten into her space without detection.

Something of which he was no doubt odiously proud.

An odd longing to lie beside him with her head on his lap as he read rose in her mind. Which—no. That was ridiculous. She didn't want or need such things.

And the fact that her mind had even conjured such an image, well, that was proof he needed to go. Now.

She cleared her throat. "What are you doing here?" she demanded. "And how did you get in?"

With an irritating calm, he closed the book and laid it back on the end table, which she really should have dusted. "You—you were a touch distracted with other tasks, so I thought I'd wait here until you were finished."

Hannah blinked at him for a moment before turning to her sister, working to keep the sharpness out of her voice. "Tamar—why don't you go downstairs and make sure all the doors are locked and the back room is organized." Because she was not having this conversation in front of her.

Tamar gazed back and forth between her and Sol, before clearing her throat and backing toward the door. "Of course," she said with a nod, though her tone was a touch odd.

Hannah waited for the snick of the latch before glaring at the man on the couch.

He needed to stop reading romantic stories—like

the one he held now—before any consequences befell them.

"I told you, you shouldn't be here. This isn't your world." She folded her arms across her chest.

"Yes, you've reminded me of that quite a few times." He rose, the worn springs beneath him creaking. "And yet here I am." He spread his arms wide, taking up even more space.

Which would not do.

Widening her own stance a touch, she threw him another dark glare. "Hence my question: What are you doing here?'"

"I had to speak with you," he said, clasping his hands together, all earnestness.

"We spoke this morning," she told him, working to keep control of the conversation. "And if you're here to tell me you can't see me again because you've found the right heiress to marry, well, a note would've sufficed. Or nothing at all. I told you, I know who I am, and you can't hurt me that way. I promise. Though, honestly, just disappearing would've been more—"

"Hannah." He stepped toward her, closing the distance between them so they were nearly nose to nose.

"What?" She whispered the word even as she forced her posture straight.

"Kiss me." The words were not fully a question and not quite a demand, but somehow, she was powerless to disobey. No, instead of shoving him out the door and out of her life, she slid her hand behind his neck, bringing his lips to hers. Opening for him, drinking him in, as he matched her with earth-shattering intensity. Sending not only pleasure through her veins, but something else, something more dangerous. Something closer to want.

Something like *need*.

His arms still wrapped around her waist, he eased his mouth back from hers, touching his lips to her forehead with an aching gentleness that threatened to shatter her senses, before gazing down at her.

"I have no desire to pursue anyone but you," he told her, his voice firm. As if that truth would never change. Or more likely, because he believed it never would. Because he was young and naïve and had never needed to see the world as it truly was. However, she knew a great deal better.

"For now." She drew away from him and moved to the window, futzing with the cord and pulling back the curtain, face toward the glass and the slush-covered, gray rooftops beyond.

"Forever," he called.

"Ha." She snorted as she whirled back around, wagging a finger at him. "You say that here, in the moment, but only because this is new. You're clever, but you're young. I'm not. I've seen this. I know how this works. I know the world. I know who I am. Trust me, once you come to your senses and see—"

"And see what?" He folded his arms over his thickly layered coat and vest and—was that a cheery orange cravat?

Heaving a great sigh, she shook her head. "I am not for you." Why could he not get that in his head? After all, she had a business to run and a sister to marry off. And money to earn. And her options to do so grew slimmer and more dangerous by the day.

The last thing she needed was this man distracting her. Tempting her. Especially when he would eventually tire of her or come to his senses and then where would she—Hannah gritted her teeth—she'd be fine. Like she had been before. Like she always would be.

He was just a man, after all.

"Who are you for, then?" he asked, interrupting her swirling but still sensible thoughts. "The man you spoke of the other night? The one you lost your temper with in the alley?"

She raised her brows. "Jealous?" Her lip twitched a little. Not because she cared, but because it served him right.

Sol contemplated her for a moment. "Very," he answered before his own lips curled into that earnest grin that caused annoying and inconvenient feelings in her chest.

Hannah rubbed the back of her neck. "You shouldn't be. My relationship with Ned was one of pure business."

"You work for him?" he asked, surprise in his voice.

"He wished." She snickered before raising her chin. "Worked, as our relationship has concluded. But I did, and always will, work for myself. I found information he needed from time to time, and he paid me accordingly."

Sol frowned as if he was turning the situation over in his head. "What did he do with the information?"

"Does. We're both still in business, just not with each other. And he uses it to hunt." She shrugged again, glancing down at the battered, aging floorboards beneath her feet. "A person, more often than not. One who owes someone money—usually to the person who hired him."

He blinked at her for a moment. "And when he finds them?" he asked, his words slow and careful.

"They pay. One way or another." And even she flinched

at the hardness in her tone. But there was no room for anything softer. Not in her life. Not if she wanted to live and not crumble. "It's not a nice business. But of course, I'm not a nice person." Her chest tightened. "Besides, I prefer being the hunter rather than the hunted. And in these parts, you're either one or the other."

Sol didn't say anything. Which was probably for the best. If what she'd told him the prior night hadn't made him see the truth, perhaps those illusions of his were being shattered here and now.

"Go home." She straightened her shoulders. "Go back to your world and forget—"

"There's no way that I'm forgetting you." And in three large steps, boots gleaming in the low light, he was back in front of her, wrapping his hands around her back. "I don't want to," he insisted. "I can't."

She shook her head. "You're a fool."

"So I've been told. But I make up for it with hard work and tenacity. And I intend to here." He loosened his grip but did not let her go. "And yes, I'm inexperienced. And I have been too distracted by the problems in my own part of the world to even think about, let alone understand, yours, but I know how to listen, how to learn, and how to know when something— *someone*—has value."

She opened her mouth to make a biting remark, but he cut her off. "My brother and I did not get to where we are—did not rise from the ashes by being afraid to demand what we wanted."

"And what do you want?" she asked, glaring. She should remove his arms. Give him a physical shove for good measure, but her hands wouldn't work.

His lip twitched. "Isn't it obvious?" he asked, gazing

down at her with heat in his thickly lashed dark eyes. "I want you."

"I—" she started but couldn't quite form the words, which was good, as apparently he wasn't finished.

"And not just for a few tumbles in the sheets—though I will never say no to that with you." It was a good thing he still had her wrapped in his arms, because he gave her that wolfish grin then that despite everything, including the fact that he was clearly meshuggeneh, still made her knees buckle. "No, I want more. I want a life with you. Not just a fraction of one. And I want you to at least consider the possibility of the same."

Hannah gaped at him. "Are you out of your head?"

"No. I just refuse to accept limits," he told her with an irritating shrug.

No, he was definitely out of his head. Or he'd spent so much time with his brother and gentile friends that he'd forgotten who he was.

"You're a Jew," she said, shaking her head. "We don't get to 'refuse to accept limits.' That's the way we die." The higher even just a few of them rose, the harder they all collectively fell. Over and over again throughout their history. A truth that never changed.

Sol tapped his fingers against her thigh and looked as if he was going to argue but clearly thought better of it. "Fine. I refuse to accept that any limit is permanent, that any limit can't be changed." He cocked his head at her. "What do you say?"

Hannah rolled her eyes. "I say that you're meshuggeneh." Because that was the only explanation for any of this.

"Why?" he asked.

Wrinkling her nose, she frowned at him. "What?"

"Why won't you consider saying yes? You were fine with just a physical engagement; why not more?" he asked again, his voice calm and serious. As if she wasn't a criminal six years his senior who would ruin everything he and his brother built the moment anyone in the light heard of their activities in the dark, let alone saw her anywhere near Sol's side.

This time she managed to gather the strength to pull away and march to the exit. The only place he belonged. "Because it's not done," she said as she turned the knob and flung open the door.

"Many things worthwhile aren't 'done.' I thought you of all people understood that," he said, for once not following, but standing firmly where she'd left him. He squinted at her. "You aren't afraid, are you?"

Afraid. As if someone like her could possibly be afraid of someone like him. Hannah sniffed a little. "No. Not in the slightest." She inhaled. "I just don't want to see you—you've worked very hard."

"You care about me?" And the smile on his face— oy, just oy.

"No." She shook her head more frantically because he needed to stop. Needed to not make her out to be someone she wasn't. Needed to go. Now. Hannah cleared her throat. "It's just—"

Sol merely grinned. "It's just what?"

"You're very irritating." She gritted her teeth.

He raised a single finger. "But attractive."

"Which is why I haven't told you that I'll no longer bed you, only that anything more is out of the question. Though that's not even possible today as I don't have time. You need to go." Rolling her eyes, she indicated the open door. "I have work to do."

"As do I. And I will leave." He adjusted his hat, brushing through the space to stand before her again. "Tell you what—take a week or two to consider. My brother told me there has been some trouble on the streets, and while I know you can handle yourself, I don't want you to take unnecessary risks. So, while Frederick is securing his marriage, we'll all be extra careful with our persons. How does that sound?"

Before she could reply, Sol bent, capturing her lips again, stirring that burning longing anew before pressing his forehead to hers.

"You really think I'm going to say yes, don't you?" she asked, working to keep her voice sharp, even as her senses reveled in his nearness.

"As you astutely guessed before, Hannah, I don't like to lose," he told her before giving her one last lingering kiss. "And I don't intend to."

And with a tip of his hat, he released her, trotting down the stairs as she stared after him.

Nary a smart retort in sight.

Chapter Fifteen

Two hours after his meeting with Hannah, hard, icy sleet pelted Sol's hat and overcoat as he hurried northward. The drop-off had been a success, the man accepting the papers with a polite "thank you" and friendly conversation afterward. No one had bothered him on the docks in any way. Actually, the workers barely even noticed him.

All and all, it was a success.

The sky darkened further as dusk began to set in. Sol wove through the thinning crowds, the faces of the remaining laborers and merchants more determined than earlier. Everyone, it seemed, was trying to rush home to a blazing fire and a meal. Like him. All he had to do now was get himself north and west—toward a nice warm bath.

Oy, he could use one. Despite the cold air, he was shvitzing. Soaking his legs and back would be quite welcome. However…he bit his lip as another image came into his head. An even more pleasing, and definitely more erotic, one.

Could his tub fit two? Perhaps if Hannah straddled him? Sol's lip curled at the concept. Yes, Hannah straddling him was definitely what he wanted and needed. Though that was just a start.

Hopefully, their conversation earlier had if not

convinced her to give him a chance, then at least planted the seed of possibility for them. He would show her that they would suit, in more places besides his bed.

A gust of wind shuddered across a puddle, splashing mud on his boots. At least this pair was old and unpolished. All he needed to do was stay out of trouble, as he'd promised, then Lady Drucilla would accept his brother's proposal and then... banns? He squinted, working to recall the nuances of gentile culture.

And after that... when Frederick's future was secure, why shouldn't he explore possibilities for his own? If certain people were amenable.

A cart rumbled past, near clipping him with its wheel. A man yelled but Sol barely registered the sound, his mind now completely focused on Hannah.

What would it take to convince her further? Arguments, obviously. That's what their people did best. However, he'd need to properly set the stage.

Gifts were a decent lure as he'd seen with the perfume. He'd already asked Isabelle to acquire another, but perhaps he needed more. What else would she like? Something for her hair? One of those special combs Lady Drucilla had worn to her brother's dinner? Or maybe some pins. With little jewels. Red ones.

No... dark blue. Dark blue would shine against Hannah's hair. And while beaded hairpins weren't practical, and she was most definitely the sort of woman who cared deeply about the practical, didn't everyone deserve to be impractical sometimes?

Or they ought to feel allowed to be. Especially considering how hard she worked. She shouldn't need to skulk about at night—finding "things" for god knows what sort of people.

The work was dangerous and how long could she do it while staying safe?

He yawned a little himself. It really was quite the walk, wasn't it? His boots pinched his toes as he ducked down, winding closer between buildings as the streets grew quieter. Despite his and Hannah's first meeting, he wasn't a complete yutz. He'd been robbed twice as a boy on late-night wanders and had developed a fairly good technique of staying in the shadows. Even as he increased in size.

Another bellow of wind battered his jacket, and he hunched even lower as it started to drizzle. Sol darted into an alley, not the safest, but the narrow passages would keep him drier as he wound back north, and east to that right edge of Mayfair, close to their home.

The rain went from the occasional plink, plank, plunk to pellets and slashes as he sloshed onward. Dash it all, he was going to be soaked to the bone by the time he got home. He'd have a bath and a long sit by the fire. With something more interesting to read than books on business or the account ledgers.

A sneeze shook his head as he pushed forward until—*crash*.

He'd been knocked to the ground, flat on his arse. Rubbing his back, he squinted through what was now snowflakes raining down from the night sky.

"What do we have here?" A dark shadow towered above him. "Lost, are we?"

Blast. Not again. And practically back in his own, supposedly safe neighborhood.

"No, not at all." Sol worked to keep his voice calm, even as he cursed in his head. "I know exactly where I'm going. It's just a bit slippery. I apologize for the inconvenience." He pressed down on the cold, icy stones with his bare palms—he really should've borrowed work gloves from a servant—and rose. "I'll just be getting on my way and—"

"Not so fast." A hand clamped down on his shoulder from behind.

"Really, gentlemen, I would love to stay and chat, but I should be going. And you should too. Don't you want to stay out of the weather?" He pointed toward the sky with one hand as he reached into his jacket pocket for the knife he'd—blast it all, he'd left it at home, hadn't he?

"Not when there's easy money to be made and fun to be had." A malevolent smile curled on the man's lips as he held up a knife.

Drat. He clenched his jaw. Time to keep them distracted for as long as he could. "Shame I'm not particularly well off. Don't even have a halfpenny on me." He turned out his empty pockets before pulling forward the front of his frock coat, using the movement to better position his body for the possibility of either fight or flight. "And just look at these buttons? Wooden. Nothing to even melt down. I'm of no interest at all. Unless you want me to tell you a rhyme. Maybe a story. I do know a few naughty tales. Have any of you ever heard the one about the woman with twelve fingers? Well, if you have—"

The sound of gravel caught his attention, and he readied for the first punch—from neither of the two men who'd spoken, but a new opponent who'd accidentally given away his position. He ducked down and rolled to the side, dodging the blow.

Fast as he could, he skittered behind a crate, just as the third turned toward him, making his approach.

"Now, come on, there's no need for that. After all,

it's late," the first said, his voice crooning. "Let's just make this nice and easy. It'll only hurt for a moment."

Sol peeked between the slats as he rose to his feet, back against the wall of—from the sound of it—a tavern. His eyes flickered side to side, looking for a back door, but none appeared, and when he looked back at his attackers, they'd tightened their circle around him. The silver of a knife glinted in the low light.

Blast. He shouldn't have taken so long at the docks. Or lingered at the apple cart before setting off on his return. Regret filled his lungs. Frederick had warned him. He just hadn't listened enough.

His hands flexed as white-hot fear coursed through him and Hannah's face flashed in his mind. How brave and clever she'd been when she saved him. What would she do now? Not go down without a fight, certainly. Well then, that was what he'd have to do, weapon or no weapon.

He couldn't disappoint her.

A harsh laugh welled in his throat, focusing him. Right. He clasped his hands together. Time to do what they did best—survive.

"Thank you for the offer," Sol managed to say. "But I think we'll have to do this the hard way."

Before any of the three could respond, he shoved the crates toward them, knocking the stack over with a deafening crash. Not waiting to see the results of his handiwork, Sol ran past them as fast as he could, not daring to look back.

Legs pumping, Sol tore down the main street, bumping into drunken strangers, teetering over the stones as he searched for safety, the snow falling harder and harder, making the ground slick.

A few glances over his shoulder told him that the three had not given up the chase, so he was going to have to lose them, somehow, someway. He did put aside the thought to consider later the strangeness of their eagerness. Surely there were far easier marks for robbery.

It was almost as if they were bent instead upon his injury—or death.

He darted through narrow passages, around cellar doors, and over troughs, but still they hounded at his heels, getting closer every time he slowed. His lungs ached as he pressed forward, clambering over stopped carts and outbuildings as they seemed to herd him eastward—away from the safety of his brother's house.

Lightning crashed through the sky, and he heard shouts, probably at the light giving them a clear view of him. Oy, he was done for if he couldn't move faster. Sol glanced around for any miracles of assistance. When his eyes lit on another stack of crates, he followed them upward and considered. It would take a bit of muscle, but if he pulled himself up hard enough...he swallowed as the shouts of his pursuers behind him grew louder.

Taking a deep breath, he pressed forward, scrambling up the creaking slats until he was close enough to grab the edge of the roof. With as much strength as he could muster, he pulled himself up so his chest was high enough that he could use it to slither his knees and feet up, tearing at his clothes and scraping the flesh beneath.

But he made it.

With a groan, Sol doubled over, before forcing

himself to his feet again. He was up. Which meant he had a chance to survive, which he would not waste. And thus, he had to move. Now. At least he could see the city better from here, and the direction that he should go.

Maybe. Hopefully. He dashed to the far edge and glanced down. Mercy, that was quite a fall, though not that much of a jump to the next building. As long as he was careful...

The wind swirled thick, sticky snowflakes in his face. With luck, the weather would help, not hurt him. All right, he swung his arms a little, closed his eyes, and—with a great leap—he cleared the first rooftop, then the second, then the third. He craned his neck; they were still following, though they had only just managed to climb to that first rooftop. Fire in his veins now, Sol ran faster, toward a high-sloped roof, probably of an inn, which, if he got around it, could probably shield him and his course for at least a little while.

The gap between buildings was greater than the last two, but not impossible, as long as he ran fast enough. He swung his arms for extra leverage, pulled back, bent his knees, and—yes, his hands hit the shingles, then his first foot and—oh no—his ankle twisted and slid.

His chest and chin hit the roof first as he fell forward. He gripped for purchase with his fingernails, kicking wildly for anything as he fell, pausing only for a second as his jacket caught.

Panting, he worked to grip anything solid. Then a terrible ripping noise cut through the air as the sleeve disintegrated.

He might have screamed as he fell; he couldn't quite tell over the wind. Only that there was a crash and a blinding pain and then nothing at all.

Chapter Sixteen

Two days after Sol had left her, Hannah found herself not eating cholent and challah at her own Shabbos table, but instead tugging her cloak tighter as she shouldered through the wind westward, her destination one of the fanciest in the city. A far cry from how she'd spent her prior evening—being pawed at by the burglary crew's mark in a rough tavern while they ransacked his home. For pay that'd barely cover a week's worth of food.

Oy. What was she doing? Hannah shook her head, disgusted with herself for every decision she'd made as of late.

Light snow stinging her cheeks, she found and nixed half a dozen new excuses to decline the tea she'd been summoned to with Isabelle Lira Ellenberg—who insisted on being called "Isabelle—and Rebecca What's-Her-Name. Not because she didn't want to see Sol's world. But because she did. More than she should, which could only lead to, well—trouble or heartbreak. Or both.

Worse, the moment she entered the gold-covered drawing room, it quickly became clear that "tea" was a mere prelude to an ambush. A Sol-initiated ambush that, after the four-mile walk, she was too tired to fight off. Something that he and his clever colleagues had probably anticipated.

Isabelle leapt from a silk fainting couch and gave her a rather tight embrace before pulling her down and practically shoving a cup of tea into her hand. "We have a gift for you," she said.

"A gift?" Hannah managed to ask, her eyes popping. "From you? I can't—"

"We're only delivering. Again. It's from Solomon Weiss," Rebecca told her, her tone dry, from her seat on a high-backed armchair.

"To be fair, I am the one who obtained it for him." Isabelle pouted a moment, before thrusting a parcel into Hannah's hand. "Open it," she all but commanded.

"That's very generous, but I really don't need gifts," Hannah tried to protest, glancing from side to side as she sank into her own chair. "I really—" she started again, before stopping at Isabelle's glare.

Sighing, she unwrapped the ribbon and all too fine paper to reveal...a book. She squinted, murmuring over the characters. Was that...? It had been a long time, but to avoid prying eyes, her parents almost exclusively wrote in...

"*Shirei Tiferet*, N. H. Wessely?" She glanced at the two women.

"Sol said you liked poetry," Isabelle said. "And he and Rebecca suspected that you could read Yiddish, and thus perhaps Hebrew, at least well enough to enjoy it." She straightened her sequined sleeves. "Not many people possess such objects, you know? It's very difficult to obtain. Though I'm not most people."

Rebecca rolled her eyes, but Hannah barely noticed.

"You shouldn't have," Hannah whispered, turning the book over in her hand before thumbing through the words. She was more than a touch out of practice and Hebrew wasn't exactly the same as Yiddish, but the letters were still the first she'd ever known. The ones that her father had taught her, despite her being a girl and despite them living in England. Her vision blurred. "You really shouldn't have."

Neither of them. Not Sol nor Isabelle Ellenberg.

"She did have to. He beat her at cards," the other woman whispered, giving her a conspiratorial wink.

"I don't lose. I just pretended to because I enjoy having the opportunity to help people get what they want," Isabelle said, taking a prim bite of cake. "Besides, my family has been involved in Hebrew printing for a great deal longer than sureties so, as I said, despite being a challenge for some, I could acquire it easily. Even on short notice."

Rebecca snorted, which Isabelle ignored and instead gave Hannah another long, lingering glance. "Has anyone ever told you that a yellow gown would do wonders for your eyes and complexion? Especially in the early spring. Before Passover. When one could marry any day one likes. I know all the best fabric distributors in the city. I can advise you on where to get the best quality for the best price."

"She means for a wedding gown for when you marry Sol," Rebecca added, as if Hannah hadn't understood.

Hannah rubbed the back of her neck. "I assure you, not only does he not want to marry me"—a small lie, true, however, only until he came to his senses—"but even if he did, I would never entertain such an offer."

"Why?" Isabelle frowned. "You like him. You must.

Don't insult my intelligence by suggesting otherwise. I've seen the way your face softens when I merely mention his name."

"I will make him miserable." How could they not see that? Hannah shook her head. "Sol wants to be loved, not reviled, and I'll bring him nothing but the latter."

That was the heart of the problem. Jews needed to separate themselves from her or lose the status they'd either already gained or hoped to secure. Any perceived sympathies toward her could—no, *would*—topple both social standing and businesses or block access to such achievements.

After all, even gentiles who feared that their hatred toward Jews would seem "old-fashioned" or "unenlightened" could safely hang on to their prejudice by separating the "good" from the "bad" Jews. And there was no doubt as to which category she'd been placed in.

Before she could remind the two women as such, there was a knock at the door and a gray-haired man stepped in the room.

"Isabelle," he said. "Roger Berab is here to see you."

The woman's dark brow furrowed. "I thought he was entertaining with his brother. Please send him in, Pena." Isabelle folded her hands in her lap as the older man exited the room, then she turned to them. "Hopefully everything is all right."

Hannah toed the fringe of the thick, floral rug in front of her seat, as the man named Pena entered with a bow, followed by another man, around her age or perhaps older, with honey-colored hair and dressed almost as fastidiously as Sol.

His eyes scanned over the occupants in the room, his cheeks coloring. When Isabelle and Rebecca each rose to greet the man, the latter stumbled, spilling her tea down the front of her gown.

Interesting.

"Oh no," Rebecca exclaimed, turning to her friend. "Please excuse me. I'll need to return home and change."

Isabelle waved a hand. "Nonsense, Pena will fetch Judith. She can find you something to wear and handle your gown." With a reluctant nod, Rebecca left the room, smiling tersely as she passed the newest visitor.

"Mr. Berab," Isabelle continued. "What a lovely surprise. Won't you come in and have some tea and cakes with us?"

"Certainly," the man murmured, strolling to Rebecca's abandoned seat. Before sitting, however, he pointed a finger in Hannah's direction before looking back at Isabelle. "She's not here because of Weiss, is she?"

"I asked Miss Moses to tea," Isabelle said primly. "She's here on my invitation."

"Naturally," the man said, his eyes drifting to the fraying edges of Hannah's gown. "You do invite the best people into our lives, don't you?"

"What would you like, Roger? If it's dramatics you're seeking, I suggest you take yourself to Drury Lane after sundown. If it's something else, now would be the time to mention it. Is everything all right with David?" Isabelle asked. "Or will he be joining us?" She glanced toward the door, as if hoping the other man would appear and save them from his brother's company.

"Later, perhaps." Roger shrugged. "Currently, he's occupied. With a Mr. Sabur."

Isabelle frowned. "Who is that?"

"A potential client that Mr. Weiss wanted to introduce

to our services. He was supposed to send him the necessary contracts before Shabbat; however, they never arrived." His tone dripped with annoyance. "Fortunately, my brother is skilled, and Mr. Sabur should become a client in truth, but David was ... concerned about our colleague's absence, so I came to search for him."

"He's not here," Hannah said, the words more intended for herself than anyone else, even as her heart began to speed, a strange nervousness pushing back the embarrassment that rose at everyone's sudden attention.

"Clearly." Roger rolled his eyes and took a step toward Hannah. "You don't happen to know where he is?"

"No." She bit her lip. "The last I saw him was two days ago. He said he had a meeting."

Her mind searched their conversation for any other clue regarding his whereabouts. Other than his concern for *her* safety and his, well, whatever-that-was, that is. She tugged at her ear. "He asked me to consider an ... offer of sorts," she said. "And after I thought on it, to contact him."

Glancing at Isabelle, she bit her lip, before adding, "His brother also warned him of trouble in the streets."

Isabelle frowned. "Strange. I'd heard nothing of the sort—nor has Aaron."

Berab heaved a sigh. "Likely Weiss forgot then. I don't appreciate my time being wasted, as my involvement in the business is rather limited—"

"Nonexistent," Isabelle said, raising her chin.

"I have other duties that are quite valuable to not only both of our families but the community as a whole," Berab retorted before turning back to Hannah. "I'd advise you to contact him sooner rather than later, whether you have 'considered' his offer or not. Even if such thinking is not your forte."

"Roger," Isabelle admonished.

The man ignored her and remained focused on Hannah, whose cheeks heated despite herself. "No one here should forget that his job is not guaranteed and does require him to actually work as well as uphold the standards our families have set for the community." His eyes bored into her as if to make sure she caught his meaning.

Even if he was being so obvious, a child would understand.

Not that he wasn't right. Here was proof: she was no good for Sol, and she respected and liked him too much to continue harming him. She would relay her refusal, as well as check on his well-being—because she knew Sol was too loyal, too hardworking to forget a meeting—as soon as she could.

"Noted." Isabelle spoke before Hannah could, rising with a dignity that she could only envy. She clasped her hands together. "Please tell David how much I appreciate his efforts, and that I'd like to meet with him after Shabbat to discuss Mr. Sabur and other matters." She glanced out the window. "Provided the weather holds."

Berab gave her a formal bow. "I most certainly will." His lip curled into a half smile. "I'm sure he'll be here soon with all the books and papers either of you could want. I'll make myself scarce for that."

He turned to Hannah and nodded. "Have a good afternoon. It's a pity we don't cross paths more often." With a small scoff, he exiting, leaving the two women alone with what now had to be cold tea and quite a few uneaten pastries. Hannah's stomach rumbled, and she cursed herself for not having eaten earlier.

Alas. Sol came first. Saving him from his own bad decisions, as well as just verifying that no harm had come to him because...she scratched her ear. It was highly unlikely, and yet still, there was an odd emptiness in her gut that had nothing to do with hunger.

She glanced at the door and back at her hostess. "I should—"

"You most certainly should." Only Isabelle plucked four tarts from the tray, wrapped them in paper, and shoved them into Hannah's arms. "Please have Sol contact me and let me know he's all right. Tell him I'm not upset with him, just concerned."

Hannah swallowed an odd lump her throat. "I will," she said. "Thank you. For your hospitality and..."

Isabelle stared at Hannah for a long moment, opening her mouth then closing it. "You're better for him than you think," she said finally.

Before Hannah could protest, a gentle hand clamped down on her arm.

"I happen to approve of that statement," Rebecca, having apparently been re-outfitted in what appeared to be a ballgown, several years out of fashion, said. "Especially if it contradicts that self-important blowhard." She pursed her lips. "But—I—It was good to see you again. Perhaps next time we all attend the Great Synagogue you shall sit with us."

"Thank you," Hannah told her. "I'd like that."

She meant the words, even if such an event happening was unlikely. But that was neither here nor there because this time—truly, this was the last—she would say goodbye to Sol for good before he lost his damned job.

Chapter Seventeen

Sol awoke to throbbing pain.

Blinking, he stared up at a cracked ceiling that was most certainly not his before looking down at an unfamiliar, worn quilt. Where was he? And—he glanced around—where were his pursuers? Had they... taken him? Ignoring the ache behind his eyes, he turned his head to see what appeared to be a small room with a sloped ceiling.

Oy, he needed a better view. And a plan.

With shaking limbs, Sol pushed down on the mattress to rise—only to immediately fall back when pain stabbed up his spine and into his head. "Ow!"

"Oh, you're awake."

Sol started at the female voice. At the foot of his bed now stood a small, white-haired woman wearing an old-fashioned cap in a rather garish shade of red.

Without preamble, she threw back the quilt over his bare knees. "Good, let me check your leg," she said. He gasped at the realization that he was completely naked—save the yarmulke he'd been wearing beneath his hat despite Frederick's earlier admonition.

Wait—was he?

He reached up to verify, and yes, the yarmulke was

still there at least. But as for the rest of his clothes...He narrowed his eyes at the woman. What was she about? Though he doubted she'd been one of those bent on robbing him—odd as their pursuit had been—she was still a stranger and he was rather vulnerable at the moment.

Not his preferred position, that was certain.

"Don't worry, I'm as good as any doctor," she said, as if her credentials were the cause for his concern. Or rather, as if that was enough of a reason not to object as she poked—*ow*. He bit his tongue to stop the rather foul stream of language ready to burst forward from his lips.

"I used to be a midwife," she continued as she prodded farther before bending down to retrieve a pillow, which she shoved under his throbbing left leg. "Retired. Of my own choice, naturally. No one forces me out of anything. And I still assist my niece and her daughter from time to time."

She grabbed a wad of cloth from her pocket and proceeded to wrap his ankle—tightly. Sol winced.

The woman tucked in the ends and wobbled his leg from side to side, presumably testing her work. "Now, that girl—my niece—could be a physician," she said, seemingly unbothered by their rather one-sided conversation. "Not that she will be, mind you, at least not if she stays here. Which she will, as where else is she to go? Prussia isn't exactly welcoming to us right now." She shook her head and sighed. "It's always opposition to one thing or the other—Jew or woman or both. But that's neither here nor there."

Sol opened his mouth then closed it, as really, how exactly did one respond to that? Or change the subject politely so he could get his questions answered?

She waved her hand a bit dismissively before giving his ankle a swat—he bit back a gasp.

"Healing nicely," she concluded. The woman—retired midwife—whatever—finally focused on his face, hands on her hips. "Turn on your side and pull down the quilt."

He gaped at her. "I—"

For possibly the first time in his life, he wasn't sure what to say. Or rather, what to say first. But that—he was naked, completely naked, and if he turned, she'd have a view of, well, everything. And while he had more pressing concerns, like identifying where he was and what had happened—and who exactly *she* was—showing a stranger, midwife or not, all his bits and pieces was not exactly a preferable alternate.

"Come on now." The woman huffed. "I saw all of it last night when we undressed you so I could stitch you up. Your garments are a tad worse for the wear, but once Shabbos is over, we can change that."

"We?" Sol started as the door swung open and two more elderly women appeared, one with a tray and another carrying a mug.

"Time for you to eat!" The first woman bounded over and plopped the tray next to him.

"Careful," the second cried, giving her friend's elbow a sharp tug. "You're going to spill it everywhere." She scowled at everyone and no one before shoving the mug at him. "Here, you need to drink, and then some rest." She released a deep yawn. "I don't know why you're all bothering him so early. He needs to heal."

The first one—first new one—the woman with the tray—oy, he needed some names—stretched her arms toward the sloped ceiling's low-hanging rafters. He'd have to be careful of those when he stood up. "I think that's Doc's job," she chirped as she pulled a spoon from her apron and proceeded to stir the porridge before scooping a bite toward his face.

"Doc?" he asked, waving her off as gently as he could. The gesture was kind, but he could most certainly eat food without assistance. His hands weren't injured, as far as he could tell.

"That's what they call me." The original woman—a former midwife, she'd said, though apparently she'd now been elevated to a doctor—was still standing at the foot of the bed, eyeing the quilt she was apparently itching to pull back. "Because of my skill in the medicinal sciences." She—Doc—gave the others a sharp look but thankfully didn't advance on him further.

"I have skills as well," the cheerful woman said, before yawning as well, a gray curl bouncing on her forehead from beneath her laced-trimmed white cap.

"Napping is not a skill," her grumpy companion snapped. "Even if we've all gotten a great deal better at it since we retired."

Sol wanted to disagree, because at the moment it was the skill he'd most definitely like to practice. Especially as he was beginning to have trouble focusing and pain was winding down his lower back. He shifted at little, but damned Doc was sharp-eyed despite her age apparently.

"It hurts, doesn't it?" she said. "As I was saying, I had to stitch you up in about half a dozen places. All which will need tending to, so you don't get an infection. You're lucky you aren't dead."

"How did I survive?" he asked, relieved to finally be getting some answers. A terrible thought occurred to him, however. "I did survive, didn't I?"

"Thanks to me, yes." Doc advanced on him again, this time lifting his leg out from the covers. He drew it back under the quilt quickly, though not before catching a glimpse of a nasty cut. Lord only knew how far up it went. She gave an irritated grunt. "You need to let me help you. Your wounds will become infected if you don't allow me to dress and change them."

He held up a finger, halting her progress toward his side. "Not until you explain a few things. You have my thanks, truly, but the last thing I remember is falling from a roof. How am I not dead? And where are we? And what happened to the men who were chasing me?"

And how do I prevent them from coming back and not only finishing me off, but you as well? Because, reluctant as he was to admit it, mere robbery couldn't explain the doggedness of their pursuit—which meant they'd intended him harm. He glanced around, inviting one, or any of the women, to speak.

They, somehow, managed a three-way glance, though no one spoke for a long while. Instead, they just stood there, toying with cuffs and fluffing aprons.

Finally, Doc broke the silence. "It appears that you're alive thanks to a fortuitously located fruit cart—an empty one, filled with hay, as the snow was still light then."

"Got it all over the house when we took you in," the unnamed, grumpy woman continued. "I should never have trusted you to clean; half the time you can't tell a broom from a bucket." She glared at her companion, waving her hands in the air, so close to his head, he had to duck.

"Shah, she's your sister," Doc said, before sneezing. The grouch handed her a handkerchief, which she accepted, blowing her nose rather loudly.

"Are you all sisters?" He squinted at them. They didn't quite look it, but he and Frederick didn't exactly look like brothers.

"Bayla and Gertrude are, but I'm not related to them," Doc explained, gesturing first to the cheerful woman, then the other. "We all used to work together. Gertrude did the books and Bayla assisted both of us. And we're friends. Very good friends." She smiled at the grumpy one—Gertrude—a gesture which her apparent friend did not return.

"But you all live together?" he asked.

"We do," Bayla—the helper—said with a nod. "There used to be more of us, seven in total, but the others moved on to Brighton for the sea air. You're in one of the rooms they vacated."

"And where are we located? What part of the city?" He fisted the edge of the quilt, his eyes on Doc. "How long have I been here? And the men, my attackers, what of them?"

"We didn't see any men lurking about when we found you after the—fall from a roof did you say? That certainly explains the extent of your injuries. We weren't entirely sure." Doc coughed—perhaps she was allergic to something? Hay or what have you, or maybe him, given his luck—then motioned to Bayla, who shoved another spoonful of porridge toward his mouth. "You're in Aldgate and it's Saturday afternoon."

Sol waved her away as his head spun. Two days. He'd been there two days. Frederick must be worried sick.

"I should be home. My family—my friends—my employer—" Sol started, his mind overwhelmed at all he'd missed. The correspondence he owed—to clients he couldn't upset. News of Frederick's courtship.

And Hannah. She'd soon receive his second gift, if she hadn't already.

He pressed his fist to his lips.

Gertrude glared at him. "Your ankle is badly injured. Not broken, thankfully, but it's still swollen. You can't walk on it, and given the storm conditions now, it would be very unwise for you to attempt to leave the premises."

"Storm? What storm?" he asked.

"The snowstorm," Doc told him. "It started Friday and hasn't stopped. It's so bad that barely a horse, let alone a cart or carriage, can move through the streets. People have been out and about but very few. I'm sure Shabbos services were not well attended."

"Is there any way I could get a message to them?" He needed to tell people what was happening, damn it. However, he considered his saviors and sighed. "Discreetly, of course."

For that was the rub. What if the men were lurking about, waiting to finish him off? His mind spun and a terrible thought occurred to him. What if Frederick had been their true target? He was the more valuable of the two of them. "My brother must be warned and apprised of the situation, at a minimum."

"Too dangerous," Gertrude said with a shake of her head. "We're not exactly steady on our feet and breaking a bone at our age..." She tutted a little, her expression sour. "We need to wait until the snow stops. And would your brother be about in this weather, besides?"

And now he felt guilty for asking. Especially since they were already taking quite a risk harboring him. He considered her point. Frederick was unlikely to leave the warmth, and safety, of their home if it was that dreadful outside. Perhaps his brother was safer with less knowledge than more. At least until he could be by Frederick's side.

"When will I be well enough to go?" he asked.

"Not for a few more days. But even for that, you're going to need to let me help you." Doc gave him a pointed stare.

"Fine." He folded his arms before glancing around. "But maybe without so many people in the room?" He winced at Gertrude and Bayla's hurt expressions. "I'm grateful for all you've done, really, but I'm a little…"

"Bashful?" Bayla yawned. "You really don't have to be." She gave him a long, lingering glance and a wink.

Oy. Sol swallowed.

"But we understand." Gertrude physically pushed her sister out the door as she exited. "We'll leave you to your task, Doc." She glanced back at him. "You should listen to her. She knows what's what. And be grateful, or you'll be here for a long time."

The door shut behind her, leaving him alone with Doc.

"Now," she said, hands on her hips. "If you're ready, we can get to work. I promise, if you're good, I'll explain everything as we go."

"Truly?" he asked, squinting.

"Truly," she said with a nod. Doc adjusted her spectacles and clapped her hands together, as if that settled the matter. "Just relax this might hurt a bit." She pulled up the quilt and tugged and—*ow*. "All right, more than a bit." She shrugged.

Right, relax. As if that were possible. Sol winced in pain once more as Doc moved a damp cloth over his already burning body.

Hannah. He would think about Hannah. Hold on to her image. He closed her eyes. Hopefully she liked the poetry. Wouldn't it be wonderful if she were there? Reading it to him?

Fuck.

He forced his fist into his mouth to hold back the word as another bandage came off, along with what had to be a clump of his hair. Dash it.

Closing his eyes again, he tried again to picture Hannah's beautiful face, especially when she was about to tease him, or more, challenge him. Yes, as long as he thought of her, he could survive anything.

And he would make sure she, and Frederick, and all his friends survived as well.

Chapter Eighteen

Hannah rubbed her eyes before pressing the wax into a seal to close the envelope. It had taken her four hours to finish writing, but now the deed was done. She could send—or more accurately, sneak—the letter into Sol's house and slip it under his door. Even if it felt rather cowardly.

If she was truly a good woman, she'd have ended things completely—told him that under no circumstances could they see each other again. But she had not.

No, instead she'd reiterated that only a physical relationship between them was possible—a relationship she'd happily enjoy for whatever brief time they had—before expressing her concern over his absence. She'd concluded by informing him that he needed to contact Isabelle Ellenberg posthaste or risk his job, and probably social standing.

A situation she shouldn't fret about, and yet...she swallowed. The idea of Sol losing his position after all his hard work or having missed his meeting due to illness or injury or what-have-you was just—*no*.

She shook her head. This was all irrelevant to her life. What she and Sol had was temporary and based on mutual lust—whether her damned heart wanted to accept that or not. And sentiment regarding anyone but Tamar had no place in her world.

Besides, Sol was clever and strong and tenacious, with far more money and connections and chances than she, and he would be fine. Especially after she got up the nerve to end *all* aspects of their relationship. Which she would do. Soon.

With a sigh, she rose and retook her cloak from where it had been drying by the fire. She peaked inside Tamar's bedroom door to find her sister snoring softly, then reclosed it as quietly as she could, and left. Hannah crept down the stairs to the alley, careful to avoid the icy patches slickening the stones. Hardly any carts had been in the streets when she'd returned from tea, and there were even fewer now, given the increasingly poor weather conditions.

The wind howled up from the river as she moved westward, carefully sticking close to buildings, especially since the falling snow dulled her hearing, leaving her more vulnerable than she preferred.

All in all, not a night anyone should be out and about, but this was something she had to do. The sooner the better. Taking a deep breath, she scurried across the lane, boots sinking in the sludge, only to duck behind a fence when she spotted Mick and George ahead. Looked like they were shaking down Siobhan, an informant—now former informant, probably—who worked the alley two buildings down, for a purse that looked too nice to be hers, likely from a customer.

Momzers. Acting like they owned these streets.

They laughed as the woman rushed away, before a familiar form approached them, palm outstretched. Hannah clenched her teeth as she watched George hand Ned the small pouch. He tipped his hat to the two, before shoving it in a pocket and leaning forward to whisper in Mick's ear. With a nod, the two thugs scurried off, presumably to relieve Ned's next target of their coin.

Her former colleague watched them for a moment before glancing over his shoulder exactly in Hannah's direction. Holding her breath, she stilled, even as her fingers itched for the knife she'd stuck in her apron pocket. He took one step and then two in her direction, then paused before turning back to the road and walking south, presumably toward a pub or some such establishment to spend some of his "earnings."

Not until he had disappeared did Hannah breathe again, her knees near knocking together as she straightened, ready to move. She took one more glance into the road to make sure no one was watching and—

A hand shoved a rag beneath her nose, an odd smell invading her senses.

She tried to scream but the leather-gloved palm clamped down on her mouth, cutting off all sound. Hugging her from behind, her attacker quickly pinned her arms as she struggled, stopping her before she could grab for her knife. As she kicked backward in a desperate attempt to escape, her boots met with nothing but air as her limbs grew heavy, movements turning sluggish until her eyes shut of their own accord.

Her vision plunged into darkness and then—nothing.

Hannah awoke with a start, her heart dashing against her ribs.

Quick as she could, she thrust her hand into her apron pocket and pulled out her knife, brandishing it, even before her eyes fully adjusted. But when she searched for her attacker, she met empty air—and when she gathered her wits, it was to find herself sprawled upon a dark velvet chair, before a great mahogany desk, a roaring fire at her side. The walls of the room were covered in dark purple silk and adorned with silver mirrors of various shapes and sizes, several placed far higher than anyone could use, creating an oddly eerie effect.

From the largest and most fearsome of all, directly behind the desk, she saw her own reflection.

Oy, she looked terrible. Dark circles marred the skin beneath her eyes, her lips were cracked from cold, and her hair had come loose, falling in nettled waves over her shoulders. Her already ill-fitting gown had bunched and—

A door creaked open and she whirled around, knife still in hand to find two men standing in the threshold—both around her age or a touch older, one dressed in simple clothes, and one dressed in richly colored silks. The former had easily forgettable features, the latter was striking, if not handsome, his brown hair slightly curled but neatly coiffed.

"Ah, Miss Moses, how good of you to grace me with your presence so soon after your Sabbath," the elegantly dressed man said, ignoring the knife. Shutting the door and rounding her chair, he stood before her, leaning against the desk. "I believe you've met my employee, Martin."

"We have." Martin raised a thick brow in challenge, making her pause at the sound of his voice, its familiarity washing over her.

She gasped. He was the man, the man from the alley, the one who'd hired her after Ned—so this must be his employer. Well, that explained the fancy getup and the expensive, if peculiar, décor. How had Martin described him? *Quite at home with a certain set.*

The unnamed employer's face broke into a handsome but oddly unsettling grin as her recognition became evident. A handsome, familiar grin. Like the shape of his brows. And the tilt of his chin, and the way he threaded his fingers and clasped his hands in front of him.

A maneuver she'd now seen multiple times from the man's brother.

"Frederick Weiss," she breathed as she hastily smoothed her skirts in a belated attempt at propriety, unable to quite meet his sharp blue eyes. So different than Sol's warm brown. He was leaner than Sol too, more angular. Older, obviously, and of a different mother. And despite the features they had in common, Frederick's felt more forbidding, somehow.

Attractive, but cold. Like all the mirrors.

"Aren't we quick?" he mused as she slipped the knife back into her pocket. "Though even dogs know not to bite the hand which feeds them."

Well, she'd not need the letter, as she could presume then that he knew about her relationship, for lack of a better word, with Sol. It should comfort her that he most certainly shared her own dim view of them continuing an association, making him an ally in her mission to do right by Sol, but his disdain felt like a kick in the gut.

"You have a beautiful home," she lied instead of replying, indicating the room. "And quite an impressive collection."

"They are, aren't they? Some are more than three hundred years old. And they hail from all parts of the world. It's why I find them fascinating—different materials, different designs, but the same center." His lips turned into an almost real smile as he glanced around.

"That is fascinating." Hannah twisted her hands in her lap, shifting uneasily on the narrow chair.

"They can be. Though I imagine you aren't actually interested in discussing my collection. No, I suspect you're curious as to why I asked you here." Frederick dipped his head forward, his curls glinting in the light.

"I suppose this means you were satisfied with my prior services," she said, working to match his tone—or at least maintain the tone necessary for her to do business, despite the ill feeling in her gut. She didn't think it would be to her benefit to point out that abducting hardly counted as asking.

"Quite." He nodded. "And I know that I'll have many uses for you in the future, provided you *keep* proving useful." Despite the nearness of the fire, she shivered at his hard stare. "How is your trade these days?" he asked, his lip twitching as if he most certainly knew how Ned's threats were taking a toll and how eager she was for additional work.

Any work.

"What information do you need, Mr. Weiss?" she asked, straightening in the chair.

"So direct," he tutted, moving around the desk to sit in the chair opposite her. He nodded at Martin, who exited from the room. "How refreshing. I've become so used to only interacting with women trained in social niceties, but you're so...the opposite. You'd create quite the stir in a ballroom. Amusing, for some people."

His eyes hardened.

This man knew things. Many things. Far more than his brother realized. At least, that's what she thought. For the way Sol spoke of Frederick, he clearly idolized the man—how betrayed would he feel should he discover his brother's illicit activities? As for her, if she was truly seen as a threat... She cleared her throat.

"Unfortunately, I doubt I'll ever see the inside of one," she said. Not a truth she hadn't already known that, but this man clearly needed reassurance. Something she shouldn't resent. After all, she'd not want herself anywhere near Tamar. And, she supposed, who was she to judge when she shielded her sister from all manner of hard truths about their life?

Frederick Weiss smiled again. "Clever, aren't you, Miss Moses. A becoming quality. It's rare to meet a person so completely aware of their place and limits." He threaded his fingers and placed his hands in his lap. "One hears tell of so many stories from your world. Of women whose work with pretty objects leads them to dream and want things which will never be theirs. Stories which end in... disappointment."

A warning if there ever was one.

"You needn't worry about me. I'm not one of those women," she said, squeezing her own hands together tighter, careful not to let go of the man's gaze.

"No, I suppose you aren't," he said softly, cocking his head to the side. "Which is why you are here, to help me with a very delicate matter."

That got her attention. "Sir?" she asked.

"My younger brother, Solomon, is unfortunately not quite as sensible as you." The temperature in his gaze seemed to drop even further. "He's a bit of a dreamer, flighty and far too trusting. So many people attempt to take advantage of him—almost have, many times…"

Frederick paused, moving his hard stare to the floor. He clenched and opened his fists once, twice, and a third time, before lifting his head back up, his expression now calm. "I apologize," he said, his voice softening for the first time. "I tend to become a touch emotional discussing him. You see, I've raised him since our parents died. He was just a child. So young, so fragile, and I tried my best, but I often worry…"

"I understand." She swallowed a hard lump. Because she most certainly did.

"Of course you do," he said, sounding almost kind. "Which is why I sent for you. Solomon didn't come home a few nights ago, and while initially I wasn't worried—" His eyes narrowed at her. "I presume I don't need to be delicate with you?"

"You do not," she said, her smile turning brittle.

"He's been distracted as of late, and in the past, he's dealt with the matter by releasing his pent-up, let's say, urges. He generally favors professionals to assist him. One of his cleverer habits. Though he does become… infatuated at times, the attachment always passes quickly enough," he told her, his eyes even more intent. Knowing.

And clearly disapproving.

Hannah willed her face not to react. After all, why should she be hurt? Yes, Sol had made passionate declarations toward her, but she'd not actually taken them seriously. And she most certainly knew the way of the world and the men in it, no matter their background or class.

"I didn't necessarily expect him home until Friday

morning, or even the afternoon; however..." Frederick frowned. "I know the weather is bad, but one would have thought he'd have at least contacted me...especially as now it's been several days."

"I understand," she told him again, thoughts turning over in her mind. She herself had also told him to seek out women who could appreciate and benefit from what he had to offer. Thus, it would've been logical for him to comply.

And if he had become temporarily stranded with one such woman due to the weather, well, good for him.

Of course, Isabelle Ellenberg would not appreciate that explanation for his absence, but that Roger Berab fellow probably would, from the look of him. And if confirming such a situation earned her money that she and her sister needed and helped Hannah finally put to bed any errant feelings and conclude their relationship for good—that was the best result for everyone involved.

Clearing her throat, she said, "Is there a particular part of the city...?"

"The West End, I suspect. There was a production of *Fra Diavolo* the other night, with what I've heard is an interesting cast," he replied without hesitation. He pursed his lips for a moment. "If he did and was waylaid as discussed, well, I'll ask you to keep this discreet. After I'm wed, which will occur shortly, I'd like to see my brother settled as well. And Solomon is very interested in marrying a good woman from the Jewish community—he's sentimental like that, and I can't help indulging him. As you are probably aware, many people in that world are a touch provincial about certain things..."

He trailed off as her chest tightened once more.

What did it matter to her if Solomon Weiss had spent several days in the arms of a woman far prettier and wittier and more amusing than she could ever hope to be? What that did to his future prospects was no skin off her nose. Being paid to find him was really his best and only use in her life.

And after this was done, her life could go back to the way it was before. No more distractions.

"I will find your brother. Don't worry, Mr. Weiss," she promised, rising from her seat.

"Thank you. I only want him to be home safe and protected. Not foolishly costing him the good, respectable life he deserves." He ran his hand over a small gilded box next to him on the desk. "You have a sister, do you not?" he asked.

"I do," she said, hand tightening into a fist.

"So you understand not wanting anything to happen to her." He smiled, but there was no warmth there, and it was impossible to miss the distinct note of warning in his tone.

"I most certainly do," she told him before taking a deep, painful, breath. "And I want nothing more than a good life for Tamar."

"Well, if you complete this task properly, such things can be arranged. Having friends in certain places is quite useful. They can put a thumb on the scale, so to speak." He rose up, as if to dismiss her, before adding, "In either direction."

"I understand," she repeated, opening the door to let herself out because what more was there to say?

"I hope you do. And Miss Moses?"

She turned back to him. "Yes?"

"Be careful," he said. "I have it on good authority that your name is on many people's lips these days. Not particularly advantageous for someone like you."

And with those words, he shut the door behind her, leaving her alone with Martin, who had apparently been waiting in the hall. He gestured for her to follow, and she did, shivering, so she could escape back into the night.

Where she belonged.

Chapter Nineteen

Pulling her hood over her head, Hannah crept out of the mouth of the alley onto the street, glancing from side to side to make sure no one was watching her. Ever since she'd left the Weiss home the other night, she couldn't shake the feeling that she was being watched.

Or more, her instincts told her that she was. Each time she'd gone out to make inquiries about Sol and his whereabouts, a chill that had nothing to do with the frigid temperatures trailed fingers down her neck. Not to mention Mick and George seemed to be getting bolder by the day, shaking down even the smallest of players on the streets with no one rising up to challenge them.

Another reason to be extra careful with her work.

The West End had been more of a dead end and nearly cost her a toe, as no one could confirm whether Sol had arrived or not. So, given the meeting Roger Berab had been on about him missing, Hannah had concluded that whatever happened to him had occurred early in the day. After he'd seen her. She pushed herself against the sides of buildings, where the snow didn't accumulate, so as not to leave tracks, and worked to wind through the small streets and cut-throughs instead of the main thoroughfares, for good measure.

Besides, she'd permitted herself to be kidnapped. Her instincts were supposed to be sharper than that. And the only kind of man who could've done that would've needed to blend on the streets—her streets— long enough to grab her. Something precious few outsiders, if any, could accomplish.

Which meant Frederick Weiss had reach into her world. Which shouldn't bother her. After all, who knew better than she what it meant to make great sacrifices in respectability to build a life for a sibling? Such sacrifices made him the best person to understand what Sol needed and wanted. The person who most certainly had the right to protect him from her.

After she found him.

Which would be soon if the tip she'd received was true. A woman desperate to sell a pair of combs had shared the strangest story: the body of a man being wheeled off in a cart by what was believed to be a group of elderly women.

Hannah shivered as another icy gust made quick work of her threadbare cloak. Her destination wasn't far, in theory, but if she was going to make it there without being followed... Was someone trying to harm the Weiss brothers? The more she learned of Frederick, both regarding his tactics and the waves he was making in gentile circles, the more she believed it to be a possibility. And it would make sense to threaten his sibling as leverage.

Though... Hannah frowned as she slid around the side of a tanner, wrinkling her nose at the stench. One would've thought that if someone was going to threaten Frederick with Sol's safety, they'd have been less circumspect— given Frederick an unmistakable message. And while it was highly doubtful the man would've shared something like that with her, one would've thought he'd have shared such a warning with Sol so his brother would've known to be on high alert.

A twinge of something like guilt twisted below Hannah's ribs.

Which was ridiculous. Yes, she'd not exactly told Tamar about Ned's threats or the burglary she'd participated in, but that was different. There just wasn't a need. The situation would right itself if they could hold on and the job was a one-time occurrence and—she froze at the edge of the alley. There was someone by her door. Cloaked in shadow. Waiting.

As quietly as possible, she bent in the snow, working her way behind the trough to get a better view without being seen. Squinting through a slat of wood, she peered through the moonlight at the unfortunately familiar figure.

Oy. Why did it have to be Ned? What could he possibly want? Nothing good, that was for certain. She really did not need this now.

But unfortunately, it wasn't as if she had a choice. Heart in her ears, she rose, and strolled toward the man with as much false confidence as she could muster.

"Fancy seeing you out here, Hannah," he said as she pulled down her hood, revealing her face and hair to the night sky, snowflakes now chilling her ears.

"I live here." She jabbed a thumb in the direction of her store before tugging her cloak tighter around her body. "Besides, I don't answer to you anymore," she told him, keeping her voice as steady as possible, so as neither to challenge him with aggression nor entice him with fear.

"How has that been going for you?" he asked with a smirk, as if to let her know that he most certainly knew about the recent struggles and was proud of any part he'd played in them.

Momzer. She bit her tongue so as not to say the word out loud. "I get by," she said instead, tucking a loose strand of now slightly wet hair behind her ear.

He cocked his head. "Do you?" he asked, his voice soft but with a distinct edge. He traipsed a step toward her, reaching out and tracing a finger down her cheek. "You know, we were good together." He moved closer so he could run his hand along the side of her neck, where he'd last left bruises. Hannah's stomach roiled, even as she schooled her features to remain nonchalant.

"I thought I was getting too old and disagreeable for you?" she told him, with a half smile, before taking a step back, just out of his grasp, her skirts swirling in the wind as she reached a hand into her pocket to finger the handle of her knife.

"That doesn't mean we can't rekindle the good times," he said, apparently unwilling to let her, or the subject, go. In two steps he was back to hovering over her. "I know you need money." His fingers dipped down the front of her gown, toying with a hole where a button they couldn't afford to replace should be.

"I can make it without you," she said, folding her arms. She could. Especially if Frederick paid what he'd promised. And maybe had other jobs for her. And perhaps whatever rumors Ned had spread about her would be forgotten. Things would turn around. She just needed to wait and survive. Like always.

Ned released a low chuckle. "You're a terrible liar. You'd think you'd be better, given what you are, but no, this gives everything away." He caressed her cheek and her throat tightened. "You should come back to me," he whispered, leaning forward and kissing her ear.

She hated his touch but didn't move away. Tears of frustration swarmed behind her eyes, and it took everything in her to hold them at bay.

"I think not," she told him. She squeezed the hilt of her weapon before pulling it out, not fulling brandishing it, but holding it between them so as to make him aware that it wouldn't be so easy to dispatch her this time.

Ned, however, did not back down. Instead, he shook his head at her, tutting. "I see you're lying to yourself as well."

Hannah blinked. "Pardon?"

"He doesn't love you. He's only interested because he's a bored rich boy and you seem dangerous and exciting. He can never make you fit into his world. Not when you belong in this one." Ned didn't need to say who "he" was. And while it bothered her that the man had seen them together, no doubt when he'd come back to threaten her again, the true punch in the gut was the fact that he was right.

Not about Sol being arrogant or spoiled, no matter how much he pretended to be both when it suited him, but that she'd never belong in his world, and he'd never belong in hers. And while he might think she was good for more than a few "tumbles in the sheets," he'd understand he was mistaken soon enough. How could he not? Even Ned of all people could see the truth...and now she'd put him in Ned's view, a dangerous position to be in no matter how well off he was.

"I've told him as much," she said, crossing her arms over her chest, a hard lump in her throat.

"Not good at listening, eh," Ned stated more than asked, with a sniff. He pounded one gloved fist into his palm. "Perhaps he should be taught a lesson," he added, a menacing edge to his tone.

This time she approached him with her knife. "Stay away from him, Ned," she warned. For the first time in the conversation her voice shook, even if that was the worst thing it could do. But she couldn't stop herself. "He's a good person and doesn't deserve—"

Before she could finish, Ned slammed a fist into her wrist, causing her hand to open and the knife to clatter to the ground. She dropped to her knees to pick it up, but he swiped it away with a quick kick before grabbing her by the hair and twisting it.

"The way I hear, he already has folks hunting for him," he whispered as she ground her teeth against the pain. "You should take your own advice, Hannah." He released her with a sharp shove. "I'm going to enjoy watching you come back to me and beg."

Hannah shivered as his footfalls faded into the distance, straining to identify the sounds of the night in between. Swiping the back of her hand against her face, she fought again and again to hold back the emotions brewing below the surface. A task that she'd once been so skilled at, but now, all her training seemed to be failing her.

She half-heartedly patted around for her knife, but it was nowhere to be found. More fool she was for losing it.

"Shmuck," she muttered, not quite sure if she was talking about herself or Ned. She brushed the snow off her soaked skirts, her knees cold and bruised, her hair clinging to her scalp.

Oy. She was a complete mess. And much too old for any of this. As if to confirm the notion, she cracked her aching back after she struggled to her feet. She would have to be careful, very careful, in verifying Sol's location. And even more careful in delivering the news to his brother.

Something was afoot, something not good, and even if she was not for Sol, and he could never actually be happy with her, she'd still do everything in her power to make sure he wasn't harmed.

Especially not due to her actions.

And once she was properly paid—hopefully Frederick would be good to his word regarding her sister. Tamar would have a place in the community, where she most certainly belonged, and Hannah...would be all right.

This was her world. The world she'd made a place for herself in, the world that had permitted her to survive when all other doors had closed. She swiped her eyes. Fakakta snowflakes, sticking in her lashes, making her vision blur.

Hannah forced herself to move forward.

She had a job to do, one she would do well or the rest wouldn't matter. And she'd not let Sol down.

After all, above all else, she was a hunter.

Chapter Twenty

Sol bit his lip as he worked to catch the yarn in his hook, the light low. The half-moon and few stars glinted through the dormer window into the house, making shadow patterns on the quilt over his legs. Now all he had to do was pull the yarn through the loop one more time and—bollocks. The pesky material dropped again.

Right, he just needed to catch it and—*ow*. His thumb. Again. Blasted crochet hook.

"You're doing very well." Bayla glanced up from her chair at the other side of the fire, where she was diligently stitching his trousers to make them wearable. She waved at the small circle—the beginning of a lace cap—he'd begun seven hours ago, quite the way to spend his third day awake with the women. "This is your first attempt, after all. With more practice, you'll be brilliant."

"I was just hoping to be of more use," he said with a sigh. "Carry my weight." Especially since he'd been unable to solve the mystery of who had tried to kill him. Was it one of their former business rivals? He couldn't help but think murder, while potentially satisfying, would not give any of them actual financial success.

Though feelings of rage over embarrassment could never be underestimated. He frowned again. No matter how he spun it, someone wanted him dead. He'd now revisited the conversation with his attackers at least two dozen times—and they'd been intent not to rob him but maim or more.

And while he still could've been a random target, the effort they'd expended in chasing him suggested otherwise. Whatever was afoot, he needed to find out, so he could properly protect himself, and all the people in his life who might be in jeopardy.

Including these women. He was determined to repay them for their generosity. They deserved much more respect and attention from the community than what they currently received.

"People do leave us food sometimes," Doc had told him when he'd asked about their situation.

"The inedible kind." Gertrude snorted. "Soothes their guilt over forgetting we exist. Like they didn't once depend on Doc's services, and they won't one day become us. Especially if they have no children of their own." She pointed to the stove. "Luckily we make much better."

Luckily indeed. He patted his stomach, filled with potatoes he'd peeled—an entirely new experience—and cooked with carrots and onions, served with a warm, hearty bread. Still, these women deserved finer things.

Perhaps a few chickens. And a new goat, given the elderly state of their current one.

"You're our guest." Bayla reached out and patted his knee as Sol reached down to pick up some crumbs that had dropped onto the floor from his meal. "You don't need to carry your weight." She grabbed a broom to tidy up the area, pressing her lips together. Oy, the woman did really like to whistle while she worked. At least she seemed to prefer a happy tune. She swept up the remaining crumbs, then gathered the yarn and hooks. "I should let you rest."

"I'm fine," he protested as she placed both their works in a basket, strolling it over to the door so it was out of his reach.

"You might believe so, but Doc thinks you shouldn't strain yourself. You still have healing to do if you want to leave when the snow clears," she told him. "And I don't want to get on her bad side, or Gertrude's."

Before he could object again, the door shut, and he was alone. Stuck. With nothing but his thoughts for company and nowhere to go.

A bang shook the rafters above his head, startling Sol. The wood groaned and creaked in a downward pattern as he stared upward. What in the world? He patted around the blanket for something to use as a weapon, but his fingers came up empty. Why did Bayla need to take the crochet hook with her?

The noises continued, unabated, as he scanned the room, his gaze finally settling on the crutch Doc had secured for him. He wrapped his fingers around the handle just as another loud thud came from outside the dormer. Sol gasped as a shadow fell over the glass, blocking the moonlight.

The window creaked open and in bounded a figure shrouded in a cloak. They rose up, shaking off snow and ice and debris before lowering their hood and—

"Hannah?" Sol whispered her name. He pinched his own arm to verify that he hadn't dozed off and was now merely dreaming her. "Hannah?" he repeated.

"So you do live." She folded her arms, pulling her cloak tight over her body.

"I do. I had quite an accident—well, not truly an accident, I was chased and fell—but I'm being tended to and healing, despite being stuck here due to the weather and having an ankle that's too swollen to walk upon," he said before peering through the dim light, working to read the rather inscrutable expression on her face. "That's why I haven't been able to get word to anyone regarding my whereabouts. I'm sure my brother is worried."

And you? You were worried too? Perhaps?

Not that he wanted her to be upset . . . Fine. That was a lie. He'd wanted her to worry. To care. To want him as much as he wanted her.

"He most certainly is. As are quite a few people." She interrupted his thoughts, as snow-laced wind billowed the curtain behind her.

"Are you one of those people?" he couldn't help but ask, raising a brow while longing to pull her close, hold her as an anchor against the muddle that he'd somehow made of his usually calculated life.

"I am—was." She tugged on her earlobe then glanced backward toward the window. "I'm glad you're safe and only a touch worse for wear—" She fiddled with the laces of her cloak, inching backward. Away from him. "But now that I've seen you, I should go tell everyone else. Especially your brother. I know how important you are to each other."

"Wait!" Sol called out. "Don't tell them. Or . . . do but warn them to stay away. At least until I'm back to fighting form again." Which would be sooner rather than later if he had his say.

He cleared his throat. "You see, I suspect someone is trying to kill me. Not that they'll be successful," he told her with a confidence that he'd not felt in a long time—but now roared through his veins.

She gave him a sharp, and thankfully not in the least bit pitying, glance before returning to his side. "You're going to stop them? How?"

"I have my ways," he told her. "You'll remember, I'm well trained in being quick and clever. My handsomeness obscures it, of course. Things I can use to my advantage." Even if there was one slight, minor problem with his plans. He rubbed the back of his neck. "Though I have to figure out who is behind it all first, naturally."

"Naturally," she repeated. "What exactly happened?"

"My brother asked me to deliver an important package," he explained. "On my return, a group of men attacked me—but they weren't interested in my purse. They chased me, far longer than a random robbery would justify, even up onto a roof."

Hannah grasped his arm. "Is that how you were injured? Falling off a damned roof?"

Sol nodded then winced at the pain the movement brought. "My brother and I have made a few enemies over the years as we don't like to ask permission." He chuckled to himself. "And given Frederick is the respectable 'face' of the family, so to speak, I suppose that makes me the likeliest target of a rival business, but I can't quite understand why one would want me attacked? Especially without exacting financial revenge."

Hannah's grip loosened, her brows drawing together. Almost to herself, she muttered, "I suspect Frederick has made enemies of his own."

Well, yes, there was Frederick's rise socially and his suit of Lady Drucilla, but Sol's death wouldn't harm either. And in either case, there was still the question of who?

"Were you 'caught' recently?" Hannah asked, interrupting his thoughts.

He started to shake his head in the negative before remembering Frederick's warning. "Not that I know. Which makes solving this mystery a touch challenging. But I'm up for the task." As he gazed up at her, his relief at having her at his side turned to heat as he realized how little space there was between them.

And how few clothes he was wearing. A fact he'd complained about prior, but now was rather grateful for.

"I'm up for many things," he said, pulling down the quilt and baring his chest to the room. He wasn't feeling tired anymore; rather, he was tired of talking.

The edge of her tongue traced her bottom lip, but rather than enjoy the view, she snapped. "Are you joking?"

"It depends on your answer." He leaned back against the pillow and stretched his arms above his head. "Whichever makes you come closer, most certainly," he added. Waiting for her to obey was agony, but obey she did, coming right to the edge.

She stopped and squinted.

"Are you wearing only a yarmulke?" she asked.

"Would you like to find out?" he countered, mischief coursing through his veins, along with the confidence that never felt as natural as it did when she was in the room.

"You're incorrigible," she told him, but she was smiling.

"Very," he said with a nod. *And you like it.* He raised a brow at her. "Is that a yes?"

She glanced behind her toward the door. "There are people in the house."

"They went to bed." He shrugged. "And the door has a lock if you care to use it." He resisted a smile as she ran her finger over the post closest to his head.

He had her. Almost.

"Someone is trying to kill you and we don't know who," she reminded him, worry etched on her brow.

"But they haven't yet," he countered before lifting her chin so her eyes could meet his—so he could properly win. "Hannah, I'm a vigorous man of many skills who has had more rest than he's had in months. I know when to fret about my safety and that time is not now." He released her chin but not her gaze. "Are you going to ask me what it is time for?"

"I'm sure you're going to tell me," she said with a small, and completely delicious, pout, which he was most certainly going to be kissing soon.

"Smart woman," he murmured. "It's time for you to get rid of those clothes and allow me to make up for the days I've lost convincing you to give me and my silver tongue a chance."

Staring into her eyes, he knew he had won. At least this battle. But that was fine.

In the end, victory would be his.

Chapter Twenty-One

She shouldn't obey.

After all, if there was one thing Sol didn't need to convince her of, it was how much her body craved his—how right the universe felt when he was inside her. Even if it was wrong.

They were undeniably perfect in bed. That was not and would never be the problem. She had to end things. Had to quit him.

But not quite yet.

Because she wasn't brave or good. No, she was, at her core, rather wicked, as the gentiles said. And the way he crooked his finger at her, a sly grin spreading over his handsome features, almost made her believe that he was the same. And if only they had been born in a different world, under different circumstances, they might have been able to allow whatever burned between them to come to fruition.

However, they lived in reality, so she would have to take what she could get. Even if a better person would resist, given his injuries, the danger he was in, and the very real possibility of the women downstairs catching them. But again, she was not a better person. And for once, at least part of her was thankful for that fact.

Taking a deep breath, she untied her cloak and let it drop to the floor. Hands only shaking a touch, she moved to undo the buttons on the back of her dress, allowing that layer to also fall away.

"There we go, gorgeous," Sol whispered, leaning forward. With a swallow she began untying the laces in the front of her corset. "Let me see you." His eyes glowed with desire in the firelight, emboldening her. And for one shining moment, she not only heard his words but believed them.

She wanted to revel in them. Tease. She lifted the hem of her chemise and unrolled her stockings, taking off one and then the other. "Like this?" she asked in her best facsimile of innocence.

It was his turn to roll his eyes. "You know, I was going to make you feel very good, very quickly, but you're convincing me to take things slow." He wagged a finger. "I could bring you so very close and..." He stared at her with what could only be described as wolfish desire. "Stop."

Her throat went dry as need filled her body. Not that she could reveal his hold on her just yet. This was too much fun.

Instead, she raised both brows. "You think you have that much control?"

"Is that a challenge?" he asked. "The ones between us haven't gone very well for you." He waved a hand at her chemise. "That too, Hannah. Get it gone. Now."

And something about his voice had her reaching for her hem with barely a thought.

"There she is," he whispered as the worn garment fell into the pile with the others. He crooked a finger at her. "Now, come here and let me make you feel very good." He grinned. "Provided you do as I say."

It took everything in her to hold back and not run to him immediately.

"You're injured," she argued, glancing at the blankets. "Aren't I supposed to be doing the work? Nursing you or some such thing?"

"I've been fussed over and coddled plenty. That is very much not what I need right now from you." As if to demonstrate his point, he threw the quilt to the floor, revealing his nearly nude body—and very ready penis.

Still, she took in the bandages around his torso, the gauze on his arms and legs, rage and something small and hurt she did not want to name distracting from the heat.

"Hannah. I've had enough of thinking about my own body." His strong hands clasped hers. "Trust me." She nodded, unable to resist, and he guided her onto the bed, her skin flush against his. "I want to play with your body now," he commanded. "Straddle my waist."

She startled as his mouth came down on one of her aching nipples. "Oh my," she gasped, throwing her head back when he took her other breast in his large palm, firm but gentle, until he began to alternate between using his teeth on one breast while caressing the other, then laving at one nipple with his tongue while pinching the other. The blissful combination made her nearly scream with desire.

"You do like that, do you?" he said more than asked in a way that ought to be obnoxiously smug but she only found utterly charming.

Nonsense was all she managed to say in response, her senses completely enveloped by him and only him.

"Yes or no, Hannah?" the momzer asked, pausing as her body hovered on the threshold of pleasure.

All smart quips fled her. "Yes. Please—"

"There we go," he cooed, caressing her breasts again, his touch softer, slower, nearly sweet. "This is good too, isn't it?"

And she could only nod as liquid heat pooled in her core.

"Would you like something even better?" he whispered before kissing the side of her neck, causing her to groan with desire.

"Will I survive it?" she finally managed to ask with a small laugh. Reluctantly, she pulled back enough to wag a finger of her own at him. "I'm not quite as young as you, you know?"

"You're perfect," he told her with such sincerity, emotion nearly felled her. He took her hand, threading her fingers in his, and brought it to his lips, kissing her knuckles. "And I'll never hurt you."

If only she could believe that.

Because he most certainly would. Even if it wasn't his fault. But she couldn't tell him that. No, instead, she'd seize all they had here and hold on to it as long as she could.

"I know, Sol," she whispered, bending and kissing his forehead.

His face lit up with a full genuine smile, which nearly broke her heart. "That's the right answer," he told her before his eyes turned wicked. "So you get a reward."

And before she could even think, let alone reach, his hands had gone to her hips, holding her in place, as he slid down. "Hold the bed," he told her as he took up his position beneath her. Hannah did as asked, squeezing the wood and—

"Oh. My. God," was all she could gasp as his tongue entered her.

"You taste so good," he near moaned himself, before lapping her once more. "Perfect and sweet. Like apples." One arm still around her waist, he slid a finger inside her, then a second, undulating, as he continued with his tongue, just a touch higher.

"Sol—I—" She could barely form the words as he stroked the tiny nub in small, deliberate circles. "Apples." She cried the word, her nails digging into the bedpost.

"Best food in the world," he said, his fingers not letting up, continuing the delicious pressure. "Except for you." Tightening his hold around her, he commanded, "On your knees and grab your breasts. I want you touching yourself too."

"You are—" she started, but obeyed, matching the rhythm he was creating, faster and harder, with his arm gripping her in place, until she cried out, "Oh—yes," as she reached for and sailed over the peak, moving through the stars and allowing the shudders to take her. And for Sol to pull her down and hold her against his chest. Which was both too much and not quite enough as their time was growing short by the second.

"Beautiful. That was absolutely beautiful," he whispered into her hair. "Like you." He kissed her ear. "I could do that all day."

"Haven't you before?" she bit out before she could hold back the words, a painful lump growing beneath her ribs. She swallowed down the memory of Frederick's words. *The attachment always passes quickly enough.*

"Are you jealous?" he teased, nipping at her ear.

"You've no cause to be. I've had past lovers, true, but none were you."

"Oh," was all she said, for foolishly enough, she wanted to believe him. Forcing herself back into the moment, she rolled on her side and smiled down at him. "But now, I'd like something else." She ran a hand through his soft, thick hair.

He rewarded her with another one of his lupine grins. "Are you asking me for something, Hannah?"

"You're ridiculous," she told him even as she could not stop smiling.

"Sometimes," he said with a shrug before turning fully toward her. "But do you want something? From me?" He raised a brow. "Very badly?" He bent and kissed her nose. "Because all you have to do..." he whispered, his eyes sparkling as he teased her.

And her heart ached a little. There was so much. So much she couldn't have. But she would take what she could.

"I want you," she told him. "I want you inside of me."

"Done," he said with a nod before pausing with a rueful smile. "Well, not done. It will be done. Correctly, but your wish is my command."

"I—" she started as she glanced downward, reminded of the quite large collection of bandages wrapped around his ankle.

He nipped her ear. "I'm young." And in an instant she was on her back and he was above her. "I know you're a touch fatigued, being old and all," he teased, grabbing her wrist to thwart her playful swat.

He bent and took her lips. "I'll take care of you. Don't you worry," he whispered, nudging her legs apart. He reached down and swirled his fingers through her wetness, worrying her small nub again. "There we go." Removing his hand, he teased her with his tip, before sliding inside her.

"Perfect," he said, stretching her, filling her.

And it was. Perfect. Slow and steady, he rocked into her, his eyes never wavering from her face, his thumb continuing to rub circles as she moaned against him.

"Wrap your legs around me," he whispered as his pace began to speed.

She did as he asked, clinging to him as he joined with her, her hips bucking as the delicious friction took her to yet another climax, him tumbling right behind her, his name on her lips. He quickly pulled out, spilling on the sheets beside them, before taking her lips again, long and hard, as if he was trying to claim something that wasn't theirs to own.

Then it was over.

And she was easing around his all too lovely body as his eyes closed. As quietly as she could, she climbed down from the bed and began gathering her garments.

"Keep bending like that. You're giving me a nice view," he called out. "However, I'm not sure you're getting this back." He held up her corset, which he'd somehow managed to snatch up from the floor.

She pulled on her stockings and turned to him, folding her arms. "So you'd have me go out in the snow with my gown unbuttoned?" she teased.

He smiled at her, that warm, genuine smile that made her long for all that she could never have. "You're rather incorrigible yourself," he told her, pulling her toward him. He took her hand, kissing her wrist. "And I love you for it."

Placing their tangled fingers over his heart, he

repeated the words, "I love you." The unflinching sincerity in his gaze nearly broke her. "*Only* you."

"Sol—" she started.

"You don't have to say it back," he said, holding her to him for another moment. "Just know it."

"All right," she managed to say but wild fear beat through her veins. When he finally let her go, handing her back her corset, she glanced around the room as she hurriedly replaced it on her body. "I should—I need to tell your brother and—"

"I know. And you should," he said as she redonned her gown and cloak. He pulled himself to the edge of the bed, catching her gaze. "But know this, Hannah. This isn't temporary. We can and will have a life with each other. In the light. And I will convince you of that. Soon."

There it was again.

The perfect time for her to do what needed to be done, to break him of his delusions, to let him go like a better woman would. But in the dim firelight, with him staring at her, so earnest and handsome and capable, so deserving of love that could most certainly not be for her, she became worse than reckless, worse than selfish, worse than *wicked*.

She became a coward.

"Be careful, Sol," she said and fled to the window before disappearing into the night.

Chapter Twenty-Two

Love. The word beat into Hannah's head as she stole through the snow, the wind howling above her as she made her way through the near empty city and away from Sol.

Why did he have to say the words? Did he not understand how dangerous it was to her? How her craving for such emotion, where it could not be, could lead to nothing but misery?

And yet he would not stop, fighting a battle that could not be won, shredding the will she needed to cling to, to keep moving, to survive.

It was funny that anyone thought her fearless. Because she was the opposite—she only understood when to be brave and when to run away, and back there, it was time to run. If not to save herself, then to save him. So that was what she would do. After she'd completed her obligations to Frederick and smoothed over any issues Sol might have with his employers, she'd remove herself from his life and stay where she belonged.

She clutched her cloak tighter as the wind howled around her, stinging through every patch in her petticoats. In all her years, Hannah had never seen such weather in London. Even in December.

And while she needed to speak with Frederick, she was best off first visiting the Berab house—well, the house where Roger Berab lived though it belonged to his late wife's family—because of its closeness. Barely able to reach the door through the snow, she managed to leave a hastily written note with the bleary-eyed butler.

Gritting her teeth, she pressed farther east. Time to finish things. And if it nagged at her that Frederick Weiss had proven to be more familiar with the darker parts of London than she'd previously believed, well, why she should it? He also had access to its bright parts. And resources she couldn't boast in a thousand years.

Who better to protect Sol than him?

Though it was quite early, the sky was still dark as she approached the Weiss house, this time from the front entrance. Martin, unsmiling as before, opened the door before she could even knock. He led her into the same office, where Frederick was waiting, impeccably dressed despite the hour, the odd mirrors reflecting the firelight.

"You must have news for me, Miss Moses," he said, glancing up from his desk as she entered. He motioned to the chair where she'd sat the last time.

"I do," she said with a nod. "I have found your brother." She sat, folding her hands in her lap. "He's very much alive, though injured. However, he will heal. He has good care and—"

"Where is he?" Frederick demanded, his tone sharp enough for her to wince, despite having been talked to in much harsher tones most of her life.

"He's in Aldgate proper," she said. "On Mitre Street, near the square. He's being tended to by one of the community's former midwives. After his meeting near the docks, he was attacked and—"

"Someone tried to rob my brother?" he asked with a frown. He pressed his fingers together then touched them to his lips. "I warned him to be careful of thieves, to pay attention to his surroundings, but did he listen..." He tutted, shaking his head. "And now he's been injured? Did they take his purse as well?"

"His purse wasn't taken," Hannah explained. "Nothing was taken, actually." She bit her lip as the man glared, as if the information somehow displeased him. An odd response.

Though perhaps it was due to the hour. After all, no one enjoyed being woken from a decent sleep.

She cleared her throat so she could continue relaying Sol's message. "He did not believe it to have been a robbery at all." She tugged on her ear. "He said it seemed more...personal."

The man's eyebrows arched. "Did they say anything to that effect? Did my brother insult one of them? Get into some sort of fisticuffs? He's not prone to bouts of temper, though he's made some odd choices as of late." His scanned her person with a sniff.

Hannah's back stiffened. He wasn't incorrect, exactly, but there was something...off about his reaction.

"Who would want to hurt Sol? He's a nobody." He shook his head then rose and strolled around the desk, bending in front at her, looking down his nose. "Unless you've gotten him into some sort of trouble."

Hannah's face heated. "I—I don't believe so." She tugged on her ear as she searched her mind for any veracity to the concept. She felt like a fool for not having considered her own enemies. There were people certainly unhappy with her, and while she'd not mentioned Sol, he'd made his presence known by hanging about her shop...

"So I will repeat myself—how does he know it was personal?" Frederick asked, interrupting her thoughts.

"They seemed more intent on killing him than on anything else, even after he ran," she said with a shrug, suspicion working its way through her gut.

There was a pause. "And who told you that?" he asked finally, tenting and folding his fingers, his voice level but she could see the warning lurking beneath his smooth veneer.

"He did."

Frederick took an audible breath and his face softened. "I'm going to let you in on a small secret concerning my brother, Miss Moses." He leaned forward, as if sharing a confidence. "Solomon has had, since childhood, an unfortunate penchant for dramatics, in the hopes that I'll pay him more attention." He gave her a small smile. "Something I always do, as he is my brother. So I fear that he's decided to create a situation where I will need to intervene and give all my focus to him."

Hannah held back a gasp. "Are you suggesting that he hired men to attack him?"

Frederick shook his head. "No. I'm not. I'm suggesting that he most likely happened upon them and insulted them in some way but left that fact out of the retelling as he knew you were going to speak with me."

She stared at Frederick, her mind unable to quite reconcile the picture he was painting with the man she knew.

If she hadn't spent so much time with Sol, perhaps it

would have made sense. She bit her lip. Or perhaps he was right? Perhaps she'd lost all her senses in thrall to their relationship and couldn't see what was real or what she wanted to. After all, Frederick did know his brother a great deal more than she.

Though, was that true? He'd been wrong about Sol being at the opera, perhaps even Sol's dalliances...

"Miss Moses, I know my brother," Frederick said, breaking her cycling thoughts. "As he might have told you, I'll be married shortly. The final banns are to be posted this Saturday, in fact. And that marriage will change our family for the first time since he was a young boy. Something which I'm sure is difficult for him to accept."

The man tutted. "I've also expected him to take on more responsibility of late, which I'm afraid has... overwhelmed him, perhaps."

Hannah frowned. She'd not exactly describe Sol's behavior as "overwhelmed." At least not at the prospect of his brother's marriage. No, the man had seemed rather motivated to *not* be an obstacle. Yes, he was failing spectacularly, but that was as much her fault as his. Probably more hers, as she was the one always sneaking in windows at night.

"He's been trying to get my attention for weeks." Frederick leaned back in his seat. "First falling off his horse, then nearly walking in front of a carriage, then tripping down the stairs." He recounted each incident on his fingers. "Not to mention the dangerous company he keeps. And now he's slipping off rooftops? I've tried to be understanding, not accusatory. However, it is apparent that tactic has not worked as his behavior has escalated."

Hannah's mind churned. Again, a logical explanation, but all her senses were screaming the opposite at her.

"The men who attacked him, they chased him for blocks. So if there's any possibility that someone truly wants him dead, wouldn't it at least be prudent to take extra precautions?" she couldn't help arguing back. After all, no matter how the incident had occurred, the consequences were still real and there was no guarantee they had dissipated.

Sol's brother wanted to protect him, so why wasn't he understanding the gravity of the situation? While the elder Weiss was clearly canny, he was not invincible. The information she'd brought him should at least put him on alert.

"How long did they truly chase him, Miss Moses?" Frederick asked, impatience dripping from his voice. He stood up and began to pace, like a barrister making his case. "You weren't a witness, and tired minds produce all sorts of nonsense."

"Be that as it may—" she started, trying to recall all Sol had said. Hadn't Frederick warned Sol about danger in the streets? Yes, she wasn't exactly the person the man would confide in himself, but what was the purpose of denying what he'd already told his brother?

"Yes, Miss Moses?" he asked.

She cleared her throat, searching for the correct words. "I don't want to—Sol might have few enemies, but you..."

"I what?" His tone was colder than the snow outside.

Hannah folded her hands in her lap, forcing herself to be calm, to think, to approach this man correctly. Manipulation wasn't her strong suit, but if ever there was a time to put all those years of being in multiple criminal situations to good use, it was now. She took a deep breath. "As you mentioned, you're on the verge of marrying a very prominent gentile woman. That has to have made people jealous."

"You have a point," he said, returning to his seat with a thoughtful half smile. The man was all too mercurial. "But targeting Sol..."

"As you know, there are worlds in which the predators reign and kill for lesser slights," she pointed out. "Hurting Sol might have just been a convenient and effective message."

His lip curled. "Aren't you clever?"

Frederick leaned forward in his chair, the mirror shimmering behind him. "You're wrong, but you're clever," he declared. His sharp glare told her exactly the kind of man she was dealing with, despite his fine clothes and soon-to-be-titled in-laws. They may both be scavengers, but rats still ate mice when the cats weren't looking. "And I didn't hire you to think."

"You did not," she said, keeping her voice steady. She forced herself not to swallow, to play the part he expected. After all, she hadn't survived as long as she had without knowing how to stare down far more dangerous men who wanted to do far worse things to her.

"A pity, as you could have been such an interesting asset." He tented his fingers and tapped them once, twice, three times. "Ah well, given your background, you were never going to be anything more than temporary help. After all, you've committed a great deal of easily provable crimes—including a rather recent burglary near here, I believe?"

He raised a brow as Hannah's throat grew dry.

"Preying on innocents to feed your lust for money—you're the worst kind of Jew. Not a person I can permit myself to be tied to," he continued. "Imagine how that could be used against me for the purposes you outlined. And think of what you might do to my brother. You believe my actions and dealings put him in danger? What about you, Miss Moses?"

She stared at him, his words like a slap in the face, before her shoulders slumped.

Because he was not wrong. Far from it. He was completely right. She'd been selfish, so, so selfish. If she cared about Sol—cared about him, not loved him, as she'd not permitted her heart to become that involved—if she truly cared about him and his safety, there was only one thing she could do.

"This was always going to be the point where our relationship would need to be terminated," Frederick continued. "Now you will promise never to so much again as breathe the same air as my brother." He smiled, but it was so cold, his voice like ice. "Have I made myself clear?"

Yes, this was not a man with whom to trifle. And no matter how much she disliked him and how terrifying his threats, a part of her had to admire his drive to protect his brother—little as he seemed to know him.

Sol deserved that. And she was grateful that he had it. Grateful that, no matter what, he would be fought for and cared for, that he would have a good life with everything he wanted when she was long gone. She swallowed again.

Frederick arched a brow. "Have I?" he repeated.

"Yes. I understand," she managed to say, making her voice as resolute as possible.

He flashed her a charming smile, which almost certainly made many women swoon. However, it only left her cold with fear.

"Thank you, Miss Moses." He bowed his head before rising. She did the same as gracefully as she could. Forcing herself to finish this encounter without shaking. Or worse, bursting into tears.

"I'll send Martin to you with the money after I fetch my brother," he told her with a dismissive wave. "Good day."

"Good day," she murmured as she exited, her mind searching for the words that would set everything right. It wasn't until later that she realized she'd never told him exactly how Sol had injured himself, and yet he'd known he'd fallen from a roof.

Chapter Twenty-Three

Sol spent the entire night and most of the morning thinking of Hannah. He was losing her. He'd felt it when she left, despite his efforts. She was going to end things because she didn't believe that they could be more. Didn't truly believe he was offering more.

And in a way, she was right to think that. How exactly was he different from those men she'd spoken of before? The ones from the community who were happy to take from her in the dark, but ignore her in the light?

He'd made pretty promises, but all were vague, at best. He'd showed her nothing. No, he'd continued to take the easy, well-traveled road. Why should she believe him?

Something he'd need to rectify.

Not the easiest task when stuck there. He glanced at his still bandaged ankle. Doc had told him he'd be able to walk without assistance in a day or two, but the wait was agony.

Especially as even if he could convince Hannah that a future was possible, he needed to be alive to have one. Which meant he needed to find out who was after him. Though the more he considered the matter, the more he came back to the attack on Stoudmire and Frederick's courtship of Lady Drucilla. Perhaps there was another rival for her affections? He needed to discuss matters with his brother. Between the two of them, they should be able to puzzle it out.

Oy. So much waiting. With a sigh, he retook his hook and started anew. Even if he could not concentrate. At all.

A knock on the door interrupted the cycling of his thoughts.

"You have visitors," Gertrude called through the door. "I trust you're presentable?"

"Visitors?" He repeated. Plural? Who would be visiting him? "I—" Sol started, patting around the bed. He placed the yarn to the side. "Yes, I'm dressed. Thank you so much for mending my garments. They and you can come in."

The door swung open before he could even finish the words.

"Sol, thank goodness," a familiar voice cried out. And the last person he expected to see burst into the room.

"Hello, Solomon," a poshly accented voice drawled as the—strike his first thought—*actual* last person he expected to see followed.

"Aaron." Grimacing only a little, he pushed himself up so he could reach out and shake his friend's hand.

However, that was clearly not good enough, as Aaron instead pulled him into a tight embrace. Not what he was used to, as Frederick had stopped holding him when he was eight in adherence to gentile parenting treatises that explained how such treatment would corrupt his character—or more, foreclose their chances to rise.

"It is so good to see you, Sol." Aaron's voice was a touch tight. "We were quite worried."

"You as well," he told Aaron, patting him on the back. Wobbling only a little, he turned and gave his companion a small nod. "And Mister—Roger. What are you doing here?" He looked back and force between them, just in time for Aaron to wrap his arm around his shoulders in a sideways embrace.

"Miss Moses paid us a call last night and let us know your whereabouts." Roger glanced around the room before strolling to the window with a rather judgmental sniff.

Hannah? Sol started at her name.

"And while it's still snowing, and I most certainly would've preferred being in my own home today"— Berab turned back around—"Mr. Ellenberg insisted on seeing you for himself and it was decided that, given the alleged circumstances of your...injuries...it would be prudent for him not to come alone."

"Fair," Sol said with a nod.

"I'm just glad you're all right," Aaron said, clasping his hands together. "You've had so many close calls lately."

"I know." Sol rubbed the back of his neck. "I'm sorry. I hadn't been sleeping enough and I've been distracted, but I promise, when I get back, I will be in top performance. You can assure Isabelle that I won't let her down." He winced as pain shot through his ankle. Oy. Not quite as ready as he'd thought.

Aaron's eyes narrowed. "That's not—" He frowned. "Isabelle isn't displeased with you, Sol. She's worried. We're all worried." He raised a finger. "I'm beginning to wonder if it hasn't been all bad luck."

Grimacing, Sol moved back to the edge of the bed, sitting himself down. "Why?" he asked as he rubbed the swollen joint. Perhaps a crutch would help.

"Because we're your friends." Aaron shook his head before nodding in Berab's direction. "Well, some of us are. And you said yourself this wasn't a normal robbery."

"I will pretend not to have heard that," the other man called as he finished clearing a chair of its sewing contents and pulling it over next to the bed. "Actually, Mr. Ellenberg, would you mind assisting the sisters, as I believe they're preparing us some tea." He took his seat, crossing his legs. "You're still good at that sort of thing, aren't you?"

"I'm going to take that as a compliment whether you meant it as one or not." Aaron sent him a withering glare.

"Skills of any sort should be cherished," Sol told him and meant it. Something he'd most certainly learned.

"I'll see you in a bit," his friend said with a roll of his eyes before exiting the room, closing the door quietly behind him.

As soon as the footfalls on the stair went quiet, Roger Berab turned to him. "You and I need to talk. Is there anyone who would benefit from your death?"

"What do you mean?" Sol asked. Oy, what was he about?

Berab folded his arms across his chest. "Threats and the like are well enough reasons to cause someone injury—"

"Says the man who once tried to kill me," he said with a sniff.

"As we've discussed, that was my brother, and again,

he merely attempted to maim you." Berab smoothed his cravat. "And that's exactly my point—your death will not cause anyone great harm or upset unless you've gotten yourself into a mess I don't know about."

Sol gaped at the callous words. "My brother—"

"—will be married within the month," he said with a wag of his finger. "The banns are being called, so there's no stopping it now. And Isabelle may be fond of you, but your loss would hardly damage the business."

Sol frowned, but, well, this was exactly what he'd been struggling with. Though Frederick had yet to propose, so what was this nonsense about banns? Berab must be mistaken—though the sentiment remained the same. If not for revenge or as a warning to Frederick— in which case, a more direct message would be all the more effective—why *would* someone want to kill him?

"I see your point," he admitted. "But I'm not sure how my dying for someone else's benefit is your conclusion. Frederick has controlling ownership, rightly so, at the bank, not that I'm suggesting *him*"—a ridiculous idea, indeed—"so he'd gainsay anyone claiming my shares. Beyond that, well . . ."

He certainly didn't lack funds. But neither did he have much that he did not already share with Frederick—or that would go to his brother in any case.

"I did judge your intelligence correctly," Berab said with a bright smile. "And as my workload is light, I'll do some digging of my own. Perhaps I'll discover you're a lost heir or some such nonsense. They like that kind of thing in their fairy stories, don't they?"

Leaning back in his chair, Berab's smile sharpened. "That would certainly be an asset if you're to acquire what you say you want in life—success in our business, success in your own, respectability to assist your brother's cause, and it seems, retaking your place in the Jewish community. Things that are easier to gain with the right wife."

Berab folded his hands in his lap and gazed at Sol, as if daring him to challenge the veracity of his statements. Well, he'd been itching to have this debate with Hannah, so he might as well take the practice.

"I do want those things, but I want Hannah as well." Sol straightened against the headboard. "And I believe I can have both, as not only do I trust my own abilities, but I trust that others, if given the proper chance—and with a little nudging—will see what I see in her."

They had to. At least the people he loved, the people he respected, had to understand, right?

"And what is that exactly?" Berab's voice was so reasonable and calm that it was unsettling. How exactly did he manage that?

"That she's beautiful," Sol said before rubbing the back of his head, searching for the right words. "Not how you think—though she is—beautiful to look at."

Oy, not articulate at all. He took a deep breath.

"She's pretty and clever and has a wicked tongue that I enjoy very much, but it's more than that. Being with her makes me want to be, well, more alive. More present. More the me I can be," he continued, the words now flowing from him. "And beyond that, she's a warrior. Someone who has battled and lost but keeps going. Someone who loves and protects with complete abandon and doesn't give up."

He shook his head. "It's funny, she says she's resigned to a great deal of things, but when you look at what she does . . . how can I not love her?"

"You might see that, but the world does not. To them, she's a villain—what we all are at our core, itching to do evil if not controlled." Berab shook his head. "She will limit your life."

Sol reached down and rubbed his ankle. "I disagree."

Berab paused. "I won't lie to you." He placed a hand on his knee. "Not even I could marry her without consequences—ones that would be felt by not only myself, but my family, and perhaps, the entire community. While you don't have the same level of responsibility I do, there are still those to whom you owe your care, and the more visible you become, the more those numbers grow." The man paused again. "And the circles your brother travels in...there are people who will snub not just you, but him and his wife-to-be. Even if they denounce the both of you."

It was as if someone had wrenched Sol's heart from his body. He closed his eyes. "I love my brother. I owe him everything. If not for him, what would have become of me?"

"If you marry her, you'll always be a hinderance to him and his ambition," Berab said firmly.

A yoke around Frederick's neck, just like he'd been his entire life. He'd worked so hard, for so many years, to repay his brother, to pull his weight, and now, when Frederick needed him most...yet when he pictured a future without Hannah, he saw only bleak gray. He'd promised to find a way, to not be another in the long line of men who'd used and disappointed her, and he loved her. Loved her so much it hurt.

Only victory was impossible. He just didn't have the cards, no matter how many times he shuffled the deck. What was he going to do?

"I don't know," Berab said, sounding oddly sympathetic. Had he spoken aloud? "And while Miss Moses's name is not one I want connected to mine in any way, you are correct—once someone is revealed as a mere human, someone with a life and wants and friends, instead of a monster on paper, it's hard to muster the same level of animosity."

Pushing back his chair, Berab stood. "What I will say is this: take care with whom you trust. And think."

As if he wasn't. Oy. Not that he could say that. For whether Berab was a person he could trust or not, it was clear he needed all the allies he could get these days.

Chapter Twenty-Four

It was well after midnight by the time Hannah was able to sneak through the window and into the room where Sol was staying. The snow had stopped enough that most of the moon and even a few stars lit the night sky, guiding her way. The same now illuminated his sleeping form.

God, she wanted him. Too much. But as she'd known from the beginning, she could not have him. That wasn't her story. That would never be her story.

She'd accepted the life she'd created. And she'd been—and would soon be again—on the cusp of giving Tamar the life she deserved. Fulfilling the promise to her parents. That would have to be enough.

She moved to the bed and gazed down at Sol. She was only here to warn him and then end things for good. Though doing so in person—an act that had seemed like a necessity when leaving the Weiss home—now, in the moonlight, Hannah had to admit that she'd been lying to herself.

A note would've most certainly sufficed. Even if her original one had been lost to the snow when Martin had taken her. Her gloved fingers flexed as the urge to touch him, to gently brush the dark curls back from his forehead, near overwhelmed her. She reached out—and nearly screamed as his hand encircled her wrist.

"Back, are we?" the bloody momzer said, opening his eyes and arching a brow.

"Only for a moment," she told him. "I'm here just to confirm that I spoke to both Roger Berab and your brother—"

"I know," he said, not releasing her. "Berab came to visit me today."

He tugged on her wrist and pulled her against his body, wrapping his arms around her. "Why are you really here, Hannah?" he asked with a rather wolfish grin.

"Not for that," she admonished, though her tone was less convincing than she'd like.

"Pity," he said. And the damned momzer licked his lips.

Her heart began beating in her ears. No. They couldn't—shouldn't—do this again.

"You're ridiculous," she said, willing herself to pull away but failing.

"Debatable," he said before grabbing her waist with one arm and nudging her up so she was straddling his chest. "As, despite how things appear, I'm even less injured than before."

This was meshuggeneh. But need pooled in her core as he reached up to twirl a lock of hair that had fallen from its cheap pins.

"You're tempted, aren't you?" he said with a sly smile. "You find me irresistible."

"How hard exactly did you hit your head when you fell from the rooftop?" She pouted but didn't pull away, instead arching into him as he ran a hand down her cheek.

"My head is just fine. It's other parts of my body that need attention." He waggled his damned eyebrows in a manner that was both suggestive and ridiculous. "Didn't you say something about nursing, last time you were here?"

"Completely incorrigible," she groaned.

"Damned straight," he told her, this time his dimple showing when he smiled. "Tenacious too. In more ways than one." He gave her a wink. "Ways you can find out, if you just let me show you."

"Tenacious, you said? Certainly, in your ability to argue until the sun comes up." She glanced out the window. "And as I'm a person of the night, I should be getting home before that occurs," she told him, even if in her heart she knew that he'd already won. Right or wrong—well, most certainly wrong—she was staying.

This one last time.

"You know, if you just dispensed with your arguments now, there could be plenty of time for what we both need." Sol tightened his grip on her waist. "Come on, Hannah, come sit...with me." He grinned at her as he moved his hand low, cupping her and making her moan. "For just a little longer."

"Incorrigible" was an understatement. But the man was right; he was still completely irresistible. Especially when he looked at her that way, both tugging at her heartstrings and making her body fizzle with heat.

"And at least let me kiss you." He leaned up against her. "Kisses certainly have healing properties."

At that she had to laugh a little. "You're not tenacious," she told him, placing her hands on her hips. "You're a nag."

"Very much." He brought her hand to his lips and

paused for a moment, giving her a questioning tilt of his head. "Which is why you're wearing the perfume I bought you." He stroked her fingers. "That and because you like it." His voice softened. "See, Hannah, when I'm right, I'm right. And regarding us, I'm often right. Is that so difficult to acknowledge?"

She should bolt for the damned window, but instead, she nodded.

And in an instant, he pulled her wrist toward him and—blew on it.

Momzer. Complete momzer. "You're arrogant and spoiled too, you know?" she added.

He chuckled. "That as well, though I still try to pull my weight—at least a little." He drew her wrist to his lips and this time—*ah*. She near melted as he first planted soft kisses on the joint before moving to licks. Hannah's toes curled. She might have moaned too.

Another laugh from him, a dark, rumbling one that tightened every muscle in her body. He moved his fingers to the buttons on her cuff, raising his brows.

She should say no. She didn't.

"I finished making a cap today," he told her as he unfastened her cuff, rolling up her sleeve. "Only took the better part of four days. My crocheting is a touch slow."

His lips connected with her skin once more and she sighed.

"And I peeled vegetables," he added as he moved down to her elbow.

"A regular person now, aren't we?" she managed between gasps. "No more the would-be dandy?"

"Would that make you kiss me?" he asked, lifting his head.

"I—" She blinked at him because, god, she wanted to, needed to, but shouldn't, really shouldn't.

But her head appeared to no longer be in control of her body. She gave him a soft push back before cupping his chin this time and—blast, he tasted so good—tart and sweet, and spicy, like apples and cinnamon and wine, and lust. She drank him in, lightning shooting through her body as he wrapped his arms around her back, holding her to him.

"Was that so bad?" he asked as she came up to breathe, lest she swoon. Though if she did, what a way to go.

Yes. And the more it happened, the more painful losing him would be. Though she feared it was already too late—that she'd be damaged irreparably once they parted.

"No," she lied out loud, shaking her head. She took a deep breath. "And it wasn't before. But that's the problem."

"Why is that the problem?" he asked, his brow pinched.

"See, this is why I shouldn't kiss you." She pushed up even though he did not let go. "When I do, I get all muddled. I stop thinking rationally. I want impossible things. Or worse, I start fooling myself into believing they're possible." Her throat thickened. "And if I do that..."

He reached up and brushed back her hair. "If you do that, what?" he asked, his voice soft.

"I'll pursue them. When I shouldn't. I need to put an end to us once and for all. Because that's what's right for both of us." And something burned behind her eyes. "Being with me—it'll cost you everything you've been working for. You can pretend you want me for more than this—convince yourself that you'll be happy that way—but in the end, when you live the life that I entail, you'll come to resent me. If my world doesn't kill you first. You say you love me, but I promise you, that love will turn to hate if you go down this path."

"Hannah—" he started, but she put a finger to his lips.

"Don't, Sol. You know as well as I do that it's true." She took a deep breath. "You need to let me go." She swallowed. "When this is over—when you are well and safe, I want you to be happy. To live a good life. With someone who can give you what you need. What you deserve." She gritted her teeth. "The community is lucky to have you back. You belong there and you belong in the world your brother is entering, at his side. Please, take your due."

He ran his thumb down her cheek, as she, like she'd done so many times in the past, willed back her tears. Remaining strong. No matter the pain.

"I don't know the correct words—the ones which will right everything. And I'm stuck in here so there are very few ways I could do to show you right now. But if you just give me time, give us time..." He shook his head. "Let this"—he pressed a hand to his chest—"let *me* speak this way, let me show you this way."

And she couldn't say no. Not to him, not when he looked at her with such longing and sheer will that all her ramparts began to crumble. With a single nod, she obeyed, allowing him to hitch her skirts all the way up so her thighs above her worn garters were exposed.

Gazing into her eyes with stern determination, he stroked the skin between her stockings and garters, his lips only quirking when she finally permitted herself a soft moan, even as her body screamed and begged for more. Almost in a trance, she fiddled with the front of her gown, squeezing, pressing her hands against her now aching nipples.

"There we go, beautiful. Those feel better now, don't they?" he whispered, gripping her side. "It drives me wild when you do that, by the way. I could watch you touch yourself for hours."

But thankfully, he didn't.

"Please, Hannah," he said as he slid one finger into her, and then a second, and a third, between her now wet folds, still watching her face. "Give me this, just once more."

She whimpered as he brushed her curls aside, finding the nub with his thumb, circling it. And in what seemed like mere moments, his ministrations turned her entire body into an inferno of need. He quirked an eyebrow as she gasped, her body teetering on the edge, nearly shaking with pleasure.

"So this is good?" he asked, the damned momzer pausing. "Tell me if it's good."

"You know it's good," she told him, her voice a strangled cry as she moved one of her hands lower to replace his, but he caught her wrist.

"And you'd like more?" he asked, a smile playing on his lips, somehow both smug and endearing. And intoxicating. But more than that. Somehow, no matter how hard she'd fought it, the dratted man had battered his way into places she'd permitted no one in years.

Soft places. Vulnerable places. Places that dreamed of more. And she could see them, even if they weren't real and could never be. Places she had to lock up tight, somehow, someway, or she'd not survive.

"I should—" she started, but Sol reached up and placed a finger on her lips.

"Please." He studied her face. "What are you so afraid of?"

*That when I leave, I will not be able to lie to myself about this. That I will not be able to call what we had mere temporary pleasure. That I will have to admit that this act, with you, is significant. And thus, for as long as I manage to survive, I'll have to live with the memory of what I lost and—*she forced the thoughts down whence they'd come.

"I told you, wanting what's not mine," she said. As that was true as well. Because what he wanted to give could never truly be hers.

He shook his head. "You don't understand; this is already yours, Hannah," he said, taking her wrist and running her palm over his own body. "I'm already yours." Shifting, he pushed the quilt down farther, revealing the rest of his very nude, very erect body.

Hannah shook her head. She wanted him too, too much in too, too many ways. And this would never be enough. Even if it was all she'd have.

"All yours," he repeated, his voice firm as he stared into her eyes. "All you have to do is take it." He cocked his head as she hesitated, her heart pounding in her ears. But how could she refuse him? She wrapped her hand around him, his soft skin stretched tight against his hardness.

"You can do that for me, can't you?" He pulled her hips closer, so the tip teased her entrance. She moaned, stroking him with her hand as she made him slick with her own wetness.

"There we go," he whispered as, god help her, she gave in, and took him inside her again.

She gasped his name as she let him fill her. The last time, she vowed to herself. She'd have to make this the last time. No matter how right it felt. If it wasn't, she would certainly not survive.

"Yes, love?" he whispered, the term of endearment shattering the last bit of protection she had, but she was beyond caring.

"Please, I need..." she said through the lump in her throat, her eyes stinging.

"I know, love, I know." He reached up and stroked her cheek before placing his thumb in that same blissful spot and moving beneath her, thrusting upward, as together they established a rhythm that was anything but elegant or gentle, but completely theirs.

She'd never felt so full, or so safe, and she gave herself over to the waves of pleasure, carrying her higher and higher.

"Touch yourself again for me," he gasped as he moved faster. "Show me you're here with me and me alone, nowhere else."

And she obliged, grabbing her breasts once more as his movements sped, taking her over the edge, her body squeezing his as she sailed off their peak. In a flash, he'd rolled her onto her back, taking his own pleasure through her waves, until he slid out of her body, wrapping her against his chest as he finished, repeating her name over and over.

"Tell me you love me," he whispered to her. "Just say the words, once, let me hear them."

She opened her mouth. Closed it.

She wanted to. So badly. But one of them had to be strong. One of them had to be reasonable. And it would have to be her.

Sol only kissed the top of her head when she said nothing. And they lay there in the silence, her body pressed against his as he stroked her hair, Hannah willing back tears as she tried not to think of the losses to come.

Chapter Twenty-Five

Sol held Hannah in his arms, his mind spinning. He needed to say something. She needed words—the right ones—ones that would make her see that they belonged together.

And he would, somehow, find a way to reconcile that with Frederick's needs. He simply required more time. If she could just trust him to rise to the occasion for once in his life. Be the man both she and Frederick needed.

Even if he wasn't quite sure how. The future was not set in stone. If not, what were any of them doing?

Hannah turned, blinking up at him before squinting at the clock across the room.

"I need to leave," she told him, rising from the bed and retying her laces, leaving him cold and alone. "And I have to finish what I was telling you before—this, this has to be good-bye." She kept her back turned to him.

"You've said that before, and yet here you are," he told her, sitting up. "Come on, Hannah, neither of us wants that, so why don't you get back into bed and help me plan a way to make that a reality."

"No," she said, bending and retaking her discarded cloak, still not turning to meet his eye. "Trust me, Sol. This has to end. There's no other option."

"Like hell there isn't." He rose and moved so he was directly in front of her. She fiddled with her buttons before sighing and glancing up at him.

Generally, the kind thing to do would be to offer her assistance, but if she believed he was going to help her leave him, she had another think coming.

"I met with your brother," she said, her voice eerily calm. "And he does not approve. Of me. Of this."

Sol froze. "You and Frederick—you met and he knew about...us?" How? Yes, Roger and Isabelle and Aaron—so likely others in the Jewish community—knew as well, but that was not a circle in which Frederick operated in the slightest.

Oy. And this was certainly not the way he'd wanted his brother to learn about them. That was for certain.

"He's a clever, powerful, man. He knows what's happening in his house," Hannah said with a shrug. "And I am not someone who belongs there." She gave him a rueful half smile, which twisted his heart. "But we knew that already."

Sol swore in his head. Not that his reaction was a surprise; he'd just wanted to manage Frederick himself, once he'd laid the groundwork. And after his brother had already succeeded in his endeavors.

"Hannah—" he started, his mind whirling as he searched for a way to salvage the conversation.

She held up a palm. "Let me finish," she said before slipping a glove over her fingers. "This is really quite difficult."

"Good. It should be," he told her, folding his arms across his chest as he certainly wasn't going to make leaving him easy for her.

Hannah rolled her eyes. "Perhaps you'll think differently about it after we discuss the rest."

He frowned. "What rest?"

There was a long pause as Hannah shifted from foot to foot. Clearly unable to fully trust him with whatever information she had, as if that wasn't another kick in the gut. "You need to talk to your brother," she said finally.

"Naturally. And I intend to. About several things, after I'm home," he told her, working to keep the annoyance out of his voice.

Hannah tugged at her ear. "I do not know the details, but I believe he...knows more about your attack than he's said."

Sol blinked at her. "Did he tell you that?" he asked.

"No. Denied it, in fact," she said with a weary half smile. "But that's not a surprise. He doesn't think particularly highly of me"—she tugged on her ear again—"not a surprise and not unwarranted, and he made it quite clear I was only hired for a limited purpose—"

"Finding me," he finished with a nod.

"And the other one," she said with a shrug. "The first job was more difficult. Did earn both fees, though. You should thank him for me."

Sol froze. She'd worked for Frederick before? Why hadn't she told him? "What other one?" he asked.

She waved a dismissive hand. "The valet of some son of some nobleman. He said it was a 'test' job, though I...well, never mind."

A valet of a—Sol stared at her. "The son of a marquess?" he whispered, his mind spinning.

Hannah nodded.

"And you found his whereabouts for...Frederick?"

A hard lump of fear grew in his chest. *Oh, Frederick, what have you done?* And it was as if a large puzzle piece that had been just out of reach fell into his hand.

"I did. That's what I was doing when I was under your window," she explained, her expression curious.

"That was the first job he hired you for?" he asked before a thought occurred to him. "How did you come to work for my brother?"

"He found me," she said, pursing her lips. "I suspect he'd seen you visit the shop—twice—so he saw an opportunity and took it." She looked away. "Though he probably had quite a bit of information on me first. Your brother doesn't strike me as the sort of person to do anything without a plan."

"No, he's not," Sol murmured in agreement, his mind still stuck on the idea of Frederick doing something so dangerous. Yes, Penrose had been working hard to take the woman he loved away, with Stoudmire as an accomplice, but this wasn't—Frederick was protective, but honorable. There must be more to the story.

Sol's heart squeezed. God, what had he done that his brother no longer shared his plans with him? Did no one trust him at all?

"But what does that have to do with anything?" she asked, interrupting his thoughts.

"That man…the marquess's son…he was also attacked recently. I suspect his valet shared his schedule." He shook his head slowly. "Vengeance for his attack is certainly a possible motive for mine." He glanced up at her. "You don't look surprised."

She looked rather stricken in fact.

Shaking her head, she straightened. "I didn't get the sense that this foray into my world was his first," she told him. "And your brother is on the verge of being powerful in a respectable way as well. Men like that often make enemies." She raised a finger. "Your brother's building you protection from all of that. But if I remain, I can only ruin it for you."

And the crack in her voice almost felled him.

Sol took a step toward her. "No, there has to be another—"

"He loves Lady Drucilla and will take steps to protect her," Hannah said, arching a brow.

He blinked at her. "What sort of—" he started before grimacing. Her meaning became clear. If she and Frederick were at odds, she feared that he might use his new power in ways that could be costly to her. Which, given what she now knew he'd done to a rival before he had his access to titled gentiles, wasn't such a great leap.

However, Hannah didn't know his brother. Not truly. Sol shook his head. "But he wouldn't actually—"

"He loves Lady Drucilla," she repeated and closed her eyes for a moment. Sol moved closer, ready to take her in his arms, but she moved away, wrapping her arms around her body. "And I don't love you."

It was as if she'd slapped him. He might've stumbled back. "What?" he whispered.

"I don't love you," she said, this time her voice clearer and stronger. "I was just using you."

She almost convinced him. Except her eyes, there was pain there. And she'd started to shiver. No, this woman should not give up the pawnshop for a career on the stage.

"Using me?" He folded his arms. "For what?" he challenged.

"The same thing I've gotten from dozens of men." She lifted her chin defiantly but did not meet his eyes. "And there are quite a few in my world, with much more to offer me. In more ways than one." She jutted out a hip and placed a hand on it.

It would've been funny how unbelievable her performance was if it wasn't also so infuriating. "You're a terrible actress," he told her.

"Then just let me go," she snapped at him. "Please, let me go."

"Why?" he demanded. "Tell me why. A real reason, not some sort of half-truth or lie."

"Because I—" she started to say then closed her mouth firmly. Her swallow was visible. "Because this is what's best for you." She folded her arms again as if she was somehow irritated with him.

That was rich.

"What's best for me?" he asked. How dare she? How absolutely dare she? He shook his head and turned away. "That's quite arrogant, isn't it?" He whirled back around and glared at her, raising a brow. "Do you think me foolish?"

She hung her head. "No," she whispered. "No. You're quite clever." Her voice increased in volume and she gestured widely. "Brilliant, actually. More than you realize, I think."

Then why? Why would she not trust him? Trust them?

He took a deep breath and stepped toward her one more time. "But you don't trust my judgment when it comes to you?" he asked softly. He reached out a hand, and her fingers flexed at her side. Sol's breath caught in his throat as he waited.

But she did not come. Instead, she backed away.

"In time, you'll see that this is best," she said in an irritatingly calm voice. "Trust me."

"You tell me that, but you refuse to trust *me*." Suddenly, he was tired. Very, very tired.

Why was he so insistent on chasing after a woman,

one who everyone else for whom he cared told him would make his life difficult, if all she did was shove him away?

Yes, her behavior contradicted her words, but didn't he deserve the words too? And yes, he understood she was scared—she'd told him as much in the story regarding her parents' deaths. But she wasn't the only one in the world who had suffered losses. He'd opened his heart to her time and time again, and while he might not be perfect, he didn't deserve—he swallowed.

Perhaps he did. She'd told him multiple times that she didn't want what he was offering. He should've taken her at her words. Oy, he should've listened to his brother. Frederick had tried so hard, but clearly, he was just not cut out for making decisions on his own.

"Fine," he said, unable to keep the frustration and hurt out of his voice. "You want to play this game? Push me away? Well, that's just fine. Because you're finally going to get your wish. If you leave now, like this, don't bother coming back. I don't want you to come back. I don't want to see you again. I'm done."

And he was. Truly. This—the pain—wasn't worth it. Bile rose in his throat as if rejecting the unspoken lie.

"Good," she whispered, turning her head from him, the catch in her voice unmistakable. And the sound near felled him. She rushed toward the window.

"I'm sorry," he managed to call out. Because he was a shmuck and he couldn't help himself. Couldn't beat the last bit of hope out of his heart, no matter how foolish and illogical.

She paused, hands on the sill, her face turned away from him. "Sorry for what?" she asked, her voice shaking.

For not being able to fix her life, let alone his own.

For not being able to give her the words, the ones that she needed.

"For not being enough for you to get over your fear," he said finally. "For not being enough to convince you that risking your heart is worth the possibility of more."

Her shoulders slumped. "You have no idea what you're worth."

"Then tell me." He slapped his hand down on the bedpost in frustration. His eyes stung. "Stop lying, stop running, and stay. Fight. With me," he pleaded.

"I can't," she told him, her hands clenching the sill. "I'm sorry."

And before he could do anything else, she'd gone. Leaving him alone with nothing but pain and regret at how he'd managed to lose so spectacularly.

Chapter Twenty-Six

The starless sky was already changing from black to a dull gray by the time Hannah trudged through the alley and up the stairs to her and Tamar's living quarters. Slumping onto the fainting couch, Hannah unbuttoned her cloak and threw it to the side, staring into the smoldering ashes of the dying fire.

She should get up and poke it. The day was about to begin and there was work to do. She might as well start.

Except her legs wouldn't budge. No, try as she might, she could not force herself to stand and do what needed to be done.

"What's the matter?" Her sister's voice startled her, and Hannah glanced over her shoulder to find Tamar at the edge of the room, still in her night rail, feet bare, thick hair breaking loose from its braid.

"Nothing," Hannah said quickly, rubbing her eyes. "I'm merely tired." This time she managed to rise and grab the poker, turning the embers so once again they could have full heat.

"Not a surprise. You've been out all night," Tamar said, taking a seat upon the couch. "A frequent occurrence for you as of late." She tucked her legs beneath the hem of her gown and motioned to Hannah to join her.

With a sigh, Hannah retook her seat, staring again, now at the flames. "It won't be anymore," she said.

"What did you do?" her sister demanded, more than asked.

"What do you mean?" Hannah pinched the bridge of her nose before yawning. Oy, she did not need this discussion. Not now. Not ever.

"You know exactly what I mean." Tamar glared at her. "You left him, didn't you?"

Hannah rolled her eyes. "There was no 'leaving' to be done. I wasn't his wife. I merely put an end to our... what do the fancy set call 'em?" She frowned, searching her tired brain for the correct word.

What was the one? From that book her sister'd been reading? She patted around until her hand hit on it, under a cushion. She glanced at the spine. "Liaison."

Tamar snorted. "You're not fancy," she said, taking the volume from her and tossing it on the table. "And even if you were, you know very well that the word is not apt regarding Mr. Weiss's intention toward you." Her sister wagged an accusatory finger at her. "I knew you were going to hurt him."

Hannah pressed her fingers over her eyes, forcing back all the emotion that was fighting to overtake her. But she couldn't let that happen. Not for Sol's sake. Not for Tamar's sake. She had to be strong. She forced down a breath and opened her eyes once again.

"I saved him," she said, her voice shaking.

"From what?" Her sister put her hands on her hips.

Hannah pressed a fist to her mouth. "From ruining his chance at a good life, where he'll be loved and adored and celebrated. Where he belongs." It was what he deserved. What being with her would prevent him from having. Her throat closed again.

"How do you know that's what he wants?" her sister asked, interrupting her thoughts.

Hannah shrugged. "He was working toward that before I came along. Rubbing elbows with the big machers and the fancy gentile set alike, courting the likes of Isabelle Ellenberg."

And soon, when he thought better of it, he'd pursue someone like Isabelle again. And one day, he'd realize that it was all for the best. Her chest ached so much that she had to press her hands against her ribs.

"And yet the moment you came along, he spent most of his time finding ways to get into our rooms instead. What does that tell you?" her sister asked, unable to take a hint.

"That he enjoyed taking me to bed?" With a huff, Hannah rose and moved to the curtains, fiddling with the ties.

Tamar glared at her. "I'm not going to even dignify that with a response."

"It doesn't matter anyway. I made quite sure he'd not come round again," Hannah told her before grabbing the broom and beginning to sweep.

"Of course you did." And now Tamar was on her feet, not only not letting the subject drop, but standing in her way. "There's nothing you like better than punishing yourself," her sister muttered.

Hannah rolled her eyes. "That's most of London's favorite pastime—why shouldn't I get in on the fun?" She couldn't help but joke, despite everything. After all, what else was there left to do? She was who she was. And her life was the same. Neither would ever change.

Tamar snatched the broom from Hannah's hand and threw it against the ground. It clattered over the wood. "That's not funny," her sister said.

"What do you want me to say?" Hannah asked before bending to pick up the broom. But her sister was too quick, slamming her foot over the handle and pressing down with all her weight.

"It's not what I want you to say, it's what I want you to do." Tamar placed her hands on Hannah's shoulders, forcing their faces to meet. "I want you to stop," she said as Hannah broke free, turning away and marching back to the window.

She pressed her face against the cold glass, willing her sister again to stop. Just stop.

Except Tamar would not, and in an instant, she was back behind Hannah.

"Do you think I enjoy watching the community spit on you? Watching you allow yourself to be pawed at by men you despise, who cheat you and toss you around as if you're not a person? Do you think it's amusing for me to watch you take a hundred risks that are likely to leave you either dead in the streets or transported or worse?" Tamar was nearly shouting now.

"And when, finally, when someone sees you, really sees you and your value the way I do, do you expect me to watch you shove him away so you can continue your—your—bloody—um—masochism?" Tamar huffed and Hannah heard a sound like something hitting the ground—her foot?

At that, Hannah turned around, frustration welling in her gut.

"It's not 'masochism'—and I don't even want to know what merchandise you read that word in—it's fortitude. Fortitude to do my duty and give you what you deserve," she told her sister. "Let you have a good life." She clasped their hands together, her voice shaking. "I promised our parents that I'd take care of you. That's why I'm here, that's why I'm still alive. That's the only reason. Nothing else matters."

And Tamar was right in her face, pulling her hand away to wag her finger furiously. "Don't you say that. Don't you dare say that. Don't you dare do that to me."

"Do what to you?" Hannah asked. What did her sister want from her? And why couldn't Tamar just let this go? Let her nurse her wounds by herself. Like she'd done for years. The scars weren't pretty, but she'd healed. She would this time too. If Tamar would permit her.

Her sister had other ideas.

"Don't you understand? I don't want you to live for me, I want you to live for you, alongside me," Tamar yelled. "And what exactly is this good life that you're always on about, Hannah?" her sister demanded, folding her arms across her chest.

"A husband who loves you, enough funds so you can live and not worry about creditors and your next meal, a community that cares for you, safety and respect, and admiration," Hannah retorted, ticking the familiar dreams off on her fingers.

"Is that what I want or what you want?" her sister countered, her mouth grim.

"It's what everyone wants." Hannah waved her hands in the air.

Tamar frowned. "All I know is that while the funds would be nice, I agree, and perhaps I'd want a husband someday, in theory, but for the rest? Why would I want to take part in a community that doesn't include the person I love and respect and admire the most?"

"Because you shouldn't love and respect and admire me," Hannah finally screamed. She'd done too much, made too many mistakes, and could not stop making them, wanting things she couldn't have. She panted, her blood pumping in her ears.

"You think I'm a fool?" her sister demanded, hands on her hips.

Do you think me foolish?

"I think you're naïve," Hannah told her, pushing away Sol's memory.

Her sister paused, before inching closer. "Do you think they were fools?" she asked, her voice soft. "Our parents."

Hannah gaped at her. "What?"

Tamar tilted her head. "You heard me. Do you think they were fools? Because they certainly loved you."

And the words were like a slap. Because they were the truth. They'd loved her. So, so much. Too much. And she'd not appreciated them enough until they were gone. If only she'd spent less time wanting love and admiration from outside their home and focused instead on what they had inside. Her eyes stung.

"And I killed them," she said through gritted teeth, hating herself more with every moment.

"You did no such thing," Tamar snapped, folding her arms tightly. "We were a target."

"I know." Hannah closed her eyes again, the guilt near overwhelming. "I made us one when I lost my temper." So how could Tamar possibly think she would bring Sol anything but misery? How could Sol?

"Stop lying to yourself. You know as well as I do that

we were a target long before that." Tamar pursed her lips. "We were always a target, the size merely changed when our parents became successful. It was only a matter of time until they fell."

She waved an arm toward the store. "Look around us. This is how we live, while the rich go about in Mayfair with golden walls and jeweled buckles that they need another person to fasten. There's rage in these streets. They seethe with it. *They* need an outlet that they can actually touch. Who better than people whose job it is to remind them of how low they are in the world?" She gave Hannah a bitter smile.

"But they still need us—or at least people like us and our parents," she continued. "They can't destroy the entire profession. They just needed a symbol, a stand-in for those they resent. Who were they going to choose? Not the good, honest gentile pawnbrokers providing a valuable service. No, they could see themselves too easily in them. They needed to really feel like they were slaying an ogre. They needed *Jews*." Her sister near spit the word.

"That's our best use, after all. Make us the face of something they hate, while they make money quietly doing the same thing. Punish us, execute us—for them, cruelty is the same as justice." She smiled grimly. "If our parents are indeed dead, and I have never counted them out, they aren't dead because of you."

"I pushed them." Hannah couldn't believe her—didn't want to believe her. Because if that were true... She clasped her hands. "I wanted too much. I wanted pretty things and a good dowry and—"

Tamar barked a harsh laugh. "Oh, so our mother didn't like her silks and perfumes? Didn't make sure she had little jewels in her hair for the holidays, parading around in front of all the women who snubbed her?" Her sister shook her head. "Our father enjoyed the finer things too. And the way he went on about that donation plaque—I was there too." Her sister stared at her. "The question is, why are you always so eager to take all the blame?"

Hannah blinked. Why? Because it had to be her fault. If it was her fault, then everything was fair and made sense and the world was livable. The losses were survivable.

Including Sol. Not that he was ever hers to lose.

She heaved a sigh and admitted the truth. "Because that's the only way I know how to stand it. That's the only way I can bear it all." And everything in her crumbled. "Including losing him," she whispered.

"Let me." Tamar wrapped her arms around Hannah, holding her against her chest. "Please," she murmured against Hannah's hair. "I'm not a child any longer. Please let me love you and protect you back." She kissed the top of Hannah's head. "And tell you when you're being an arrogant fool."

"That's what he called me," she said between sobs. "But I'm not. I'm not at all. I love him too much to let him throw away his life for me."

And there. She'd said the words. Out loud. Admitting them to herself and—she inhaled—it hurt, god it hurt—not the love, but the loss, acute and sharp beneath her breast. How was she going to stand living without him?

She wasn't sure how long she leaned against her sister and cried, but when she was finally able to swipe her eyes on her sleeve, her throat was dry and raw.

She gazed up at Tamar. "Being with him could hurt you too," she finally shared. "His brother made it very clear that I was not welcome in their family, and that if I don't stay away, well, he'll use his power and influence to get rid of me. And you."

Which could not—would not happen. No matter what. Love or no love.

"Did you tell Sol this?" Tamar asked as Hannah sat up fully.

"No," she confessed, smoothing her hair as best she could, twisting and repinning it. She'd tried—not very well, she could admit—to hint at his brother being a threat, but Sol didn't seem to believe Frederick capable of such a thing.

"So he could talk to his brother and change his mind," her sister suggested, as if it were so easy.

Hannah adjusted the buttons on her gown. "He's... not that kind of man. He knows our world too well." Tamar lifted an eyebrow. Well, might as well tell her the whole of it. "He hired me to do the same sort of work I did for Ned. And he's marrying the sister of a titled gentile now. He and his wife would be snubbed if they were associated with me," she explained with a sigh. "And me being gone—permanently—would be the easiest solution. And then Sol would be forced to choose."

And she couldn't do that to him. For either way, he'd hate himself.

"So you and his brother made the choice for him?" Tamar asked with a pout.

"We're protecting him," she said firmly. "Each in our own way." Whether or not she agreed with Frederick's methods.

"No, you're both arrogant," Tamar snapped. She pursed her lips. "And you're also scared." She shook her head. "I just can't figure out if you're more scared that he'll choose his brother or that he'll choose you." She swiped a loose strand of hair off Hannah's forehead and tucked it behind her ear. "I suspect the latter."

It was Hannah's turn to pout. "Of course I'm scared. I'll make him miserable," she said. "How could I not? He might think it's romantic in the moment, but in the end, when he realizes the extent of what I cost him, he'll come to resent me, and watching that happen... I'm not strong nor brave enough."

Blast it all, her eyes were misting again. She swiped at them with her bare hand.

"I think you are," Tamar said, taking Hannah's hands in hers. "You're the strongest, bravest person I know." Her voice caught, and in an instant, Hannah threw her arms around her sister, holding her like she'd done so many times over the years.

Except this time, it was Hannah who was scared. Terrified.

"It doesn't matter," she whispered. "Even if I was brave, he's done with me now."

"I'm not so sure, but now is not the time to argue more," Tamar whispered as she stroked Hannah's hair. "You should sleep. And when you have your strength, we can revisit this discussion and perhaps you'll see another perspective."

She opened her mouth to protest—to tell her sister that it was highly unlikely that her "perspective" would change—but only a yawn came out.

Blast, they had work to do. There were fires to tend and chores and a shop to open. However, she was tired. So very tired.

"Only for a moment," she said to Tamar as she closed her eyes. Then she fell into a deep sleep.

Chapter Twenty-Seven

Sol spent the rest of the morning abed. None of the women came to disturb him, as if they had a sense of what had transpired and how, despite the fact his mind was clearer than it had been in days, he felt no peace. Only guilt and regret. He'd failed, but damned if he could figure out how he could have succeeded.

Or perhaps he couldn't have. Perhaps he'd just been wrong about everything. Perhaps he was too naïve, too foolish, too spoiled to face reality. He pressed his hands to his temples, pain now brewing.

His brother was right. He was completely incompetent. How he believed he could succeed...

But no longer.

Unwinding his bandage, he rubbed his ankle. The moment he could get into a carriage, he'd be going home, and they would talk—be completely honest with each other. He'd tell Frederick everything that had happened, all the mistakes he'd made, and beg his brother's forgiveness. And then he'd plead with Frederick to share the truth with him as well.

About Lady Drucilla—he'd checked the papers and Berab had been right, which had been a kick to his gut—about the matter of the marquess's son, about

Hannah, even if whatever they'd had between them was done.

Yet try as he might, one voice, one image, one person would not leave his mind, would not stop haunting him and his thoughts. She'd left but wouldn't leave him.

He gritted his teeth. Well, he'd just have to forget, like she'd said he would. He'd find a way. No matter how much it hurt. Because she wasn't coming back.

Buttoning his shirt, Sol took to the stairs, his feet bare, but for the first time since his fall, he was able to put weight on both. Yes, the injured side was still swollen, but he'd be able to get home easily, either that day or the next, just as Doc had promised.

Hopefully that day. He was ready. He needed to get on with it all.

His stomach growled.

Fine, he'd get on with it after he ate.

Sol ducked into the parlor. "Doc, Gertrude, Bayla?" He frowned at the empty room. "Where is everyone?" The fire was going, though it was more embers than flame. He poked at it and glanced at the mantel clock.

After eleven. They should all be about. He craned his neck, but the dining room was empty as well. He poked his head out into the back lane. The snow had thankfully stopped, the sun even shining, but it was likewise empty. And quiet.

Actually, so was the street, which meant... Sol tapped his chin. It wasn't Shabbos, but perhaps it was... market day. If that was correct, they and all their closer neighbors were most likely bargaining and wouldn't be home for hours. Especially if the weather stayed nice after so many days of downpour. Everyone's larder probably needed refilling.

He drew himself back inside and latched the door.

Just his mazel, the day he was ready to leave and he had to wait to say good-bye. He wrinkled his nose. He was not going back to bed; he was too keyed up. Perhaps he'd read. Sol marched back into the parlor and grimaced at Doc's collection of medical texts and Gertrude's rabbinical books.

Perhaps not.

His stomach rumbled. Well, at least that was something he could do. He moved into the kitchen to poke around and find what Bayla had left. Maybe there was something from that basket Aaron and Roger Berab had brought? If it wasn't completely finished. The jam had been divine.

He looked around the empty worktable to the space beyond. The cupboard held a few crusts of bread, but the room looked to be near empty, except...he glanced toward the small windowsill. There, perched atop, likely set out to cool—and lure a dozen thieves, not to mention birds—was an entire cake.

An applecake. His favorite.

Sol's mouth watered. He shouldn't—or, well, he should wait until everyone came home and they could eat together. Her stomache twisted again, this time painfully.

Though perhaps if he just cut a small piece from the outside, a thin sliver, then no one would notice any was missing...

Before he could rethink his plan, he'd grabbed a knife and crossed the room. He brought the plate down and set it on the table. Squinting, he saw one side was a bit uneven, thus cutting a piece off would assist the cake's total appearance. Really, eating just a little would be doing everyone a favor.

Or at least that was what he would argue to anyone
who asked. Smiling, he sliced in and cut off the narrow-
est piece. Quick as he could, he stuffed it in his mouth.
It tasted like paradise, golden and sweet and tart. He
closed his eyes and...the room began to spin.

Sweat prickled his brow and he grabbed the table for
purchase as his knees began to buckle. His eyes itched
and he started to gasp for air.

No.

He tried to scream for help, but his throat wouldn't
work. What was going on?

An old memory rose in his mind. He'd been young.
Only seven or eight. His father hadn't been dead for a
year. A friend of his brother's had come for a visit and
brought some salted nuts he'd purchased on a trip to
Spain. Sol had been fine the first day, but on the second,
the reaction had been swift.

Hannah.

Regret filled his mind. He should have fought
harder. Should have gone after her. Should have told her
he loved her enough for them both.

Sol tried to cry out, but his eyes swelled shut and the
darkness took him as he crashed to the floor.

Hannah woke with a start, still on the fainting couch,
her cloak draped over her, the fire a comfortable
warmth at her back. Rubbing her eyes, she sat up, pushing strands of loose hair out of her eyes.

"Tamar?" she called, glancing around as she rebuttoned her cuffs. "Tamar?"

"I'm here," her sister said, reentering the room, this

time fully dressed. She gave Hannah a once-over, then ducked back into the bedroom. "Let me grab a brush."

"What time is it?" Hannah asked with a yawn.

"Almost one," her sister said as she reemerged. She moved behind Hannah, her hands working with impressive speed.

"We need to open." Hannah finished rebuttoning her gown. She'd change later, when there was a lull in customers.

"I can open alone," Tamar said, finishing with Hannah's hair and taking her work apron from the hook. "Especially if you want to go somewhere else." She gave her a pointed stare.

Oy. Unable to meet her sister's eye, she moved to the basin and splashed water on her face. She shook her head. What she'd told her sister before was correct. They were done. *He* was done. She'd hurt him too much and any other action would be pouring salt in their wounds.

She needed to stay away.

"The longer you wait, the harder it will become," Tamar called.

No, the longer she waited, the more he'd realize he'd been right to tell her enough.

"We have a shop to run right now," Hannah said as she dried her hands with a cloth. She returned to the sitting room. "I need to keep our business afloat so we can have food in our bellies and a roof over our heads."

"Don't you trust me?" her sister asked, wagging the piece of bread she was nibbling on at her. She brushed the crumbs off her skirt.

With a roll of her eyes, Hannah grabbed the broom, but before she could answer, the two were interrupted by a loud banging, followed by shouts. Tamar gasped, wide-eyed, as Hannah squeezed the broom handle, adjusting the tool in her hands so it might be used as a weapon.

Pushing her sister behind her, she crept toward the staircase.

"What is that?" her sister asked, eyes wide. She clutched Hannah's arm, peering over her shoulder toward the entrance to their living quarters.

"I don't know," Hannah said, her heart beginning to pound. There was no jangle from the front door's bell, and the door to the alley was supposed to be locked. *Was* locked. She'd definitely locked it, right? She always locked the door.

"You stay here," she told Tamar before unlatching the upper lock and peering out. Nothing.

Quiet as she could, still armed with the broom, she edged down the staircase. She rounded the corner, brandishing her weapon, only to find Isabelle and Rebecca, both panting as they rushed toward her.

"Thank goodness you're here. We saw the shop was closed and"—Isabelle grasped Hannah by the shoulders, gasping—"It's Sol. You need to come with us. Now."

"What's happened?" Panic rose in her mind. "Has he been attacked again? Are the women all right?" Because Sol would hate himself if anything happened to his rescuers.

Isabelle shook her head, her brow pinched. "He's— it's hard to explain but he's not well."

"Not that very hard," Rebecca said, shooting Isabelle a look before drawing closer. "My great-aunt believes he's been poisoned."

"Poisoned?" How was that possible? And how had the other women not been affected?

"He's alive but unable to wake." Isabelle clutched her gloved hands together.

"My aunt's been treating him and I'm helping, but we thought that perhaps, hearing your voice, knowing you're there, might give more reason to fight," Rebecca added, her face serious.

"I can't," she told them, shaking his head. "The way we ended things—the way I ended things—he does not want to see me again. Trust me." Hannah swallowed. "And even if he did, his brother doesn't want me anywhere near him and has told me that if I do, he'll have me arrested for a crime I very much did commit. Which will not merely ruin Tamar's life again but also damage the community and—"

"His brother is not there," Rebecca snapped. "No one's there with him, except my aunt and her companions. Who care about him, but who are not you."

"He's in love with you, Hannah." Isabelle's deep, near black eyes brimmed with tears as the smaller woman shook with emotion, her thick black hair bouncing beneath her bonnet. "Just as you're in love with him. If you don't come now, you will regret it. Trust me. You only get so many chances, so much time. Please don't squander what you have."

Her features tightened and she added, "Besides, if Frederick Weiss is angered by your presence, I'll personally make sure that no such action is taken against you or your sister. He *will* listen to my family. No matter who he is now and who he's going to marry."

"Solomon's fighting for his life," the midwife said, slapping a hand against her skirts as if to emphasize her point. She eyed Hannah. "Don't tell me you're too much of a coward to do right by him. Don't tell me that we've misjudged you, that you don't love him enough to do all you can to keep him from dying and are prepared to let him go without even saying good-bye."

Hannah's heart clenched and she balled her fists. She'd never permit Sol to die.

Sol had to live. There was no other possibility. And she would risk anything to make it so.

"All right," she said. "I'll go."

Chapter Twenty-Eight

The ride through Aldgate proper was a blur as Isabelle's carriage bumped along the winding streets. The lane where the house stood was too narrow for them to travel down so they had to walk. The sleet mixed with snow had started anew and Hannah shivered beneath her cloak. They rushed through the near empty streets, passing only a few stragglers from the market.

Panting, they reached the front door to the house—quite a change for her from the window—then took the stairs two at a time. Hannah pushed through the door to Sol's room first and gaped at the motionless body on the bed, her view blocked by the pair of older women surrounding him.

"How long has he been like that?" She rushed forward, not even bothering to unfasten her cloak as she knelt beside the bed. Isabelle, of all people, removed it for her, sliding it off her shoulders.

"We don't know." A cross-looking woman shook her head and motioned to the bed. "This is how we found him. But he couldn't have been that way for very long."

"What happened?" She grimaced at the inflamed skin covering his arms. Hadn't Rebecca said he'd been poisoned?

"There was a cake downstairs," the same woman said. "Not made here and not something any of us remember seeing in any of the deliveries we've received as of late. We have no idea how he got it."

"That's not what's concerning," interrupted the other woman—the one actually sitting on the bed—before Hannah could ask what exactly a cake had anything to do with this? She reached over and dotted his lips with a cloth, blocking most of Sol's upper half. "What's concerning is his face."

The woman leaned back, finally giving them a clear view and—*my god*. In all her years, and she'd seen quite a few nightmarish acts of cruelty, between the streets and Newgate—Hannah shuddered—she'd never quite seen anything like this.

"He was beaten?" she whispered, unable to look away from his swollen eyes and lips, which looked worse next to the red splotches, probably the beginning of bruises, all over his skin. She balled her hands into fists. "Because if he was—I will—I'll go and find whoever—"

"Oh, none of that," Isabelle scoffed at her. "The last thing we need is to divert Rebecca or her aunt's attention away from Sol to patch up your wounds. Besides, it'll not help him in any way. Neither will leaving and burning London to the ground or whatever you seem set on doing right now."

That was—she wasn't going to—Hannah glared at the woman but relaxed her hands. "What will help?"

"We'll get to that, but first look." The older woman, the one who must be Rebecca's aunt, pointed a finger at Sol's face. "This swelling, it's not from a beating; it's his innards fighting something. See how his chest isn't properly rising; he's struggling to breathe even though he's asleep."

Hannah pressed a hand over her mouth so as not to cry out.

"We—well, I—believe there was something in the cake that poisoned his body," she continued. "I checked his airway and there's no food lodged in it, just swelling. So much swelling that I've had to put some additional air inside him myself."

"My god," Hannah whispered. She raced around to the other side of the bed and grabbed Sol's hot, but limp hand, holding it to her chest. "Tell me what I can do for him—anything." Because there had to be something— some way she could help. If only she could fight it for him, give him her breath and her lungs. She clutched his fingers tighter.

The woman with the kindly face brushed off her apron. "Doc needs someone to administer the treatment…" She gestured to a bowl filled with dark liquid on the first woman's lap.

"Coffee," she—Doc?—offered. "Though I'm not sure it's helping. At least it isn't hurting him." She demonstrated dipping the cloth before parting Sol's lips and squeezing the rag gently, dripping down the liquid, a little at a time. "If you can handle this, there's a combination of herbs I can make to reduce the swelling so he can breathe better and hopefully wake." She paused. "Truly, what he needs is for his body to fight for its own survival."

"Let me do this." Hannah reached for the bowl. "So you can go mix whatever potion will help him in any way." She swallowed, summoning all her strength. "Please, just let me be of use, let me help because—"

And her voice caught. Damn it. She wouldn't cry. The world had no use for her tears. Sol most certainly didn't.

With a nod, the woman handed her the cloth. "Just a few drops at a time," she instructed Hannah before securing the bowl on her lap. "I'll make sure we have the ingredients." She tapped her chin. "Apples, nettles, bark, perhaps juice of an orange…"

"I can fetch anything you need," Isabelle volunteered.

"And I can help you prepare the remedy," the kindly woman said. "After all, the kitchen is my domain." She glanced at Isabelle. "And I should feed you, especially if you're going to run out in the snow again. Perhaps you can give me some ideas of what Miss Moses would like."

"I'll stay," the grim woman said. "I'll grab you if anything changes."

Everyone nodded as Hannah turned back to Sol, dipping the rag in again and copying what she'd been shown. The door creaked but Hannah didn't glance up, her focus only on him.

"I'm sorry," she whispered as she swiped liquid off his lips because what else was there to say? Hannah's throat stung. "I'm so sorry." She thought back to their last conversation, guilt choking her, and brushed her fingers over his sweaty brow.

"What are you sorry for?" a rather annoyed voice snapped. "Did you give him the cake?" Hannah raised her head to find the scowling, grumpy woman still in the room, standing with her hands on her hips.

"No." She squinted at the woman. "Do I look like I could afford a fruitcake? I can barely afford meat for Shabbos these days." She sniffed before returning to

Sol. "And as for the ability to make one, well, let's just say that was not one of the skills I was taught." She gave the rag another dip.

"Not particularly clever. Just like him," the woman scoffed. "It'd be just like a man to eat food without knowing its source." She walked back around the bed, peering over Hannah's shoulder at Sol's motionless form.

After a moment, she gave her an awkward pat on the back. "He'll be all right."

"I know he will," Hannah retorted, her voice tight. Because he had to be. Because if he wasn't—she swallowed once more. "He'll live and go on to do great things. And he'll be happy, so very happy..."

The woman just stood there, silent.

A hot dash of liquid fell on Hannah's hand and another and another. She swiped at her blasted eyes with the back of her hand.

"I'm not crying." She sniffed. "Crying is useless."

It only showed weakness, and the weak were preyed upon at best and crushed at worst, and it certainly wouldn't help Sol. No, air would help him and Doc and Rebecca and—tears continued to stream despite her arguments.

"Quite," the woman said with a small squeeze of her hand. "And you're a practical, sensible person."

"I'm a woman who has learned from experience," she sniffed again.

"A survivor."

"Yes," Hannah whispered. If only she could make him one too.

"He's strong," her companion continued, "in his own way. And shrewd. And rather good at heart, if not a touch arrogant. And quite the persistent noodge.

Getting him to stay still for his ankle to heal…
ridiculous."

Hannah giggled but it quickly turned into a sob. She
clutched Sol's hand to her breast, wishing that his fingers would flex, or more likely, considering him, inap-
propriately squeeze, just where she enjoyed it most,
despite the fact that they were not alone.

He could strip her naked and have his way with her
in the middle of the synagogue for all she cared, as long
as he was alive.

"But we all are, aren't we?" the older woman asked.

"What?" Hannah glanced back at her.

"A bit ridiculous," she continued. "Pretending we
can plot and plan and control our fates. Know what the
future will hold."

"We can guess well enough," Hannah snapped. "I
don't—this isn't the time."

"I'm just saying, dear"—the woman's voice was
sharp—"any of us can leave this earth at any given
time. We don't control that. We only get to choose how
we spend the time we have and with whom. And finding someone whose window we can't help but sneak
into is a rarity. Far rarer than business opportunities
or invitations to gentile balls or even prominently dis-
played donation plaques. And certainly rarer than people making us their villains then slaying us." She gave
Hannah another pat. "Not that you'll believe the likes
of me. I'm just the daughter of a scholar, one descended
from Tzvi Ashkenazi." She paused. "Actually, my name
is Gertrude."

Hannah could only nod as the blasted tears fell
harder.

"Here," Gertrude whispered, "I'll go see how the

others are doing. Give you two some privacy. Even if there never really is any in this house."

Before Hannah could respond, the door creaked again, leaving her and Sol alone.

"I'm sorry," she choked out before laying her head on his chest, letting the beat of his heart, somehow still steady, comfort her. "I'm so sorry. I should have protected you. I would give anything for you to live."

The tears returned, no matter how hard she fought them back. Finally, she whispered, "I love you, Sol. Even if I shouldn't. Even if you're a hundred times too good for me and always will be. I know I'm the one who ruined us, but you deserved to have heard me say it. To know it. You have always and will always be enough. You're everything. And I love you."

Bending down, she planted the softest kiss as possible on his forehead. A single tear splashed on his nose, and she pressed her lips there as well, and finally to his lips, as swollen as they were, blowing a little air inside his lungs as if the action could somehow fix everything, could somehow make his body stop struggling against itself and heal.

Heaving a sigh, she dipped the rag back in the bowl, repeating the ministrations as she waited. And hoped.

Chapter Twenty-Nine

Sol was getting tired of waking in pain with no idea why—or where he was and how he'd gotten there. And yet here he was in the same situation once again.

What had happened? Sol blinked into the darkness as burning pain enveloped his body. His skin pulsed and nettled, his chest ached, and worst of all, the back of his head—oy—it was as if someone had taken an ax to it. He reached back to rub it, only to near fall back in dizziness.

He frowned, working to remember. He'd been in the kitchen with the cake and—nothing.

A soft snoring started him, and his eyes grew wide. He reached out and his hand landed on another body. Sol worked to turn his head to the side and gasped. There, sleeping beside him, was...

"Hannah?" he whispered, his throat aching and his voice thin. He touched his neck, movement coming easier now. What had happened? Not that it fully mattered, if it had brought her back to him. Given him another chance at what he knew, in his heart of hearts, was the only thing he wanted.

Her head shot up, and her eyes grew wide. She pushed herself into a sitting position, pressing a hand to her mouth. "Sol." She gasped his name before throwing her arms around him and clutching him to her body.

Her hair was mussed and coming down from its pins at odd angles. Her gown was wrinkled and the circles under her eyes were deeper than ever, but she'd never been quite so beautiful.

"You're awake," she whispered, wonderment in her voice. "You're all right."

"I'm not sure if I'd say that. I'm, well, I'm not sure what I am other than achy." He grimaced.

"You're speaking, though, and breathing and your eyes are open." There was clear relief on her face when she pulled back. "You've been asleep for almost four days. We thought you'd never wake up." Her swallow was visible and there was a catch in her voice, which would never do.

He grasped her hand. "No one can sleep forever, not even the laziest among us. And I'm certainly not lazy." And now he was babbling, but he didn't care. "Especially not when I'm still working to get what I want." *And I want you.* He still did. No matter how things had ended. He always would. And now that he'd been given another chance at living, he was going to use it to try again.

Not try—succeed.

Which meant he needed to fully rally. He cleared his throat, but the coughing turned to rasping, and Hannah drew back in horror, dropping his hand.

"Let me get Doc," she told him, squeezing his shoulder. "She and Rebecca, they've been working so hard, they'll..."

Before he could say anything else, or more, say what needed to be said, she sprang from the bed and jogged out of the room. Sol flopped back down against the pillow, working not to become frustrated.

Especially since he'd just near recovered from his other injuries.

Footfalls pounded on the stairs as Doc and Rebecca burst into the room, rushing to his side and taking hold of different parts of his body to poke and prod. Hannah returned as well, but stayed away from the bed, back to the wall. Much too far from him, but with all the ministrations, he couldn't even signal with his chin, let alone call out and insist—or at least ask—that she come to him once more.

"What do you remember?" Doc asked as she pressed first a hand, then a cloth, to his forehead. "Tell me the last things you remember."

Sol inhaled, pushing back in his memory to recall the events leading up to him being incapacitated, well, yet again. It was good that Hannah didn't seem to expect him to be some sort of warrior-man.

Though it was rather frustrating that he hadn't been able to show the full range of his physical prowess for a while, especially in bed. Something that he would need to rectify, posthaste. After he convinced her that he still wanted her—and proved that it was her and only her, no matter what.

"Mr. Weiss?" Doc gave him a quizzical gaze. He blinked at her before coughing—drat, his ribs. What did she want from—right, what he remembered. He pursed his apparently swollen lips.

"I'd overslept on market day and the house was empty. I had come downstairs to get a bite of food, and well, there was a cake in the window." He grimaced, still feeling a touch guilty. "It was very pretty and obviously for later, but I presumed one small shaving wouldn't harm anyone and then..." He shook his head because everything after was fuzzy.

"And then, you had some sort of—your body behaved rather oddly and you had trouble breathing and swooned. Is that right?" Rebecca asked, peering at him through her spectacles.

Yes. Sol nodded as more memories flooded back. With his elbows, he pushed himself up. "I remember— my body, it was, like you said, odd. Thick and tingly." As parts of it, the tips of his fingers and toes especially, were still behaving strangely.

"Has anything like that happened before?" Rebecca leaned forward. "Have you ever, say, eaten anything and become ill that way?"

"Yes." He craned his neck to check on Hannah as both women were blocking her from view now. He huffed in frustration, but continued on, supposing this was probably relevant to his treatment. "Years ago. My brother's friend, a Spanish fellow who had come to England for school, brought us these spiced nuts." He nodded toward Doc. " 'Peanuts,' I believe. Obviously not particularly common—someone mentioned something about them being from the Americas perhaps? I haven't seen them much since. The first time I ate them I was fine, though I realized later they'd made me itchy, but the second time I had trouble breathing right after. Gave everyone a scare. They've been easy enough to avoid since."

Rebecca nodded. "That's what I suspected, given that mekhasheyfe of a stray cat who's always about snuck in through the window and ravaged the rest of the cake." She pointed a thumb at the door. "I persuaded

Roger Berab—who, of all people, came to see if he could be of assistance—to take the little beast. And hopefully keep him." The woman's lip twitched in what Sol thought might be a smile.

Sol's eyes grew wide. "So the cat was all right?"

"Entirely." Rebecca brushed at her apron. "Nothing amiss at all. If it had been something like rat poison, the cat would've also been ill."

"As it wasn't," Doc added, "I also suspect that the cause was a specific food—in this case, those nuts—that only certain people react to."

"There are foods like that?" Sol frowned. Really? Food was supposed to be food.

"Shellfish is a common one," Rebecca offered. "We all wouldn't know because we don't eat it but there are other foods that make people sick, like strawberries."

"They irritate the body so much that it fights itself, which is what I believe happened to you," Doc explained. "None of us know where the cake came from, and it wasn't on the windowsill before we left. We think it was left by whoever is trying to kill you."

Rebecca turned to Doc. "And nuts can be made into an oil, can't they? It fits, since oil is used in applecake to make it parve..."

"But how would anyone know peanuts would have that effect?" he asked, frowning. "I haven't thought of the incident in years and the only people who were there were our family physician and Frederick's friend." Sol's temples began to thud. "And...both men are long gone." The doctor had passed several years ago, and... hadn't Frederick told him his friend returned abroad or some such?

The women all shared a look, their faces grim.

No. There had to be another explanation.

Because yes, Frederick hadn't been pleased with him of late. Not for some time, to be honest. And yes, his brother was unhappy with his return to the Jewish community, not to mention distrustful of his friendships with Aaron and Roger Berab. And Hannah... she'd tried to tell him, hadn't she? That he'd more than disapproved of her, that he'd warned her off.

But his threats were mere words. Merely a ploy.

His brother could wield smoke and mirrors with the best of them, but he'd never intentionally attack someone. His actions were always in defense. Besides, Frederick was the smart one, the clever one, the planner. But... the marquess's son, Hannah... that was risky.

That was *foolish*.

His throat tightened. Frederick wouldn't. He loved his brother. And Frederick loved him.

After all, Frederick had raised him. Made him who he was. If that wasn't love... *No.* Sol shook his head. It couldn't be Frederick. It couldn't.

Only... all his brother's words from the last few months—god, maybe longer—whirled in his mind. How he'd not been able to make his brother happy, no matter what he tried. How his successes seemed to anger Frederick as much as his failures. How his brother only held disdain for everything Sol was or cared for. Especially his Jewishness.

And how his brother had been imagining his future—without him.

We should invent some sort of fashionable disease for you.

He closed his eyes. *Fuck*. That was the only appropriate word for the situation.

Fuck, fuck, fuck, fuck.

The backs of his eyes burned as he realized the truth. It would never be enough for Frederick—he could never repay him for stealing his youth, never make up for the unfairness his presence had brought. The unforgivable sin of his existence—the yoke that hung around Frederick's neck—would never permit his brother to love him back.

Frederick had never—and would never—love Sol in the way Hannah loved her sister, no matter what he had thought. What she did for Tamar—how she felt, how she loved her sister—there was no debt between them. Hannah thought Tamar deserved the world—it was only herself she did not think worthy of the same.

It was so clear now that he'd bothered to really look, instead of only seeing what he wanted.

But still...to want to kill him?

"Impossible," he muttered, but he knew that it wasn't. It was the only explanation that made sense.

Sol closed his eyes, hating himself and his own incompetence. He was never committed enough, never followed through, never did what needed to be done. Just like his brother always said. Why wasn't he—and he nearly laughed in despair.

His brother always said. Not Isabelle. Not David Berab. Not the ever-judgmental Rebecca Adler and Roger Berab—oy—if ever there were two people who thought highly of their own judgment...he sniffed.

You're brilliant, actually. More than you know.

Hannah's words rang in his ears. Now, that was a touch of an overstatement. If anything, he was closer to merely clever, he was—wait—Hannah—he craned his neck, searching for her. She'd not spoken in a while and—

"Where's Hannah?" he asked. "Where did she go?"

Rebecca and Doc exchanged frowns.

"What?" he asked. The two moved back to reveal an entirely empty room.

"She left several minutes ago," Gertrude shared, appearing in the doorway. "Said you were well taken care of so she wasn't needed anymore, but that we should tell you that she wishes things could've been different. And that you are, and always will be, everything to her, and that she wishes you all the happiness in your life."

His sadness over Frederick turned to supreme annoyance. Could the woman not wait long enough for him to talk to her? Well, he wasn't giving up on them again, and he would show her or tell her or—definitely both. She needed both.

If he could just get to her. He pushed down on the bed to stand, but dizziness quickly overtook him, and he fell back against the pillows, muttering a curse beneath his breath.

Doc and Rebecca made their escape, sliding around Gertrude to exit the room. "We'll get something to dress your wound," Doc called before closing the door behind her with a soft snick.

"Don't you dare do that," Gertrude snapped, crossing to stand in front of him.

"What?" he asked, folding his arms because he was most certainly not in the mood for her scoldings.

"Feel sorry for yourself," she retorted.

He glared. She had to be joking.

"I'm not feeling sorry for myself. I'm sad, I'm hurt, and I'm annoyed. Very annoyed."

He paused.

"And maybe a touch sorry for myself; however, I think I've earned it," he told her with a sniff. "I've been nearly killed twice, my head aches, my body hurts, and everything tingles, but in a very, very bad way."

Sol counted each incident off on his fingers.

"Not to mention the fact that my own brother would like me dead. And given his ambitions, wants the woman I love dead as well, whether we're together or not, whether I'm alive or not. She knows far too much and is far too much of a threat to him." He squeezed the coverlet in frustration. "And naturally, at the moment I need to speak with her most, if not to convince her that she's wrong about us, then to at least warn her regarding my brother, she's run off. Yet again. While I'm, once again, stuck here."

"First, you're healing rather rapidly," Gertrude said. "As for the girl, I'm not sure convincing her that she's wrong will be so difficult." She pointed a finger at him. "She sat with you the whole time, administering remedies in tiny, minuscule drops so as not to choke you. Rubbed your hands and forehead too and talked to you."

She raised an eyebrow at him. "Told you she was sorry and that she loved you."

"I thought that was a dream," Sol murmured as a memory whispered through his mind. "I thought I conjured it and her because I wanted her—that—so badly."

"For now, I would focus your energy on the matter with your brother," Gertrude advised. "That's the most challenging situation, it seems. He's proven himself quite driven and, I fear, has become quite powerful. It would take someone even more powerful, I imagine, to resolve this in a way that will keep you and Miss Moses safe." She folded her arms. "You don't happen to know anyone like that, do you?"

Did he? Isabelle, David, and Roger all had money and influence that stretched outside the Jewish community, but not enough to counter the gentry—or the law for that matter. And Frederick would have the power of both behind him. Especially after he married Lady Drucilla.

Sol frowned as an idea—or more so, a person—popped into his head. Someone who did not care for his brother but was almost certainly going to have to live with him. And thus, might be interested in a way to manage him.

He closed his eyes. Frederick would see it as a clear betrayal. It would most certainly end his relationship with his brother forever. He inhaled slowly.

It didn't matter. Well, it did, but not in the way it should. He had tried, he had done everything, and now it was time to admit that you couldn't make someone love you. That you could only protect those who did, who made you so happy. That you could only love without expecting it in return.

Though he'd need a touch extra proof first. Or at least facts. Which meant for once, he, not Hannah, was the one who'd be gathering information.

Chapter Thirty

After the last customer had left for the night and Tamar had gone to their quarters to start dinner, Hannah locked the cashbox and lugged it into the back room. Like she did every day. Like she would keep doing every day. That was her life. That would always be her life.

Sol deserved better. That was the long and the short of it. And now that he'd recovered, he'd have it. Without her.

And she'd find some way to bear the pain.

"This is the way it has to be," she whispered, wiping away the dust irritating her eyes, making them water. "It was always going to end this way. He's made for better things. He deserves better." She repeated the words again and again as she cleaned and put objects away. If she said them enough, her heart would come to the same realization as her head.

"Bavajadas. And here I thought you were clever," a voice—one that made Hannah's blood thump in her ears—said from the front of the shop.

Heart thudding, Hannah whirled around, only to find a well-dressed elderly woman, supported by a cane topped by a carved bird head, standing in the entryway.

It couldn't be. Panic rose in Hannah's brain as recognition spread through her body. The voice was familiar, as was the form, but what were the chances that—

"It's been a while," the woman said, strolling to the counter. "Ten years, give or take, though the last time, you rudely didn't give me the chance to introduce myself." She gave a small, formal bob, despite her age. "Luckily, you've been more pleasant to my granddaughter, Isabelle."

Isabelle...Isabelle Ellenberg? So this woman—her old enemy from the Jewish Orphan's Home—was... Isabelle's beloved grandmother?

"Don't tell me the cat that is currently terrorizing the Berab household got your tongue." The woman—Mrs. Lira—thumped her cane as if to command Hannah's attention. "Permit me to amend my prior statement, I have never thought you clever, only presumptuous, poorly mannered, bad-tempered, reckless, careless, self-centered, and odiously stubborn. While several of those qualities served you more than hindered you in the interceding years—more than even I believed possible—that's neither here nor there. Nor is whether or not Sol Weiss deserves 'better,' as you say. The man wants to marry you. While I have always found him a touch...much, he's not without quite a few positive qualities. And should not be easily dismissed."

"By the likes of you" was so clearly implied that Hannah rolled her eyes. As if that was not the point. A view this woman certainly shared.

"I know. He's told me as such—multiple times. But the fact he can form the words doesn't make them true," Hannah retorted, unable to help herself even as she searched for the closest exit, even if she was in her own bloody store, as no other good way to rectify the situation came to mind.

Isabelle's grandmother, however, did not appear to be listening. Instead, she'd rounded the counter and was now yanking out the stool her sister kept beneath it.

"Don't you love him?" she asked as she hoisted herself up so she could sit. She wagged her finger at Hannah. "I have it on good authority that he loves you. And given that you both—"

"Love is not enough to overcome reality. Overcome the world in which we live," Hannah argued back. "That sort of thing only happens in the storybooks Tamar favors." And even in those, such endings rarely occurred for Jews. Especially not the bad ones, like her.

"Ah yes, Tamar. How old is she now?" Mrs. Lira asked, glancing around. "You don't have any tea, do you?"

Hannah gaped. She had to be joking.

"We have coffee. But it's almost certainly cold at this hour," she finally said. "And it's upstairs."

"Provided it's properly strong, I take it with sugar." The other woman waved her hand. As if she'd actually been offered the beverage.

They stared at each other for a long moment, and yet, several minutes later, Hannah found herself—after a hasty conversation with Tamar—returning down the stairs with the woman's request.

"Tamar is twenty now," Hannah said as she handed Mrs. Lira the rather plain, but thankfully not chipped, teacup she'd selected. "But you know that."

"Yes...an interesting age. It's funny, I remember it better now at seventy than I did at sixty." The older woman's voice was prim. She took a sip of her drink before placing it on the counter and returning her gaze to Hannah.

"If you think I'm going to apologize for my words the last time we met, you, as you say, are out of your head," she declared. "You made bad choices then and I have it on good authority that you make plenty of them now."

Hannah's spine stiffened before she folded her arms and grumbled, "Tell me something I don't know." She tucked a stray lock of hair behind her ear.

"Guay de mi, you have the worst manners. I haven't finished," the woman said before sighing. "I'll admit that, at the time, I didn't look at all the angles. Something quite unlike me." She gave a rueful smile. "Your sister is your only family, correct?"

Hannah frowned. "Yes, she's all I have left," she said slowly, searching for the trick in the question. "And while I might not be the sort of woman someone like Sol Weiss marries, Tamar is. She's the sort of woman any man from the community would be proud to marry." She ground her teeth. "I made sure of it."

"Yes, you created the space to permit her that life. Made providing for her and her future your primary role," the older woman said with a nod. She took another sip of what was, at best, lukewarm coffee. "You know, my late husband had a specific role in his family."

There was a long pause. Hannah glanced up to meet Mrs. Lira's stern gaze.

Oh, for fuck's sake. If this woman thought she was going to perform some sort of deferential, goyishe… though if she ever wanted the woman to leave… Hannah ground her teeth but forced herself to respond.

"Yes?" she asked, with as much politeness as she could muster.

"Look at you, learning manners so quickly. I should have visited earlier." Mrs. Lira pressed her gloved hands together in faux applause. She took another sip of coffee before resuming. "Indeed. He was the oldest son of the head of the Jewish Council back in Livor—Leghorn—and was expected to take on his father's role, after marrying the wealthy and beautiful daughter of one of his father's most important allies."

"What happened to her?" she muttered reluctantly, even if the question was most certainly not polite. As even if, at seventy, Mrs. Lira was breathtakingly stunning in a way she could never dream of.

"How do you know he didn't marry who he was supposed to?" Mrs. Lira asked, raising both brows.

Hannah's cheeks heated. "I—"

"I'm toying with you, dear," the woman said with a sniff. "You should be flattered. If I didn't think you were formidable enough, I'd have treated you like a simpleton instead."

She shifted in her seat. "Anyway, as you correctly guessed, I was what happened to all those plans and expectations. And while I was the prettier option, it was more than that. My husband was meant for a different life and just needed the right motivation to guide him down that path. Moreover, there was someone better suited to the role to which he was assigned." She raised a finger. "His youngest brother, who no one saw in that light, is currently the head and—well, the rest is, as they say, history."

"And what does this have to do with me?" Hannah asked, glancing at the clock on the mantel. It was nearly midnight.

The woman rolled her eyes. "You're a smart girl. You

know the Torah stories," she said. "Birth is not destiny. And expectations and assumptions can be changed."

Oy. Had Mrs. Lira's mind started to go? She was no Jacob or Joshua or Moses or whatever this woman was implying.

"Not when there is truth to the assumptions," she countered.

"If you truly believed that our bad choices define our character for all time, then why even bother attending services on Yom Kippur?" Mrs. Lira asked. "And don't deny that you appear each year. As well as on all the other holidays. Just because you stick to the shadows doesn't mean you don't count."

If it were only so simple. Hannah shook her head. "But even if I make better choices," she started, "there will still be people who will never forget, never forgive, never—"

"I never said it would be easy. Or even successful, but it would be a shame not to even try." Finishing the last bit of coffee, she set down her cup. "Especially when assistance is being offered." She gave Hannah a pointed glance.

Wait. Was the woman suggesting that *she* would assist her in convincing London that Hannah, of all people, was the right sort of Jew? Like some sort of… she bit her lip… what was that other goyishe book Tamar had her read? *Emma*?

And how well had that woman's misguided guidance turned out? She shook her head. "It'll never work."

"Not if you don't try," Mrs. Lira said, thankfully rising from the stool and grabbing her cane. "And certainly not if you keep insulting the very people you want to accept you when they're attempting to help." She gave her another glare.

As if she wasn't saving the woman time and embarrassment by refusing.

Hannah shook her head again. "It won't be enough. Not for everyone. Not for most people." Because even if certain people, like the Liras and Berab, could, at times, afford to take certain risks, most people couldn't. And given her background, the price of association might be too steep even for them. And that was only the Jews. She sighed. "Especially not the goyim. And when I fail, it'll hurt him in multiple ways, and I can't stand—"

"You do realize that while Mr. Weiss is a man, he's still an adult, with his own mind," the woman interrupted. "A rather clever one, at that. Would it not be prudent to, after humoring me so I don't complain about both of you to everyone who'll listen, permit him to decide?"

She pursed her lips. "And doesn't he also deserve your best efforts, to at least try and fail, instead of quitting before you've started? Wouldn't that be the action worthy of him and his love? Unless you're too afraid," she added, sounding very much like her granddaughter.

Mrs. Lira was right, not that Hannah would ever admit it.

She was also so, so, so damned scared. But Sol did deserve to be fought for.

"You should do it."

It was her sister who said the words, standing in the shadows near the stairs. She strolled over to Hannah and gave her a kiss on the cheek, before turning to Mrs. Lira. "Take her to your home. She needs a break from the store." She wrapped an arm around Hannah's waist and squeezed. "It'll be fine. Please be brave and take this gift. Please. I believe in you. More so, I want you to live for *you*."

She gazed at her sister's large, pleading eyes. The ones she truly couldn't ever say no to.

Besides, even if it was all for naught, she was already in so much pain from missing him—this could not hurt her more.

Swallowing, she turned back to Mrs. Lira. "All right," she said before raising a finger. "But just for a few days."

"Excellent." Mrs. Lira gave them a bright, still beautiful smile, before snapping her fingers in Hannah's direction. "Come along, dear," she said, threading her free arm in hers.

Now? Hannah gestured to the staircase. "Shouldn't I pack some—"

"Not unless you want them burned," Mrs. Lira said, guiding her outside.

Oy. What exactly had she gotten herself into?

Chapter Thirty-One

It was two evenings later when Sol finally strode into this—no, his brother's, it had always been his brother's—town house, armed only with the information given to him by the Viscount Penrose. And surprisingly, Roger Berab.

He sighed as he entered the house in which he'd been born for probably the last time. The swelling on his face was better, though not completely gone; thankfully, the blotches weren't as noticeable. And while he was wearing a borrowed waistcoat and cravat, they were a rather welcome change from his sick clothes.

And fitted enough to give him the confidence he needed now.

Aaron walked behind him. He'd wanted to go alone, but his friend had been convinced that he needed at least a little assistance, especially as he was still a touch shaky on his feet, despite drinking more of Doc and Rebecca's concoctions than he thought his stomach could hold.

"Hello, Martin," he said to the butler, who had most likely known of, if not outright assisted in, what now was apparent had been many attempts on his life, "Is my brother home?" Without waiting for an answer, he strode into the front parlor. "Tell him I've arrived, and we need to meet straightaway." Sol turned to Aaron. "Why don't you wait for me here?"

His friend gave a quick nod. "Call for me if you need anything."

With a nod of his own, Sol hobbled down the corridor and into his brother's office, settling himself down on a wide chaise across from one of the more ornate gilded mirrors. He glanced at himself and grimaced. Blast, his jaw had always been a touch large, but with the continued swelling, it was gigantic.

Actually, this gave him a pugnacious appearance, which wasn't the worst look, all things considered.

"Sol." His brother's voice from the door startled him.

"Surprised to see me alive, Frederick?" Sol rose in greeting.

"No—I mean, yes, I mean, I was so worried about you. Are you all right?" Frederick asked, brushing into the room and taking a seat on the other side of his desk, not even making an attempt to touch him. Sol worked to keep at bay the rage and hurt and, well, disappointment that pumped through his veins.

"I'm fine. A bit worse for the wear." He gestured up and down his body. "But nothing time won't heal. Luckily, I did manage to secure a new client for the surety company. Apparently, despite my absence, they are still rather pleased with my work and want to keep me in their employ."

Something David and Isabelle had taken care to assure him of, despite the actions he would be taking starting today.

"Well, I wish you could have done more for our bank." Frederick glared from behind his spectacles. "Your focus has been, let's say, lacking as of late."

You don't say. Sol sighed to himself, for once rather tired of the thinly veiled criticism even as its now obvious falseness amused him. He coughed to cover a harsh laugh, jabbing his own fist into his chest. "I apologize, but I'm sure the bank will be much more stable in the future." He crossed his legs. "Congratulations are in order, I hear."

"Yes, Lady Drucilla and I were married this morning." This time when Frederick smiled, it was a real one.

Sol's heart squeezed, not just because he'd missed the event, but because the love there was genuine. And the idea that he'd not be able to share in the joy, when he would have done anything and everything in his power to help bring it about...

"Mazel tov," he managed as brightly and sincerely as he could because, despite everything, a part of him was glad for Frederick. His brother had worked so hard and had sacrificed so much to be with Lady Drucilla and a part of her world that he deserved at least congratulations.

His brother's smile fell. "I hope you haven't been using that language outside the house. I would have thought I had taught you better."

Sol winced. Well, that was his cue. It was time to end the polite conversation.

"Or maybe you taught me just enough." Sol tented his hands. "I had another look at the books for the bank, which made a great deal more sense after I visited Father's solicitor thanks to Roger Berab's suggestion."

"My, my, you've been busy," his brother said, his voice calm—but his right eye twitched.

"Busier than you think," Sol told him. "I'm now privy to quite a bit of information, including Lady

Drucilla's debt and that trust you've been skimming from." His fists clenched. "Why didn't you just ask me for the money? I would've given it to you, plus my share of the bank, if only you had asked."

"I highly doubt it." Frederick sniffed. "I know how you'd have viewed her and the situation."

No—that was only how Frederick would have viewed the situation, had it been Sol coming to him.

"Do you? Do you truly think I would've judged her—for what her first husband did? Or more, denied you the help because of it? That I'm so greedy, I would have allowed you to suffer to, what, indulge my own material tastes?" He adjusted the lapel of the borrowed jacket. "Did you believe that I love you so little?"

Frederick waved a hand at him. "Stop being melodramatic, Sol."

"I wish I was." He sighed. He wished that so very much.

"It's admirable. How much you love Lady Drucilla. How much you were willing to do for her. You'd worked so hard—spent nearly half your life paying off our father's debts, only to start paying them for someone else anew." He leveled his best disappointed gaze at Frederick—after all, he'd learned from the finest—and added, "I know, Frederick. I know."

For a moment, he believed his brother would continue to deny it, but instead, his shoulders slumped.

"I had to." Frederick jabbed a finger in his direction. "If I didn't prove to Drucilla that I could be a good husband—the husband she needed—she'd have chosen Stoudmire. He's the one her brother wanted. He could more than afford to both pay the debt and fund her charities, without needing to prove his money wasn't tainted. He has good blood—a father and brother with titles. All I have is *you*." He near spit the word, resentment dripping from his lips. "Perhaps if you had converted, spent more time learning how to behave properly instead of wallowing even further in the habits of your mother, I might have trusted you to help. But it was clear I couldn't."

He crossed his arms. "And what I did? Was it so wrong? Stoudmire is still alive. But if not for his absence, Penrose would have thwarted me."

"I don't doubt that." Or more, the man had said as much. Which made the fact that the banns had already been posted at the time of their chat rather convenient, at least for Sol, as it had bound the viscount to their side. "Trouble is, what you did was still a crime. One you could be imprisoned for. Or worse."

"Every person I hired can be controlled. Easily," his brother said with a coldness that he'd never heard before. Or never paid enough attention to notice. "If not, there are other ways. I have enough information on each of them that if one was to point the authorities in the proper direction... well, they'd regret it."

Sol gaped at his brother. "You may not think highly of the people you hired, but they're still people. No worse than either of us. Or Penrose or Drucilla. I thought you still knew that, still understood that." At least he'd hoped so, deep down. That even with all the rest, his brother was at least a shadow of the man he'd believed him to be.

"It's not—I wasn't the one who told them to commit their crimes—without me, they were always two steps away from a hang—it's different. They always knew the—" His brother lifted his chin. "There are some people the world is better off without."

And it took everything in him not to take a swing at the man Sol had loved with all his heart. Instead, Sol willed matching ice into his gaze and tone. "Like me, apparently."

"I had no choice. You insisted on staying with those... people...ones who can only hold us back. Then I needed the trust in full. More than *you* ever did." His brother leaned back against his chair, knitting his fingers together. "We're too far apart now, Solomon. We can no longer understand each other. And thus, to save what we had, I thought it might be better if we ended things with only good memories."

Sol stared at his brother a long moment, trying to comprehend what he had heard. He thought he might be sick again, but no, it was merely his heart that hurt. He shook his head in disappointment.

"I'll always love you, Frederick, but I think you're wrong. I understand you perfectly. It took me a long time to get here, but it's all clear now." He shrugged. "Oddly enough, everything about you has been clear to Penrose for a while."

"The viscount?" His brother's eyes grew wide at the mention of his brother-in-law. He leaned forward in his seat. "What have you done? What did you tell him?" The mirrors surrounding them reflected Frederick's horror tenfold. Rage flew over his countenance and he stood, leaning over the desk. "This is why I never trusted you. You're not smart enough to understand all the consequences your—"

"Funny that," Sol said. "Most people seem to think I understand things just fine." He shrugged then relaxed back in his chair as if he hadn't a care in the world.

"And my recent plans have served me, my health,

and the health of those I love a great deal better than anything you've done in quite a while." He lifted his chin. "As for Penrose, I didn't tell him anything he didn't already know. I merely paid him a visit."

Sol leaned forward again. "You see, I was, well, I had denied the truth for quite a while, but he had not. While I loved you—still love you, for that matter—he also loves his sister very much and paid close attention to her situation. In the past and now. He has quite a lot of information. Enough to either protect you or, if necessary, force you to hang."

"Not without the others," Frederick sputtered. "Including the little criminal that you can't seem to stop fucking. If I hang, so does she." He glared at Sol. "I will point to her as my accomplice in the attack on Stoudmire."

He paused then cocked his head and retook his seat. "Though, considering your behavior today, perhaps I'll just take care of her now. I have information already on a little burglary she assisted in recently. The Crown would love to settle the grumbling in the streets with a good hanging. Especially of the worst sort of Jew. The ones you all would've gotten rid of yourself, if you were truly civilized."

Sol closed his eyes, hating how much his brother was proving right every terrible possibility Roger Berab had raised when he'd gone to him for advice before his discussion with Penrose.

"We anticipated you might say that." Sol forced his voice and body to hold steady. "And while it's true that the viscount doesn't care very much about what happens to Hannah, I do. So I struck a bargain with him that, in the end, benefits both of you. Ties your fates together even tighter, actually."

"What?" His brother whipped off his spectacles and stared at him. "What did you do?"

Saved us all. Not that his brother would truly see it that way, but perhaps in time. Sol's ribs ached. No, he couldn't—he just had to keep going.

"You're going to do whatever Penrose says, Frederick, which means staying out of trouble—including no more attempts on anyone's life. Perhaps you'll start with a long honeymoon on the Continent." He raised a single finger. "However, if you do break your word, he'll see that you're dealt with as he sees fit. And as you know, the gentry has many ways to take care of dangerous relatives without involving the law, so I'd watch your step."

"And that's that?" his brother asked, squinting.

"Not quite. That was the original offer. And while I liked the viscount's plan, I didn't think it adequately protected Hannah." He shifted his ankle. Mercy, he was really going to need to be careful as that healed. "Both you and I are going to be selling the bank."

Frederick blinked at him.

"Don't worry, it's for a fair price. And it's not as if you'll need the income. Lady Drucilla's family will see that you both are cared for and live in a lifestyle that suits her. The initial proceeds will pay off her remaining debts and then be used to make sure neither Stoudmire's family nor anyone on the street ever speaks of this matter again. The victim of that burglary you keep using as a threat will also be made whole in exchange for his agreement to never prosecute." He knitted his fingers. "Any leftover proceeds shall go into a trust for your wife's exclusive benefit."

His brother opened and closed his mouth, but for the

first time Sol could remember, appeared to have been rendered speechless.

"In addition, I'm giving you my inheritance—well, I'm giving it to your wife," Sol continued. "Just as you wanted." He couldn't help if the words were a touch bitter. "I can do perfectly fine without it." Glady and freely. And possibly better than he ever had been before.

Frederick sniffed.

"Even if I can't, being here, in this world, as you've demonstrated, comes at much too high a cost and I shall be happy to be rid of it and the poison it oozes." He smiled grimly. "This is the money's best use. After all, giving it to Lady Drucilla is what bought Hannah and her sister's freedom and protection. So for that I'm quite willing to live only on my salary from the surety company."

"You won't last a week without your fancy boots and fine linens and the connections that I bring you," his brother scoffed.

This time Sol did laugh because after everything he'd been through . . .

"I think I lasted for almost two so far, actually," he said. "And I'm ready to last a lifetime." He rose. "Goodbye, Frederick. I wish you and Lady Drucilla well. I do truly want you to be happy—I always did. I regret that I can't be a part of it, but I do . . . Take care of your wife, love her, and I'm sure everything will turn out fine."

Before his brother could say anything more, he marched into the hall, refusing to look back—only to run into Aaron, whose arms were laden with trunks and bags.

"I thought I told you to stay in the foyer," he said, eyeing the load before grabbing two pieces, only teetering a little at the weight.

"The staff took the liberty of helping me pack up your room," Aaron said, panting. "Isabelle might pay you decently, but your wardrobe has been an asset to your position, and it would be a shame to leave it behind. I know with the decision you're making regarding Miss Moses, it's highly unlikely you'll ever be made partner—though David was rather impressed with your plan to drum up business from less respectable gentile institutions—"

"Gaming hells need to plan for losses too," Sol pointed out. "There are fires and fights and who knows when the Crown will change various rules."

His friend smiled. "My wife does know who to hire. Anyway, since you've rented your own home, you might as well have some comforts."

Which was a very kind thought. And while it didn't soften the blow of Frederick's betrayal, it would be nice to hold on to some of his things. Especially as he worked out running a household and budgeting, for the first time ever.

"Fair enough," Sol said with a nod.

"Ready to leave?" Aaron asked, indicating the front door with his elbow.

Sol glanced around the house he'd lived in all of his life, expecting to feel regret or guilt or sadness, but all he felt was... excited. And hopeful. Provided he figured out what to do about Hannah.

He turned to Aaron and grinned. "Yes. Very much."

Chapter Thirty-Two

Hannah stood in the guest bedroom at the Lira family town house, staring at the mirror at her borrowed gown, a beautiful navy with bold yellow threaded through it. Isabelle's maid, a woman named Judith, had futzed with her hair, making it, well, appear a great deal thicker and shinier than it was.

She looked...different. Perhaps pretty, even. And not just for her age. No, prettier than she'd probably been at twenty.

She should be happy. Though she still needed additional work on her manners—not to mention her dancing so she could be properly presentable to gentiles before they threw her out of their homes—Mrs. Lira had given her a priceless gift in celebration of her progress.

Tamar was going to have the opportunity to explore futures besides marriage and working in a pawnshop. She and Isabelle were already plotting, looking to place her in a temporary position as a nurse with an influential Jewish family, which would no doubt be wonderful. With an entire new wardrobe to bring along.

However, there was still the matter of Sol. She'd not spoken to him since she'd left his bedside once it was clear he would recover. And while Mrs. Lira had not so subtly noodged her to call on him—several times—she'd not quite worked up the courage.

What exactly could she say? Especially after the way they'd left things.

A noise at the window made her jump, and Hannah rushed across the room to peer over the sill. For a moment she could only gape. There, clinging on to the building for dear life, was Sol. Dressed in what looked like dark velvet, but without the proper overcoat for the fleetly falling December snow that was drifting over his bare knuckles.

"What are you doing out there?" she called.

"Climbing into your window, if you couldn't tell." He glanced up at her and grinned, as if he weren't completely freezing and slippery and likely cutting up his hands, as if he needed more injuries.

Which she should really warn him about. However, when she opened her mouth, all she said was, "How did you know it was my window?"

"Aaron told me," he said, as if it were obvious, as if this was something men just regularly discussed, where different guests slept and the like.

"If Aaron told you and the family knows you're here, why didn't you just come in the front door?" she asked, because they would have certainly allowed him in and then, well, called her down to the parlor or something if he wanted to see her. "They believe in etiquette and propriety, but not so much that it results in death."

"I'm not going to die." He rolled his eyes. "You've climbed in my window several times, so I figured it was my turn." He shrugged as if that made sense, only to sway in the wind enough for her to gasp again.

"I'm quite secure," he assured her.

It was her turn to roll her eyes.

"You're dangling. And I only climbed through your window in Aldgate." She placed a hand on her hip. "It was a much shorter height and there was a trough and a few crates and... are you climbing a lattice?" She squinted down again through the squall, which was now picking up. "You know those aren't intended to hold people, correct? And you aren't a small man."

Not small in the slightest, and it was one of the things she enjoyed most about him, especially given how tall she was. While he was more average in height, his broadness balanced things and... she licked her lips before shaking her head. What was she doing?

"Yes, I've noticed," he responded with another smirk, as if reading her thoughts. Which should embarrass her but instead filled her with heat. Though she was still concerned for his damned safety, even if he apparently was not.

"Don't forget you're injured." She gestured to his body.

"My ankle is feeling much better, actually. As are my face and my tongue." He stuck out the latter, catching a snowflake with a grin.

"Clearly not your head." She sniffed.

"I promise you, my brain and my thought processes are just fine," he said. "Better than fine. Spectacular even."

"So you say." She rolled her eyes once more, staring down at him with a smile. The wind gusted again and she shivered.

Sol tightened his hold and grimaced. "Can I, um, have a—well, just a smidge of assistance?" he asked. "I could do it myself, but perhaps, to save us some time..."

Oy, right. He should come inside, appropriate or not, because she could not let him fall.

"Oh, yes, certainly." Hannah bent over as far as she could, while keeping her hips firmly below the edge of the sill, and extended both arms to him. He grasped them and she pulled, as he climbed from below, using her more for leverage than anything else.

"Thank you," he panted as he swung his legs over the side of the window and squeezed into the room. He rose and brushed off his garments, straightening his shirt. "Here I was attempting to rescue a damsel in a tower..."

"And she had to rescue you instead." Hannah snickered as she beckoned him to stand closer to the fire. "Though as I told you before, I'm no damsel."

"True. But can you at least humor me and pretend I'm knight-like?" He rubbed his hands together in front of the flames. "And as for the rescue, why don't we call it mutual?"

"I suppose. Though I'm not sure I want to be rescued per se." She waved around at the rather posh quarters. "After all, I do have a very nice tub in here."

Sol gave her a rather serious nod. "I'm not sure I can compete with that."

"Can't you?" she asked, biting her lip. After all, the last time she'd checked, his room was ten times the size of this one and his tub was quite large.

"Well, I do have a tub, though it isn't quite as fancy." He placed his hands in his jacket pockets. "It was one of the few luxuries I insisted on in my new house."

"New house?" Hannah squinted at him. Since when had that happened?

"I'm in Aldgate, near Doc and Gertrude and the

other ladies actually," he told her. "I'm renting right now, but I hope to buy in the future, provided the Crown continues to permit it." He ducked his head, rubbing the back of his neck. "It's rather empty and I do need some help setting it up as I've never quite done that by myself. Budgeting too, since I'm only living on my salary from the surety company."

She gaped at him. "What happened?"

"I gave up the rest. Gave it to Frederick's wife. I made a bargain with the Viscount Penrose, you see. It was a small price to pay to make sure no one, especially not my brother, tries to kill either of us again." He gave her a rather cryptic smile before his eyes turned serious. "He was not the man I thought him to be."

Her stomach twisted at the pain in his eyes. She'd give anything to take that away. She shook her head, her voice catching. "Sol, I'm . . . I mean, I'm so sorry."

And she was. While she had no great love for the man who'd threatened her, it was clear Sol had loved him—still loved him, from the look on his face—and he was his family. That sort of betrayal could only be devastating.

"It wasn't your fault." Sol shrugged. "I was so consumed with this image of my brother, of him being the person I wanted him to be—actually, in a way we both were. We both wanted each other to be something we weren't, or couldn't be. He wanted the image of love and loyalty, but all he saw was the reflection."

Her eyes welled, because it wasn't fair. He deserved better, so much better.

"What's wrong?" he asked, moving toward her. He reached out and took both her hands in his. A gesture she also didn't deserve.

She shook her head. "It's...it's that you are so open and so loving and so loyal and you give so much but—you deserved for him to love you and I...I do love you, but I withheld the words because I was frightened—frightened of your realizing that I'm not enough, that my love isn't enough and that was unfair. You're so brave and I'm such a coward that I insisted you didn't know your own mind. I thought I was protecting us both but was really only hurting us."

He clucked his tongue. "Well, this is a mess."

"What?" she asked, blinking back at him.

He released one of her hands, gesturing around the room. "This wasn't my plan. I'm supposed to rescue you from a metaphoric tower, tell you of my triumphs in battle, like a good knight, and properly propose marriage. And maybe, hopefully, you'll permit me to take you up against a wall or in the room that I want to have furnished but now only has a bit of bedding on the floor and my trunks." He retook her hand and squeezed.

"Your trunks?" She wrinkled her nose.

"You think I would have left my garments behind? Never. As I said, some luxuries are necessary." He stepped back, spreading his arms wide and gazing over her body with that hungry expression that always undid her. "Like that gown on you. Is it Isabelle's? Do you think she'll let me buy it for you?" His voice came out a bit strangled, as if he truly did like it. As if he still wanted her.

"Just beautiful," he whispered. "You should have a dozen like that."

"You can't afford a dozen," she managed to say. Which was probably true. After all, how much could the Lira and Berab families really pay him? And even if he did have some items of value in the trunks, it took quite a bit of money to start a household and—

"Yet." He held up a finger. "I know it won't come as easily as planned, or perhaps not even at all, but that doesn't matter. No amount of money or status or respect could replace you. And having any of the above without you to share them with would be meaningless and empty." He shook his head. "You said I'd grow to resent you if you stayed, but it's the opposite. Without you, nothing in my life seems to have worth. So I intend to make you mine. And to do whatever it takes to make you feel happy and loved, because I love you very much too."

He pulled her against his body and cupped her chin. "I was wrong to have even considered you might be right. That I would be happy any other way. I won't. I should have found the words to explain this to you weeks ago. And I promise, if you have me, while I won't not make mistakes—I'm far from perfect—I'll do my best to make as few of them as possible where you're concerned. And to keep you safe and love you with all my heart." He bit his lip. "Would you accept that?"

"Yes, Sol. Very much, yes." She nodded, on the verge of tears, and this time, she didn't even care. "But I don't deserve—"

"Shh." He bent down and brushed her lips with his, halting her protest and making her melt. Then he pulled back and stared down at her, his eyes serious once more.

"The one thing I ask is you never say that about yourself, ever again. No one makes all the right choices, and no one can stand alone. We just do the best we can in the world in which we're placed." He gripped her hands again. "You're a wonderful sister, a wonderful daughter, a wonderful person, and if anyone says otherwise—including you—well, they should be careful as I have friends in high places." He smirked.

"I love you, Hannah. Being with you makes me happy and there is no one else with whom I'd rather build a life. So will you let me rescue you?"

She brushed her lips against his before pulling back. "As long as we can use the front door, yes. And so long as you'll take my rather paltry dowry to help with expenses. I do have one, apparently, as my sister decided that she'll only accept half of what I intended for her."

She smiled a little to herself before gazing back at him, happiness glowing within her. "I love you too, Sol. With you, no matter where, I'll be happy forever, I know it."

He pulled her into him, embracing her fully. "So long as we're together, we can make all our dreams come true."

Epilogue

October 3, 1836
Aldgate, London, England

It was near midnight. Far too late for respectable people to be awake. But Hannah Moses, now Hannah Weiss, was not and would never be respectable. Not for the gentiles, or any part of the Jewish community. Including her own. A fact that bothered her a great deal less than it used to.

It helped that when she attended services, she no longer looked at the spot where her family's plaque used to be. Perhaps one day she and Sol would donate the money for another one. Perhaps not. But these days, she found it difficult to muster even the mildest consternation.

Same for the gossips' whispers and stares. Which had become considerably less accusatory in nature.

It didn't hurt that someone—Rebecca, Isabelle, Gertrude, Doc, Bayla, or some combination of the five—always sat with her. Useful as the stairs to and from the synagogue's balcony were a touch narrow and winding. Especially for someone as close to birthing her second child as she was.

Luckily, three-year-old Moses Weiss was so enthralled with the procession in the main part of the sanctuary—the swirling march of Torahs, with their silver crowns and polished and gleaming plates, flanked by flags—that he'd not even noticed she wasn't with them, let alone not the one carrying him. Not that she could blame him. His father was certainly enthralling.

And in her humble opinion, the handsomest man ever to celebrate Simchat Torah in all of England, let alone London.

She'd watched Sol clap and sing through each of the hakafot, even if he was still a touch shaky with the Hebrew, tallis pulled over his head, Moses bouncing on his shoulders. And when he leaned forward and encouraged their son to kiss each Torah—well, someone had to hand her a handkerchief.

It had been quite a night. But it was late, and services would be early the next morning. She washed behind Moses's ears before slipping his nightshirt over his head and leading him over to his bed, which was far too large for a three-year-old.

He'll grow into it, Sol had said when the workmen carried it into the room across from theirs in the house they still rented, though hopefully not for too many more years. Their friends gave generous wedding gifts. And baby gifts. And bonuses.

And while he would probably never have his name on the door at the sureties company, Sol had proven himself a valuable asset, both behind the scenes and in bringing in clients, the sort whose businesses were often overlooked but still turned a profit. And who liked the idea of "peace of mind." Especially how Sol sold it.

"Come on, Moses, hop on up." Hannah patted the brocade quilt before placing her hand on her hip.

"Not...tired, Mama." Blinking his large, dark brown eyes that were so much like his handsome father's, Moses shook his head and yawned.

"Naturally," Hannah said as she took her son's soft little hand and helped him climb up. "We're creatures of the night, and thus it's quite early for us."

"I want another apple," Moses told her, but he lay his head against his pillow, dark brown waves flopping on his forehead, and allowed her to cover him up with the bedding.

"How many did you catch?" she asked, smiling to herself. That had always been her favorite part of the holiday. How when the processions ended, the children were all gathered and the community leaders threw bushels of apples to them as treats. Moses, on Sol's shoulders, had been a formidable hunter.

"This many," he told her, holding up two rather adorable fingers.

"And your father?" she asked as she seemed to recall him munching on at least three.

"I caught five."

Hannah turned around to find the man himself leaning in the doorway, arms crossed, jacketless, his shirt half unbuttoned, dark chest hair tempting her. Much more delicious than any fruit. She raised a brow. "And have eaten..."

"Only two. Our son has had three and there are two left." He strolled into the room to stand next to her. "Come along, Moses, let's hear your Shema," he said, reaching over and running his hand through the little boy's hair.

"Cover your eyes, Papa," their son said, his hand already over his own.

"Thank you for reminding me," Sol said, equally serious. He placed one hand around Hannah's waist, before placing the other over his eyes. Hannah did the same, and the three of them recited the words together, each at their own slightly off-key pitch, Hannah continuing through the full paragraph to the end, even as Moses started to softly snore.

"Is he..." Sol whispered against her ear.

"He is," she said as she snuggled beneath her husband's arm and stared at the absolutely breathtaking sight she once could never have imagined existing but now could not imagine living without. She patted her stomach. So much joy. Even if she still wasn't sure she deserved it, she was damned well never letting it go.

"Excellent," he told her before swiping his tongue over the edge of her ear, making her toes curl. "Because it's time for you to come to the bedroom too, my lovely creature of the night." He thread his fingers through hers and lead them toward their chamber.

"Most certainly," she more yawned than said. Oy, perhaps she was not quite as nightly as she'd once been.

"Keep those eyes open a little longer if you can," he said.

"Sol..." she started before yawning again. Their bed was quite nice. Almost as nice as Moses's. And so warm...especially by the fire.

"It'll be worth it," he assured her, squeezing her hand. "Though, of course, I'm always worth it." He kissed her on the head and pushed open the door.

At that, she couldn't stop smiling. "Yes, you are."

Sol laughed. "You must be quite tired if you're not serving me a quip now."

"Just wait. When the baby is born, they'll come back to me." Hannah snickered a little and patted her stomach before glancing up at her husband with a wink. "I'm hoping whatever you have planned might involve your hands in certain places…"

"That can definitely be arranged," he told her, trailing his fingers against her side before tipping his chin toward their room. "Shortly." He squeezed her hip as she glanced inside, her eyes falling on—her mouth dropped open.

"Is that…" she whispered, moving away from Sol and toward the largest tub she'd ever seen, filled with steaming water and—she sniffed—oils. Jasmine oils. She ran a finger along the side.

Gorgeous, absolutely gorgeous. Not that their original tub hadn't been completely lovely, but…

Sol came up behind her and placed his chin on her shoulder. "I felt the other one would be useful for our children and thus we might want one for just us," he said.

"How did you…" she whispered, barely believing it was real.

"I received a bonus for a few recent clients," he said. "It's big enough for two." He wrapped his now completely bared arms around her.

"I can see," she said before whirling around and starting. "How are you already undressed?"

"I'm a man of many talents." He bent to take her lips. "Turn around," he whispered again. "Let me assist you." His hands were already undoing her laces. "So the water stays nice and hot." He slid her gown off her shoulders, then her short stays, leaving her in just her chemise, her nipples already hard and tight.

Something he must have noticed as in an instant his hands were on her breasts, teasing them through the fabric. Hannah moaned and rocked back against him.

"I thought we were going to wait until the tub," she managed to say as he slipped the garment down off her hips and moved his large hands over her skin, lower and lower...and...she gasped.

"Who in the world said that?" He nipped her ear once more. "I certainly didn't." He kissed her again, making her near lose her blasted mind.

"If I trip and you can't get me off the floor..." she huffed.

"Relax, I have you." He wrapped an arm around her body, holding her for a moment before sliding away. "Now, let me get in first..."

He stepped into the tub and sat down. "Here, take my hand." He reached and gave her that absolutely irresistible smile.

"All right..."

"There we go," he whispered as he settled her against him, wrapping his legs around her. He leaned forward and kissed her neck. "Perfect."

She leaned into him. "It absolutely is."

Because it was. No matter what the future held, this was more than she could ever have imagined and she was going to damn well savor it as much as she could. Like her parents had taught her. For better or worse.

Sol brought her hand to his lips and kissed her knuckles.

"I love you," her husband told her, holding her tight. "You're all my dreams come true."

Tears streamed down Hannah's cheeks. She swiped a hand over her eyes as her throat tightened.

Blasted pregnancy.

But she was never going to fail at saying the words her husband needed to hear again. Unless her mouth was otherwise occupied, that is.

"I love too, Sol." She took his hand and kissed it right back. "Forever."

Acknowledgments

Writing is hard and publishing is harder. It takes a ton of professionals and supporters and colleagues and cheerleaders to create the magic and I have been so lucky to have the best of all of that in my life.

Thank you to my incredible agent, Becca Podos, without whom I could not competently function in this industry by any stretch of the imagination. You keep me as sane as I can possibly be and help me focus on what's important. No one has more patience. You are incredible, and none of this would happen without you.

Thank you to Sam Brody, the most amazing editor anyone could ask for, who works tirelessly to make my overwriting and overplotting turn into something wonderful. The work is so much better with you and your talents, and I'm so grateful.

Thank you to copyeditor extraordinaire Joan Matthews for painstaking, careful, excellent work. And surviving all my writing tics. Thank you to Dana Cuadrado for all her fantastic marketing and for working so hard to make sure this book got into the hands of readers who (hopefully) enjoyed it. Thank you to everyone who worked on the cover: amazing art director Daniela Medina, cover artist Aleta Rafton, fabulous photographer David Wagner, and the best cover models ever, Aurelia Scheppers and Elijah Van Zanten. It is amazing.

Thank you to all the wonderful writers and beta readers from all the communities I am so lucky to be included in, especially Romance Shmooze and Jewish Women Talk About Romance Books.

Thank you to Jessica Lepe, KD Casey, Liana De la Rosa, Jessica Lepe, Jean Meltzer, Sara Goodman Confino, Meredith Schorr, Yaffa Santos, and Heidi Shertok— all of you are wonderful, and your support and friendship means everything to me.

Thank you to Lisa Lin and Stacey Agdern—you are the best of writing friends, best of people, and I am so lucky to know you.

Thank you to A. R. Vishny, Julie Block, and S. A. Simon—you make me smarter and better and are fun and fabulous doing it. And you put up with all my most annoying qualities, and I'm eternally grateful. I love you all so much, which is why you all know where ALL the bodies are buried.

Thank you to Maureen Marshall. Nothing I write is any good without you. You are brilliant and fabulous, and I will love and adore you forever and always, no matter what.

Finally, thank you to my family. Mom and Marni, you are the best mother and sister anyone could have, and I'm lucky you are mine. Dan, kiddos, I love you all more than anything in the world and hope I make you just a little bit proud.

Author's Note

Antisemitism has been a significant feature of English-speaking culture since the first permanent Jewish community arrived in England from France in 1066. Those Jews were subjected to a plethora of legal restrictions as well as seizures of property, continual harassment, scapegoating, and violent attacks by the populace.

The idea of Jews as villains crept into British art and literature almost immediately, and continued well after that initial group of Jews was expelled by Edward I in 1290, forced back to France, from which they were then expelled a century later, and forced farther and farther east through a series of subsequent expulsions (incidentally creating the populations from which Sol and Hannah are each descended, now commonly referred to as Ashkenazi Jews, denoting their community's distinct scholarship and customs originating in the Frankish kingdom just before the rule of Charlemagne).

Anti-Jewish Anglophone art and literature continued even during the period before Cromwell, when Jews were not legally permitted to reside in England. Jews were not officially welcomed back until the reign of William and Mary, who ushered in a new wave of Jewish immigration to England, this time primarily from the Netherlands, made up mostly from descendants of the Jews expelled from Spain and Portugal in the fifteenth and sixteenth centuries, commonly referred to as Sephardi Jews (like Roger Berab and Isabelle Lira-Ellenberg).

Those Jews, who were permitted admittance due to their ability to move in Dutch society as well as their relative financial stability, worked hard to appear as assets to England lest they be expelled again—something which was attempted multiple times and almost succeeded in the 1730s.

As the eighteenth century drew on and the nineteenth century began, additional Jews arrived in England. Most of these immigrants had recently lived in the Germanic states, were of varying means, but lacked freedoms and stability in central Europe. However, a small percentage came from farther east, whose lives were in danger due to Tsarina Catherine the Great's plan to decrease the Russian Empire's population of Jews by two thirds by any means necessary. This included violence and starvation, a program carried on by each of her successors into the twentieth century, with more and more extreme means as both a governmental project and as a way to gain support of other ethnic groups with their own antisemitic prejudices. These groups, like with many populations before and after them, used extra governmental actions, which were often more deadly than anything the ruling "elites" could accomplish.

Indeed, one of the quirks of Jewish history in Europe and beyond is that legal and social antisemitism have been equally dangerous, with the latter often being more deadly if it is attendant to populism.

From this period, arguably the most famous Jew in nineteenth-century British literature, possibly in all of

English-language literature, was created—a character named Fagin, in Charles Dickens's *Oliver Twist*, a fence who manipulated young gentile boys to steal for him. He in turn inspired arguably the most famous Jew in all of historical romance, Georgette Heyer's evil pawnbroker Goldhanger in *The Grand Sophy*.

Fagin's image, born from already-existing antisemitic lore, became synonymous with the dreaded "Jew." He is a greedy, inherently dishonest, devious, and untrustworthy monster committing a sort of secular, modern blood libel—and therefore a danger to good, innocent gentiles, and their children. Fagin exists as a warning to potential "victims" of the Jews and as a lesson to other Jews to "behave," and never, ever appear to have any power or money over gentiles, or face severe punishment.

Fear of Fagin has been used not merely to influence the perception of Jews in English-language culture and media, but also to justify laws aimed to protect gentiles by limiting Jews' rights in English-speaking societies. It was additionally used bolster support for immigration law in England and the United States that limited the number of Jewish refugees admitted during the ethnic cleansing surrounding the Russian Revolution, in which the Red Army, White Army, Polish Nationalists, and Ukrainian Nationalists with the help of the populace killed somewhere between fifty thousand and five hundred thousand Jews for being Jews, as well as during and after the Holocaust.

One of the oft-cited defenses of this caricature is that Fagin was "based on a real person," a man named Isaac "Ikey" Solomon, a pawnbroker and fence in Regency England. A man whose trial was indeed covered by

Charles Dickens. However, unlike Fagin, Ikey Solomon was married with children. He didn't manipulate and prey upon young gentile boys. Instead, like his father before him, he and his family ran a pawnshop and occasionally dealt in illegal goods. A profession never exclusive to Jews, though at various periods one of the very few open to them.

Solomon was only noteworthy as his business was profitable and he was quite clever at escaping the law. He fled to Argentina and was caught only when his family was arrested, tried, and sent to the penal colony in Australia. He was subsequently arrested during a daring rescue attempt of his family.

The Solomons' relationship was rather messy with many breakups and reunifications. They did not live together at the end of their lives, but had both an epic and extremely human story. One that barely resembled the portrait created and used against him and multiple Jewish communities by people like Dickens and Heyer. A portrait that is still used against Jews today.

Out of that history, Hannah Moses and her family, characters much closer to Ikey and his family and the multitude of real Jews who operated businesses like pawnshops, were born. The "bad Jews" of their time who seem to symbolize everything the society around them believed was evil, even though they were merely regular people attempting to live in a world they neither created nor controlled. These "bad Jews" were ultimately quite vulnerable, both legally due to their lack of rights and various restrictions and socially due to their small numbers and unpopularity. After all, in Jewish history the masses and the "elites" are equally as deadly.

Today, the idea that merely running a pawnshop and occasionally receiving stolen goods, or charging too much interest, would make someone a fiend worthy of extreme punishment seems comical. However, at the time, this was how many people felt if the pawnbroker in question was a Jew.

The nineteenth century was a time of great upheaval, socially, politically, and technologically, as well as one of rising wealth inequality in England. In such climates, people seek villains, preferably ones who they cannot see themselves in, to rally them together and to vanquish. More importantly, they seek villains who can absolve people they like and respect, as well as themselves, of guilt and responsibility for the problems in their society. Much easier and less costly than working to fix the problems collectively.

For many people, especially those of culturally Christian descent, that villain is the Jew. The details of Jews' villainy changes according to what the culture finds most heinous at the time, whether the majority fits the charge or not or whether the charge is objectively truly "evil," in hindsight.

After all, many nineteenth-century gentiles who rallied against the Ikey Solomons of the world and believed any story of their alleged evil without question laughed at their Crusader ancestors' "holy" bloodlust for the Jews of the Rhine as "backward" and "superstitious." They scoffed at the peasants who accused Jews of ritually using the blood of non-Jewish children in their matzah for Passover as "ignorant." They might even have found locked ghettos and forced wearing of yellow hats and scarves cruel if not antiquated (ironic, given their revival in the next century).

However, each of these generations sincerely believed that ridding themselves of Jews—at least the "bad ones"—was necessary to create a better, more righteous, more just world and were prepared to use any power available to them to make it happen.

And thus, for the average gentile in 1830s England, it is easy to hate the Liras and Berabs with all their money or the Hannahs who earn a living off people's debts—never mind their lack of political rights, professional options, and precarious status in society—rather than blame the Penroses who have made the rules for centuries, built a society to retain their power, and control all the physical resources, all while being afforded the veneer of righteous innocence.

The fact that antisemitism posits Jews as inherently dishonest "supervillains" capable of any evil is reflective of the fears of those who propagate the prejudice. It can take alternative forms in a single society, making it very difficult to spot and even more difficult to combat. There are many people today who resemble Penrose, Ned, the customer and his relatives who had Hannah and her family arrested, and even Frederick with his internalized antisemitism. They just often can't see it.

And yet, still, like Hannah and Sol and Moses, we will march around with the Torahs and wave our flags for Simchat Torah—my favorite holiday, not just due to the apples I've always loved since I was little—with its message that our work is not done so we will continue it forward, generation after generation, that we will keep striving to be guided to create a better world, and that we, as a people, will preserve, and outlive all who want our lights to go out.

About the Author

Felicia Grossman is the author of historical romance, usually featuring Jewish protagonists and lots of food references. Originally from Delaware, she now lives in the Rustbelt with her family and Scottish terrier. When not writing romance, she enjoys eclairs, cannolis, and Sondheim musicals.

You can learn more at:
FeliciaGrossmanAuthor.com
Facebook.com/FeliciaGrossmanAuthor
Instagram @FeliciaGrossmanAuthor

Get swept off your feet by charming dukes and sharp-witted ladies in Forever's historical romances!

A SPINSTER'S GUIDE TO DANGER AND DUKES
by **Manda Collins**

Miss Poppy Delamare left her family to escape an odious betrothal, but when her sister is accused of murder, she cannot stay away. Even if she must travel with the arrogant Duke of Langham. To her surprise, he offers a mutually beneficial arrangement: a fake betrothal will both protect Poppy and her sister and deter Society misses from Langham. But as real feelings begin to grow, can they find truth and turn their engagement into reality—before Poppy becomes the next victim?

ALWAYS BE MY DUCHESS
by **Amalie Howard**

Because ballerina Geneviève Valery refused a patron's advances, she is hopelessly out of work. But then Lord Lysander Blackstone, the heartless Duke of Montcroix, makes Nève an offer she would be a fool to refuse. Montcroix's ruthlessness has jeopardized a new business deal, so if Nève acts as his fake fiancée and salvages his reputation, he'll give her fortune enough to start over. Only neither is prepared when very *real* feelings begin to grow between them…

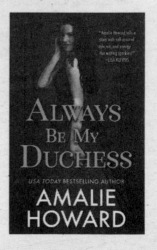

Connect with us at Facebook.com/ReadForeverPub

Discover bonus content and more on
read-forever.com

THE DUKE'S ALL THAT
by Christina Britton

Miss Seraphina Athwart never wanted to abandon her husband, but she
did what was necessary to keep herself and her sisters safe. And while
she's missed Iain, she's made a happy life without him. But all that is put at
risk when Iain arrives on the Isle of Synne, demanding a divorce. Despite
their long separation, the affection and attraction between them still burn
strong. But with so much hurt and betrayal simmering as well, can they
possibly find their way back to each other?

Meet your next favorite book with @ReadForeverPub on TikTok

THE PARIS APARTMENT
by Kelly Bowen

2017, London: When Aurelia Leclaire inherits an opulent Paris apartment, she is shocked to discover her grandmother's secrets—including a treasure trove of famous art and couture gowns.

Paris, 1942: Glamorous Estelle Allard flourishes in a world separate from the hardships of war. But when the Nazis come for her friends, Estelle doesn't hesitate to help those she holds dear, no matter the cost.

Both Estelle and Lia must summon hidden courage as they alter history—and the future of their families—forever.

WAKE ME MOST WICKEDLY
by Felicia Grossman

To repay his half-brother, Solomon Weiss gladly pursues money and influence—until outcast Hannah Moses saves his life. He's irresistibly drawn to her beauty and wit, but Hannah tells him she's no savior. To care for her sister, she heartlessly hunts criminals for London's underbelly. Which makes Sol far too respectable for her. Only neither can resist their desires—until Hannah discovers a betrayal that will break Sol's heart. Can she convince Sol to trust her? Or will fear and doubt poison their love?